Also by John Updike

COUPLES

John Updike

COUPLES

Alfred A. Knopf   New York

1968

THIS IS A BORZOI BOOK
PUBLISHED BY ALFRED A. KNOPF, INC.

W

TO MARY

Chapters

COUPLES

i. *Welcome to Tarbox*

"WHAT did you make of the new couple?"

The Hanemas, Piet and Angela, were undressing. Their bed-chamber was a low-ceilinged colonial room whose woodwork was painted the shade of off-white commercially called eggshell. A spring midnight pressed on the cold windows.

"Oh," Angela answered vaguely, "they seemed young." She was a fair soft brown-haired woman, thirty-four, going heavy in her haunches and waist yet with a girl's fine hard ankles and a girl's tentative questing way of moving, as if the pure air were loosely packed with obstructing cloths. Age had touched only the softened line of her jaw and her hands, their stringy backs and reddened fingertips.

"How young, exactly?"

"Oh, I don't know. He's thirty trying to be forty. She's younger. Twenty-eight? Twenty-nine? Are you thinking of taking a census?"

He grudgingly laughed. Piet had red hair and a close-set body; no taller than Angela, he was denser. His flattish Dutch features, inherited, were pricked from underneath by an acquired American something—a guilty humorous greed, a wordless question.

His wife's languid unexpectedness, a diffident freshness born of aristocratic self-possession, still fascinated him. He thought of himself as coarse and saw her as fine, so fair and fine her every gesture seemed transparently informed by a graciousness and honesty beyond him. When he had met her, Angela Hamilton, she had been a young woman past first bloom, her radiance growing lazy, with an affecting slow mannerism of looking away, the side of her neck bared, an inexplicably unscarred beauty playing at schoolteaching and living with her parents in Nun's Bay, and he had been laboring for her father, in partnership with an army friend, one of their first jobs, constructing a pergola in view of the ocean and the great chocolate-dark rock that suggested, from a slightly other angle, a female profile and the folds of a wimple. There had been a cliff, an ample green lawn, and bushes trimmed to the flatness of tables. In the house there had been many clocks, grandfather's and ship's clocks, clocks finished in ormolu or black lacquer, fine-spun clocks in silver cases, with four balls as pendulum. Their courtship passed as something instantly forgotten, like an enchantment, or a mistake. Time came unstuck. All the clocks hurried their ticking, hurried them past doubts, around sharp corners and knobbed walnut newels. Her father, a wise-smiling man in a tailored gray suit, failed to disapprove. She had been one of those daughters so favored that spinsterhood alone might dare to claim her. Fertility at all costs. He threw business his son-in-law's way. The Hanemas' first child, a daughter, was born nine months after the wedding night. Nine years later Piet still felt, with Angela, a superior power seeking through her to employ him. He spoke as if in self-defense: "I was just wondering at what stage they are. He seemed rather brittle and detached."

"You're hoping they're at our stage?"

Her cool thin tone, assumed at the moment when he had believed their intimacy, in this well-lit safe room encircled by the April dark, to be gathering poignant force enough to vault them over their inhibitions, angered him. He felt like a fool. He said, "That's right. The seventh circle of bliss."

"Is that what we're in?" She sounded, remotely, ready to believe it.

They each stood before a closet door, on opposite sides of an unused fireplace framed in pine paneling and plaster painted azure. The house was a graceful eighteenth-century farmhouse of eight rooms. A barn and a good square yard and a high lilac hedge came with the property. The previous owners, who had had adolescent boys, had attached a basketball hoop to one side of the barn and laid down a small asphalt court. At another corner of the two acres stood an arc of woods tangent to a neighboring orchard. Beyond this was a dairy farm. Seven miles further along the road, an unseen presence, was the town of Nun's Bay; and twenty miles more, to the north, Boston. Piet was by profession a builder, in love with snug right-angled things, and he had grown to love this house, its rectangular low rooms, its baseboards and chair rails molded and beaded by hand, the slender mullions of the windows whose older panes were flecked with oblong bubbles and tinged with lavender, the swept worn brick of the fireplace hearths like entryways into a sooty upward core of time, the attic he had lined with silver insulation paper so it seemed now a vaulted jewel box or an Aladdin's cave, the solid freshly poured basement that had been a cellar floored with dirt when they had moved in five years ago. He loved how this house welcomed into itself in every season lemony flecked rhomboids of sun whose slow sliding revolved it with the day, like the cabin of a ship on a curving course. All houses, all things that enclosed, pleased Piet, but his modest Dutch sense of how much of the world he was permitted to mark off and hold was precisely satisfied by this flat lot two hundred feet back from the road, a mile from the center of town, four miles distant from the sea.

Angela, descended from piratical New Bedford whaling captains, wanted a property with a view of the Atlantic. She had mourned when the new couple in town, the Whitmans, had bought, through the agency of Gallagher & Hanema, Real Estate and Contracting, a house she had coveted, the old Robinson place, a jerrybuilt summer house in need of total repair. It had a huge view of the salt marshes and a wind exposure that would defy all insulation. She and Piet had gone over it several times in the winter past. It had been built as a one-story cottage around 1900. In the early twenties it had been jacked up on posts and a new first floor built under it, with a long screened porch that darkened the living room. Then new owners had added a servants' wing whose level differed by two steps from the main structure. Piet showed Angela the shabby carpentry, the crumbling gypsum wallboard, the corroded iron plumbing, the antique wiring with its brittle rubber insulation, the rattling sashes chewed by animals and rain. A skylight in the main bedroom leaked. The only heat came from a single round register in the living-room floor, above a manually fed coal furnace in an unwalled clay hole. A full cellar would have to be excavated. Solid interior walls and a complete heating system were essential. The roof must be replaced. Gutters, sashes. Ceilings. The kitchen was quaint, useless; servants had run it, summers only, making lobster salads. On the two windward sides the cedar shingles had been warped and whitened and blown away. Forty thousand the asking price, and twelve more immediately, minimum. It was too much to ask him to take on. Standing at the broad slate sink contemplating the winter view of ditch-traversed marsh and the brambled islands of hawthorn and alder and the steel-blue channel beyond and the rim of dunes white as salt and above all the honed edge of ocean, Angela at last agreed. It was too much.

Now, thinking of this house from whose purchase he had escaped and from whose sale he had realized a partner's share of profit, Piet conservatively rejoiced in the house he had held. He felt its lightly supporting symmetry all around him. He pictured his two round-faced daughters asleep in its shelter. He gloated upon the sight of his wife's body, her fine ripeness.

Having unclasped her party pearls, Angela pulled her dress, the black décolleté knit, over her head. Its soft wool caught in her hairpins. As she struggled, lamplight struck zigzag fire from her slip and static electricity made its nylon adhere to her flank. The slip lifted, exposing stocking-tops and garters. Without her head she was all full form, sweet, solid.

Pricked by love, he accused her: "You're not happy with me."

She disentangled the bunched cloth and obliquely faced him. The lamplight, from a bureau lamp with a pleated linen shade, cut shadows into the line of her jaw. She was aging. A year ago, she would have denied the accusation. "How can I be," she asked, "when you flirt with every woman in sight?"

"In sight? Do I?"

"Of course you do. You know you do. Big or little, old or young, you eat them up. Even the yellow ones, Bernadette Ong. Even poor little soused Bea Guerin, who has enough troubles."

"You seemed happy enough, conferring all night with Freddy Thorne."

"Piet, we can't keep going to parties back to back. I come home feeling dirty. I hate it, this way we live."

"You'd rather we went belly to belly? Tell me"—he had stripped to his waist, and she shied from that shieldlike breadth of taut bare skin with its cruciform blazon of amber hair—"what do you and Freddy find to talk about for hours on end? You huddle in the corner like children playing jacks." He took a step forward, his eyes narrowed and pink, party-chafed. She resisted the urge to step backwards, knowing that this threatening mood of his was supposed to end in sex, was a plea.

Instead she reached under her slip to unfasten her garters. The gesture, so vulnerable, disarmed him; Piet halted before the fireplace, his bare feet chilled by the hearth's smooth bricks.

"He's a jerk," she said carelessly, of Freddy Thorne. Her voice was lowered by the pressure of her chin against her chest; the downward reaching of her arms gathered her breasts to a dark crease. "But he talks about things that interest women. Food. Psychology. Children's teeth."

"What does he say psychological?"

"He was talking tonight about what we all see in each other."

"Who?"

"You know. Us. The couples."

"What Freddy Thorne sees in me is a free drink. What he sees in you is a gorgeous fat ass."

She deflected the compliment. "He thinks we're a circle. A magic circle of heads to keep the night out. He told me he gets frightened if he doesn't see us over a weekend. He thinks we've made a church of each other."

"That's because he doesn't go to a real church."

"Well Piet, you're the only one who does. Not counting the Catholics." The Catholics they knew socially were the Gallaghers and Bernadette Ong. The Constantines had lapsed.

"It's the source," Piet said, "of my amazing virility. A stiffening sense of sin." And in his chalkstripe suit pants he abruptly dove forward, planted his weight on his splayed raw-knuckled hands, and stood upside down. His tensed toes reached for the tip of his conical shadow on the ceiling; the veins in his throat and forearms bulged. Angela looked away. She had seen this too often before. He neatly flipped back to his feet; his wife's silence embarrassed him. "Christ be praised," he said, and clapped, applauding himself.

"Shh. You'll wake the children."

"Why the hell shouldn't I, they're always waking me, the little bloodsuckers." He went down on his knees and toddled to the edge of the bed. "Dadda, Dadda, wake up-up, Dadda. The Sunnay paper's here, guess what? Jackie Kenneny's having a *baby!*"

"You're so cruel," Angela said, continuing her careful undressing, parting vague obstacles with her hands. She opened her closet door so that from her husband's angle her body was hidden. Her voice floated free: "Another thing Freddy thinks, he thinks the children are suffering because of it."

"Because of what?"

"Our social life."

"Well I have to have a social life if you won't give me a sex life."

"If you think *that* approach is the way to a lady's heart, you have a lot to learn." He hated her tone; it reminded him of the years before him, when she had instructed children.

He asked her, "Why shouldn't children suffer? They're supposed to suffer. How else can they learn to be good?" For he felt that if only in the matter of suffering he knew more than she, and that without him she would raise their daughters as she had been raised, to live in a world that didn't exist.

She was determined to answer him seriously, until her patience dulled his pricking mood. "That's positive suffering," she said. "What we give them is neglect so subtle they don't even notice it.

We aren't abusive, we're just evasive. For instance, Frankie Appleby is a bright child, but he's just going to waste, he's just Jonathan little-Smith's punching bag because their parents are always together."

"Hell. Half the reason we all live in this silly hick town is for the sake of the children."

"But we're the ones who have the fun. The children just get yanked along. They didn't enjoy all those skiing trips last winter, standing in the T-bar line shivering and miserable. The girls wanted all winter to go some Sunday to a museum, a nice warm museum with stuffed birds in it, but we wouldn't take them because we would have had to go as a family and our friends might do something exciting or ghastly without us. Irene Saltz finally took them, bless her, or they'd never have gone. I like Irene; she's the only one of us who has somehow kept her freedom. Her freedom from crap."

"How much did you drink tonight?"

"It's just that Freddy didn't let me talk enough."

"He's a jerk," Piet said and, suffocated by an obscure sense of exclusion, seeking to obtain at least the negotiable asset of a firm rejection, he hopped across the hearth-bricks worn like a passageway in Delft and sharply kicked shut Angela's closet door, nearly striking her. She was naked.

He too was naked. Piet's hands, feet, head, and genitals were those of a larger man, as if his maker, seeing that the cooling body had been left too small, had injected a final surge of plasma which at these extremities had ponderously clotted. Physically he held himself, his tool-toughened palms curved and his acrobat's back a bit bent, as if conscious of a potent burden.

Angela had flinched and now froze, one arm protecting her breasts. A luminous polleny pallor, the shadow of last summer's bathing suit, set off her surprisingly luxuriant pudenda. The slack forward cant of her belly remembered her pregnancies. Her thick-thighed legs were varicose. But her tipped arms seemed, simple and symmetrical, a maiden's; her white feet were high-arched and neither little toe touched the floor. Her throat, wrists, and triangular bush appeared the pivots for some undeniable effort of flight, but like Eve on a portal she crouched in shame, stone. She held rigid. Her blue irises cupped light catlike, shallowly. Her skin breathed hate. He did not dare touch her, though her fairness gathered so close dried his tongue. Their bodies hung upon them as clothes too gaudy. Piet felt the fireplace draft on his ankles and became sensitive to the night beyond her hunched shoulders, an extensiveness pressed tight against the bubbled old panes and the frail mullions, a blackness charged with the ache of first growth and the suspended skeletons of Virgo and Leo and Gemini.

She said, "Bully."

He said, "You're lovely."

"That's too bad. I'm going to put on my nightie."

Sighing, immersed in a clamor of light and paint, the Hanemas dressed and crept to bed, exhausted.

As always after a party Piet was slow to go to sleep. There had not been many parties for him as a child and now they left him overexcited, tumescent. He touched his own self to make himself sleepy. Quickly his wife was dead weight beside him. She claimed she never dreamed. Pityingly he put his hand beneath the cotton nightie transparent to his touch and massaged the massive blandness of her warm back, hoping to stir in the depths of her sleep an eddy, a fluid fable she could tell herself and in the morning remember. She would be a valley and he a sandstorm. He would be a gentle lion bathing in her river. He could not believe she never dreamed. How could one not dream? He always dreamed. He dreamed last night he was an old minister making calls. Walking in the country, he crossed a superhighway and waited a long time on the median strip. Waiting, he looked down into a rural valley where small houses smoked from their chimneys. He must make his calls there. He crossed the rest of the road and was relieved when a policeman pulled up on a motorcycle and, speaking German, arrested him.

The party had been given by the Applebys in honor of the new couple, the what, the Whitmans. Frank had known Ted, or Dan, at Exeter, or Harvard. Exeter, Harvard: it was to Piet like looking up at the greenhouse panes spattered with whitewash to dull the sun. He shut out the greenhouse. He did not wish to remember the greenhouse. It was a cliff.

Stiffly his fingers tired of trying to give his wife a dream: a baby on the river of herself, Moses in the Nile morning found snagged in the rustling papyrus, Egyptian handmaids, willowy flanks, single lotus, easy access. Sex part of nature before Christ. *Bully*. Bitch. Taking up three-quarters of the bed as if duty done. Mouthbreathing with slack lips. Words in and out. Virgins pregnant through the ear. Talk to me psychologee. He touched in preference again himself. Waxen. Wilted camellia petals. In his youth an ivory rod at will. At the thought of a cleft or in class a shaft of sun laid on his thigh: stand to recite: *breathes there a man with soul so dead*. The whole class tittering at him bent over. The girl at the desk next wore lineny blouses so sheer her bra straps peeped and so short-sleeved that her armpits. Showed, shaved. Vojt. Annabelle Vojt. One man, one Vojt. Easy Dutch ways. Married a poultry farmer from outside Grand Rapids. Wonderful tip of her tongue, agile, squarish. Once after a dance French-kissed him parked by the quarry and he shot off behind his fly. Intenser then, the duct narrower, greater velocity. Not his girl but her underpants satiny, distant peaty odor, rustle of crinoline, formal dance. Quick as a wink, her dark tongue saucy under his. His body flashed the news nerve to nerve. Stiff in an instant. Touch. A waxworks petal laid out pillowed in sensitive frizz: wake up. Liquor. Evil dulling stuff. Lazes the blood, saps muscle tone. He turned over, bunched the pillow, lay flat and straight, trying to align himself with an invisible grain, the grain of the world, fate. Relax. Picture the party.

Twisting. Bald Freddy Thorne with a glinting moist smirk put on the record. Chubby. *Huooff: cummawn naioh evvribuddi less* Twist! Therapy, to make them look awful. They were growing old and awful in each other's homes. Only Carol had it of the women, the points of her pelvis making tidy figure eights, hands aloof like gentle knives, weight switching foot to foot, a silent clicking, stocking feet, narrow, hungry, her scrawny kind of high-school beauty, more his social level, the motion, coolly neat, feet forgotten, eyelids elegantly all but shuttered, making a presumed mist of Frank Appleby bouncing opposite, no logic in his hips, teeth outcurved braying, gums bared, brown breath, unpleasant spray. Everybody twisted. Little-Smith's black snickering feet. Georgene's chin set determinedly as if on second serve. Angela, too soft, rather swayed. Gallagher a jerking marionette. John Ong watched sober, silent, smiling, smoking. Turning to Piet he made high friendly noises that seemed in the din all vowels; Piet knew the Korean was worth more than them all together in a jiggling jouncing bunch but he could never understand what he said: *Who never to himself has said.* Bernadette came up, broad flat lady in two dimensions, half-Japanese, the other half Catholic, from Baltimore, and asked Piet, *Twist?* In the crowded shaking room, the Applebys' children's playroom, muraled in pink ducks, Bernadette kept bumping him, whacking him with her silken flatnesses, crucifix hopping in the shallow space between her breasts, thighs, wrists, bumping him, the yellow peril. *Whoofwheeieu. Wow.* Better a foxtrot. Making fools of themselves, working off steam, it's getting too suburban in here. The windows had been painted shut. Walls of books.

Piet felt, brave small Dutch boy, a danger hanging tidal above his friends, in this town where he had been taken in because Angela had been a Hamilton. The men had stopped having careers and the women had stopped having babies. Liquor and love were left. Bea Guerin, as they danced to Connie Francis, her drunken limpness dragging on his side so his leg and neck ached, her steamy breasts smearing his shirt, seemed to have asked why he didn't want to fuck her. He wasn't sure she had said it, it sounded like something in Dutch, *fokker, in de fuik lopen,* drifting to him from his parents as they talked between themselves in the back room of the greenhouse. Little Piet, Amerikander, couldn't understand. But he loved being there with them, in the overheated warmth, watching his father's broad stained thumbs packing moss, his mother's pallid needling fingers wrapping pots in foil and stabbing in the green price spindles. Once more with the eyes of a child Piet saw the spools of paper ribbon, the boxes holding colored grits and pebbles for the tiny potted tableaux of cactuses and violets and china houses and animal figurines with spots of reflection on their noses, the drawerful of stacked gift cards saying in raised silver HANEMA, his name, himself, restraining constellated in its letters all his fate, *me, a man, amen ah.* Beside the backroom office where Mama did up pots and Papa paid his bills were the icy dewy doors where cut roses and carnations being dyed and lovely iris and gladioli leaned, refrigerated, dead. Piet tensed and changed position and erased the greenhouse with the party.

The new couple. They looked precious to themselves, self-cherished, like gladioli. Cambridge transplants, tall and choice. Newcomers annoyed Piet. Soil here not that rich, crowding. Ted? Ken. Quick grin yet a sullen languor, a less than ironical interest in being right. Something in science, not mathematics like Ong or miniaturization like Saltz. Biochemistry. Papa had distrusted inorganic fertilizer, trucked chicken dung from poultry farms: *this is my own, my native land.* She was called oddly Foxy, a maiden name? Fairfox, Virginia? A southern flavor to her. Tall, oak and honey hair, a constant blush like windburn or fever. She seemed internally distressed and had spent two long intervals in the bathroom upstairs. Descending the second time she had revealed her stocking-tops to Piet, reclining acrobatically below. Tawny ashy rims in an upward bell of shadow. She had seen him peek and stared him down. Such amber eyes. Eyes the brown of brushed fur backed by gold.

Bea. What did you say? I must be deaf.

Sweet Piet, you heard. I must be very drunk. Forgive me.

You're dancing divinely.

Don't poke fun. I know I can't matter to you, you have Georgene, and I can't compare. She's marvelous. She plays such marvelous tennis.

That's very flattering. You really think I'm seeing Georgene?

It's all right, singingly, gazing into a blurred distance, *don't bother to deny it, but Piet—Piet?*

Yes? I'm here. You haven't changed partners.

You poke fun of me. That's mean, that's not worthy of you, Piet. Piet?

Hello again.

I'd be kind to you. And someday you're going to need some-body to be kind to you because—now don't get cross—you're surrounded by unkind people.

For instance who? Poor Angela?

You're cross. I feel it in your body you're cross.

No, he said, and stood apart from her, so her dragging was no longer upon his body, and she sagged, then pulled herself erect, blinking, injured, as he went on, *it happens every time I try to be nice to a drunk. I wind up getting insulted.*

Oh!—it was a breathless cry as if she had been struck. *And I meant to be so kind.*

Whitewash wore away after two or three rains, but after the war the chemical companies came up with a compound that lasted pretty well until winter. In winter there could not be too much light. The Michigan snows piled in strata around the glass walls and within the greenhouse there was a lullaby sound of dripping and a rasping purring in the pipes rusted to the color of dirt as they snaked along the dirt floor flecked with tiny clover. A child cried out in her sleep. As if being strangled in a dream. From the voice he guessed it had been Nancy. She, who could tie her shoes at the age of three, had lately, now five, begun to suck her thumb and talk about dying. *I will never grow up and I will never ever in my whole life die.* Ruth, her sister, nine last November, hated to hear her. *Yes you will die everybody will die including trees.* Piet wondered if he should go to Nancy's room but the cry was not repeated. Into the vacuum of his listening flowed a rhythmic squeaking insistent as breathing. A needle working in the night. For her birthday he had given Ruth a hamster; the little animal, sack-shaped and russet, slept all day and ran in its exercise wheel all night. Piet vowed to oil the wheel but meanwhile tried to time his breathing with its beat. Too fast; his heart raced, seemed to bulge like a knapsack as into it was abruptly stuffed two thoughts that in the perspective of the night loomed as dreadful: soon he must begin building ranch houses on Indian Hill, and Angela wanted no more children. He would never have a son. *Eek, ik, eeik, ik, eeek.* Relax. Tomorrow is Sunday.

A truck passed on the road and his ears followed it, focused on its vanishing point. As a child he had soothed himself with the sensation of things passing in the night, automobiles and trains, their furry growling sounds approaching and holding fast on a momentary plateau and then receding, leaving him ignored and untouched, passing on to Chicago or Detroit, Kalamazoo or Battle Creek or the other way to the snow, stitched with animal tracks, of the northern peninsula that only boats could reach. A bridge had since been built. He had pictured himself as Superman, with a chest of steel the flanged wheels of the engines could not dent, passing over him. The retreating whistles of those flatland trains had seemed drawn with a pencil sharpened so fine that in reality it broke. No such thing in nature as a point, or a perfect circle, or infinitude, or a hereafter. The truck had vanished. But must be, must. Must. Is somewhere.

Traffic this late in this corner of New England, between Plymouth and Quincy, between Nun's Bay and Lacetown, was sparse, and he waited a long stretch for the next truck to come lull him. Angela stirred, sluggishly avoiding some obstacle to the onflow of her sleep, a dream wanting to be born, and he remembered the last time they had made love, over a week ago, in another season, winter. Though he had skated patiently waiting for her skin to quicken from beneath she had finally despaired of having a climax and asked him simply to take her and be done. Released, she had turned away, and in looping his arm around her chest his fingers brushed an unexpected sad solidity.

Angel, your nipples are hard.
So?
You're excited and could have come too.
I don't think so. It just means I'm chilly.
Let me make you come. With my mouth.
No. I'm all wet down there.
But it's me, it's my wetness.
I want to go to sleep.
But it's so sad, that you liked my making love to you after all.
I don't see that it's that sad. We'll all be here another night.

He lay on his back like a town suspended from a steeple. He felt delicate on his face a draft from somewhere in his snug house, a loose storm window, a tear in the attic foil, a murderer easing open a door. He rolled over on his stomach and the greenhouse washed over him. The tables like great wooden trays, the flowers budding and blooming and dropping their petals and not being bought. As a child he had mourned the unbought flowers, beseeching the even gray greenhouse light with their hopeful corollas and tepid perfume. He surveyed the party for a woman to bring home and picked Bea Guerin. *Dear Bea, of course I want to fuck you, how could I not, with your steamy little body so tired and small and kind. Just about all lilies, aren't you? Now spread your legs. Easy does it. Ah.* The moisture and light within the greenhouse had been so constant and strong that even weeds grew; even when bright snow was heaped against the glass walls like a sliced cross section in a school book, clover from nowhere flourished around the legs of the tables and by the rusty pipes, and the dirt floor bore a mossy patina and was steeped in an odor incomparably quiet and settled and profound. He saw them, his father and mother, *vader en moeder*, moving gently in this receding polyhedral heart of light carved from dank nature, their bodies transparent, and his mind came to a cliff—a slip, then a skidding downward plunge. Left fist clenched upon himself, he groped in his mind for the party, but it was no longer there.

God help me, help me, get me out of this. *Eek ik, eeik ik.* Dear God put me to sleep. Amen.

A golden rooster turned high above Tarbox. The Congregational Church, a Greek temple with a cupola and spire, shared a ledgy rise, once common pasturage, with a baseball backstop and a cast-iron band pavilion used only on Memorial Day, when it sheltered shouted prayers, and in the Christmas season, when it became a crêche. Three edifices had succeeded the first meetinghouse, a thatched fort, and the last, renovated in 1896 and 1939, lifted well over one hundred feet into the air a gilded weathercock that had been salvaged from the previous church and thus dated from colonial times. Its eye was a copper English penny. Deposed once each generation by hurricanes, lightning, or repairs, it was always, much bent and welded, restored. It turned in the wind and flashed in the sun and served as a landmark to fishermen in Massachusetts Bay. Children in the town grew up with the sense that the bird was God. That is, if God were physically present in Tarbox, it was in the form of this unreachable weathercock visible from everywhere. And if its penny could see, it saw everything, spread below it like a living map. The central square mile of Tarbox contained a hosiery mill converted to the manufacture of plastic toys, three dozen stores, several acres of parking lot, and hundreds of small-yarded homes. The homes were mixed: the surviving seventeenth-century saltboxes the original Kimballs and Sewells and Tarboxes and Cogswells had set along the wobbly pasture lanes, quaintly named for the virtues, that radiated from the green; the peeling Federalist cubes with widow's-walks; the gingerbread mansions attesting to the decades of textile prosperity; the tight brick alleys plotted to house the millworkers imported from Poland; the middle-class pre-Depression domiciles with stubby porches and narrow chimneys and composition sidings the colors of mustard and parsley and graphite and wine; the new developments like even pastel teeth eating the woods of faraway Indian Hill. Beyond, there was a veiny weave of roads, an arrowing disused railroad track, a river whose water was fresh above the yellow waterfall at the factory and saline below it, a golf course studded with bean-shapes of sand, some stubborn farms and checkerboard orchards, a glinting dairy barn on the Nun's Bay Road, a field containing slowly moving specks that were galloping horses, level breadths of salt marsh broken by islands and inlets, and, its curved horizon marred, on days as clear as today, by the violet smudge that was the tip of Cape Cod, the eastward sea. Casting the penny of its gaze straight down, the cock could have observed, in dizzying perspective, the dotlike heads of church-goers congregating and, hurrying up the gray path, the red head of Piet Hanema, a latecomer.

The interior of the church was white. Alabaster effects had been skillfully mimicked in wood. Graceful round vaults culminated in a hung plaster ceiling. A balcony with Doric fluting vertically scoring the parapet jutted as if weightless along the sides of the sanctuary and from under the painted Victorian organ in the rear. The joinery of the old box pews was still admirable. Piet seldom entered the church without reflecting that the carpenters who had built it were dead and that none of their quality had been born to replace them. He took his accustomed place in a left back pew, and latched the paneled door, and was alone with a frayed grape-colored pew cushion—a fund drive to replace these worn-out cushions had only half succeeded—and a pair of powder-blue Pilgrim hymnals and a hideous walnut communion-glass rack screwed to the old pine in obedience to a bequest. Piet always sat alone. His friends did not go to church. He adjusted the cushion and selected the less tattered of the two hymnals. The organist, a mauve-haired spinster from Lacetown, rummaged through a Bach prelude. The first hymn was number 195: "All Hail the Power." Piet stood and sang. His voice, timid and off-key, now and then touched his own ears. ". . . on this terrestrial ball . . . let angels prostrate fall . . . and crown him, Lorhord of all . . ." On command, Piet sat and prayed. Prayer was an unsteady state of mind for him. When it worked, he seemed, for intermittent moments, to be in the farthest corner of a deep burrow, a small endearing hairy animal curled up as if to hibernate. In this condition he felt close to a massive warm secret, like the heart of lava at the earth's core. His existence for a second seemed to evade decay. But church was too exciting, too full of light and music, for prayer to take place, and his mind slid from the words being intoned, and skimmed across several pieces of property that concerned him, and grazed the faces and limbs of women he knew, and darted from the image of his daughters to the memory of his parents, so unjustly and continuingly dead.

They had died together, his mother within minutes and his father at the hospital three hours later, in a highway accident the week before the Christmas of 1949, at dusk. They had been driving home to Grand Rapids from a Grange meeting. There was an almost straight stretch of Route 21 that was often icy. The river flowed near it. It had begun to snow. A Lincoln skidded head-on into them; the driver, a boy from Ionia, survived with lacerations. From the position of the automobiles it was not clear who had skidded, but Piet, who knew how his father drove, as ploddingly as he potted geraniums, one mile after the other, did not doubt that it had been the boy's fault. And yet—the dusk was confusing, his father was aging; perhaps, in an instant without perspective on that deceptive flat land, at the apparition of on-rushing headlights, the wheels for a moment slithering, the old man had panicked. Could there have been, in that placid good gardener, with his even false teeth and heavy step and pallid stubby lashes, a fatal reserve of unreason that had burst forth and destroyed two blameless lives? All those accumulated budgets, and hoarded hopes, and seeds patiently brought to fruition? Piet pictured shattered glass strewn across the road and saw snow continue to descend, sparkling in the policemen's whirling lights. He had been a sophomore at Michigan State, studying toward an architect's certificate, and felt unable to continue, on borrowed money and the world's sufferance. There was a shuddering in his head he could not eliminate. He let his brother Johan— Joop—cheaply buy his share of the greenhouses and let himself be drafted. Since this accident, the world wore a slippery surface for Piet; he stood on the skin of things in the posture of a man testing newly formed ice, his head cocked for the warning crack, his spine curved to make himself light.

". . . and we lift our hearts in petition for those who have died, who in the ripening of time have pierced the beyond . . ." Piet bent his thought toward the hope of his parents' immortality, saw them dim and small among clouds, in their workaday greenhouse clothes, and realized that if they were preserved it was as strangers to him, blind to him, more than an ocean removed from the earthly concerns of which he had—infant, child, boy, and beginning man—been but one. *Kijk, daar is je vader. Pas op, Piet, die hond bijt. Naa kum, it makes colder out. Be polite, and don't go with girls you'd be ashamed to marry.* From the odd fact of their deaths his praying mind flicked to the odd certainty of his own, which the white well-joined wood and the lucent tall window beside him airily seemed to deny.

Piet had been raised in a sterner church, the Dutch Reformed, amid varnished oak and dour stained glass where shepherds were paralyzed in webs of lead. He had joined this sister church, a milder daughter of Calvin, as a compromise with Angela, who believed nothing. Piet wondered what barred him from the ranks of those many blessed who believed nothing. Courage, he supposed. His nerve had cracked when his parents died. To break with a faith requires a moment of courage, and courage is a kind of margin within us, and after his parents' swift death Piet had no margin. He lived tight against his skin, and his flattish face wore a look of tension. Also, his European sense of order insisted that he place his children in Christendom. Now his daughter Ruth, with his own flat alert face and her mother's stately unconscious body, sang in the children's choir. At the sight of her submissively moving her lips his blood shouted *Lord* and his death leaned above him like a perfectly clear plate of glass.

The children's choir's singing, an unsteady theft of melody while the organ went on tiptoe, ceased. In silence the ushers continued their collection of rustles and coughs. Attendance was high today, Palm Sunday. Piet held his face forward, smiling, so that his daughter would see him when, as he foresaw, she searched the congregation. She saw him and smiled, blushed and studied her robed knees. Whereas with Nancy his manhood had the power to frighten, with Ruth it could merely embarrass. The ushers marched up the scarlet carpet, out of step. Crossing a bridge. Vibration. The minister extended his angel-wing arms wide to receive them. The golden plates were stacked. The hymn: "We Are Climbing Jacob's Ladder." Amid Yankees trying to sing like slaves, Piet nearly wept, knowing the Dutch Reformed would never have stooped to this Christian attempt. "Sinner, do you love your Jesus?" Abolitionism. Children of light. "Every rung goes higher, higher . . ." Two of the four ushers sidled into the pew in front of Piet and one of them had satyr's ears, the holes tamped with wiry hair. The back of his neck crisscrossed, pock-marked by time. Minutes. Meteors. Bombarding us. The sermon commenced.

Reverend Horace Pedrick was a skeletal ignorant man of sixty.

His delusions centered about money. He had never himself had enough. A poor boy from a Maine fishing family, he had entered the ministry after two business bankruptcies brought about by his extreme caution and fear of poverty. Too timid and old to acquire a city church, worn out with five-year-stints in skimping New England towns, he imagined his flock to be composed of "practical men," businessmen whose operations had the scope and harshness of natural processes. In the pulpit, his white hair standing erect as the water on it dried, he held himself braced against imagined mockery, and his sermons, with contortions that now and then bent his body double, sought to transpose the desiccated forms of Christianity into financial terms. "The man Jesus"—one of his favorite phrases—"the man Jesus does not ask us to play a long shot. He does not come to us and say, 'Here is a stock for speculation. Buy at eight-and-one-eighth, and in the Promised Land you can sell at one hundred.' No, he offers us *present security*, four-and-a-half per cent compounded every quarter! Now I realize I am speaking to hard-headed men, businessmen whose decisions are far-ranging in the unsentimental world beyond this sanctuary . . ."

Piet wondered if the hair sprouting from the ears in front of him were trimmed. A cut-bush look: an electric razor, quickly. He fingered his own nostrils and the tickling itch spidered through him; he fought a sneeze. He studied the golden altar cross and wondered if Freddy Thorne were right in saying that Jesus was crucified on an X-shaped cross which the church had to falsify because of the immodesty of the position. Christ had a groin. Not much made of His virginity: mentioned in the Bible at all? Not likely, Arab boys by the age of twelve, a rural culture, sodomy, part of nature, easy access, Egyptian lotus. Coupling in Africa right in the fields as they work: a sip of water. Funny how fucking clears a woman's gaze. Christ's groin Arab but the lucent air vaulted by the ceiling of this church His gaze. Piet feared Freddy Thorne, his hyena appetite for dirty truths. Feared him yet had placed himself in bondage to him, had given him a hostage, spread X-shaped, red cleft wet. Freddy's wise glint. The head with cross-etched wrinkles on the back of its barbered neck under Piet's gaze rotated and the ear orifice became a round brown eye. In Pedrick's sermon the palms spread across Jesus's path had become greenbacks and the theft of the colt a troubled disquisition on property rights. Pedrick struggled and was not reconciled. How blithe was God, how carefree: this unexpected implication encouraged Piet to live. "And so, gentlemen, there *is* something above money, believe it or not: a power which treats wealth lightly, which accepts an expensive bottle of ointment and scorns the cost, which dares to overturn the counting tables of respectable bankers and businessmen like yourselves. May we be granted today the light to welcome this power with hosannahs into our hearts. Amen."

They sang "Lift Up Your Heads, Ye Mighty Gates" and sat for prayer. Prayer and masturbation had so long been mingled in Piet's habits that in hearing the benediction he pictured his mistress naked, a reflected sun pooled between her breasts, her prim chin set, her slightly bulging green eyes gazing, cleared. Erotic warmth infused Piet's greetings as he edged down the aisle, through a china-shop clutter of nodding old ladies, into the narthex redolent of damp paper, past Pedrick's clinging horny handshake, into the open.

At the door Piet was given a palm frond by a combed child in corduroy shorts.

Waiting for his daughter to emerge, he leaned by a warm white pillar, the frond in his left hand, a Lark in the right. Outside the sanctuary, the day was surpassingly sentimental: a thin scent of ashes and sap, lacy shadows, leafless trees, the clapboarded houses around the rocky green basking chalkily. The metal pavilion, painted green, sharpened the gay look of a stage set. The sky enamel-blue, layer on layer. Overhead, held motionless against the breeze, its feet tucked up like parallel staples, a gull hung outlined by a black that thickened at the wingtips. Each pebble, tuft, heelmark, and erosion gully in the mud by the church porch had been assigned its precise noon shadow. Piet had been raised to abhor hard soil but in a decade he had grown to love this land. Each acre was a vantage. Gallagher liked to say they didn't sell houses, they sold views. As he gazed downhill toward the business district, whose apex was formed where Divinity Street met Charity Street at Cogswell's Drug Store and made a right-angled turn up the hill, Piet's vision was touched by a piece of white that by some unconscious chime compelled focus. Who? He knew he knew. The figure, moving with averted veiled head, moved with a bride's floating stiffness. The color white was strange this early in the year, when nothing had budded but the silver maples. Perhaps like Piet she came from a part of the country where spring arrives earlier. She carried a black hymnal in a long glove and the pink of her face was high in tone, as if she were blushing. He knew. The new woman. Whitman. Evidently she was an Episcopalian. St. Stephen's Episcopal Church, unsteepled fieldstone, sat lower down the hill. Walking swiftly, Mrs. Whitman walked to a black MG parked at the foot of the green, far from her church. Perhaps like Piet she habitually came late. A subtle scorn. Thinking herself unseen, she entered her car with violent grace, hitching her skirt and sinking backwards into the seat and slamming the door in one motion. The punky sound of the slam carried to Piet a moment after the vivid sight. The distant motor revved. The MG's weight surged onto its outside tires and she rounded the island of rocks downhill from the green and headed out of town toward her house on the marshes. The women Piet knew mostly drove station wagons. Angela drove a Peugeot. He tipped back his head to view again the zenith. The motionless gull was gone. The blue fire above, layer on layer of swallowed starlight, was halved by a dissolving jet trail. He closed his eyes and imagined sap rising in blurred deltas about him. A wash of ashes. A chalky warmth. A nice bridal taste. Shyly, fearing to wake him, his elder daughter's touch came into the palm of his hanging hand, the hand holding the frond welcoming Jesus to Jerusalem.

After what seemed to Foxy far too long a cocktail time, while the men discussed their stocks and their skiing and the new proposal to revive the dead train service by means of a town contract with the MBTA, and Ken who drove to B.U. in his MG sat looking fastidious and bored, with an ankle on his knee, pondering the intricacies of his shoelaces as if a code could be construed there, Bea Guerin as hostess hesitantly invited them to dinner: "Dinner. Please come. Bring your drinks if you like, but there's wine." The Guerins lived in an old saltbox on Prudence Street, the timbers and main fireplace dating at least from 1680. The house had been so expensively and minutely restored it had for Foxy the apprehensive rawness of a new home; Foxy empathized with childless couples who conspire to baby the furniture.

Rising and setting down their drinks, the company moved to the dining room through a low varnished hallway where on a mock cobbler's bench their coats and hats huddled like a heap of the uninvited. It was Foxy's impression that this set of couples—the Guerins, the Applebys, the Smiths, whom everybody called the little-Smiths, and the Thornes—comprised the "nicer" half of the little society that was seeking to enclose her and Ken. To put herself at ease she had drunk far too much. Under the mechanical urging of her inflexibly frowning host she had accepted two martinis and then, with such stupid false girlishness, a third; feeling a squirm of nausea, she had gone to the kitchen seeking a dilution of vermouth and had whispered her secret to her hostess, a drunken girlish thing to do that would have outraged Ken, yet the kind of thing she felt was desired of her in this company. In a breathy rush Bea Guerin had said, laying a quick tremulous hand on Foxy's forearm, *How wonderful of you.* Though up to this moment Bea had seemed vulnerable to Foxy, defensively whimsical and tipsy, wearing a slightly too naked red velvet Empire dress with a floppy bow below the bosom that Foxy would have immediately snipped, she became now the distinctly older woman, expertly slapping the martini down the sink, retaining the lemon peel with a finger, replacing the gin with dry vermouth. *Don't even pretend to drink if you don't want to. The oven is funny, we had it put in a fireplace and the wind down the chimney keeps blowing out the pilot light, that's why the lamb isn't doing and everything is so late.* It appealed to Foxy that Bea, though Roger was so rich his money was a kind of joke to the others, so rich he apparently barely pretended to work and went in to Boston mostly to have lunch and play squash, was her own cook, and so indifferent at it. Janet Appleby had told her that one of the things they and their friends *loved* about Tarbox was that there were no country clubs or servants; it's so *much* more luxurious to live *simply*. Bea opened the oven door and gingerly peeked in and shut it in a kind of playful fright. The flesh of her upper arm bore a purplish oval blue that might have been a bruise. When she laughed an endearing gap showed between her front teeth. *My dear, you're wonderful, I'm so envious. So envious.* Now the touch of her hand was wet, from handling the drink. Foxy left the kitchen feeling still unsettled.

April was her second month of pregnancy and she had hoped the primordial queasiness would ebb. It offended her, these sensations of demur and rebuke from within. She had long wanted to be pregnant and, having resented her husband's prudent postponement, his endless education, now wondered, at the age of twenty-eight, if the body of a younger woman would have felt less strain. She had imagined it would be like a flower's unresisted swelling, a crocus pushing through snow.

Candlelight rendered unsteady a long table covered by an embroidered cloth. Foxy held herself at attention; her stomach had lifted as if she were in flight above this steaming miniature city of china and goblets and silver flickering with orange points. Namecards in a neat round hand had been arranged. Roger Guerin seated her with a faintly excessive firmness and precision. She wanted to be handled driftingly and felt instead that a long time ago, in an incident that was admittedly not her fault but for which she was nevertheless held to account, she had offended Roger and made his touch hostile. The cloud of the consommé's warmth enveloped her face and revived her poise. In the liquid a slice of lemon lay at fetal peace. Foxy waited instinctively for grace. Instead there was the tacit refusal that has evolved, a brief bump of silence they all held their breaths through. Then Bea's serene spoon tapped into the soup, the spell was broken, dinner began.

Roger on her right asked Foxy, "Your new house, the Robinson place. Are you happy in it?" Swarthy, his fingernails long and buffed, her host seemed older than his age; his dark knitting eyebrows made constant demands upon the rest of his face. His mouth was the smallest man's mouth she had ever seen, a snail's foot of a mouth.

She answered, "Quite. It's been primitive, and probably very good for us."

The man on her left, the bald dentist Thorne, said, "Primitive? Explain what you mean."

The soup was good, clear yet strong, with a garnish of parsley and a distant horizon of sherry: she wanted to enjoy it, it was lately so rare that she enjoyed food. She said, "I mean primitive. It's an old summer house. It's cold. We've bought some electric heaters for our bedroom and the kitchen but all they really do is roast your ankles. You should see us hop around in the morning; it's like a folk dance. I'm so glad we have no children at this point." The table had fallen silent, listening. She had said more than she had intended. Blushing, she bent her face to the shallow amber depths where the lemon slice like an embryo swayed.

"I understand," Freddy Thorne persisted, "the word 'primitive.' I meant explain why you thought it was good for you."

"Oh, I think any hardship is good for the character. Don't you?"

"Define 'character.' "

"Define 'define.' " She had construed his Socratic nagging as a ploy, a method he had developed with women, to lead them out. After each utterance, there was a fishy inward motion of his lips as if to demonstrate how to take the bait. No teeth showed in his mouth. It waited, a fraction open, for her to come into it. As a mouth, it was neither male nor female, and not quite infantile. His nose was insignificant. His eyes were lost behind concave spectacle lenses that brimmed with tremulous candlelight. His hair once might have been brown, or sandy, but had become a colorless fuzz, an encircling shadow, above his ears; like all bald heads his had a shine that seemed boastful. So repulsive, Freddy assumed the easy intrusiveness of a very attractive man.

Overhearing her rebuff, the man across the table, Smith, said, "Give it to him, girl," adding as if to clarify: "*Le donnez-lui.*" It was evidently a habit, a linguistic tic.

Roger Guerin broke in. Foxy sensed his desire, in this presuming group, to administer a minimal code of manners. He asked her, "Have you hired a contractor yet?"

"No. The only one we know at all is the man who's the partner of the man who sold us the place. Pi-et . . . ?"

"Piet Hanema," the Smith woman called from beyond Freddy Thorne, leaning forward so she could be seen. She was a petite tense brunette with a severe central parting and mobile earrings whose flicker communicated across her face. "Rhymes with sweet."

"With indiscreet," Freddy Thorne said.

Foxy asked, "You all know him?"

The entire table fully laughed.

"He's the biggest neurotic in town," Freddy Thorne explained. "He's an orphan because of a car accident ten years or so ago and he goes around pinching everybody's fanny because he's still arrested. For God's sake, don't hire him. He'll take forever and charge you a fortune. Or rather his shyster partner Gallagher will."

"Freddy," said his wife, who sat across from Foxy. She was a healthy-looking short woman with a firm freckled chin and narrow Donatello nose.

"Freddy, I don't think you're being quite fair," Frank Appleby called from the end of the table, beyond Marcia little-Smith. His large teeth and gums were bared when he talked, and there was a salival spray that sparkled in candlelight. His head was florid and his eyes often bloodshot. He had big well-shaped hands. Foxy liked him, reading an intended kindness into his jokes. "I thought at the last town meeting that the fire chief was voted the most neurotic. If you had another candidate you should have spoken up." Frank explained to Foxy, "His name is Buzz Kappiotis and he's one of these local Greeks whose uncles own the town. His wife runs the Supreme Laundry and she's pretty supreme herself, she's even fatter than Janet." His wife stuck out her tongue at him. "He has a pathological fear of exceeding the speed limit and screams whenever the ladder truck goes around a corner."

Harold little-Smith, whose uptilted nose showed a shiny double inquisitive tip, said, "Also he's afraid of heights, heat, water, and dogs *L'eau et les chiens.*"

Appleby continued, "The only way you can get your house insured in this town is to give Liberty Mutual even odds."

Little-Smith added, "Whenever the alarm goes off, the kids in town all rush to the spot with marshmallows and popcorn."

Roger Guerin said to Foxy, "It is true, the rates in town are the highest in Plymouth County. But we have so many old wooden houses."

"Yours is beautifully restored," Foxy told him.

"We find it inhibiting as far as furniture goes. Actually, Piet Hanema was the contractor."

Seated between Ken and little-Smith, Janet Appleby, a powdered plump vexed face with charcoal lids and valentine lips, cried, "And that alarm!" Leaning toward Foxy in explanation, she dipped the tops of her breasts creamily into the light. "You can't hear it down on the marsh, but we live just across the river and it's the absolutely worst noise I ever heard anything civic make. The children in town call it the Dying Cow."

"We've become slaves to auctions," Roger Guerin was continuing. From the square shape of his head Foxy guessed he was Swiss rather than French in ancestry.

Her side was nudged and Freddy Thorne told her, "Roger thinks auctions are like Monopoly games. All over New Hampshire and Rhode Island they know him as the Mad Bidder from Tarbox. Highboys, lowboys, bus boys. He's crazy for commodes."

"Freddy exaggerates," Roger said.

"He's very discriminating," Bea called from her end of the table.

"That's not what I'm told they call it," Harold little-Smith was saying to Janet.

"What are you told, dear?" Janet responded.

Harold dipped his fingers into his water goblet and flicked them at her face; three or four drops, each holding a spark of reflection, appeared on her naked shoulders. "*Femme méchante,*" he said.

Frank Appleby intervened, telling Ken and Foxy, "The phrase the children use when the alarm goes would translate into decent language as, 'The Deity is releasing gas.' "

Marcia said, "The children bring home scandalous jokes from school. The other day Jonathan came and told me, 'Mother, the governor has two cities in Massachusetts named after him. One is Peabody. What's the other?'"

"Marblehead," Janet said. "Frankie thought that was the funniest thing he'd ever heard."

Bea Guerin and the silent wife of Freddy Thorne rose and took the soup plates away. Foxy had only half-finished. Mrs. Thorne politely hesitated. Foxy rested her spoon and put her hands in her lap. The soup vanished. Oh thank you. Circling the table, Bea said singingly, "My favorite townsperson is the old lady with the *National Geographics*."

Little-Smith, aware that Ken had not spoken a word, turned to him politely; fierily illuminated, the tip of his nose suggested something diabolical, a cleft foot. "Did Frank tell me you were a geographer, or was it geologist?"

"Biochemist," Ken said.

"He should meet Ben Saltz," Janet said.

"The fate worse than death," Freddy said, "if you don't mind my being anti-Semitic."

Foxy asked the candlelit air, *"National Geographics?"*

"She has them all," the little-Smith woman said, leaning not toward Foxy but toward Ken across the table. From Foxy's angle she was in profile, her lower lip saucily retracted and her earring twittering beside her jaw like a tiny machine. Ken abruptly laughed. His laugh was a boy's, sudden and high and disproportionate. In private with her, he rarely laughed.

Encouraged, the others went on. The old lady was the very last of the actual Tarboxes, and she lived in one or two rooms of a big Victorian shell on Divinity Street toward the fire station, crammed in among the shops, diagonally across from the post office and Freddy's office, and her father, who had owned the hosiery mill that now makes plastic ducks for bath tubs, and teething rings, had been a charter subscriber. They were neatly stacked along the walls, twelve issues every year, since 1888.

"The town engineer," Frank Appleby pronounced, "calculates that with the arrival of the issue of November 1984, she will be crushed to death."

"Like a character in Poe," little-Smith said, and determinedly addressed his wife. "Marcia, which? *Not* 'The Pit and the Pendulum.' "

"Harold, you're confused by 'The House of Usher,' " she told him.

"*Non, non,* tu *es confuse,*" he said, and Foxy felt that but for the table between them they would have clawed each other. "There *is* a story, of walls squeezing in."

Janet said, "It happens on television all the time," and went on in general, "What *can* we do about our children watching? Frankie's becoming an absolute zombie."

Frank Appleby said, "It's called 'The Day the Walls Squeezed In.' As told to Jim Bishop."

Ken added, "By I. M. Flat, a survivor in two dimensions," and laughed so hard a candle flame wavered.

Marcia said, "Speaking of television, you know what I just read? By the year 1990 they're going to have one in every room, so everybody can be watched. The article said"—she faltered, then swiftly proceeded—"nobody could commit adultery." An angel passed overhead.

"My God," Frank said. "They'll undermine the institution of marriage."

The laughter, Foxy supposed, was cathartic.

Freddy Thorne murmured to her, "Your husband is quite witty. He's not such a stick as I thought. I. M. Flat in two dimensions. I like it."

Harold little-Smith was not amused. He turned the conversation outward, saying, "Say. Wasn't that a shocker about the *Thresher?*"

"What shocked you about it?" Freddy asked, with that slippery thrusting undertone. So it wasn't just women he used it on.

"I think it's shocking," little-Smith iterated, "that in so-called peacetime we send a hundred young men to be crushed at the bottom of the sea."

Freddy said, "They enlisted. We've all been through it, Harry boy. We took our chances honeymooning with Uncle, and so did they. *Che sarà sarà,* as Dodo Day so shrewdly puts it."

Janet asked Harold, "Why 'so-called'?"

Harold snapped, "We'll be at war with China in five years. We're at war with her now. Kennedy'll up the stakes in Laos just enough to keep the economy humming. What we need in Laos is another Diem."

Janet said, "Harold, that's reactionary shit. I get enough of that from Frank."

Roger Guerin said to Foxy, "Don't take them too seriously. There's nothing romantic or eccentric about Tarbox. The Puritans tried to make it a port but they got silted in. Like everything in New England, it's passé, only more so."

"Roger," Janet protested, "that's a rotten thing for you to be telling this child, what with our lovely churches and old houses and marshes and absolutely grand beach. I think we're the prettiest unself*con*scious town in America." She did not acknowledge that, as she was speaking, Harold little-Smith was blotting, with the tip of his index finger, each of the water drops he had flicked onto her shoulders.

Frank Appleby bellowed, "Do you two want a towel?"

A leg of lamb and a bowl of vegetables were brought in. The host stood and carved. His hands with their long polished nails could have posed for a cookbook diagram: the opening wedge, the lateral cut along the lurking bone, the vertical slices precise as petals, two to a plate. The plates were passed the length of the table to Bea, who added spring peas and baby potatoes and mint jelly. Plain country fare, Foxy thought; she and Ken had lived six years in Cambridge, a region of complicated casseroles and Hungarian goulashes and garlicky salads and mock duck and sautéed sweetbreads. Among these less sophisticated eaters Foxy felt she could be, herself, a delicacy, a princess. Frank Appleby was given two bottles to uncork, local-liquor-store Bordeaux, and went around the table twice, pouring once for the ladies, and then for the men. In Cambridge the Chianti was passed from hand to hand without ceremony.

Freddy Thorne proposed a toast. "For our gallant boys in the *Thresher*."

"Freddy, that ghoulish!" Marcia little-Smith cried.

"Freddy, really," Janet said.

Freddy shrugged and said, "It came from the heart. Take it or leave it. *Mea culpa, mea culpa.*"

Foxy saw that he was used to rejection; he savored it, as if a dark diagnosis had been confirmed. Further she sensed that his being despised served as a unifying purpose for the others, gave them a common identity, as the couples that tolerated Freddy Thorne. Foxy glanced curiously at Thorne's wife. Sensing Foxy's perusal, she glanced up. Her eyes were a startling pale green, slightly protruding, drilled with pupils like the eyes of Roman portrait busts. Foxy thought she must be made of something very hard, not to show a scar from her marriage.

"Freddy, I don't think you meant it at all," Janet went on, "not at all. You're delighted it was them and not you."

"You bet. You too. We're all survivors. A dwindling band of survivors. I took my chances. I did my time for God and Uncle."

"You sat at a steel desk reading Japanese pornography," Harold told him.

Freddy looked astonished, his shapeless mouth inbent. "Didn't everybody? We've all heard often enough about you and your geishas. Poor little underfed girls, for a pack of cigarettes and half of a Hershey bar."

His wife's bottle-green eyes gazed at the man as if he belonged to someone else.

"You wonder what they think," Freddy went on, swimming, trying not to drown in their contempt, his black mouth lifted. "The goddam gauges start spinning, the fucking pipes begin to break, and—what? Mother? The flag? Jesu Cristo? The last piece of ass you had?"

A contemptuous silence welled from the men.

"What I found so touching," Bea Guerin haltingly sang, "was the way the tender—is that what it is?—"

"Submarine tender, yes," her husband said.

"—the way the tender was called *Skylark*. And how all morning it called and circled, in the sea that from underneath must look like a sky, circling and calling, and nobody answered. Poor *Skylark*."

Frank Appleby stood. "Too much of water hast thou, poor Ophelia. I propose a toast, to the new couple, the Whitmans."

"Hear," Roger Guerin said, scowling.

"May you long support our tax rolls, whose rate is high and whose benefits are nil."

"Hear, hear." It was little-Smith. "*Écoutez.*"

"Thank you," Foxy said, blushing and feeling a fresh wave of rebuke rising within her. She quickly put down her fork. The lamb was underdone.

Little-Smith tried again with Ken. "What do you do, as a biochemist?"

"I do different things. I think about photosynthesis. I used to slice up starfish extremely thin, to study their metabolism."

Janet Appleby leaned forward again, tipping the creamy tops of her breasts into the warm light, and asked, "And then do they survive, in two dimensions?" Through a lucid curling wave of nausea Foxy saw that her husband was being flirted with.

Ken laughed eagerly. "No, they die. That's the trouble with my field. Life hates being analyzed."

Bea asked, "Is the chemistry very complex?"

"Very. Incredibly. If a clever theologian ever got hold of how complex it is, they'd make us all believe in God again."

Ousted by Bea, Janet turned to them all. "Speaking of that," she said, "what does this old Pope John keep bothering us about? He acts as if we all voted him in."

"I like him," Harold said. "*Je l'adore.*"

Marcia told him, "But you like Khrushchev too."

"I like old men. They can be wonderful bastards because they have nothing to lose. The only people who can be themselves are babies and old bastards."

"Well," Janet said, "I tried to read this *Pacem in Terris* and it's as dull as something from the UN."

"Hey Roger," Freddy called across Foxy, his breath meaty, "how do you like the way U Whosie has bopped Tshombe in the Congo? Takes a nigger to beat a nigger."

"I think it's *lovely*," Bea said emphatically to Ken, touching his sleeve, "that it's so complex. I don't want to be understood."

Ken said, "Luckily, the processes are pretty much the same throughout the kingdom of life. A piece of yeast and you, for example, break down glucose into pyruvic acid by exactly the same eight transformations." This was an aspect of him that Foxy rarely saw any more, the young man who could say "the kingdom of life." Who did he think was king?

Bea said, "Oh dear. Some days I *do* feel moldy."

Freddy persisted, though Roger's tiny mouth had tightened in response. "The trouble with Hammarskjöld," he said, "he was too much like you and me, Roger. Nice guys."

Marcia little-Smith called to her husband, "Darling, who isn't letting you be a wonderful old bastard? Terrible me?"

"Actually, Hass," Frank Appleby said, "I see you as our local Bertrand Russell."

"I put him more as a Schweitzer type," Freddy Thorne said.

"You bastards, I mean it." The tip of his nose lifted under persecution like the flowery nose of a mole. "Look at Kennedy. There's somebody inside that robot trying to get out, but it doesn't dare because he's too young. He'd be crucified."

Janet Appleby said, "*Let's* talk news. We always talk people. I've been reading the newspaper while Frank reads Shakespeare. *Why* is Egypt merging with those other Arabs? Don't they know they have Israel in between? It's as bad as us and Alaska."

"I love you, Janet," Bea called, across Ken. "You think like I do."

"Those countries aren't countries," Harold said. "They're just branches of Standard Oil. *L'huile étendarde.*"

"Tell us some more Shakespeare, Frank," Freddy said.

"We have laughed," Frank said, "to see the sails conceive, and grow big-bellied with the wanton wind. *Midsummer Night's Dream.* Isn't that a grand image? I've been holding it in my mind for days. Grow big-bellied with the wanton wind." He stood and poured more wine around. Foxy put her hand over the mouth of her glass.

Freddy Thorne leaned close to her and said, "You don't have much of an appetite. Tummy trouble?"

"Seriously," Roger Guerin said on her other side, "I'd have no hesitation about calling Hanema and at least getting an estimate. He does very solid work. He's one of the few contractors left, for instance, who puts up honest plaster walls. And his job for us, though it took forever, was really very loving. Restoration is probably his forte."

Bea added, "He's a dear little old-fashioned kind of man."

"You'll be so-orry," Freddy Thorne said.

Frank Appleby called, "And you can get him to build a dike for you so Ken can farm the marsh. There's a fortune to be made in salt hay. It's used to mulch artichokes."

Foxy turned to her tormentor. "Why don't you like him?" She had abruptly remembered who Hanema was. At Frank's party, a short red-haired man clownishly lying at the foot of the stairs had looked up her dress.

"I *do* like him," Freddy Thorne told her. "I love him. I love him like a brother."

"And he you," little-Smith said quickly.

Thorne said, "To tell the truth, I feel homosexually attracted to him."

"Freddy," Thorne's wife said in a level voice hardly intended to be heard.

"He has a lovely wife," Roger said.

"She *is* lovely," Bea Guerin called. "So serene. I envy the wonderful way she *moves*. Don't you, Georgene?"

"Angela's really a robot," Frank Appleby said, "with Jack Kennedy inside her, trying to get out."

"I don't know," Georgene Thorne said, "that she's so perfect. I don't think she gives Piet very much."

"She gives him social aplomb," Harold said.

Freddy said, "I bet she even gives him a bang now and then. She's human. Hell, everybody's human. That's my theory."

Foxy asked him, "What does he do neurotic?"

"You heard Roger describe the way he builds. He's anally neat. Also, he goes to church."

"But *I* go to church. I wouldn't be without it."

"Frank," Freddy called, "I think I've found the fourth." Foxy guessed he meant that she was the fourth most neurotic person in town, behind the fire chief, the Dutch contractor, and the lady doomed to be crushed by magazines.

Foxy came from Maryland and partook of the aggressiveness of southern women. "You *must* tell me what you mean by 'neurotic.' "

Thorne smiled. His sickly mouth by candlelight invited her to come in. "You haven't told me what you mean by 'character.' "

"Perhaps," Foxy said, scornfully bright, "we mean the same thing." She disliked this man, she had never in her memory met a man she disliked more, and she tried to elicit, from the confusion within her body, a clear expression of this.

He leaned against her and whispered, "Eat some of Bea's lamb, just to be polite, even if it is raw." Then he turned from her, as if snubbing a petitioner, and lit Marcia's cigarette. As he did so, his thigh deliberately slid against Foxy's. She was startled, amused, disgusted. This fool imagined he had made a conquest. She felt in him, and then dreaded, a desire to intrude upon, to figure in, her fate. His thigh increased its pressure and in the lulling dull light she experienced an escapist craving for sleep. She glanced about for rescue. Her host, his eyebrows knitted tyrannically above the bridge of his nose, was concentrating on carving more lamb. Across the table her husband, the father of her need for sleep, was laughing between Bea Guerin and Janet Appleby. The daggery shadow in the cleft between Janet's lush breasts changed shape as her hands darted in emphasis of unheard sentences. More wine was poured. Foxy nodded, in assent to a question she thought had been asked her, and snapped her head upright in fear of having dropped asleep. Her thigh was nudged again. No one would speak to her. Roger Guerin was murmuring, administering some sort of consolation, to Georgene Thorne. Ken's high hard laugh rang out, and his face, usually so ascetic, looked pasty and unreal, as if struck by a searchlight. He was having a good time; she was hours from bed.

As they drove home, the night revived her. The fresh air was cool and the sky like a great wave collapsing was crested with stars. Their headlights picked up mailboxes, hedgerows, crusts of dry snow in a ditch. Ken's MG swayed with each turn of the winding beach road. He asked her, "Are you dead?"

"I'm all right now. I wasn't sure I could get through it when we were at the table."

"It *was* pretty ghastly."

"They seemed so excited by each other."

"Funny people." As if guilty, he added, "Poor Fox, sitting there yawning with her big belly."

"Was I too stupid? I told Bea."

"For God's sake, why?"

"I wanted a pretend martini. Are you ashamed of my being pregnant?"

"No, but why broadcast it? It'll show soon enough."

"She won't tell anybody."

"It doesn't matter."

How little, Foxy thought, *does matter to you.* The trees by the roadside fell away, and rushed back in clumps, having revealed in the gaps cold stretches of moonlit marsh. The mailboxes grew fewer. Fewer houselights showed. Foxy tightened around her her coat, a fur-lined gabardine cut in imitation of a Russian general's greatcoat. She foresaw their cold home with its flimsy walls and senile furnace. She said, "We *must* get a contractor. Should we ask this man Hanema to give us an estimate?"

"Thorne says he's a fanny-pincher."

"That's called projection."

"Janet told me he almost bought the house himself. His wife apparently wanted the view."

Janet, is it?

Foxy said, "Did you notice the antagonism between Frank and the little-Smith man?"

"Aren't they both in stocks somehow? Maybe they're competing."

"Ken, you're so work-oriented. I felt it had to do with s-e-x."

"With Janet?"

"Well, she was certainly trying to make some point with her bosom."

He giggled. *Stop it,* she thought, *it isn't you.* "Two points," he said.

"I knew you'd say that," she said.

There was a rise in the road, cratered by frost heaves, from which the sea was first visible. She saw that moonlight lived on the water, silver, steady, sliding with the motion of their car, yet holding furious myriad oscillations, like, she supposed, matter itself. Ken worked down there, where the protons swung from molecule to molecule and elements interlocked in long spiral ladders. A glimpse of dunes: bleached bones. The car sank into a dip. There were four such rises and falls between the deserted, boarded-up ice-cream stand and their driveway. They lived near the end of the road, an outpost in winter. Foxy abruptly craved the lightness, the freedom, of summer.

Ken said, "Your friend Thorne had a very low opinion of Hanema."

"He is *not* my friend. He is an odious man and I don't understand why everybody likes him so much."

"He's a dentist. Everybody needs a dentist. Janet told me he wanted to be a psychiatrist but flunked medical school."

"He's awful, all clammy and cozy and I kept feeling he wanted to get his hands inside me. I cut him short and he thought I was making a pass. He played kneesies with me."

"But he sat beside you."

"Sideways kneesies."

"I suppose it can be done."

"I think his poor opinion should be counted as a plus."

Ken said nothing.

Foxy went on, "Roger Guerin said he was a good contractor. He did their house. With their money they could have afforded anybody."

"Let's think about it. I'd rather get somebody nobody knows. I don't want us to get too involved in this little nest out here."

"I thought one of the reasons we moved was so our friendships wouldn't be so much at the mercy of your professional acquaintance."

"Say that again?"

"You know what I said. I didn't have any friends of my own, just chemical wives."

"Fox, that's what we all are. Chemicals." He knew she didn't believe that, why did he say it? When would he let her out of school?

A mailbox rammed by a snowplow leaned vacantly on the moonlight. The box belonged to summer people and would not be righted for months. Foxy wrapped her greatcoat tighter around her and in the same motion wrapped her body, her own self, around the small sour trouble brewing in her womb, this alien life furtively exploiting her own. She felt ugly and used. She said, "You really *liked* those women, didn't you, with their push-me-up bras and their get-me-out-of-this giggles?" The women they had known in Cambridge had tended to be plain Quaker girls placidly wed to rising grinds, or else women armored in a repellent brilliance of their own, untouchable gypsy beauties with fiery views on Cuban sovereignty and German guilt. Foxy sighed as if in resignation. "Well, they say a man gets his first mistress when his wife becomes pregnant."

He looked over at her too surprised to speak, and she realized that he was incapable of betraying her, and marveled at her own disappointment. She puzzled herself; she had never been in their marriage more dependent upon him, or with more cause for gratitude. Yet a chemistry of unrest had arisen within her body, and she resented his separation from it. For she had always felt and felt now in him a fastidious, unlapsing accountability that shirked the guilt she obscurely felt belonged to life; and thus he left her with a double share.

He said at last, "What are you suggesting? We were invited. We went. We might as well enjoy it. I have nothing against mediocre people, provided I don't have to teach them anything."

Ken was thirty-two. They had met when he was a graduate student instructing in Biology 10 and she was a Radcliffe senior in need of a science credit. Since her sophomore year Foxy had been in love with a fine-arts major, a bearish Jewish boy from Detroit. He had since become a sculptor whose large welded assemblages of junk metal were occasionally pictured in magazines. There had been a clangor about him even then, a snuffly explosive air of self-parody, with his wiglike mop of hair, combed straight forward, and a nose so hooked its tip appeared to point at his lower lip. The curves of his face had been compressed around a certain contemptuousness. His tongue could quickly uncoil. *Eat me up, little shiksa, I'm a dirty old man. I sneeze black snot. I pop my piles with a prophylactic toothbrush.* He scorned any sign of fear from her. He taught her to blow. His prick enormous in her mouth, she felt her love of him as a billowing and gentle tearing of veils inside her. Before he took her up she had felt pale, tall, stiff, cold, unusable. His back was hairy and humpily muscular across the shoulder blades and thickly sown, as if by a curse, with moles.

With a tact more crushing than brute forbidding her parents gradually made her love grotesque and untenable. She did not know how they did it: it was as if her parents and Peter communicated through her, without her knowing what was being said, until the *No* came from both sides, and met beneath her ribs. That schoolgirl ache, and all those cigarettes. Her senior year at Radcliffe, it had snowed and snowed; she remembered the twittering of the bicycles pushed on the paths, the song of unbuckled galoshes, the damp scarf around her neck, the fluttering of crystals, meek as thoughts, at the tall serene windows of the Fogg. She remembered the bleached light that had filled her room each morning before she awoke to the soreness in her chest.

Ken appeared, was taller than she, wanted her, was acceptable and was accepted on all sides; similarly, nagging mathematical problems abruptly crack open. Foxy could find no fault with him, and this challenged her, touched off her stubborn defiant streak. She felt between his handsomeness and intelligence a contradiction that might develop into the convoluted humor of her Jew. Ken looked like a rich boy and worked like a poor one. From Farmington, he was the only son of a Hartford lawyer who never lost a case. Foxy came to imagine his birth as cool and painless, without a tear or outcry. Nothing puzzled him. There were unknowns but no mysteries. After her own degrading miscalculation—for this was what her first romance must have been, it ended in such a flurry of misery—Foxy sought shelter in Ken's weatherproof rightness. She accepted gratefully his simple superiority to other people. He was better-looking, better-thinking, a better machine. He was fallible only if he took her, on the basis of the cool poise her tallness had demanded, for another of the same breed.

She was, Elizabeth Fox from Bethesda, known to herself in terms of suppressed warmth. Applaudingly her adolescent heart had watched itself tug toward stray animals, lost children, forsaken heroines, and toward the bandaged wounded perambulating around the newly built hospital, with its ugly tall rows of windows like zipped zippers. They had moved from east Washington in the spring of 1941, as the hospital was being built. Her father was a career navy man, a lieutenant commander with some knowledge of engineering and an exaggerated sense of lineage. One of his grandfathers had been a Virginia soldier; the other, a New Jersey parson. He felt himself to be a gentleman and told Foxy, when she came to him at the age of twelve inspired to be a nurse, that she was too intelligent, that she would someday go to college. At Radcliffe, looking back, she supposed that her sense of deflected tenderness dated from her father's long absences during World War II; the accident of global war had deprived her of the filial transition to heterosexual relationships free of slavishness, of the expiatory humiliations she goaded Peter to inflict. Now, herself married, milder and less mathematical in her self-analyses, she wondered if the sadness, the something broken and uncompleted in her upbringing, was not older than the war and belonged to the Depression, whose shadowy air of magnificent impotence, of trolley cars and sinusitis, still haunted the official mausoleums of Washington when she visited her mother. Perhaps the trouble had merely been that her mother, though shrewd and once pretty, had not been a gentlewoman, but a Maryland grocer's daughter.

Foxy had no sooner married than her parents had gotten divorced. Her father, his thirty years of service expired, far from retiring, took a lucrative advisory job to the shipbuilding industry, and moved to San Diego. Her mother, as if defiantly showing that she too could navigate in the waters of prosperity, remarried: a wealthy Georgetown widower, a Mr. Roth, who owned a chain of coin-operated laundromats, mostly in Negro neighborhoods. Foxy's mother now made herself up carefully, put on a girdle even to go shopping, kept a poodle, smoked red-tipped filtered cigarettes, was known to their friends as "Connie," and always spoke of her husband as "Roth."

The couple Foxy's parents had been had vanished. The narrow shuttered frame house on Rosedale Street. The unused front porch. The tan shades always drawn against the heat. The electric fan in the kitchen swinging its slow head back and forth like an imbecile scolding in monotone. The staticky Philco conveying Lowell Thomas. The V-mail spurting through the thrilled slot. The once-a-week Negro woman, called Gracelyn, whose apron pockets smelled of orange peels and Tootsie Rolls. Veronica their jittery spayed terrier who was succeeded by Merle, a slavering black-tongued Chow. The parched flowerless shrubbery where Elizabeth would grub for bottlecaps and "clues," the long newspaper-colored ice-cream evenings, the red-checked oilcloth on the kitchen table worn bare at two settings, the way her mother would sit nights at this table, after the news, before putting her daughter to bed, smoking a Chesterfield and smoothing with a jerky automatic motion the skin beneath her staring eyes: these images had vanished everywhere but in Foxy's heart. She went to church to salvage something. Episcopalianism—its rolling baritone hymns to the sea, its pews sparkling with the officers' shoulder-braid—had belonged to the gallant club of Daddy's friends, headed by caped Mr. Roosevelt, that fought and won the war.

She was graduated and married in June of 1956.

Every marriage is a hedged bet. Foxy entered hers expecting that, whatever fate held for them, there were certain kinds of abuse it would never occur to her husband to inflict. He was beyond them, as most American men are beyond eye-gouging and evisceration. She had been right. He had proved not so much gentle as too fastidious to be cruel. She had no just complaints: only the unjust one that the delay while she waited barren for Ken to complete his doctorate had been long. Four intended years of post-graduate work had been stretched into five by the agonies of his dissertation; two more were spent in a post-doctoral fellowship granted by the U.S. Public Health Service; and then Ken squandered another as an instructor in the vicinity of the same magnetic Harvard gods, whose very names Foxy had come to hate. For her, there had been jobs, little research assistantships amid Flemish prints or Mesozoic fern fossils in comfortable dusty Harvard basements, a receptionist's desk at University Hall, an involvement in a tutoring project for mentally disturbed children that had led her to consider and then to run from a career in social work, some random graduate courses, a stab at a master's degree, two terms of life-drawing in Boston, vacations, even flirtations: but nothing fruitful. Seven years is long, counted in months paid for with a punctual tax of blood, in weeks whose pleasure is never free of the belittling apparatus of contraception, longer than a war. She had wanted to bear Ken a child, to brew his excellence in her warmth. This seemed the best gift she could offer him, since she grew to know that there was something of herself she withheld. A child, a binding of their chemistries, would be an honest pledge of her admiration and trust and would remove them for good from the plane where the sufficiency of these feelings could be doubted. Now this gift was permitted. Ken was an assistant professor at the university across the river, where the department of biochemistry was more permeable to rapid advancement. Their reasons for happiness were as sweeping as the view from their new house.

The house had been Ken's choice. She had thought they should live closer to Boston, in Lexington perhaps, among people like themselves. Tarbox was an outer limit, an hour's drive, and yet he, who must do the commuting, seized the house as if all his life he had been waiting for a prospect as vacant and pure as these marshes, those bony far dunes, that rim of sea. Perhaps, Foxy guessed, it was a matter of scale: his microscopic work needed the relief of such a vastness. And it had helped that he and the real-estate man Gallagher had liked each other. Though she had raised all the reasonable objections, Foxy had been pleased to see him, after the long tame stasis of student existence, emerge to want something new, physical, real. That he had within him even the mild strangeness needed to insist on an out-of-the-way impractical house seemed (as if there had been a question of despair) hopeful.

The house tonight was cold, stored with stale chill. Cotton, their cat, padded loudly toward them from the dark living room and, stiff from sleep, stretched. He was a heavy-footed caramel tom that in years of being their only pet had acquired something of a dog's companionableness and something of a baby's conceit. Courteously he bowed before them, his tail an interrogation mark, his front claws planted in the braided rag rug the Robinsons had abandoned in the hall. Cotton pulled his claws free with a dainty unsticking noise and purred in anticipation of Foxy's picking him up. She held him, his throaty motor running, beneath her chin and like a child wished herself magically inside his pelt.

Ken switched on a light in the living room. The bare walls leaped into being, the exposed studs, the intervals of varnish, the crumbling gypsum wallboard, the framed souvenirs of old summers—fan-shaped shell collections and dried arrays of littoral botany—that the Robinsons had left. They had never met them but Foxy saw them as a large sloppy family, full of pranks and nicknames for each other and hobbies, the mother watercoloring (her work was tacked all around upstairs), the older boys sailing in the marsh, the girl moonily collecting records and being teased, the younger boy and the father systematically combing the shore for classifiable examples of life. The room smelled as if summer had been sealed in and yet had leaked out. The French windows giving onto a side garden of roses and peonies were boarded. The shutters were locked over the windows that would have looked onto the porch and the marsh. The sharp-edged Cambridge furniture, half Door Store and half Design Research, looked scattered and sparse; the room was a good size and of a good square shape. It had possibilities. It needed white paint and walls and light and love and style. She said, "We *must* start doing things."

Ken felt the floor register with his hand. "The furnace is dead again."

"Leave it to morning. No warmth gets upstairs anyway."

"I don't like being outsmarted. I'm going to learn how to bank this bastard."

"I'm more worried about dying in my sleep of coal gas."

"No chance of that in this sieve."

"Ken, please call Hanema."

"You call him."

"You're the man of the house."

"I'm not sure he's the right man."

"You like Gallagher."

"They're not twins, they're partners."

"Then find somebody else."

"If you want him, you call him."

"Well I just might."

"Go ahead. Fine." He went to the door that led down into the narrow hole that did for a basement. The register began to clank and release a poisonous smell. Foxy carried Cotton into the kitchen, plugged in the electric heater, and poured two bowls of milk. One she set on the floor for the cat; the other she broke Saltines into, for herself. Cotton sniffed, disdained the offering, and interrogatively mewed. Foxy ignored him and ate greedily with a soup spoon. Crackers and milk had been a childhood treat between news and bedtime; her craving for it had come over her like a sudden release from fever, a gust of health. While the glow of the heater and the begging friction of fur alternated on her legs, she spread butter thickly on spongy white bread, tearing it, overweighting it, three pieces one after the other, too ravenous to bother with toast, compulsive as a drunk. Her fingertips gleamed with butter.

Washing them, she leaned on her slate sink and gazed from the window. The tide was high; moonlight displayed a silver saturation overflowing the linear grid of ditches. Against the sheen was silhouetted a little houseless island of brambles. In the distance, along the far arm of Tarbox Bay, the lights of another town, whose name she had not yet learned, spangled the horizon. A revolving searchlight rhythmically stroked the plane of ocean. Its beam struck her face at uneven intervals. She counted: five, two, five, two. A double beam. Seconds slipping, gone; five, two. She hastily turned and rolled up the cellophane breadwrapper; a voluminous sadness had been carved for her out of the night. It was after midnight. Today was Easter. She must get up for church.

Ken returned from the furnace and laughed at the traces of her hunger—the gouged butter, the clawed crumbs, the empty bowl.

She said, "Yes, and it's the cheap bread I feel starved for, not Pepperidge Farm. That old-fashioned rubbery kind with all the chemicals."

"Calcium propionate," he said. "Our child will be an agglutinated monster."

"Did you mean it, I should call this Dutchman?"

"Why not? See what he says. He must know the house, if his wife wanted it."

But she heard doubt in his even voice and changed the subject. "You know what bothered me about those people tonight?"

"They were Republicans."

"Don't be silly, I couldn't care less. No what bothered me was they wanted us to love them. They weren't lovable, but that's what they wanted."

He laughed. Why should his laugh grate so? "Maybe that's what *you* wanted," he told her.

They went to bed up a staircase scarred and crayoned by children they had never seen. Foxy assumed that, with the revival of her appetite, she would enjoy a great animal draught of sleep. Ken kissed her shoulder in token of the love they should not in this month make, turned his back, and quickly went still. His breathing was inaudible and he never moved. The stillness of his body established a tension she could not quite sink through, like a needle on the skin of water. Downstairs, Cotton's heavy feet padding back and forth unsatisfied seemed to make the whole house tremble. The moon, so bright it had no face, was framed by the skylight and for an hour of insomnia burned in the center of her forehead like a jewel.

Monday morning: in-and-out. A powdery blue sky the color of a hymnal. Sunshine broken into code by puffs and schooners of cumulus. The Thornes' sunporch—the tarpaper deck-roof of their garage, sheltered from the wind by feathery tall larches, entered by sliding glass doors from the bedroom—cupped warmth. Every year Georgene had the start of a tan before anyone else. Today she looked already freckled, austere and forbidding in her health.

She had spread her plaid blanket in the corner where she had tacked reflecting sheets of aluminum broiling foil to the balustrade. Piet took off his suède apricot windbreaker and sank down. The sun, tepid and breezy to a standing man, burned the skin of his broad face and dyed his retinas red. "Bliss," he said.

She resumed her place on the blanket and her forearm touched his: the touch felt like a fine grade of sandpaper with a little warm sting of friction left. She was in only underwear. He got up on his elbow and kissed her belly, flat and soft and hot, and remembered his mother's ironing board and how she would have him lay his earaches on its comforting heat; he put his ear against Georgene's belly and overheard a secret squirm of digestion. Still attentive to the sun, she fingered his hair and fumblingly measured his shoulders. She said, "You have too many clothes on."

His voice came out plucking and beggarly. "Baby, I don't have time. I should be over on Indian Hill. We're clearing out trees." He listened for the rasp and spurt of his power saws; the hill was a mile away.

"Please stay a minute. Don't come just to tease me."

"I can't make love. I don't tease. I came to say hello and that I missed you all weekend. We weren't at the same parties. The Gallaghers had us over with the Ongs. Very dreary."

"We talked about you at the Guerins Saturday night. It made me feel quite lovesick." She sat up and began to unbutton his shirt. Her lower lip bent in beneath her tongue. Angela made the same mouth doing up snowsuits. All women, so solemn in their small tasks, it tickled him, it moved him in a surge, seeing suddenly the whole world sliding forward on this female unsmilingness about things physical—unbuttoning, ironing, sunbathing, cooking, lovemaking. The world sewn together by such tasks. He let her fumble and kissed the gauzy sideburn, visible only in sun, in front of her ear. Even here a freckle had found itself. Seed. Among thorns. Fallen. She opened the wings of his shirt and tried to push the cloth back from his shoulders, an exertion bringing against him her bra modestly swollen and the tender wishbone blankness above. The angle of her neck seemed meek. He peeled his shirt off, and his undershirt: weightless as water spiders, reflected motes from the aluminum foil skated the white skin and amber hair of his chest.

Piet pulled Georgene into the purple shadow his shoulders cast. Her flesh gentle in her underthings possessed a boyish boniness not like Angela's elusive abundance. Touch Angela, she vanished. Touch Georgene, she was there. This simplicity at times made their love feel incestuous to Piet, a connection too direct. Her forbearance enlarged, he suspected, what was already weak and overextended in him. All love is a betrayal, in that it flatters life. The loveless man is best armed. A jealous God. She opened wide her mouth and drew his tongue into a shapeless wet space; fluttering melted into a forgetful encompassing; he felt lost and pulled back, alarmed. Her lips looked blurred and torn. The green of her eyes was deepened by his shadow. He asked her, "What was said?"

Gazing beyond him, she groped. "The Whitmans were wondering—she's with chi-yuld, by the way—the Whitmans were wondering if you should be the contractor for their house. Frank said you were awful, and Roger said you were great."

"Appleby talked me down? That son of a bitch, what have I done to him? I've never slept with Janet."

"Maybe it was Smitty, I forget. It was just one remark, a joke, really."

Her face was guarded in repose, her chin set and the corners of her mouth downdrawn, with such a studied sadness. The shadows of the larch boughs shuffled across them. He guessed it had been her husband and changed the subject. "That tall cool blonde with the pink face is pregnant?"

"She told Bea in the kitchen. I must say, she did seem rude. Freddy was being a puppy dog for her and she froze over the soup. She's from the South. Aren't those women afraid of being raped?"

"I watched her drive away from church a Sunday ago. She burned rubber. There's something cooking in that lady."

"It's called a fetus." Her chin went firm, crinkled. She added, "I don't think as a couple they'll swing. Freddy thinks *he's* a stick. I sat right across the table from *her*, and I must say, her big brown eyes never stopped moving. She didn't miss a thing. It was insulting. Freddy was being his usual self and I could see her wondering what to make of *me*."

"None of us know what to make of you."

Pretending to be offended yet truly offended, Piet felt, by his interest in the Whitman woman, Georgene drew herself from his arms and stretched out again on the blanket. Giving the sun his turn: whore. The reflecting foil decorated her face with parabolic dabs and nebulae and spurts: solar jism. Piet jealously shucked his shoes and socks and trousers, leaving his underpants, Paisley drawers. He was a secret dandy. He lay down beside her and when she turned to face him reached around and undid her bra, explaining, "Twins," meaning they should both be dressed alike, in only underpants.

Her breasts were smaller than Angela's, with sunken paler nipples, and, uncovered, seemed to cry for protection. He brought his chest against hers for covering and they lay together beneath the whispering trees, Hansel and Gretel abandoned. Shed needles from the larches had collected in streaks and puddles on the tarpaper and formed rusty ochre drifts along the wooden balustrade and the grooved aluminum base of the sliding glass doors. Piet stroke the uninterrupted curve of her back, his thumb tracing her spine from the knucklelike bones at the nape of her neck to the strangely prominent coccyx. Georgene had the good start of a tail. She was more bone than Angela. Her presence pressing against him seemed so natural and sisterly he failed to lift, whereas even Angela's foot on his instep was enough, and he wondered, half-crushed beneath the span of sky and treetops and birdsong, which he truly loved.

Before their affair, he had ignored Georgene. She had been hidden from him by his contempt for her husband. His, and Angela's, dislike of Freddy Thorne had been immediate, though in their first years in Tarbox the Thornes as a couple had rather courted them. The Hanemas in response had been so rude as to refuse several invitations without an excuse or even a reply. They had not felt much in need of friends then. Piet, not yet consciously unhappy with Angela, had dimly dreamed of making love to other women, to Janet or to stately gypsy-haired Terry Gallagher, as one conjures up fantasies to induce sleep. But two summers ago the Ongs built their tennis court and they saw more of Georgene; and when, a summer ago, Piet's dreams without his volition began to transpose themselves into reality, and unbeknownst to himself he had turned from Angela and become an open question, it was Georgene, in a passing touch at a party, in the apparently unplanned sharing of a car to and from tennis, who attempted an answer, who was there. She said she had been waiting for him for years.

"What else?" he asked.

"What else what?" Behind the sunstruck mask of her face her senses had been attending to his hand.

"What else with you? How's Whitney's cold?"

"Poor little Whit. He had a fever yesterday but I sent him off to school in case you decided to come."

"You shouldn't have done that."

"He'll be all right. Everybody has a spring cold."

"You don't."

She carried forward the note of contention. "Piet, what did you mean, a minute ago, when I told you Frank criticized you, you said you had never slept with Janet?"

"I never have. It's been years since I wanted to."

"But do you think—stop your hand for a second, you're beginning just to tickle—that's why Freddy doesn't like you? I lied, you know. It was Freddy who told the Whitmans you were a bad contractor."

"Of course. The jerk."

"You shouldn't hate him."

"It keeps me young."

"But do you think he *does* know, about us? Freddy."

Her curiosity insulted him; he wanted her to dismiss Freddy

utterly. He said, "Not as a fact. But maybe by osmosis? Bea Guerin implied to me the other night that everybody knows."

"Did you admit it?"

"Of course not. What's the matter? *Does* he know?"

Her face was hushed. A thin bit of light lay balanced across one eyelid, trembling; a stir of wind was rippling the sheets of foil, creating excited miniature thunder. She said carefully, "He tells me I must have somebody else because I don't want him as much as I used to. He feels threatened. And if he had to write up a list of who it might be, I guess you'd be at the top. But for some reason he doesn't draw the conclusion. Maybe he knows and thinks he's saving it to use later."

This frightened him, altered the tone of his body. She felt this and opened her eyes; their Coke-bottle green was flecked with wilt. Her pupils in the sun were as small as the core of a pencil.

He asked her, "Is it time to break off?"

When challenged, Georgene, the daughter of a Philadelphia banker, would affect a playful immigrant accent, part shopgirl, part vamp. "Dunt be zilly, fella," she said, and sharply inched upward and pressed her pelvis against his, so that through his cotton he felt her silk. She held him as if captive. Her smooth arms were strong; she could beat him at tennis, for a set. He wrestled against her hold and in the struggle her breasts were freed, swung bulbous above him, then spilled flat when, knees on thighs and hands on wrists, he pinned her on her back. Tarpaper. Her glistening skin gazed. Wounded by winning, he bowed his head and with suppliant lips took a nipple, faintly salt and sour, in. Suddenly she felt to be all circles, circles that could be parted to yield more circles. Birds chirped beyond the rainbow rim of the circular wet tangency holding him secure. Her hand, feathery, established another tangency, located his core. If her touch could be believed, his balls were all velvet, his phallus sheer silver.

Politely he asked, "Do we have on too many clothes?"

The politeness was real. Lacking marriage or any contract, they had evolved between them a code of mutual consideration. Their adultery was divided precisely in half. By daring to mention their breaking up, by rebuking her with this possibility, Piet had asked

Georgene to cross the line. Now it was her turn to ask, and his to cross. She said, "What about those trees on Indian Hill?"

"They can fall without me," he said. The sun was baking a musty cidery smell from the drift of needles near his face, by the blanket's edge. The tarpaper scintillated. Good quality: Ruberoid Rolled Roofing, mineralized, $4.25 a roll in 1960. He had laid this deck. He added, "I'm not sure you can."

"Oh I'm not so fallen," Georgene said, and quickly sat up, and, kneeling, flauntingly stretched her arms to the corners of the sky. She possessed, this conscientious clubwoman and firm mother, a lovely unexpected gift. Her sexuality was guileless. As formed by the first years of her marriage with Freddy, it had the directness of eating, the ease of running. Her insides were innocent. She had never had an affair before and, though Piet did not understand the virtue she felt in him, he doubted that she would ever take another lover. She had no love of guilt. In the beginning, deciding upon adultery with her, Piet had prepared himself for terrible sensations of remorse, as a diver in midair anticipates the under-water rush and roar. Instead, the first time—it was September: apples in the kitchen, children off at school, except for Judy, who was asleep—Georgene led him lightly by one finger upstairs to her bed. They deftly undressed, she him, he her. When he worried about contraception, she laughed. Didn't Angela use Enovid yet? *Welcome*, she said, *to the post-pill paradise*, a lighthearted blasphemy that immensely relieved him. With Angela the act of love had become overlaid with memories of his clumsiness and her failure to tolerate clumsiness, with the need for tact and her irritation with the pleadingness implicit in tact, her equal disdain of his pajama-clad courting and his naked rage, his helpless transparence and her opaque disenchantment. Georgene in twenty minutes stripped away these laminations of cross-purpose and showed him something primal. Now she kneeled under the sun and Piet rose to be with her and with extreme care, as if setting the wafery last cogwheels of a watch into place, kissed the glossy point of her left shoulder bone, and then of her right. She was double everywhere but in her mouths. All things double. Without duality, entropy. The universe God's mirror.

She said, "You're in my sun."

"It's too soon to have a tan." Politely: "Would you like to go inside?"

The sliding glass door led off the sun deck through a playroom into their big bedroom, a room adorned with Chinese lanterns and African masks and carved animal horns from several countries. Their house, a gambrel-roof late-Victorian, with gingerbread eaves and brackets, scrolling lightning rods, undulate shingling, zinc spouting, and a roof of rose slates in graduated ranks, was furnished in a style of cheerful bastardy—hulking black Spanish chests, Chippendale highboys veneered in contrasting fruitwoods flaking bit by bit, nondescript slab-and-tube modern, souvenir-shop colonial, Hitchcock chairs with missing rungs, *art nouveau* rockers, Japanese prints, giant corduroy pillows, Philippine carpets woven of rush rosettes. Unbreakable as a brothel, it was a good house for a party. Through his illicit morning visits Piet came to know these rooms in another light, as rooms children lived in and left littered with breakfast crumbs as they fled down the driveway to the school bus, the *Globe* still spread open to the funnies on the floor. Gradually the furniture—the antic lamps, the staring masks—learned to greet him, the sometimes man of the house. Proprietorially he would lie on the Thornes' king-size double bed, his bare toes not touching the footboard, while Georgene had her preparatory shower. Curiously he would finger and skim through Thorne's bedside shelf—Henry Miller in tattered Paris editions, Sigmund Freud in Modern Library, *Our Lady of the Flowers* and *Memoirs of a Woman of Pleasure* fresh from Grove Press, inspirational psychology by the Menningers, a dove-gray handbook on hypnosis, *Psychopathia Sexualis* in textbook format, a delicately tinted and stiff-paged album smuggled from Kyoto, the poems of Sappho as published by Peter Pauper, the unexpurgated Arabian Nights in two boxed volumes, works by Theodor Reik and Wilhelm Reich, various tawdry paperbacks. Then Georgene would come in steaming from the bathroom, a purple towel turbaned around her head.

She surprised him by answering, "Let's make it outdoors for a change."

Piet felt he was still being chastised. "Won't we embarrass God?"

"Haven't you heard, God's a woman? Nothing embarrasses Her." She pulled the elastic of his underpants toward her, eased it down and around. Her gaze became complacent. A cloud passingly blotted the sun. Sensing and fearing a witness, Piet looked upward and was awed as if by something inexplicable by the unperturbed onward motion of the fleet of bluebellied clouds, ships with a single destination. The little eclipsing cloud burned gold in its tendrilous masts and stern. A cannon discharge of iridescence, and it passed. Passed on safely above him. Sun was renewed in bold shafts on the cracked April earth, the sodden autumnal leaves, the new shoots coral in the birches and mustard on the larch boughs, the dropped needles drying, the tarpaper, their discarded clothes. Between the frilled holes her underpants wore a tender honey stain. Between her breasts the sweat was scintillant and salt. He encircled her, fingered and licked her willing slipping tips, the pip within the slit, wisps. Sun and spittle set a cloudy froth on her pubic hair: Piet pictured a kitten learning to drink milk from a saucer. He hurried, seeking her forgiveness, for his love of her, on the verge of discharge, had taken a shadow, had become regretful, foregone. He parted her straight thighs and took her with the simplicity she allowed. A lip of resistance, then an easeful deepness, a slipping by steps. His widening entry slowly startled her eyes. For fear of finding her surrendered face plain, he closed his lids. The whispering of boughs filtered upon them. Distant saws rasped. The breeze teased his squeezing buttocks; he was bothered by hearing birds behind him, Thorne's hired choir, spying.

"Oh, sweet. Oh so sweet," Georgene said. Piet dared peek and saw her rapt lids veined with broken purple and a small saliva bubble welling at one corner of her lips. He suffered a dizzying impression of waste. Though thudding, his heart went mournful. He bit her shoulder, smooth as an orange in sun, and traveled along a muffled parabola whose red warm walls she was and at whose end she also waited. Her face snapped sideways; drenched feathers pulled his tip; oh. So good a girl, to be there for him, no matter how he fumbled, to find her way by herself. In her strange space he leaped, and leaped again. She said, "Oh."

Lavender she lay in his shadow, the corners of her lips flecked. Politely Piet asked her, "Swing?"

"Dollink. Dunt esk."

"I was sort of poor. I'm not used to this outdoor living."

Georgene shrugged under him. Her throat and shoulders were slick. A speck of black construction dust, granular tar from his hair, adhered to her cheek. "You were you. I love you. I love you inside me."

Piet wanted to weep, to drop fat tears onto her deflated breasts. "Did I feel big enough?"

She laughed, displaying perfect teeth, a dentist's wife. "No," she said. "You felt shrimpy." Seeing him ready, in his dilated suspended state, to believe it, she explained solemnly, "You hurt me, you know. I ache afterwards."

"Do I? Do you? How lovely. How lovely of you to say. But you should complain."

"It's in a good cause. Now get off me. Go to Indian Hill."

Discarded beside her, he felt as weak and privileged as a child. Plucking needs agitated his fingers, his mouth. He asked at her side, "What did Freddy say about me that was mean?"

"He said you were expensive and slow."

"Well. I suppose that could be true."

He began dressing. The birds' chirping had become a clock's ticking. Like butter on a bright sill her nakedness was going rancid. She lay as she must often lie, accepting the sun entirely. The bathing-suit boundaries were not distinct on her body, as on Angela's. Her kitten-chin glutinous with jism. The plaid blanket had been rumpled and pulled from under her head, and some larch needles adhered to her hair, black mixed with gray. Because of this young turning of her hair she kept it feather-cut short.

"Baby," he said, to fill up the whispering silence surrounding his dressing, "I don't care about Freddy. I don't want the Whitmans' job. Cut into these old houses you never know what you'll find. Gallagher thinks we've wasted too much time restoring old heaps for our friends and the friends of our friends. He wants three new ranch houses on Indian Hill by fall. The war babies are growing up. That's where the money is."

"Money," she said. "You're beginning to sound like the rest of them."

"Well," he told her. "I can't be a virgin forever. Corruption had to come even to me."

He was dressed. The cool air drew tight around his shoulders and he put on his apricot windbreaker. With the manners that rarely lapsed between them, she escorted him from her house. He admired and yet was slightly scandalized that she could walk so easily, naked, through doors, past her children's toys, her husband's books, down stairs, under a shelf of cleansing agents, into her polished kitchen, to the side door. This side of the house, where the firewood was stacked and a single great elm cast down a gentle net of shade, had about it something rural and mild unlike the barbaric bulk of the house. Here not a brick or stone walk but a path worn through grass, now muddy, led around the corner of the garage, where Piet had hidden his pick-up truck, a dusty olive Chevrolet on whose tailgate a child had written WASH ME. Georgene, barefoot, did not step down from the threshold but leaned silent and smiling in the open doorway, leaving framed in Piet's mind a complex impression: of a domestic animal, of a fucked woman, of a mocking boy, of farewell.

Next Sunday, a little past noon, when Foxy had just returned from church and with a sigh had dropped her veiled hat onto the gate-legged table where the telephone sat, it impudently rang. She knew the voice: Piet Hanema. She had been thinking of calling him all week and therefore was prepared, though they had never really spoken, to recognize his voice, more hesitant and respectful than that of the other local men, with a flattish blurred midwestern intonation. He asked to speak to Ken. She went into the kitchen and deliberately didn't listen, because she wanted to.

All week she had been unable against Ken's silent resistance to call the contractor, and now her hands trembled as if guiltily. She poured herself a glass of dry vermouth. Really, church was getting to be, as the weather grew finer, a sacrifice. Magnolia buds swollen by heat leaned in the space of air revealed by the tilted ventilation pane of commemorative stained glass, birds sang in the little late-Victorian cemetery between the church and the river, the sermon dragged, the pews cracked restlessly. Ken came back from the phone saying, "He asked me to play basketball at two o'clock at his place."

Basketball was the one sport Ken had ever cared about; he had played for Exeter and for his Harvard house, which he had told her as a confession, it had been so unfashionable to do. Foxy said, "How funny."

"Apparently he has a basket on his barn wall, with a little asphalt court. He said in the spring, between skiing and tennis, some of the men like to play. They need me to make six, for three on a side."

"Did you say you would?"

"I thought you wanted to go for a walk on the beach."

"We can do that any time. I could walk by myself."

"Don't be a martyr. What is that, dry vermouth?"

"Yes. I developed a taste for it at the Guerins'."

"And then don't forget we have Ned and Gretchen tonight."

"They won't get here until after eight, you know how arrogant Cambridge people are. Call him back and tell him you'll play, it'll do you good."

Ken confessed, "Well, I left it that I might show up."

Foxy laughed, delighted at having been deceived. "Well if you told him yes why are you being so sneaky about it?"

"I shouldn't leave you here alone all afternoon."

Because you're pregnant, the implication was. His oppressive concern betrayed him. They had gone childless too long; he feared this change and added weight. Foxy made herself light, showed herself gay. "Can't I come along and watch? I thought this was a wives' town."

Foxy was the only wife who came to basketball, and Angela Hanema came out of the house to keep her company. The day was agreeable for being outdoors; nothing in the other woman's manner asked for an apology. The two together carried a bench, a weathered moist settee with a spindle-rung back, from beside the barn to a spot on the gravel driveway where simultaneously they could see the men play, have the sun on their faces, and keep an eye on the many children running and hiding in the big square yard and the lacy screen of budding woods beyond.

Foxy asked, "Whose children are all these?"

"Two are ours, two girls. You can see one of them standing by the birdbath sucking her thumb. That's Nancy."

"Is thumb-sucking bad?" It was a question probably naïve, another mother wouldn't have asked it, but Foxy was curious and felt she could hardly embarrass herself with Angela, who seemed so graceful and serenely humorous.

"It's not aesthetic," she said. "She didn't do it as an infant, it just started last winter. She's worried about death. I don't know where she gets it from. Piet insists on taking them to Sunday school and maybe they talk about it there."

"I suppose they feel they should."

"I suppose. The other children you see—the happy loud ones belong to our neighbors who run the dairy farm and the rest came with their proud daddies."

"I don't know all the daddies. I see Harold—why is it *little-*Smith?"

"It's one of those jokes that nobody knows how to get rid of. There were some other Smiths in town once, but they've long left."

"And that big imposing one is our real-estate man."

"Matt Gallagher. My husband's partner. The bouncy one with red hair is my husband."

Foxy thought, how funny that he is. She said, "He was at the Applebys' party for us."

"We all were. The one with the beard and grinning is Ben Saltz. S-a-l-t-z. I think it's been shortened from something."

"He looks very diabolical," Foxy said.

"Not to me. I think the effect is supposed to be rakish but it comes out Amish. It's to cover up pockmarks; when we first moved to town it was bushier but now he cuts it square. It's misleading, because he's a terribly kind, uxorious man. Irene is the moving spirit behind the League and the Fair Housing group and whatever else does good in town. Ben works in one of those plants along 128 that look as though they make ice cream."

"I thought that was a Chinaman."

"Korean. That's John Ong. He's not here. The only things he plays are chess and very poor tennis. His chess is quite good, though, Freddy Thorne tells me. He's a nuclear physicist who works in MIT. *At* MIT? Actually, I think he works *under* MIT, in a huge underground workshop you need a password to get into."

Foxy asked, "With a cyclotron?"

Angela said, "I forget your husband's a scientist too. I have no idea. Neither he nor Ben can ever talk about their work because it's all for the government. It makes everybody else feel terribly excluded. I think a little tiny switch in something that missed the moon was Ben's idea. He miniaturizes. He once showed us some radios that were like fingernails."

"At the party, I tried to talk to—who, Ong?—you all have such funny names."

"But aren't all names funny until you get used to them? Think of Shakespeare and Churchill. Think of Pillsbury."

"Anyway I tried to talk and couldn't understand a word."

"I know. His consonants are not what you expect. He was some kind of booty in the Korean War; I can't believe he defected, he doesn't seem to have that kind of opinion. He was very big with them I guess; for a while he taught at Johns Hopkins and met Bernadette in Baltimore. If they ever dropped an H-bomb on Tarbox it would be because of him. Like the Watertown arsenal. But you're right. He's not sexy."

Her tone implied a disdain of sex mixed with the equanimous recognition that others might chose to steer by it. Studying the other woman's lips, pale in the sunlight, composed around the premeditation of a smile, Foxy felt as if she, Foxy, were looking up toward a luxurious detached realm where observations and impressions drifted nodding by one another like strolling aristocrats. Every marriage tends to consist of an aristocrat and a peasant. Of a teacher and a learner. Foxy, though by more than an inch the taller, felt beneath Angela, as a student, at once sheltered and challenged. Discovering herself blushing, she hastily asked, "Who's the quick one with the ghostly eyes?"

"I guess they are ghostly. I've always thought of them as steely but that's wrong. His name is Eddie Constantine. He's an airline pilot. They just moved a year or so ago into a grim big house on the green. The tall teen-ager who looks like the Apollo Belvedere is a neighbor's boy he brought along in case there weren't six. Piet didn't know if your husband would come or not."

"Oh. Ken has made the sides uneven?"

"Not at all, they're delighted to have another player. Basketball isn't very popular, you can't do it with women. He's very good. Your husband."

Foxy watched. The neighbor boy, graceful even ill at ease, was standing aside while the six grown men panted and heaved, ducked and dribbled. They looked clumsy, crowded on the little piece of asphalt whose edges fell off into mud softened and stamped by sneaker footprints. Ken and Gallagher were the tallest and she saw Ken, whose movements had a certain nice economy she had not seen displayed for years, lift the ball to the level of his forehead and push it off. It swirled around the rim and flew away, missing. This pleased her: why? He had looked so confident, his whole nicely poised body had expressed the confidence, that it would go in. Constantine seized the rebound and dribbled down low, protecting the ball with an outward elbow. Foxy felt he had been raised in a city. His eyes in their ghostly transparence suggested photographic paper now silver, now black, now clear, depending upon in what they were dipped. His sharp features flushed, little-Smith kept slapping his feet as if to create confusion. He had none of the instinctive moves and Foxy wondered why he played. Saltz, whom she was prepared to adore, moved on the fringes cautiously, stooped and smiling as if to admit he was in a boys' game. His backside was broad and instead of sneakers he wore black laced shoes, such as peek from beneath a priest's robe. As she watched, Hanema, abruptly fierce, stole the ball from

Constantine, braving his elbow, pushed past Ken in a way that must be illegal, hipped and hopped and shot. When the ball went in he jumped for a joke on Gallagher's back. The Irishman, his jaws so wide his face was pentagonal, sheepishly carried his partner on a jog once around the asphalt.

"Discontinuous," Saltz was protesting.

"And you fouled the new guy," Constantine said. "You are an unscrupulous bastard."

Their voices were adolescently shrill. "All right crybabies, I won't play," Hanema said, and waved the waiting boy into his place. "Shall I call Thorne to come and make four on a side?"

Nobody answered; play had already resumed. Hanema draped a sweater around his neck and came and stood above the watching pair of women. Foxy could not study his face, a circular purple shadow against the sun. A male scent, sweat, flowed from him. His grainy courtly voice asked his wife, "Shall I call Thorne or do you want to? He's your friend."

Angela answered, "It's rude to call him this late, he'll wonder why you didn't call him sooner." Her voice, lifted toward the man, sounded diminished to Foxy, frightened.

He said, "You can't be rude to Thorne. If rudeness bothered him he'd have left town long ago. Anyway everybody knows on Sundays he has a five-martini lunch and couldn't have come earlier."

"Call him then," Angela said. "And say hello to Foxy."

"Pardon me. How are *you*, Mrs. Whitman?"

"Well, thank you, Mr. Hanema." She was determined not to be frightened also, and felt that she was not.

Sun rimmed his skull with rainbow filaments. He remained an upright shadow in front of her, emanating heat, but his voice altered, checked by something in hers. "It's very endearing," he said, and repeated, "en*dear*ing of you to come and be an audience. We need an audience." And his sudden explosion of energy, his bumping of Ken, his leap to Gallagher's back, were lit in retrospect by the fact of her watching. He had done it for her to see.

"You *all* seem very energetic," Foxy said. "I'm impressed."

He asked her, "Would you like to play?"

"I think not," she answered, wondering if he knew that she was pregnant, remembering him looking up her skirt, and guessing that he did. He would make it his business to know.

"In that case I better call Thorne," he said, and went into his house.

Angela, her casual manner restored, told Foxy, "Women sometimes do play. Janet and Georgene are actually not too bad. At least they look to me as if they know what they're doing."

Foxy said, "Field hockey is my only game."

"What position did you play? I was center halfback."

"You played? I was right inner, usually. Sometimes wing."

"It's a lovely game," Angela said. "It was the one time in my life when I enjoyed being aggressive. It's what men must have a lot of the time." There was a flow and an authority in the drifting way she spoke that led Foxy to agree, to nod eagerly, as the sun drifted lower into a salmon overcast. Keeping their pale faces lifted to the pale light, they talked, these two, of hockey ("What I liked about halfback," Angela said, "was you were both offensive and defensive and yet nobody could blame you for anything."); of sports in general ("It's so good," Foxy said, "to see Ken playing at anything. I think being with students all the time makes you unnecessarily old. I felt ancient in Cambridge."); of Ken's profession ("He never talks to me about his work any more," Foxy said. "It used to be starfish and that was sort of fun, we went to Woods Hole one summer; but now it's more to do with chlorophyll and all the breakthroughs recently have been in other fields, DNA and whatnot."); of Piet's house ("He likes it," Angela said, "because everything is square. I loved the house you have now. So many things could be done with it, and the way it floats above the marsh! Piet was worried about mosquitoes. Here we have these terrible horseflies from the dairy. He's from inland, you know. I think the sea intimidates him. He likes to skate but isn't much of a swimmer. He thinks the sea is wasteful. I think *I* prefer things to be somewhat formless. Piet likes them finished."); and of the children who now and then emerged from the woods and brought them a wound, a complaint, a gift:

"Why, Franklin, thank you! What do you think it can be?"

"A coughball," the boy said. "From an owl or a hawk." The boy was eight or nine, intelligent but slow to form, and thin-skinned. The coughball lay in Angela's hand, smaller than a golf ball, a tidy dry accretion visibly holding small curved bones.

"It's beautiful in its way," Angela said. "What would you like me to do with it?"

"Keep it for me until they take me home. Don't let Ruthie have it. She says it's hers because it's her woods but I want to start a collection and I saw it *first* even though she did pick it up." Making this long statement brought the child close to tears.

Angela said, "Frankie, go tell Ruth to come see me." He blinked and turned and ran.

Foxy said, "Isn't that Frankie Appleby? But Frank himself isn't here."

"Harold brought him. He's friends with their Jonathan."

"I thought the Smith boy was years older."

"He is, but of course they're thrown together."

Of course?

Three children returned from the woods—four, counting little Nancy Hanema, who hung back near the birdbath and, thumb in mouth, fanned her fingers as if to hide her face from Foxy's gaze.

Ruth was a solid tall round-faced girl. Her body jerked and stamped with indignant energy. "Mother, he says he saw it *first* but he didn't see it at all until *I* picked it up. Then he said it was *his* because he saw it *first*."

The taller boy, with a clever flickering expression, said, "That's the truth, Mrs. Hanema. Old Franklin Fink here grabs every-thing."

Young Appleby, without preamble, broke into sobs. "I don't," he said, and would have said more, but his throat stuck shut.

"Boo hoo, Finkie," the Smith boy said.

"Mother," Ruth said, stamping her foot on the gravel to re-trieve Angela's attention. "Last *summer* we found a bird's nest and *Frankie* said it was *his* for a *collection* and grabbed it out of my hand and it all came apart and fell into *nothing,* all because of *him!*" She flounced so hard her straight hair fanned in space.

Jonathan little-Smith said, "Lookie, Finkie's crying again. Boo hoo, oh dear, goodness gracious me oh my oh."

With a guttural whimper the younger boy attacked his friend with rotating fists. Jonathan laughed; his arm snaked out and flipped the frantic red face aside; he contemptuously pushed. Angela rose and parted them, and Foxy thought how graceful yet solid she looked, and imagined her as a hockey player standing abstracted yet impenetrable in the center of the limed field, in blue bloomers. Her body in turning showed a trace of the process that makes middle-aged women, with their thickened torsos and thinned legs, appear to be engaged in a balancing act.

"Now Jonathan," Angela said, holding each boy's hand equally, "Frankie wants to start a collection. Do you want to have a collection too?"

"No I don't give a fart about some old bird's throw-up. It's Ruthie he stole from."

"Ruthie is here all the time and I *know* she can find another in the woods. I want you all to help her. There's an owl hoots every night in that woods and if you find his tree I bet you'll find lots more coughballs. You help too, Nancy."

The child had approached closer. "Mouse died," she said, not removing her thumb.

"Yes," Ruth said, wheeling, her hair lifting winglike, "and if you don't watch out this enormous owl will come and eat you and your thumb will be sticking out from an enormous coughball with eyes on it!"

"Ruth!" Angela called, too late. Ruth had run back to the woods, her long legs flinging beneath her flying skirt. The boys, united by need for pursuit, followed. Nancy came to her mother's lap and was absent-mindedly caressed. "You have all this," Angela said to Foxy, "to look forward to."

Her pregnancy, then, was common knowledge. She discovered she didn't mind. She said, "I'll be glad when it's at that stage. I feel horrible half the time, and useless the rest."

"Later," Angela said, "it's splendid. You're so right with the world. Then this little package arrives, and it's utterly dependent, with these very clear sharp needs that you can *sat*isfy! You have everything it wants. I loved having babies. But then you have to raise them." The eyes of the child half lying in her lap listened wide open. Her lips around her thumb made a secret, moist noise.

"You're very good with children," Foxy told her.

"I like to teach," Angela said. "It's easier than learning."

With a splashing sound of gravel, a yellow convertible, top down, came into the driveway and stopped not a yard from their bench. The Thorne man was driving; his pink head poked from the metal shell like the flesh of a mollusc. Standing in the back seat were a sickly-looking boy who resembled him and a younger girl, six or so, whose green eyes slightly bulged. Foxy was jarred by the readiness with which Angela rose to greet them. After an hour of sharing a bench and the sun with her, she was jealous. Angela introduced the children: "Whitney and Martha Thorne, say hello to Mrs. Whitman."

"I know you," the boy told her. "You moved in down the road from us into the spook house." His face was pale and his nostrils and ears seemed inflamed. Possibly he had a fever. His sister was definitely fat. She found herself touched by these children and, lifting her eyes to their father, even by him.

"Is it a spook house?" she asked.

"He means," Angela intervened, "because it stood empty so long. The children can see it from the beach."

"All shuttered up," Whitney said, "with smoke coming out of the chimneys."

"The kid hallucinates," his father said. "He chews peyote for breakfast."

Whitney defended himself. "Iggy Kappiotis said he and some guys snuck up on the porch one time and heard voices inside."

"Just a little innocent teen-age fucking," Freddy Thorne said, squinting at the sallow spring sun. By daylight his amorphous softness was less menacing, more pitiable. He wore a fuzzy claret sports shirt with an acid-green foulard and hightop all-weather boots such as children with weak ankles wear.

"Hey, big Freddy," Harold little-Smith called from the basketball court. The thumping and huffing had suspended.

"It's Bob Cousy!" Hanema called from the porch.

"Looks more like Goose Tatum to me," said Gallagher. "You

can always tell by de whites ob dare eyes."

"What whites?" Hanema asked. He hurried over and, taking Thorne by the elbow, announced, "This man is living gin."

"Those are not official sneakers," Ben Saltz protested.

"Those are Frankenstein shoes," Eddie Constantine said. He went mock-rigid and tottered the few steps needed to bump into Thorne's chest. He sniffed Thorne's breath, clutched his own throat, and screamed, "Aagh! The fumes! The fumes!"

Thorne smiled and wiped his mouth. "I'll just watch," he said. "You don't need me, you got plenty of people. Why did you call?"

"We *do* need you," Hanema insisted, handling the man's elbow again and seeming to exult in his relative shortness. "Four on a side. You guard me. You belong to Matt, Eddie, and Ben."

"Thanks a holy arse-licking bunch," Constantine said.

"How many points are you spotting us?" Gallagher asked.

"None," Hanema said. "Freddy will be all right. He's an asset. He's loose. Take a practice shot, Freddy." He slammed the ball off the asphalt into Thorne's stomach. "See how loose he is?"

From the stiff-fingered way Thorne handled the ball Foxy saw he was nothing of an athlete; he was so waddly, so flat-footed, she averted her eyes from the sight.

Beside her, Angela said, "I suppose the house may have been broken into by a few young couples. They have so few places to go."

"What were the people like who owned it before?"

"The Robinsons. We hardly knew them. They only used it summers and weekends. A middle-aged couple with pots of children who suddenly got divorced. I used to see her downtown with binoculars around her neck. Quite a handsome woman with hair in a bun and windburn in tweeds. He was an ugly little man with a huge voice, always threatening to sue the town if they widened the road to the beach. But Bernadette Ong, who knew them, says it was *he* who wanted the divorce. Evidently he played the cello and she the violin and they got into a string quartet with some people from Duxbury. They never did a thing for the house."

Foxy blurted, "Would your husband be willing to look at the house for us? And give us an estimate or some notion as to where to begin?"

Angela gazed toward the woods, a linear maze where children's bodies were concealed. "Matt," she said carefully, "wants Piet to concentrate on building new houses."

"Perhaps he could recommend another contractor then. We must make a beginning. Ken seems to like the house as it is but when winter comes it will be impossible."

"Of course it will." The curtness startled Foxy. Gazing toward the trees, Angela went on hesitatingly, as if her choice of words were distracted by a flowering of things unseen. "Your husband—perhaps he and Piet could talk. Not today after basketball. Everybody stays for beer."

"No, fine. We must hurry back, we have some friends coming from Cambridge."

Thus a gentle rift was established between them. The two faced differently, Angela toward the woods full of children and Foxy toward the men's game. Four on a side was too many. The court, now deep in the shadow of the barn, was crowded and Thorne, with his protrusive rear and confused motions, was in everyone's way. Hanema had the ball. Persistently bumped by Thorne in his attempts to dribble amid a clamor of shouts, he passed the ball on the bounce to the Constantines' neighbor's boy; in the same stride he hooked one foot around Thorne's ankle and by a backwards stab of his weight caused the bigger man to fall down. Thorne fell in stages, thrusting out an arm, then rolling face down on the muddy asphalt, his hand under him.

Play stopped. Foxy and Angela ran to the men. Hanema had kneeled to Thorne. The others made a hushed circle around them. Smearily smiling, his claret shirt muddy, Thorne sat up and showed them a trembling hand whose whitened little finger stuck out askew. "Dislocated," he said in a voice from which pain had squeezed all elasticity.

Hanema, kneeling, blurted, "Jesus Freddy, I'm sorry. This is terrible. Sue me."

"It's happened before," Thorne said. He took the injured hand in his good one and grimaced and pulled. A snap softer than a twig breaking, more like a pod popping, shocked the silent circle. Freddy rose and held his hand, the little finger now aligned, before his chest as something tender and disgraced that must not be touched. He asked Angela, "Do you have surgical tape and anything for a splint—a tongue depressor, a popsicle stick? Even a spoon would do."

Rising with him, Hanema asked, "Freddy, will you be able to work?"

Thorne smirked down at the other's anxious face. He was feeling his edge enlarge, Foxy felt; she thought only women used their own pain as a weapon. "Oh," he said, "after a month or so. I can't go into somebody's mouth wearing a plaster cast, can I?"

"Sue me," Hanema said. His face was a strange stretched mixture of freckles and pallor, of the heat of battle and contrition. The other players had divided equally into two sympathizing rings. Freddy Thorne, holding his hand before him, led Angela and Constantine and the neighbor boy and Saltz into the house, in triumph. Yet Foxy's impression remained that he had been, in the minute before exploitation set in, instinctively stoical.

"You didn't do it on purpose," little-Smith told Hanema. Foxy wondered why he, Thorne's friend, had stayed outdoors, with the guilty. The patterns of union were many.

"But I *did*," Piet said. "I deliberately tripped the poor jerk. The way he bumps with his belly gets me mad."

Gallagher said, "He doesn't understand the game." Gallagher would have been handsome but for something narrowed about the mouth, something predetermined and closed expressed by the bracketlike creases emphasizing the corners: prim tucks. Amid the whiskery Sunday chins his jaws were smooth-shaved; he had been to mass.

She said, "I think you're all awfully rough with each other."

"*C'est la guerre,*" little-Smith told her.

Ken, in the lull, was practicing shots, perfecting himself. Foxy felt herself submerged in shadows and cross-currents while he was on high, willfully ignorant, hollow and afloat. His dribbling and the quivering rattle of the rim irritated her like any monologue.

Hanema was beside her. Surprisingly, he said, "I hate being a shit and that's how it keeps turning out. I beg him to come play and then I cripple him."

It was part confession, part brag. Foxy was troubled that he would bring her this, as if laying his head in her lap. She shied, speechless, angered that, having felt from an unexpected angle his rumored force, his orphan's needful openness, she had proved timid, like Angela.

The gravel driveway splashed again. An old maroon coupe pulled in, its windshield aswarm with reflected branches and patches of cloud. Janet Appleby got out on the driver's side. She carried two sixpacks of beer. Georgene Thorne pushed from the other door holding in her arms a child of a cumbersome age, so wadded with clothes its legs were spread like the stalks of an H. By the scorched redness of its cheeks the child was an Appleby.

Little-Smith and Hanema quickly went to greet them. Gallagher joined Ken at shooting baskets. Not wishing to eavesdrop, yet believing her sex entitled her to join the women, Foxy walked slowly down the drive to them as little-Smith caperingly described Freddy's unfortunate finger—"*le doigt disloqué.*"

Georgene said, "Well, I've told him not to try sports when he's potted." Her upper lids were pink, as if she had been lying in the sun.

Piet Hanema told her, "But I asked him especially to come, so we could have four on a side." Such a sad broad face, growing old without wisdom, alert and strained.

"Oh, he would have come anyway. You don't think he'd sit around all Sunday afternoon with just *me.*"

"Why not?" Piet said, and Foxy imagined hostility in his eyes as he gazed at her. "Don't you want to go inside and see how he is?"

"He's all right," she said. "Isn't Angela with him? Let them alone. He's happy."

Janet and Harold were conferring urgently, in whispers. Their conversation seemed logistical, involving schedules and placement of cars and children. When the Appleby infant seized a cat on the lawn and tried to lift it by its hindquarters, as if spilling a bag of candy out, it was little-Smith who went and pried it loose, while

Janet held her face in this idle moment up to the sun. The cat, calico, with a mildewed eye, ran off and hid in the lilac hedge. Foxy asked Hanema, "Is that yours?"

"The cat or the child?" he asked, as if also aware that the child's parentage seemed in flux.

"The calico cat. We have a cat called Cotton."

"*Do* bring Cotton to the next basketball game," Georgene Thorne said. She added, throwing an athletic arm toward the woods, "I can't see the children for the trees," as if this explained the rudeness of her first remark, with its implied indignation at Foxy's being here at all.

Hanema explained, "She belongs to the dairy down the road but the children sometimes feed it. They let the damn thing into the house full of fleas and now I have them."

Freddy Thorne came out of the house. His little finger was bandaged to a green plastic picnic spoon. The pad of his fingertip rested prettily in the bowl and the curve of the handle made a very dainty fit. That Angela had improvised this strengthened Foxy's sense of illicit affection between these two. Freddy was plainly proud.

"Oh Freddy," Janet said, "it's just gorgeous." She was wearing white slacks so snug they had horizontally wrinkled along her pelvis. The nap of her turquoise velour jersey changed tint as it rounded the curve of her breasts; as she moved her front was an electric shimmer of shadow. The neck was cut to reveal a slash of mauve skin. Her lips had been painted to be a valentine but her chalky face needed sleep. Like her son she was thin-skinned and still being formed.

Freddy said, "The kid did it."

Constantine's young neighbor explained, "At camp last summer we had to take First Aid." His voice emerged reedy and shallow from manhood's form: a mouse on a plinth.

Eddie Constantine said, "He comes over to the house and massages Carol's back."

Freddy asked, "Oh. She has a bad back?"

"Only when I've been home too long."

Ken and Gallagher stopped playing and joined the grown-ups.

The sixpacks were broken open and beer cans were passed around. "I *despise* these new tabs," little-Smith said, yanking. "Everybody I know has cut thumbs. It's the new stigmata." Foxy felt him grope for the French for "stigmata."

Janet said, "I can't do it, I'm too weak and hung. Could *you?*" She handed her can to—Ken!

All eyes noticed. Harold little-Smith's nose tipped up and his voice rose nervously. "Freddy Thorne," he taunted. "Spoonfinger. The man with the plastic digit. *Le doigt plastique.*"

"Freddy, honestly, what a nuisance," Georgene said, and Foxy felt hidden in this an attempt to commiserate.

"No kidding," Constantine said, "how will you get in there? Those little crevices between their teeth?" He was frankly curious and his eyes, which Foxy for a moment saw full on, echoed, in the absence of intelligence, aluminum and the gray of wind and the pearly width low in the sky at high altitudes. He had been there, in the metallic vastness above the boiling clouds, and was curious how Freddy would get to where *he* had to go.

"With a laser beam," Thorne said, and the green spoon became a death ray that he pointed, saying *zizz* between his teeth, at Constantine, at Hanema, at herself. "*Zizz.* Die. *Zizz.* You're dead."

The people nearest him laughed excessively. They were courtiers, and Freddy was a king, the king of chaos: though struck dead, Foxy refused to laugh. At her back, Georgene and Piet, ignoring Freddy, exchanged words puzzling in their grave simplicity:

"How are you?"

"So-so, dollink."

"You've been on your sunporch."

"Yes."

"How was it? Lovely?"

"Lonely."

Overhearing, Foxy was rapt, as when a child she listened to her parents bumbling and grunting behind a closed door, intimacy giving their common words an exalted magic.

Ben Saltz's voice overenunciated; his moving lips had an air of isolation, as if they were powered by a battery concealed in his beard. He was saying, "All kidding aside, Freddy, they really can do great things now with nontactile dentistry."

"Whoops," Freddy Thorne said, "that lets tactile types like me out," and he slapped the biform seat of Janet's tense white pants. She whirled from cozying with Ken to give Freddy a look less of surprise than of warning, a warning, Foxy felt, that had to do less with the pat than with its being witnessed.

Saltz seized the chance to latch on to Ken. "Tell me, if you can spare a minute, have you felt the effects of laser beams in biochemistry yet? I was reading in the *Globe* the other week where they've had some success with cancer in mice."

"Anybody can do miracles with mice," Ken stated, ruefully staring down at Janet's backside. He was not comfortable, Foxy had noticed years ago, talking to Jews; he had competed unsuccessfully against too many.

"Do me a favor," Saltz went on, "and tell me about DNA. How the blazes, is the way my thinking runs, how the blazes could such a complex structure spontaneously arise out of chaos?"

"Matter isn't chaos," Ken said. "It has laws, legislated by what can't happen."

"I can see," Saltz said, "how out in our western states, say, the Grand Canyon is the best example, how a rock could be carved by erosion into the shape of a cathedral. But if I look inside and see a lot of pews arranged in apple-pie order, in rows, I begin to smell a rat, so to speak."

"Maybe," Ken said, "you put those pews there yourself."

Ben Saltz grinned. "I like that," he said. "I like that answer." His grin was a dazzling throwback, a facial sunburst that turned his eyes into twinkling slits, that seized his whole face like the snarl on the face of a lion in an Assyrian bas-relief. "I like that answer a lot. You mean the Cosmic Unconscious. You know, Yahweh was a volcano god originally. I think it's ridiculous for religious people to be afraid of the majesty and power of the universe."

Angela called from the porch, "Is anybody except me chilly? Please come into the house, anybody."

This signaled some to go and some to stay. Eddie Constantine crushed his beer can double and handed it to Janet Appleby. She placed it above her breast, as if it were a tin corsage. He crossed to his Vespa and, passing close to Foxy, tapped her stomach. "Suck in your gut." Those were his words. The neighbors' boy got on the Vespa behind him, clinging possumlike. Constantine kicked off, and a spray of stones leaped from his rear wheel as he went down the drive and banked into the road beyond the lilac hedge, which was losing transparence to the swelling of buds. The cat raced from the hedge in terror and ran silently across the lawn, elongating. Children were emerging from the darkening woods. Half of them were crying. Really, it was only Frankie Appleby crying. Jonathan Smith and Whitney Thorne had tied him to a tree with his own shoelaces and then couldn't undo the knots so they had to cut them and now he had no shoelaces and it wasn't his *fault*. His feet stumbled and flopped to illustrate and Harold little-Smith ran to him while Janet his mother stood cold, plump and pluming, on the porch gazing to where the sun, a netted orange, hung in the thin woods. Across the lawn came the rosy Hanema girls and a beautiful male child like a Gainsborough in the romantic waning light, curly black hair and a lithe self-solicitous comportment. With a firm dismissing nod Gallagher took this luxurious child by the hand and led him to their car, the gray Mercedes from whose tall clean windows Foxy had first viewed Tarbox. Saltz and the Thornes moved to go in. In the narrow farmhouse doorway the two men, one bearded and one bald, bumped together and Thorne unexpectedly put his arm, the arm with the crippled green-tipped hand, around the Jew and solidly hugged him sideways. Saltz flashed upward his leonine grin and said something to which Thorne replied, "I'm an indestructible kind of a prick. Let me tell you about dental hypnosis." The pleasant house accepted them. Foxy and Ken moved to go.

"Don't all leave," Angela begged. "Wouldn't you like to have a *real* drink?"

Foxy said, "We must get back," truly sad. She was to experience this sadness many times, this chronic sadness of late Sunday afternoon, when the couples had exhausted their game, basketball or beachgoing or tennis or touch football, and saw an evening weighing upon them, an evening without a game, an evening spent among flickering lamps and cranky children and leftover food and the nagging half-read newspaper with its weary portents and atrocities, an evening when marriages closed in upon themselves like flowers from which the sun is withdrawn, an evening giving like a smeared window on Monday and the long week when they must perform again their impersonations of working men, of stockbrokers and dentists and engineers, of mothers and housekeepers, of adults who are not the world's guests but its hosts.

Janet and Harold were arguing in whispers. Janet whirled and proclaimed, "Sweet, we *can't*. We *must* rescue Marcia and Frank, they're probably *deep* in conversation." She and little-Smith collected their scrambled children and left in her maroon car. As they backed from the driveway, the sinking sun for an instant pierced the windshield and bleached their two faces in sunken detail, like saints under glass.

"Good-bye," Piet Hanema said politely from the porch. Foxy had forgotten him. He seemed so chastened by the finger incident that she called to him, "Cheer up."

Safe in their MG, Ken said, "Zowie, I'm going to be stiff tomorrow."

"But wasn't it fun?"

"It was exercise. Were you terribly bored?"

"No. I *loved* Angela."

"Why?"

"I don't know. She's gracious and careless and above it all at the same time. She doesn't make the *demands* on you the others do."

"She must have been a knockout once."

"But not now? I must say, your painted friend Janet with her hug-my-bottom sailor pants does *not* impress me aesthetically."

"How does she impress you, Fox?"

"She impresses me as less happy than she should be. She was meant to be a jolly fat woman and somehow missed."

"Do you think she's having an affair with Smith?"

Foxy laughed. "Men are so observant. It's so obvious it must be passé. I think she had an affair with Smith some time ago, is having one with Thorne right now, and is sizing you up for the future."

His flattered languid answering laugh annoyed her. "I have a confession," she said.

"You're having an affair with Saltz. God, Jews are ponderous. They *care* so much. The Cosmic Unconscious, Jesus."

"No. But almost as bad. I told Angela we wanted to have her husband look at our house."

His voice withdrew, acquired a judging dispassion. "Did you set a date?"

"No, but I think we should now. You should call. She didn't think he'd be interested anyway."

Ken drove swiftly down the road they already knew by heart, so both leaned a little before the curve was there. "Well," he said after silence, "I hope his basketball isn't a clue as to how he builds houses. He plays a pretty crusty game."

Ruth, standing beside the bed with almost a woman's bulk, was crying and by speaking woke him from a dream in which a tall averted woman in white was waiting for him at the end of a curved corridor. "Daddy, Nancy says the dairy cat got an animal downstairs and the hamster's not in his cage and I'm afraid to look."

Piet remembered the *eek eeik* by which he had learned to lull himself to sleep and slid from the bed with fear lumping in his stomach. Angela sighed moistly but did not stir. The floor and stairs were cold. Nancy, huddled in her pink nightie on the brown living-room sofa in the shadowless early-morning light, removed her thumb from her mouth and told him, "I didn't mean to, I didn't mean to, it was a 'stake!"

His mouth felt crusty. "Mean to what? Where's the animal?"

The child looked at him with eyes so pure and huge a space far bigger than this low-ceilinged room seemed windowed. The furniture itself, surfacing from the unity of darkness, seemed to be sentient, though paralyzed.

He insisted, "Where is the animal you told Ruthie about, Nancy?"

She said, "I didn't mean to," and succumbed to tears; her

smooth face disintegrated like a prodigy of embalming suddenly exposed to air, and Piet was numbed by the force that flowed through the hole her face made in the even gray light.

Ruth said, "Crybaby, crybaby, sit-and-wonder-whybaby," and Nancy plugged her face again with her thumb.

The little animal, sack-shaped, lay belly up in the center of the kitchen linoleum. The dairy cat watched at a distance, both cowardly and righteous, behind the rungs of a kitchen chair. Its quick instinctive work had been nicely done. Though scarcely marked, the hamster was dead. Its body yielded with a sodden resilience to the prodding of Piet's finger; its upper lip was lifted to expose teeth like the teeth of a comb and its eyes, with an incongruous human dignity, were closed. A trace of lashes. The four curled feet. The lumpy bald nose.

Ruth asked, though she was standing in the kitchen doorway and could see for herself, "Is it him?"

"Yes. Sweetie, he's dead."

"I know."

The adventure was easy to imagine. Ruth, feeling that her pet needed more room for running, suspecting cruelty in the endless strenuousness of the wheel, not believing with her growing mind that any creature might have wits too dim to resent such captivity, had improvised around his tiny cage a larger cage of window screens she had found stacked in the attic waiting for summer. She had tied the frames together with string and Piet had never kept his promise to make her a stronger cage. Several times the hamster had nosed his way out and gone exploring in her room. Last night he had made it downstairs, discovering in the moon-soaked darkness undreamed-of continents, forests of furniture legs, vast rugs heaving with oceanic odors; toward morning an innocent giant in a nightgown had admitted a lion with a mildewed eye. The hamster had never been given cause for fear and must have felt none until claws sprang from a sudden heaven fragrant with the just-discovered odors of cat and cow and dew.

Angela came downstairs in her blue bathrobe, and Piet could not convey to her why he found the mishap so desolating, the dim-witted little exploration that had ended with such a thunderclap of death. The kitchen linoleum, the color of grass, felt slick beneath him. The day dawning outside looked stale and fruitless and chill, one more of the many with which New England cheats spring. Angela's concern, after a glance at him and Ruth and the body of the hamster, was for Nancy; she carried her from the living room into the relative brightness of the kitchen. Squeamishly Piet enfolded the russet corpse, disturbingly dense and, the reins of blood slackened, unstable, in a newspaper. Nancy asked to see it.

Piet glanced at Angela for permission and unfolded the newspaper. KENNEDY PRAISES STEEL RESTRAINT. Nancy stared and slowly asked, "Won't he wake up?"

Ruth said, her voice forced through tears, "No stupid he will not wake up because he is dead and dead things do not wake up ever ever ever."

"When will he go to Heaven?"

All three looked to Piet for the answer. He said, "I don't know. Maybe he's up there already, going round and round in a wheel." He imitated the squeaking; Ruth laughed, and it had been her he had meant to amuse. Nancy's anxious curiosity searched out something he had buried in himself and he disliked the child for seeking it. Angela, holding her, seemed part of this same attempt, to uncover and unman him, to expose the shameful secret, the childish belief, from which he drew his manhood.

He asked Nancy roughly, "Did you see it happen?"

Angela said, "Don't, Piet. She doesn't want to think about it."

But she did; Nancy said, staring at the empty floor where it had happened, "Kitty and Hamster played and Hamster wanted to quit and Kitty wouldn't let him."

"Did you know the hamster was downstairs when you let Kitty in?"

Nancy's thumb went back into her mouth.

"I'm sure she didn't," Angela said.

"Let me see him once more," Ruth said, and in disclosing to her the compact body like a stiffening heart Piet saw for himself how the pet had possessed the protruding squarish bottom of the male of its species, a hopeful sexual vanity whose final denial seemed to

Piet a kind of relief. With Ruth he knew now the strange inner drying, a soft scorching, that follows the worst, when it has undeniably come true. She went off to school, walked down the crunching driveway in her yellow Easter coat to await the yellow school bus, with all her tears behind her, under a cloudy sky that promised no rain.

Piet had promised her a new hamster and a better cage. He buried the old hamster in the edge of the woods, near a scattering of scilla, little lillies of a wideawake blue, where the earth was soft and peaty. One shovelful did for the grave; two made it deep. The trees were beginning to leaf and the undergrowth was sketchy, still mixed, its threads of green, with winter-bleached dead stalks delicate as straws, as bird bones. In a motion of the air, the passionless air which passively flows downhill, spring's terror washed over him. He felt the slow thronging of growth as a tangled hurrying toward death. Timid green tips shaped like tiny weaponry thrust against nothing. His father's green fond touch. The ungrateful earth, receptive. The hamster in an hour of cooling had lost weight and shape to the elements. All that had articulated him into a presence worth mourning, the humanoid feet and the groping trembling nose whose curiosity, when Ruth set him out on her blanket, made her whole bed lightly vibrate, had sunk downward toward a vast absence. The body slid nose down into the shoveled hole. Piet covered him with guilty quickness. In the nearly five years they had lived here a small cemetery had accumulated along this edge of woods: injured birds they had vainly nursed, dime-store turtles that had softened and whitened and died, a kitten slammed in a screen door, a chipmunk torn from throat to belly by some inconclusive predator who had left a spark of life to flicker all one long June afternoon. Last autumn, when the robins were migrating, Nancy had found one with a broken back by the barn, groveling on the asphalt basketball court in its desire to fly, to join the others. Lifted sheerly by the beating of its heart, it propelled itself to the middle of the lawn, where the four Hanemas gathered in expectation of seeing it take wing, healed. But the bird was unhinged, as Piet's own father with his shattered chest and spine would have been unhinged had his lungs let him live; and the children, bored by the bird's poor attempt to become a miracle, wandered away. So only Piet, standing helpless as if beside a party guest who refuses to leave, witnessed the final effort, an asymmetric splaying of the dusty wings and a heave that drove the robin's beak straight down into the sweetish weedy shadowy grass. The bird emitted a minute high cry, a point of noise as small as a star, and relaxed. Only Piet had heard this utterance. Only Piet, as now, attended the burial.

Angela came across the lawn to him where he stood with the shovel. She was dressed in an English-appearing suit of salt-and-pepper tweed; today, Tuesday, was her day to be a teaching parent at Nancy's nursery school. "How unfortunate," she said, "that of all of us it had to be Nancy who saw it happen. Now she wants me to take her to Heaven so she can see for herself that there's room for her, and a little wheel. I really do wonder, Piet, if religion doesn't complicate things worse than they'd have to be. She can see that I don't believe it myself."

He stooped beside the shovel and assumed the manner of an old yeoman. "Ah," he said, "thet's all verra well for a fine leddy like yerself, ma'am, but us peasants like need a touch o' holy water to keep off the rheumatism, and th' evil eye."

"I de*test* imitations, whether you do them, or Georgene Thorne. And I detest being put in the position of trying to sell Heaven to my children."

"But Angel, the rest of us think of you as never having left Heaven."

"Stop trying to get at me and sympathize with the child. She thinks of death all the time. She doesn't understand why she has only two grandparents instead of four like the other children."

"You speak as if you had married a man with only one leg."

"I'm just stating, not complaining. Unlike you, I don't blame you for that accident."

"Ah, thank ye kindly, ma'am, and I'll be makin' a better hamster cage today, and get the poor kid a new hamster."

"It's not Ruth," Angela said, "I'm worried about." These were the lines drawn. Angela's heart sought to enshrine the younger child's innocence; Piet loved more the brave corruption of the older, who sang in the choir and who had brusquely pushed across the sill of fear where Nancy stood wide-eyed.

Angela and Nancy went off to nursery school together. Piet drove the pick-up truck into downtown Tarbox and at Spiros Bros. Builders & Lumber Supply bought five yards of galvanized cage mesh, a three-by-four-piece of ¾" plywood, twenty feet of 2" pine quality knotless stock, a half pound of 1½" finishing nails, and the same quantity of the finer gauge of poultry staples. Jerry Spiros, the younger of the two brothers, told Piet about his chest, which since Christmas had harbored a congestion that ten days in Jamaica did not clear up. "Those fucking blacks'd steal," Jerry said, "the watch right off your wrist," and coughed prolongedly.

"Sounds like you've been sniffing glue," Piet told him, and charged the hamster-cage materials to the Gallagher & Hanema account, and threw them into the back of his truck, and slammed shut the tailgate that said WASH ME, and drove to Indian Hill, taking the long way around. He swung by his office to see if Gallagher's gray Mercedes was there. Their office was a shacklike wing, one-story, upon an asphalt-shingled tenement, mostly unoccupied, on Hope Street, a little spur off Charity, a short cut to the railroad depot. Charity, the main business street, met Divinity at right angles, and Divinity carried up the hill, past Cogswell's Drug Store. The church bulked white on the green.

Huge airy thing. Twenty-four panes in each half window, forty-eight in all, often while Pedrick wrestled he counted them, no symbolism since when it was built there weren't that many states in the Union, Arizona, Oklahoma, Indian Territory. The lumber those people had. To burn. Waste? Gives the town a sense of itself. Dismal enough otherwise. On this heavy loveless day everything looked to need a coat of paint. The salt air corrupts. In Michigan barns stayed red for ages.

The green was hourglass-shaped, cut in two by a footpath, the church's section pinched off from the part holding the backstop and basepaths. Swinging left along the green's waist, Piet looked toward the Constantines' side yard hoping to see Carol hanging out wash with upstretched arms and flattened breasts. At Greek dances, leading the line, hair in spit curls, slippered toe pointed out, the neighbors' boy linked to her by a handkerchief, lithe. Lower classes have that litheness. Generations of hunger. Give me your poor. Marcia brittle, Janet fat. Angela drifty and that Whitman gawky, a subtle stiffness, resisting something, air. Eddie's Vespa but no Ford, Carol's car. He home and she shopping. Buying back liniment. *I ache afterwards.* Funeral home driveway held a Cadillac hearse and a preschool child playing with pebbles. Growing up in odor of embalming oil instead of flowers, corpses in the refrigerator, a greenhouse better, learn to love beauty, yet might make some fears seem silly. Death. Hamster. Shattered glass. He eased up on the accelerator.

Forsythia like a dancing yellow fog was out in backyards and along fences and hedges and garages, the same yellow, continuous, dancing yard to yard, trespassing. Forgive us. Piet drove on down Prudence Street past the Guerins'. Nicely restored, six thou, one of their first jobs in Tarbox, Gallagher not so greedy then, Adams and Comeau did all the finish work, nobody under sixty knows how to hang a door. The whole frame had sagged. Dry rot. The uphill house sill buried in damp earth. They had threaded a reinforcing rod eighteen feet long through the summer beam up through a closet to an ironshod A-brace in the attic. Solid but still a touch off true. *Why don't you want to fuck me?* Good question. Loyalty to Georgene, offshoot loyalty, last year's shoot this year's limb, mistress becomes a wife. Sets. Determined set of Georgene's chin. Not always attractive. Coke-bottle eyes, nude like rancid butter, tarpaper grits, Freddy's spies. Piet's thoughts shied from a green plastic spoon.

Downhill a mailman gently sloped away from the pull of his bag. Blue uniform, regular hours, walk miles, muscles firm, live forever. At the corner two dogs were saying hello. Hello. Olleh.

He drove along Musquenomenee Street, along the river, tidal up to the factory waterfall, low at this moment, black salt mud gleaming in wide scummy puddled flats, the origin of life. Across the river were high-crowned streets of elms and homes with oval windows and leaded fanlights built in the tinkling decades of ice wagons. Knickers, mustaches, celluloid collars: nostalgic for when he had never been. Piet saw no one. No one walked now. The silver maples were budding in reddish florets but the elms in tan tassels. Rips in a lilac sky. Nature, this sad grinding fine, seed and weed.

His spirits slightly lifted as he passed the Protestant cemetery, fan-shaped acres expanding from a Puritan wedge of tilted slate stones adorned with winged skulls and circular lichen. Order reigned. Soon cemeteries and golf courses the last greenswards. Thronging hungry hoardes, grain to India. On the golf course he spotted two lonely twosomes. Too early, mud, heavy lies, spikes chew up the green, proprietors greedy for fees, praise restraint, earth itself hungry, he had thrown it a sop. Pet. Pit. He drove through pastel new developments, raw lawns and patchwork façades, and up a muddy set of ruts beside which hydrants and sewer ports were already installed, in obedience to town ordinances, to his site on Indian Hill.

The bulldozer had arrived. This should have pleased him but the machine, a Case Construction King with hydraulic back hoe and front loader, crushed him with its angry weight, its alarming expense. Twenty-five dollars to move it in, twenty-two fifty per hour with the driver, a large coveralled Negro from Mather. Sitting on his jarring throne, he conveyed the impression that the machine's strength was his strength, and that if the gears ceased to mesh he would himself swing down and barehanded tear the stumps from the outraged red earth. By no extension of his imagination could Piet believe that he had helped cause this man and machine to be roaring and churning and chuffing and throttling here, where birds and children used to hide. Yet the Negro hailed him, and his young foreman Leon Jazinski eagerly loped toward him across the gouged mud, and the work was going smoothly. Stumps whose roots were clotted with drying mud and boulders blind for aeons had been heaped into a towering ossuary that must be trucked away. Now the Negro was descending, foot by foot, into the first cellar hole, diagrammed with string and red-tipped stakes. This house would have the best view, overlooking the fan-shaped cemetery toward the town with its pricking steeple and flashing cock. The other two would face more southerly, toward

Lacetown, an indeterminate area of gravel pits and back lots and uneconomic woods strangely intense in color, purple infused with copper; and should bring a thousand or two less. Piet saw the first house, the house where he stood, pine siding stained redwood and floor plan C, seeded terrace lawn linked by five fieldstone steps to the hardtopped driveway of the under-kitchen garage, smart flagstone stoop and three-chime front doorbell, baseboard oil-fired forced-hot-water heating and brick patio in the rear for summer dining and possible sunbathing, aluminum combination all-weather sash and rheostated ceiling fixtures set flush, efficient kitchen in Pearl Mist and Thermopane picture window, as bringing $19,900, or at a knockdown eighteen five if Gallagher panicked, a profit above wages paid even to himself, one-fifty weekly, of three or four, depending on how smoothly he dovetailed the subcontractors, which suddenly didn't seem enough, enough to placate Gallagher, enough to justify this raging and rending close at his back, this rape of a haven precious to ornamental shy creatures who needed no house. Builders burying the world God made. The two-headed tractor, the color of a school bus, trampled, grappled, growled, ramped. Blue belches of smoke flew upward from the hole. The mounted Negro, down to his undershirt, a cannibal king on a dragon dripping oil, grinned and shouted to Piet his pleasure that he had not encountered ledge.

"This is the soft side of the hill," Piet shouted, and was not heard. He felt between himself and the colored man a continental gulf, the chasm between a jungle asking no pity and a pampered rectilinear land coaxed from the sea. The Negro was at home here, in this tumult of hoisted rocks, bucking reversals of direction and shifting gears, clangor and fumes, internal combustion, the land of the free. He was Ham and would inherit. Piet tried to picture the young couple who would live in this visualized home and he did not love them. None of his friends would live in such a home. He stooped and picked a bone from its outline in the earth, where the grid of the dozer's tread had pressed it, and showed it curiously to Jazinski.

"Cow bone," Leon said.

"Doesn't it seem too delicate?"

"Deer?"

"Don't they say there was an Indian burying ground some-where on this south side?"

Jazinski shrugged. "Beats me." Leon was a weedy, hollow-chested young man originally from Nashua, New Hampshire. He was one of the three men that Gallagher & Hanema kept on the payroll all year long. The other two were venerable carpenters, Adams and Comeau, that Piet had inherited from Ed Byrd, an excessively amiable Tarbox contractor who had declared bank-ruptcy in 1957. Piet had himself singled out Jazinski from a doz-en summer laborers two summers ago. Leon had a good eye and a fair head, an eye for the solid angle and the overlooked bind and a sense for the rhythmic mix of bluff and guess whereby a small operator spaces men and equipment and rentals and prom-ises to minimize time, which is money. Gallagher, who discreetly craved the shoddy—vinyl siding versus wood, pressed wallboard panels versus plaster—had intended to lay Jazinski off last winter; Piet had begged him to hold the boy, offering to drop his own salary to one-twenty-five, fearing that something of himself, his younger self, would be lost if they failed to nurture a little longer Leon's uneducated instinct for the solid, the tight, the necessary.

Piet felt that the bone in his hand was human. He asked Leon, "Have you seen any arrowheads turn up? Beads, bits of pot?"

Leon shook his slow slender head. "Just crap," he said. "Mother Earth."

Embarrassed, Piet said, "Well, keep your eyes open. We may be on sacred ground." He let the bone, too small to have been a thigh, perhaps part of an arm, drop. On Leon's face, downcast beneath a blond eave of hair, Piet spied the smudge of a sneer. In his tone that meant business, the warmth withdrawn, Piet asked, "When can we pour? Early next week?"

"Depends." The boy was sulking. "I'm here all by myself, if Adams and Comeau could stop diddling with that garage . . ."

"They're not to be hurried."

"Waterproofing the foundation takes at least a day."

"It has to be done."

"If it wasn't, who'd be the wiser?"

Piet said swiftly, seeing he must pounce now, or the boy would be a cheat forever, "We would. And in a few years when the house settled and the basement leaked everybody would. Let me tell you about houses. Everything outs. Every cheat. Every short cut. I want the foundation damp-proofed, I want polyethylene under the slab, I want lots of gravel under the drain tile as well as over it, I want you to wrap felt around the joints or they'll sure as hell clog. Don't think because you cover something up it isn't there. People have a nose for the rotten and if you're a builder the smell clings. Now let's look at the drawings together."

Leon's avoiding cheek flushed under the discipline. He gazed at the hole growing in the earth and said, "Those old clunkers have been a month on a garage me and two kids could have put up in a week."

Piet's pedagogic spurt was spent. He said wearily, "They're winding up, I'll go over and see if they can't be up here by to-morrow. I'll call for a load of gravel this afternoon and see if we can set up Ready-Mix over in North Mather for next Monday, do the three at once, that'll give you a day each, I'll help myself if we can't squeeze some trade-school kids out of Gallagher." For an hour, using as a table a boulder under the low boughs of a great oak that would overshadow the patio, he and Leon analyzed the blueprints bought by mail from an architectural factory in Chicago. Piet felt the younger mind picking for holes in his, testing, resenting. It grew upon him as they plotted their campaign together that Leon disliked him, had heard enough about his life to consider him a waster, a drinker, an immigrant clown in the town's party crowd, unfaithful to his wife, bored by his business. This appraisal blew coolly on Piet's face as he traced lines and dimensions with his broad thumbnail and penciled in adjustments demanded by this sloping site. Leon nodded, learning, yet did not let up this cool pressure, which seemed part of the truth of these woods, where the young must prey upon the not-so-young, the ambitious upon the preoccupied. Piet was impatient to leave the site.

In parting, he turned for a moment to the Negro, who had retired with a lunch box and thermos bottle to the edge of the excavation. The sliced sides showed a veined logic of stratification. Pages of an unread book. Impacted vegetable lives. Piet asked him, "Do you ever find Indian graves?"

"You see bones."

"What do you do when you see them?"

"Man, I keep movin'."

Piet laughed, feeling released, forgiven, touched and hugged by something human arrived from a great distance, imagining behind the casually spoken words a philosophy, a night life.

But the Negro's lips went aloof, as if to say that laughter would no longer serve as a sop to his race. His shoulder-balls bigger than soccer balls. His upper lip jeweled with sweat. A faint tarry tigerish smell. Piet, downwind, bowed.

Pardon me, Dr. King.

Piet left the two men in the clearing and drove into town, to the far end of Temperance Avenue, where Adams and Comeau were building a garage at the rear of a house lot. Comeau was thin and Adams was fat, but after years of association they moved as matched planets, even at opposite corners of the garage revolving, backs turned, with an unspoken gravitational awareness of the other. Passing to the toolbox, on a board between sawhorses, they crossed paths but did not bump. Neither acknowledged Piet. He stood in the empty rectangle that awaited a track-hung spring-lift garage door; he inhaled the scent of shaved lumber, the sense of space secured. Except for the door, the structure seemed complete. Piet cleared his throat and asked, "When do you gentlemen think we can call it quits here?"

Adams said, "When it's done."

"And when might that be? I don't see a day's work here, just the door to come."

"Odds and ends," Comeau told him. He was applying a plane to the inside of the window sash, though the sash was factory-made. Adams was screwing in L-shaped shelf brackets between two studs. Adams smoked a pipe and wore bibbed overalls with as many pockets as a hardware store has drawers; Comeau's blue shirts were always freshly laundered and cigarettes had stained his fingers orange. He added, "Once we finish up, the widow'll have to manage herself." The property belonged to a young woman whose husband, a soldier, had been killed—knifed—by the German boy friend of his girl friend in Hamburg.

"It ought to be left neat," Adams said.

Piet, inspecting, paused at a detail of the framing. A two-by-four diagonal brace intersected a vertical stud and, though the angle was not an easy one, and this was rough work, the stud had been fitted as precisely as a piece of veneer. Waste. Piet felt as if he had been handed a flower; but had to say, "Leon needs you on the hill to knock together the basement forms."

"Jack be nimble," old Comeau said, shaking out a match. It was their nickname for Jazinski.

"Door isn't come up yet from Mather," Adams said.

Piet said, "I'll call them. If it isn't brought this afternoon, come up to the hill tomorrow morning anyway. This is a beautiful garage for the widow, but at six-fifty an hour enough is enough. She'll have boy friends who can put up shelves for her. I must get back to the hill."

As he walked around the garage to the street, he heard Comeau, who was still planing at the window, say, "Greedy Gally's on his back."

Piet drove home. The square yard and house were welcoming, empty. He carried the wood and wire he had bought into his basement workshop, which he hadn't used all winter. He cut some segments of the 2″ pine but discovered that the warpage of the rolled wire was so strong that a cumbersome system of braces would be needed to hold the sides straight. So he formed in his mind another design, using the warp of the wire as a force, and rooted a parabolic curve of mesh on either side of the plywood with the poultry staples, and then cut an oval of wire to seal the cage shut. But one end had to be a door. He improvised hinges from a coat hanger and fitted sticks for the necessary stiffness. As he worked, his hands shook with excitement, the agitation of creation that since childhood had often spoiled his projects— birdhouses, go-carts, sand castles—in the final trembling touches. The cage, completed, seemed beautiful to him, a transparent hangar shaped by laws discovered within itself, minimal, invented,

Piet's own. He foresaw Ruth's pleased surprise, Angela's grudging admiration, Nancy's delight and her insistence on crawling inside this child-sized shelter. He carried the cage upstairs to the kitchen and, needing to share his joy of accomplishment, dialed the Thornes' number. "Is this the Swedish bakery?" It was their formula, to which she could say No.

Georgene laughed. "Hi, Piet. How *are* you?"

"Miserable."

"Why?"

He told her about the hamster and the dismal work on Indian Hill, but could not specifically locate the cause of his depression, his sense of unconnection among phenomena and of falling. The lack of sun and shadows. Angela's aloofness. The Negro's snub. The slowness of spring to come.

Georgene said, "Poor Piet. My poor little lover."

He said, "Not much of a day for the sunporch, is it?"

"I've been in the house cleaning. I'm having the League Board tonight and Irene frightens me, she's so efficient and worthy."

"How's Freddy's finger?"

"Oh, fine. He took it out of the spoon yesterday."

"I felt crummy about that. I don't see why I should want to hurt him since in a way, without knowing it of course, he lets me have you."

"Is that the way you think of it? I thought *I* let you have me."

"You do, you do. Thank you. But why do I have such a hatred of him?"

"I have no idea." Always, over the telephone, there was the strangeness of their not being able to touch, and the revelation that her firm quick voice could be contentious.

He asked politely, "Could I—would you like me to come visit you for a minute? Just to say hello, we don't have time to make love. I must get back to the hill."

Her pause, in which they could not touch, was most strange. "Piet," she said, "I'd love you to—"

"But?"

"But I wonder if it's wise right this noon. I've had something happen to me."

Pregnant. By whom? There was a mirror above the telephone table and in it he saw himself, a pale taut-faced father, the floor tipped under him.

She went on, hesitating, she who had confided everything to him, her girlish loves, her first sex with Freddy, when they made love now, her periods, her mild momentary yearnings toward other men, everything, "I think I've discovered that Freddy is seeing Janet. I found a letter in the pocket of a suit I was taking to the cleaner's."

"How careless of him. Maybe he wanted you to find it. What did it say?"

"Nothing very much. It said, 'Let's break it off, no more phone calls,' et cetera, which might mean anything. It could mean she's putting on pressure for him to divorce me."

"Why would she want to marry Freddy?" He realized this was tactless and tried to disguise it with another question. "You're sure it's her?"

"Quite. She signed it J and anyway her handwriting is unmistakable, big and fat and spilly. You've seen it on her Christmas cards."

"Well. But sweet, it's been in the air for some time, Freddy and Janet. Does it really shock you?"

"I suppose," Georgene said, "there's something called female pride. But more than that. I'm shocked by the idea of divorce. If it comes to that I don't want him to have anything to throw back at me, for the children to read about in the paper. It wouldn't bother Freddy but it would me."

"So what does this do to us?"

"I suppose nothing, except that we must be very careful."

"How careful is careful?"

"Piet. I'm not going to tell you how much you mean to me. I've said that in ways a woman can't fake. I just don't think I could enjoy you today and I don't want to waste you. Also it's too near noon."

"Have you confronted Freddy with your discovery?" The man in the mirror had begun to squint, as his pang of fear relaxed into cunning.

Georgene, growing franker, said, "I'm too chicken. He'll tell Janet, then she'll know *I* know, and until I have some plan of action I'd rather just *know*."

"I'm touched by how much Freddy means to you."

"Vell, honeybunch, he *is* my husband."

"Sure enough. You picked him, he's all yours. Except I don't see why I must be sacrificed because Freddy is naughty."

"Maybe he is because I am. Because we are. Anyway you sound as though you rather *want* to be sacrificed."

"Tell me when I can see you."

"Oh love, anytime, just not today. I'm not myself."

"Sweet Georgene, forgive me. I'm being very stupid and full of threatened egotism."

"I *love* your egotism. Oh hell. Come on over now if you want, she isn't brought back from nursery school until twelve-thirty."

"No, of course not. I don't want it unless you feel right about it. You feel guilty. You feel you've driven poor old God-fearing monogamous Freddy into the arms of this harlot."

"I *like* Janet. I think she's quite funny and gutsy. I think Frank is impossible and she does quite well considering."

Piet liked Frank; he resisted the urge to quarrel. Every new assertion of Georgene's, as she relaxed into the certainty that he would not come, advanced his anger. "Anyway," he said, "I just heard the noon whistle blow. I don't want Judy coming back from school saying, 'Mommy, what's that lump under the covers? It smells like Nancy's daddy.'" Smells: the woods, the earth, the Negro's skin, the planed pine of the garage, the whiskey on Bea Guerin's breath.

"Piet. Am I putting you off? I do want you."

"I know. Please don't apologize. You've been a lovely mistress."

She ignored his tense. "When I found the note, the first thing I wanted to do was call you and—what? Cry on your shoulder. Crawl into bed beside you. It was Monday night, Freddy was at Lions'. Suddenly I was terrified. I was alone in a big ugly house with a piece of paper in my hand that wouldn't go away."

"Don't be terrified. You're a lovely doubles partner and a fine wife for Freddy. Who else could stand him? If he lost you it would be the worst thing that's happened to him since he flunked

medical school." Did she notice his unintended equation of her
with dentistry—both practical, clean, simple, both a recourse? By
this equation was Angela something difficult that he, Piet, had
flunked? "Anyway," he went on, "I don't think either Freddy or
Janet have it in them these days to give themselves much to
anybody."

She said, "It's so sad. You call to be reassured and end up by
reassuring me. Oh my Lord. Bernadette's VW is coming up the
drive. Nursery school let out early. Is today a holiday?"

"April twenty-third? The paper said Shakespeare's birthday.
He's three hundred and ninety-nine years old."

"Piet. I must run. There's a lot we haven't said. Let's see each
other soon."

"Let's," Piet said, and her kiss ticked as he had halfway returned his receiver to the cradle. The man in the mirror was
hunched, a shadow ready to spring, sunless daylight filtering into
the room behind him. He looked, he thought, young, his crow's
feet and the puckering under his eyes smoothed into shadow. A
fragment came to him of the first conversation he and Georgene
had had as lovers. She had been so gay, so sporting, taking him
upstairs to her bed that fresh September day, he could hardly
believe he was her first lover. Reflected autumnal brilliance had
invaded her house and infused with warmth her exotic furniture
of bamboo and straw rosettes and batik and unbleached sailcloth.
Gaudy Guatemalan pillows heaped against the kingsized headboard had surprised him. *Here? In Freddy's very bed?*

It's my bed too. Would you rather use the floor?

No, no. It's luxurious. Whose books are all these?

*Freddy's pornography, it's disgusting. Please pay attention to
me.*

*I am, Jesus. But . . . shouldn't we do something about not
making a little baby?*

*Sveetie. You're so naieef. You mean Angela doesn't take Eno-
vid yet?*

You do? It works?

Of course it works, it's wonderful. Welcome, Georgene said, *to
the post-pill paradise.*

Piet remembered, standing alone in his low-ceilinged living

room, where the wallpaper mourned its slanting visitor the sun
and the spare neat furniture reflected his and Angela's curiously
similar austerity of taste, how Georgene's cheeks, freckled from a
summer of sunbathing, had dryly creased as she made this joke.
Her manner had been a feathery teasing minimizing his heart's
clangor, and always until now she had brought to their affair, like
a dowry of virginal lace, this lightness, this guiltlessness. If she
was now sullied and spoiled because of Freddy's dabbling, where
would he find supplied such absolution? That first time, had she
bathed? No, it became her habit when he revealed he liked to kiss
between her thighs. And had her easy calm gaiety been a manner
she had contrived to suit some other crimp in his manner of be-
stowing love, perhaps an untoward seriousness that threatened
her marriage? His praise had amused her; she had always responded that all women liked to make love, that all women were
beautiful, like a toilet bowl, when you needed one. But by daylight he had discovered on her rapt Roman face an expression,
of peace deeper than an infant's sleep, that the darkness of night
had never disclosed on the face of his wife. Furtive husbandly
visitant, he had never known Angela as he had often known his
lovely easy matter-of-fact morning lay. The line of her narrow
high-bridged nose a double arabesque. Her white hairs belying
her body's youth. Her bony bit of a tail.

Her receding hollowed the dull noon. Tipped shoots searched
for wider light through sunless gray air. The salami he made
lunch from was minced death. He went at last to his office. His
telephone voice grew husky, defeated. Garage doors of the type
needed were out of stock in Mather and were being ordered from
Akron. The price of gravel had gone up two dollars a ton and
a truckload could not be delivered before Friday. The urban
renewal in Boston had sucked the area dry of carpenters and six
phone calls turned up only two apprentices from a trade school
twenty miles away. Spring building had begun and he had been
slow. Gallagher's silences, though his conversation was commiser-
ating, breathed accusation.

Piet had met Matt in the army, in Okinawa, in 1951. There,
then, in that riverless flatland of barracks and sand, of beer in
blank cans and listless Luchuan prostitutes, where the danger of

death in battle was as unreal as the homeland whose commercial music twanged in the canteens, Piet was attracted by Matt's choir-boy prankishness, his grooming, his black hair and eyes, his freedom from the weary vocabulary of dirt and disdain, his confident ability to sell. He had sold Piet on himself as a short cut to architecture and, both discharged, had brought him to New England, into this life. Piet's loyalty was lately strained. He found Matt grown brittle, prim, quick to judge, Jesuitical in finance. He dreamed of corrupting whole hillsides, yet wished to keep himself immaculate. He secured his wife and only child behind a wall of Catholicism. In the little transparent world of couples whose intrigues had permeated and transformed Piet, Matt stood out as opaquely moral.

When the phone on his desk rang, Piet feared it would be Georgene, seeking a reconciliation. He hated paining Matt with his duplicity; he thought of Matt with the same pain as he thought of his father, that ghost patiently circling in the luminous greenhouse gloom, silently expecting Piet to do right, to carry on.

It was not Georgene but Angela. Nancy at nursery school had burst out crying because of the hamster. The child suddenly saw with visionary certainty that its death had been her fault. *Daddy said,* she said. Her hysterics had been uncontrollable. Angela had carried her from the room and, since she was teaching, the class ended early. They did not go home. There was nothing to eat at home but ham. In hopes of distracting Nancy with syrup and ice cream, Angela had taken her to eat at the Pancake House in North Mather. Now the child, sucking her thumb and running a slight fever, had fallen asleep on the sofa.

Piet said, "The kid sure knows how to get herself sympathy."

"But not from her own father, evidently. I didn't call just to touch you with this, though as a matter of fact I do think you handled it stupidly. Stupidly or cruelly. I called to ask you to meet Ruth after school and drive to the pet shop in Lacetown for a new hamster. I think we should do it *in*stantly."

Magic. The new hamster by sleight of hand would become the old one, the one moldering nose-down underneath the scilla. A religion of genteel pretense. The idea of a hamster persists, eternal. Plato. Piet was an Aristotelian. He said he couldn't possibly do it this afternoon, he had a thousand things to do, the first quarter's accounts to check, he was trying to move the houses on the hill, a million details, the construction trade was going to hell. He was heavily conscious of Gallagher listening. Softer-voiced, he added, "I wasted half the morning making a new cage. Did you notice it in the kitchen?"

Angela said, "Oh is that what it is? We didn't know what it was for. Why is it such a funny shape? Nancy thought it was a little prison you were going to put *her* in."

"Tell the kid I love her lots and to shape up. Good-bye."

The books showed less than the twenty per cent Gallagher liked to clear. Spiros Bros. had attached to their monthly statement a printed threat to stop the account; the balance owed was $1189.24. Gallagher liked to let bills run long, on the theory that money constantly diminished in value. The figures made a gray hazy net around Piet and to compound his claustrophobia the Whitman woman, who had come to basketball uninvited, phoned and asked him to come look at her house. He didn't want the job, he didn't like working for social acquaintances. But in his hopeless mood, to escape the phone and the accounts and Gallagher's binding nearness, he got into the truck whose tailgate said WASH ME and drove down.

The marshes opened up on his right, grand in the dying day. A strip of enameled blue along the horizon of the sea. Colored tiles along a bathtub. The first drops of a half-hearted rain, cold and dry, struck the backs of his hands as he climbed from the truck. The lilacs by the door of the Robinson place were further along that those of Piet's own roadside hedge. More sun by the sea. More life. Tiny wine-colored cones that in weeks would be lavender panicles of bloom. Drenched. Dew. Salt. Breeze. Buttery daffodils trembled by his cuffs, by the bare board fence where they enjoyed reflected warmth. Piet lifted the aluminum latch, salt-corroded, and went in. Even under close clouds, the view was prodigal, a heart-hollowing carpeted span limited by the purity of dunes and ocean. He had been wrong, overcautious. It should be Angela's.

. . .

Ken Whitman's field of special competence, after his early interest in echinoid metabolism, was photosynthesis; his doctoral thesis had concerned the 7-carbon sugar sedoheptulose, which occupies a momentary place within the immense chain of reactions whereby the five-sixths of the triosephosphate pool that does not form starch is returned to ribulose-5-phosphate. The process was elegant, and few men under forty were more at home than Ken upon the gigantic ladder, forged by light, that carbon dioxide descends to become carbohydrate. At present he was supervising two graduate students in research concerning the transport of glucose molecules through cell walls. By this point in his career Ken had grown impatient with the molecular politics of sugar and longed to approach the mysterious heart of CO_2 fixation—chlorophyll's transformation of visible light into chemical energy. But here, at this ultimate chamber, the lone reaction that counterbalances the vast expenditures of respiration, that reverses decomposition and death, Ken felt himself barred. Biophysics and electronics were in charge. The grana of stacked quantasomes were structured like the crystal lattices in transistors. Photons excited an electron flow in the cloud of particles present in chlorophyll. Though he had ideas—why chlorophyll? why not any number of equally complex compounds? was the atom of magnesium the clue?—he would have to put himself to school again and, at thirty-two, felt too old. He was wedded to the unglamorous carbon cycle while younger men were achieving fame and opulent grants in such fair fields as neurobiology, virology, and the wonderful new wilderness of nucleic acids. He had a wife, a coming child, a house in need of extensive repair. He had overreached. Life, whose graceful secrets he would have unlocked, pressed upon him clumsily.

As if underwater he moved through the final hour of this heavy gray day. An irreversible, constricted future was brewing in the apparatus of his lab—the fantastic glass alphabet of flasks and retorts, the clamps and slides and tubes, the electromagnetic scales sensitive to the hundredth of a milligram, the dead experiments probably duplicated at Berkeley or across the river. Ken worked on the fourth floor of a monumental neo-Greek benefaction, sooty without and obsolete within, dated 1911. The hall window, whose sill held a dreggish Lily cup, overlooked Boston. Expressways capillariously fed the humped dense center of brick red where the State House dome presided, a gold nucleolus. Dusty excavations ravaged the nearer ground. In the quad directly below, female students in bright spring dresses—dyed trace elements—slid along the paths between polygons of chlorophyll. Ken looked with a weariness unconscious of weariness. There had been rain earlier. The same rain now was falling on Tarbox. The day was so dull the window was partly a mirror in which his handsomeness, that strange outrigger to his career, glanced back at him with a cocked eyebrow, a blurred mouth, and a glint of eye white. Ken shied from this ghost; for most of his life he had consciously avoided narcissism. As a child he had vowed to become a saint of science and his smooth face had developed as his enemy. He turned and walked to the other end of the hall; here, for lack of space, the liquid-scintillation counter, though it had cost the department fifteen thousand, a Packard Tri-Carb, was situated. At the moment it was working, ticking through a chain of isotopically labeled solutions, probably Neusner's minced mice livers. A thick-necked sandy man over forty, Jewish only in the sleepy lids of his eyes, Neusner comported himself with the confidence of the energetically second-rate. His lectures were full of jokes and his papers were full of wishful reasoning. Yet he was liked, and had established forever the spatial configuration of one enzyme. Ken envied him and was not sorry to see, at four-thirty, his lab empty. Neusner was a concertgoer and winetaster and womanizer and mainstay of the faculty supper club; he traveled with the Cambridge political crowd and yesterday had confided to Ken in his hurried emphatic accents the latest Kennedy joke. *One night about three a.m. Jackie hears Jack coming into the White House and she meets him on the stairs. His collar is all rumpled and there's lipstick on his chin and she asks him, Where the hell have you been? and he tells her, I've been having a conference with Madame Nhu, and she says, Oh, and doesn't think any more about it until the next week the same thing happens and this time he says he was sitting up late arguing ideology*

with Nina Khrushchev . . . A sallow graduate student was tidying up the deserted labs. A heap of gutted white mice lay like
burst grapes on a tray. Pink-eyed cagefuls alertly awaited anni-
hilation. Neusner loved computers and statistical theory and his
papers were famous for the sheets of numbers that masked the
fantasy of his conclusions. Next door old Prichard, the department's prestigious ornament, was pottering with his newest play-
thing, the detection and analysis of a memory-substance secreted
by the brain. Ken envied the old man his childlike lightness, his
freedom to dart through forests of evidence after such a bluebird.
Neusner, Prichard—they were both free in a way Ken wasn't.
Why? Everyone sensed it, the something wrong with Ken, so intelligent and handsome and careful and secure—the very series
expressed it, an unstable compound, unnatural. Prichard, a saint,
tried to correct the condition, to give Ken of himself, sawing the
air with his papery mottled hands, nodding his unsteady gaunt
head, whose flat cheeks seemed rouged, spilling his delicate stam-
mer: *The thing of it, the thing of it is, Wh-Whitman, it's just
t-tinkering, you mustn't s-s-suppose life, ah, owes us anything,
we just g-get what we can out of the b-bitch, eh?* Next to his lab,
his narrow office was a hodgepodge encrusted with clippings,
cartoons, snapshots of other people's children and grandchildren,
with honorary degrees, gilded citations, mounted butterflies and
framed tombstone tracings and other such detritus of the old
man's countless hobbies. Ken halted at the door of this living
scrapbook wistfully, wanting a moment of encouragement, wondering why such a sanctified cell would never be his. The old
man was unmarried. In his youth there had been a scandal, a wife
who had left him; Ken doubted the story, for how could any
woman leave so good a man?

Inspiration came to him: Prichard's virtues might be a product
of being left, a metabolic reduction necessary to growth, a fruitful fractionation. Inspiration died: he looked within himself and
encountered a surface bafflingly smooth. On Prichard's cluttered
desk today's newspaper declared, ERHARD CERTAIN TO SUCCEED
ADENAUER.

Morris Stein was waiting for him with a problem, an enzyme

that couldn't be crystallized. Then it was after five. He drove
home expertly, a shade arrogantly, knifing along the Southeastern
Expressway like a man who has solved this formula often, changing lanes as it suited him, Prichard and Neusner and Stein revolving in his head while automobiles of differing makes spun and
shuffled, passed and were passed, outside his speeding windows.
He wondered about the people in Tarbox, how Hanema could
drive that filthy clanking pick-up truck everywhere and the
Applebys stick with that old maroon Mercury when they had the
money. He wondered why Prichard had never won the Nobel
and deduced that his research was like his hobbies, darting this
way and that, more enthusiasm than rigor. He thought of photosynthesis and it appeared to him there was a tedious deep flirtatiousness in nature that withheld her secrets while the church
burned astronomers and children died of leukemia. That she
yielded by whim, wantonly, to those who courted her offhand,
with a careless ardor he, Ken, lacked. *The b-b-bitch.*

The smokestacks and gasholders of South Boston yielded to
the hickory woods of Nun's Bay Road. He arrived home before
dark. Daylight Saving had begun. Alone in the living room Cotton was curved asleep in the sling chair from Design Research.
Ken called Foxy's name. She answered faintly from the porch.
Someone had torn away the boards that had sealed the French
doors. She sat on a wicker chair, a tall gin drink in her hand,
looking through rusted porch screens toward the sea. The sky
was clearing after the brief rain. Dark-blue clouds thin as playing
cards seen edgewise duplicated the line of the horizon. The lighthouse was tipped with an orange drop of final sun. He asked her,
"Aren't you cold?"

"No, I'm warm. I'm fat."

He wanted to touch her, for luck, for safety, as when a child
in Farmington after a long hide in the weeds shouts *Free!* and
touches the home maple. Gazing in the dying light across the
greening marsh, she had a tree's packed stillness. Her blond hair
and pink skin and brown eyes were all one shade in the darkness
of the porch. With a motion almost swift, the light had died.
Bending to kiss her, he found her skin strange; she was shiver-

ing. Her arms showed goosebumps. He begged her, "Come in the house."

"It's so pretty. Isn't this what we're paying for?"

He thought the expression strange. They had never given much thought to money. Advancement, distinction: these were the real things. As if having overheard his thoughts, she went on, "We all rather live under wraps, don't we? We hardly ever really open ourselves to the loveliness around us. Yet there it is, every day, going on and on, whether we look at it or not. Such a splendid waste, isn't it?"

"I'm going in to make a drink." She followed him in and told him about her day. She had weeded and raked in the side yard. She had decided she wanted roses, white and red mixed, along the blind southern wall of the servants' wing. The Plymouth agency had called and said her car—a secondhand station wagon they had bought for her, since without a vehicle she was virtually a prisoner at this end of the beach road—would be ready Thursday, with license plates and an inspection sticker. Ken had forgotten about this car, though obviously she needed it. In Cambridge they had done so long without any car at all. Just before lunchtime Irene Saltz, with tiny Jeremiah in a papooselike arrangement on her back, had dropped in on her way back from the beach. She was a conservationist and distressed that the winter storms had flattened a number of dunes. Any town but Tarbox would ages ago have put up fences and brush hedges to hold the sand. She asked Foxy to join the League of Women Voters and drank three cups of coffee. With such a monologuist for a husband, you probably have to develop another erotic outlet, but the trouble with people who have poured themselves into good works is they expect you to do the same, pour away, even if they have husbands as handsome, charming, and attentive as, dear, yourself . . . Ken sipped his drink and wondered what she was driving at. In the living-room light she looked pale, her ears and nostrils nipped pink. She was high on something.

What else happened? Oh, yes, in the middle of her nap, and by the way she had gotten to volume two of Painter's life of Proust, which looked to be much the duller, since Proust was no longer having his childhood, Carol Constantine had called, inviting them to a May Day party; it sounded rather orgiastic. And finally she had got up her nerve and called this man Hanema to come look at the house.

"When will he come?"

"Oh, he came."

"And what did he say?"

"Oh he said fifteen thousand, more or less. It depends on how much you want to do. He'd like to see us with a full basement but a crawl space with I think he said plastic film over the earth might do for the kitchen half. He prefers hot-water heat but says hot air would be cheaper since we can put the ducts right in the walls we're going to have to build anyway. You'll have to talk to him yourself. Everything seemed to depend on something else."

"What about the roof and the shingles?"

"New roof. He thinks we can patch the shingles for now."

"Does this fifteen thousand include doing anything to those ugly upstairs dormers and that leaky skylight?"

"We didn't go upstairs. Of course he knows the house already. He thought the big issue was the basement. He was rather quaint and cute. He kept talking about babies crawling around on a nice warm floor and glancing at my tummy."

Ken felt a weight descend but persisted. "And the kitchen?"

"He sees about four thousand there. He wants to knock out the pantry partition and have new everything except the sink. He agreed with me, the slate sink must be kept. But the plumbing should be done over top to bottom. And the wiring. Have some more bourbon, baby."

She took his glass and smoothly, like a sail pushed by wind, moved toward the kitchen. "Very weak," he said, and, when she returned with the drink, said, "Well. But did you like him?"

Foxy stood a moment, her pale mouth shaped as if to hum. "I can manage him. He seemed a little forlorn today. His daughter's pet hamster was eaten by a neighbor's cat." Ken remembered Neusner's tray of gutted mice and wondered how some men still could permit themselves so much sentiment.

"You're the one," Ken said, "who'll have to deal with him."

She again moved with that airy quickness, as if she had considered a possibility and dismissed it. "I don't think he wants the job. He and your friend are building new houses for the population explosion."

"Gallagher's not my friend especially. Did Hanema recommend any other contractor?"

"I asked him to. He said there wasn't anybody he'd trust us with offhand. He was very indecisive. He seemed to feel possessive about this house."

"His wife had wanted it."

"You keep *saying* that." Her reactions had a quickness, her eyes a hard brightness, that was unusual; he felt an unseen factor operating, an unaccounted-for chemical. She had disliked Hanema: this guess, flattering to himself, inevitable in the light of himself, disposed him to the man, and he told her, "I think, why not put him to work? Exert your charm."

She was moving, swiftly, lightly, about the room, taking a kind of inventory perhaps, touching rough surfaces that soon would be smooth, saying goodbye to the ugly mementos, the fan-shaped shell collection, the dried sprigs of beach pea and woolly hudsonia, that had housed her for this while, this pregnant month. She changed the subject. "How was your day?"

He confessed, "I feel bogged down."

She thought, *You need another woman.* She said, "It's too much commuting."

"It's too much mediocre mental grinding. On my part. I should have gone into law. That we can do. The old man has two flat feet for a brain, and everybody in Hartford thinks he's nifty." She laughed, and he looked up startled; his vocabulary became boyish when he thought of Hartford, and he was unconscious of it. He went on sadly, "I was thinking about Prichard today and it made me realize I don't really have it. The flair. It all just looks like a bunch of details to me, which is the way it looks to every boob."

"Prichard's an old man. You're young. Old men have nothing serious to think about." By "serious" she meant the shadow within herself, her child, the dark world of breeding.

"Except death," Ken said, a touching strange thing for him to say. She had pictured him as thinking no more about death than a watch does about running down. She had assumed he from birth had solved it and had worked out her own solution apart from him.

Foxy said eagerly, "Oh no, when you're young you think about that. So when you're old you have nothing to do but be happy for each new day." She drifted to where a scantling shelf horizontal between two studs held a single forgotten amber marble, striped with a swirl of honey-white. She held it in her pink oval palm and tried to see into its center and imagined God as a man so old each day makes Him absolutely happy. She wondered why she could not share God with Ken, it was so innocent, like this marble, meek and small but there. She didn't ask him to believe in more than this. But in his presence she became ashamed, felt guilty of duplicity.

Ken looked up as if awaking. "Who took the boards off the porch doors?"

"He did. Hanema."

"With his bare hands?"

With your bare hands?

Sure. Why not? Why haven't you done this yourselves?

We thought it served some purpose.

It did, but winter's over. Welcome to spring. Now. This should turn, with a little love. Ah, It does. Come on.

Oh. I've hardly ever been on the porch. Are the screens still mendable?

He had taken a loose piece of rusted screening and crumpled it and showed her the orange dust like pollen in his palm. *New screens will be one of the least of your expenses. Alcoa makes nice big panels we can fit into runners along here. And here. Take them down in the fall. In summer this porch is the best room in the house. Grab the breeze.*

But it makes the living room so dark. I was thinking of having it torn away.

Don't tear away free space. You bought the view. Here's where it is.

Do you think we were silly? To buy it.

Not at all. This could be a dandy house. You have the skeleton and the size. All it needs now is money.

It was my husband who fell in love with it. I thought of us living nearer to Boston, in Lexington or Newton.

You know—Instead of finishing, he had jogged up and down on the boards, where the line of the porch sagged, testing.

Yes?

Your porch sill is missing a support. Don't hold any square dances out here.

You started to say something.

Not really.

She had waited.

I was going to say that your view makes me sad, because my wife loved it, and I didn't have the courage to do what your husband has done, take this place on.

Do you think courage is what it took? It may have been more a matter of self-esteem.

Perhaps.

Maybe it's just not your kind of place.

Thank you. I didn't feel it was. I'm not a seaside type. I like to feel lots of land around me, in case of a flood.

I suppose me too. I hate wet feet.

But you're happy here, aren't you? Somebody told me you said you were. It's none of my business, of course.

He had seemed so courtly and embarrassed, so ready to put himself back into the hired-man role, that her tongue hastened to ease his presumption. *Yes, I'm happy enough. I'm a little bored. But I like the town and I like the people I've met.*

You do?

You say that with such surprise.

Don't mean to. I guess I'm past asking myself if I like them or not. They're mine.

And you're theirs?

In a way. Watch out. It can happen to you.

No, Ken and I have always been independent. We've never gotten involved with people. I suppose we're both rather cold.

He had taken out a knife and, having turned his back on her, was prying. *Your window sashes should all be replaced.*

Wouldn't storm windows make that unnecessary?

Some of these frames are too rotten to screw a storm sash into. I hope—

You hope what?

I was going to say, I hope we can have your wife down, you and your wife, when the house is fixed up. Already I'm frightened she won't approve of what we do to it.

He had laughed—his laugh came from deeper within him than the laugh of most men, was warmer, a bit disconcerting, more invading.

She had tried to defend herself. *I don't know why I should be worried about your wife's approval. She's a lovely person.*

His laugh repeated. *And your husband's a lovely man.*

ii. *Applesmiths and Other Games*

Foxy was both right and wrong about Janet. Janet had never actually slept with Freddy Thorne, though she and Freddy had held earnest discourse about it, and her affair with Harold little-Smith had proved to be unexpectedly difficult to untangle and end.

The Applebys and little-Smiths had moved to Tarbox in the middle Fifties, unknown to each other, though both men worked in securities on State Street, Harold as a broker, Frank as a trust officer in a bank. Frank had gone to Harvard, Harold to Princeton. They belonged to that segment of their generation of the upper middle class which mildly rebelled against the confinement and discipline whereby wealth maintained its manners during the upheavals of depression and world war. Raised secure amid these national trials and introduced as adults into an indulgent economy, into a business atmosphere strangely blended of crisp youthful imagery and underlying depersonalization, of successful small-scale gambles carried out against a background of rampant diversification and the ultimate influence of a government whose taxes and commissions and appetite for armaments set limits everywhere, introduced into a nation whose leadership allowed a toothless moralism to dissemble a certain practiced cunning, into a culture where adolescent passions and homosexual philosophies were not quite yet triumphant, a climate still *furtively* hedonist, of a country still too overtly threatened from without to be ruthlessly self-abusive, a climate of time between, of standoff and day-by-day, wherein all generalizations, even negative ones, seemed unintelligent—to this new world the Applebys and little-Smiths brought a modest determination to be free, to be flexible and decent. Fenced off from their own parents by nursemaids and tutors and "help," they would personally rear large intimate families; they changed diapers with their own hands, did their own housework and home repairs, gardened and shoveled snow with a sense of strengthened health. Chauffered, as children, in black Packards and Chryslers, they drove second-hand cars in an assortment of candy colors. Exiled early to boarding schools, they resolved to use and improve the local public schools. Having suffered under their parents' rigid marriages and formalized evasions, they sought to substitute an essential fidelity set in a matrix of easy and open companionship among couples. For the forms of the country club they substituted informal membership in a circle of friends and participation in a cycle of parties and games. They put behind them the stratified summer towns of their upbringings, with their restrictive distinctions, their tedious rounds of politeness, and settled the year round in unthought-of places, in pastoral mill towns like Tarbox, and tried to improvise here a fresh way of life. Duty and work yielded as ideals to truth and fun. Virtue was no longer sought in temple or market place but in the home—one's own home, and then the homes of one's friends.

In their first years in Tarbox, the social life of the Smiths and Applebys was passed among older men and women. Neighboring aunts dutifully called and were politely received and, in the end, resolutely snubbed. "How dreary," Marcia would say, "these horsey people are," and as she and Janet became intimate they coined a term, the "big H," to signify all those people, hopefully put behind them and yet so persistently attentive, who did all the right things, a skein of acquaintance and cousinship that extended from Quogue to Bar Harbor. Discovering each other at a horsey party, in Millbrook or Scituate, that each with a great show of wifely resignation had agreed to attend, Janet and Marcia would, by way of greeting, neigh at one another. Janet's delicate nostrilly snort, accompanied by a hoofing motion of one foot, was very piquant; she was slimmer then. In truth, they rarely declined these invitations, though as they failed to return them their number slowly diminished. For among these mocked people, however nasal and wooden-headed, the Applebys and Smiths were given presence on the strength of their names and parents' names; it was years before Tarbox provided them with a society as flattering and nutritious as the scorned "big H."

The Thornes and the Guerins were in Tarbox already, but there was something uncomfortable about both couples, something unexplained and embarrassed about the men—one a dentist, and the other seemingly not employed at all, though frequently in Boston. Both wives were shy; Bea did not drink so much then, and would sit quiet and tensely smiling for an entire evening. When Roger glared, she would freeze like a rabbit. Harold called them *Barbe bleu et Fatime*. They all found Freddy Thorne's smirking pretensions and coziness ridiculous. In those days he still had some hair—wavy fine flax grown long and combed across a bald spot. Georgene was plainly another well-trained, well-groomed filly from the Big H, Philadelphia branch. The couples entertained each other with infrequent stiff dinners, and exchanged maternity clothes—except that Bea was never pregnant.

The people who did throw parties were a decade older and seemed rather coarse and blatant—Dan Mills, the bronzed, limping, and alcoholic owner of the abortive Tarbox boatyard; Eddie Warner, the supervisor of a Mather paint plant, a bullet-headed ex-athlete who could still at beery beach picnics float the ball a mile in the gull-gray dusk; Doc Allen; good old Ed Byrd; a few male teachers in the Tarbox schools, defensive plodders; and their wives, twitchy women full of vicarious sex and rock-and-roll lyrics, their children being adolescent. To Janet they seemed desperate people, ignorant and provincial and loud. Their rumored infidelities struck her as pathetic; their evident heavy drinking disgusted her. She herself had just produced a baby,

Franklin, Jr.—eight pounds, six ounces. The skin of his temples exquisitely pulsed as he sucked her breasts, so that not only the hoarsely joshing voices and unsweet breaths but the imperfect complexions of the "boatyard crowd," as she and Marcia had christened it, offended her; lepers should not insist on dancing. The boatyard crowd, a postwar squirearchy of combat veterans, locally employed and uncollegiate, knew that it was patronized by these younger cooler couples and suffered no regrets when they chose to form a separate set and to leave them alone with their liquor and bridge games and noisy reminiscences of Anzio and Guadalcanal.

Had they been less uncongenial, Janet would hardly have made social overtures to the Saltzes and the Ongs, who moved to opposite ends of the town in 1957 and who at least were college graduates. John Ong, indeed, was supposedly very brilliant. He worked in Cambridge, mathematically deciphering matter, in a program underwritten by the government. He should have been fascinating but his English was impossible to understand. His wife, Bernadette, was a broad-shouldered half-Japanese from Baltimore, her father an immigrant Portugese. She was exotic and boistrous and warm and exhausting, as if she were trying to supply by herself enough gregariousness for two. The Saltzes were killingly earnest but Irene could be fun after the third martini, when she did imitations of all the selectmen and town officials her crusading spirit brought her up against. Ben had only one imitation, which he did unconsciously—a rabbi, with scruffy beard and bent stoop, hands clasped behind him, and an air of sorrowing endurance. But it was not until, in 1958, Hanema and Gallagher set up their office on Hope Street that the final ecology of the couples was established. With these two men, the Irishman and Dutchman, shaped together like Don Quixote and Sancho Panza, began the round of sports—touch football, skiing, basketball, sailing, tennis, touch football again—that gave the couples an inexhaustible excuse for gathering: a calendrical wheel of unions to anticipate and remember, of excuses for unplanned parties. And the two new women, Terry and Angela, brought a style with them, an absent-minded amiability from which the other women were able to imitate the only tone, casual and amused, that could make bearable such a burden of hospitality and intermingling. In 1960 the Constantines moved into their sinister big house on the green; Carol painted, and Eddie flew. As a couple, they had an appealingly dangerous air. And now, in 1963, the Whitmans had moved into the old Robinson place.

These years had seen the boatyard crowd go from decay to disintegration. Two couples had been divorced, the schoolteachers had failed to get tenure and had quit or been dismissed, poor alcoholic Danny Mills had lost his boatyard to the bank and gone to Florida without his wife, whose hard stringy legs had been so quick to master the newest dance step. The only remaining contact with the boatyard crowd was by phone, when one called to ask one of their teen-age daughters to babysit. Their existence, which might have been forgotten entirely, was memorialized by a strange vestige, irksome to Harold and Marcia, within the younger group of couples. There had been, in those first Tarbox years, another couple called Smith, a pair of big-headed, ruddy, humorless social pushers who had since moved to Newton but who were, for a year, present at the same parties the smaller Smiths were invited to. So the modifiers had been coined as a conversational convenience and had outlived the need for any distinction, and become part of Harold and Marcia, though by now few of their friends knew who the big-Smiths had been, or could envision their ponderous, flushed, doll-like faces, always eagerly nodding, like floats in a Shriners parade. It was an annual cause for hilarity when, with that inexorable plodding friendliness that had been their method of attack, the Smiths from faraway Newton Centre favored the Thornes, the Guerins, the Applebys, and their name-twins with a hectographed Christmas letter. In the salutation to Harold and Marcia they unfailingly put "little" in quotes—*to our Tarbox doppelgängers the "little" Smiths.*

The affair among the Applesmiths began—gossip wrongly assumed that Janet initiated things—with Marcia noticing Frank's hands. In turn the beauty of his hands had emerged from their former pudgy look by way of an ulcer diet brought on by the sharp market slump of April and May of 1962. This slump, which more affected Frank's trusts (he had just been promoted from junior officer) than Harold's brokerage business, and which furthermore caught Frank with thousands of his own in electronics and pharmaceuticals, brought the couples closer than usual that spring and summer. It became their custom, Sunday nights, after tennis, to eat together fried clams or lobster fetched in steaming paper bags from a restaurant in North Mather. One night, as they sat on cushions and chairs around the little-Smiths' tesselated coffee table, Marcia became hypnotized by the shapely force with which Frank's fingers, their tips greasily gleaming, manipulated onion rings. His diet had shorn a layer of fat from them, so the length of the fingers, with something especially sculptured about the knuckles and nail sheaths, was revealed as aristocratic; his thumbs were eloquent in every light. Along the fleecy wrists, through the cordlike tributary veins raised on the backs of his hands, down into the tips, a force flowed that could destroy and shape; pruning roses had given Frank's hands little cuts that suggested the nicks a clammer or sculptor bears, and Marcia lifted her eyes to his face and found there, beneath the schoolboy plumpness, the same nicked, used, unconscious look of having done work, of belonging to an onflowing force whose pressure made his cheeks florid and his eyes bloodshot. He was a man. He had a battered look of having been swept forward past obstacles. After this revelation every motion of his altered Marcia's insides with a slight turning, a purling in the flow within her. She was a woman. She sensed now in him a treasurable dreadfulness; and, when they rose to leave and Janet, eight months pregnant, lost her balance and took Frank's quickly offered hand for support, Marcia, witnessing as if never before the swift sympathetic interaction of the couple, felt outraged: a theft had been brazenly executed before her eyes.

Née Burnham, Marcia was the daughter of a doctor and the granddaughter of a bishop. Her detection of a masculine beauty in Frank Appleby at first took the form of an innocent glad lightness in the company of the other couple and a corresponding dreariness on weekends when they were not scheduled to see them—though she usually managed to call Janet and arrange for at least a drink together, or a sail with their boys in the Applebys' catboat. Her possessive and probing fondness was hardly distinguishable from their old friendship, though at dances or at parties where they danced she did feel herself lifted by a willingness to come into Frank's hands. He had never been a dancer, and Marcia, locked into his bumping shuffle, aware of her toes being stubbed and her cool lotioned hand vanishing in the damp adhesion of his grip and his boozy sighs accumulating on her bare neck like the patch of mist a child will breathe onto a windowpane, sometimes watched enviously her husband and Janet or Carol Constantine waltzing from corner to corner around the shadowy rim of the room whose bright dead center she and Frank statically occupied. Harold was an adroit, even flamboyant, dancer, and sometimes after a long set with Frank she would make him take her and whirl her around the floor to relieve the crick in her neck and the ache, from reaching too high, across her shoulder blades. But there was a solidity in Frank that Harold lacked. Harold had never suffered; he merely dodged. Harold read *Barron's* or Ian Fleming on the commuting train; Frank read Shakespeare.

What Marcia didn't know was that she preceded Shakespeare: for Frank the market slump, the sleepless nights of indigestion, the birth of his second child, and his friend's wife's starry glances and strange meltingness were parts of one experience, an overture to middle age, a prelude to mortality, that he answered, in the manner of his father, an ardent amateur Sinologist, by dipping deep into the past, where peace reigned. *When all aloud the wind doth blow/And coughing drowns the parson's saw/And birds sit brooding in the snow* . . . Those vanished coughs, melted snow, dead birds seemed sealed in amber, in something finer than amber, because movement could occur within it. *I'll have a starling shall be taught to speak/Nothing but "Mortimer," and give it him/To keep his anger still in motion:* in Frank's contemplation of such passion, perfectly preserved, forever safe, his stomach forgot itself. He was not a natural reader, couldn't focus on two lines of Dante or Milton, disliked plays on the stage and novels, and found this soothing quality, of flux confined with all its colors, only in Shakespeare.

"Everything is in him," he told Marcia, flirtatiously, for he talked about Shakespeare with no one, especially not Janet, who took his reading as a rebuke of her, for not finishing college, but marrying him instead, "everything we can hope to have, and it all ends badly."

Marcia asked, "Even the comedies?"

"They end in marriage, and Shakespeare's marriage was unhappy."

"I feel," Marcia said, for she was a tight-wound nervous woman who had to have things clear, "you're trying to tell me *we* would end badly."

"Us? You and me?"

So he hadn't meant at all to tell her his own marriage was unhappy. But she went on, "If we . . . started anything."

"Should we start something? I'll buy that idea. Yes." His large red head seemed to settle heavier on his shoulders as the notion sank in. "What about Harold and Janet? Should we consult them first? Let's not and say we did."

He was so clumsy and ironical, she took offense. "Please forget whatever I said. It's a female fault, to try and sexualize friendship. I want you only as a friend."

"Why? You have Janet as a friend. Please sexualize me. It sounds like a good process. With this sloppy marketing running, it's probably the best investment left." They were leaning in the summer heat against the maroon fender of the Applebys' Mercury, after tennis, beside the Gallaghers' rather fortresslike brick house on the back road to North Mather. Matt had got permission to use a neighbor's court. Harold was inside the house, drinking; Janet was home nursing the baby. It had been a girl, whom they had named Catharine, after an aunt Frank remembered as a heap of dusty velvet, knobbed with blood-red garnets.

Marcia said to him, but after laughing enjoyably, "You're shocking, with your doubled responsibilities."

"Double, double, toil and trouble. Janet's been a bitch for nine months plus. Let's at least have lunch together in Boston. I need a vacation. How are your Tuesdays?"

"Car-pool day."

"Oh. Wednesdays I usually have lunch with Harold at the

Harvard Club. All he does is sniff. Shall I cancel him?"

"No, no. Harold hates any change of routine. Let me see if I can get a sitter for Henrietta for Thursday. Please, Frank. Let's understand each other. This is just to talk."

"Of course. I'll tell you of men whose heads do grow beneath their shoulders."

"Othello?"

"Right."

"Frank, listen. I've become fixated on you, I know it's absurd, and I'm asking for your help. As a friend."

"Pre- or post-sexualization?"

"Please be serious. I've never been more serious. I'm fighting for my life. I know you don't love me and I don't think I love you but I *need* to talk. I need it so much"—and here, half artfully, she lowered her face to hide tears that were, after all, real—"I'm frightened."

"Dear Marcia. Don't be."

They had lunch, and lunch often again, meeting at the corners of new glass buildings or in the doorways of flower shops, a toothy ruddy man with a soft air of having done well at school and a small dark efficient woman looking a little breathless, hunting hand in hand through the marine stenches of the waterfront and the jostling glare of Washington Street for the perfect obscure restaurant, with the corner table, and the fatherly bartender, and the absence of business acquaintances and college friends. They talked, touching toes, quickly brushing hands in admonishment or pity, talked about themselves, about their childhoods spent behind trimmed hedges, about Shakespeare and psychiatry, which Marcia's lovely father had practiced, about Harold and Janet, who, as they obligingly continued to be deceived, were ever more tenderly considered, so that they became almost sacred in their ignorance, wonderful in their fallibility, so richly forgiven for their frigidity, demandingness, obtuseness, and vanity that the liaison between their spouses seemed a conspiracy to praise the absent. There was a cottage north of Boston—and thus extra safe and remote from their real lives—belonging to one of Frank's aunts, who hid the key on a little sill behind one of the fieldstone foundation-pillars. To Frank as a child, groping for this key cached here had seemed a piratical adventure, the pillaging of a deep grotto powerfully smelling of earth and creosote and rodent dung. Now the key seemed pathetically accessible, and he wondered how many others, strangers to the family, had used these same bare mattresses, had borrowed these same rough army blankets from the cedar chest, and had afterwards carefully tipped their cigarette ashes into the cellophane sealer slipped from the pack. In the kitchen there had been a dead mouse in a trap. Dying, it had flipped, and lay belly up, dirty white, like a discarded swab in a doctor's office. Frank and Marcia stole some sherry from the cupboard but had not disturbed the mouse. They were not here. The cottage was used only on weekends. From its security amid pines and pin oaks it overlooked the slender peninsula of Nahant. The seaside smell that leaked through the window sashes was more saline and rank that that of Tarbox Beach, where Janet and the children would be sunning. Marcia had felt to Frank strangely small, more athletic and manageable than Janet, without Janet's troubled tolling resonance but with a pleasing pointed firmness that reminded him, in his passage into her body, of the little mistresses of the French court, of Japanese prostitutes that Harold had once drunkenly described, of slim smooth boys who had been Rosalind and Kate and Ophelia. There was in Marcia a nervous corruptibility he had never tasted before. Her thin shoulders sparkled in his red arms. Her face, relaxed, seemed, like an open lens, to be full of his face. "I love your hands," she said.

"You've said that before."

"I loved being in them. They're huge."

"Only relatively," he said, and regretted it, for he had brought Harold into bed with them.

Knowing this, knowing they could never be alone, she asked, "Did I feel different than Janet?"

"Yes."

"My breasts are so small."

"You have lovely breasts. Like a Greek statue. Venus always has little breasts. Janet's—Janet's are full of milk right now. It's kind of a mess."

"What does it taste like?"

"What? Janet's milk?"

"You don't have to tell me."

"No, why not? Sweet. Too sweet, really."

"You're such a gentle man," Marcia said. "I'm not used to being loved so gently." Thus she conveyed, weakening them as lovers but strengthening them as confidants, the suggestion to Frank that he had been too gentle, that Harold was rougher, more strenuous and satisfying with, no doubt, a bigger prick. As if hailing a dim stubby figure on a misted shore, Frank mournfully confronted the endomorph in himself. His demanding deep-socketed mistress, ectomorphic, lay relaxed at his side; their skins touched stickily along her length. The neural glitter of her intelligent face was stilled; a dangling earring rested diagonally forward from her ear lobe, parallel to the line of her cheekbone; the severe central parting of her black hair had been carried off by a kind of wind. Was she asleep? He groped beside the bed, among his under-clothes, for his wristwatch. He would soon learn, in undressing, to leave it lying discreetly visible. Its silent gold-rimmed face, a tiny banker's face, stated that he had already been out to lunch an hour and forty minutes. A sour burning began to revolve in his stomach.

Their affair went two months undetected. It is not difficult to deceive the first time, for the deceived possesses no antibodies; unvaccinated by suspicion, she overlooks latenesses, accepts absurd excuses, permits the flimsiest patchings to repair great rents in the quotidian. "*Where* have you been?" Janet asked Frank one Saturday.

"At the dump."

"At the dump for two *hours?*"

"Oh, I stopped at the drug store and talked to Buzz Kappiotis about the tax rate and the firemen's four-per-cent increase."

"I thought Buzz was fishing in Maine." Their cleaning lady was a neighbor.

"I don't mean Buzz, I mean Iggy Galanis, I must be losing my mind."

"I'll say. You're so twitchy in bed you give me insomnia."

"It's my blue-eyed baby ulcers."

"I don't see what you're so nervous about lately. The market's happy again, they've reduced the margin rate. And *how* did your clothes get so rumpled?"

He looked down at himself and saw a long black hair from Marcia's head adhering to the fly of his corduroy pants. Glancing there, he felt the little limb behind the cloth as warm and used, softly stinging. Sun had streamed through the dusty windshield glass onto her skin. He pulled the hair off and said, "From handling the trash cans."

But an affair wants to spill, to share its glory with the world. No act is so private it does not seek applause. In public Frank could scarcely contain his proud and protective feeling toward Marcia; the way at the end of an evening he held her coat for her and slipped it around her was as different from the way he would help Georgene Thorne as receiving the Host is from eating an hors d'oeuvre. All the empty pauses and gropings of this simple social action were luxuriously infused with magic: his fingers in adjusting her collar brushed the nape of her neck; her hands pressed her own lapels secure if they were his hands clasped upon her breasts; her eyes rolled Spanishly; and this innocent pantomime of robing was drenched in reminiscence of their nakedness. Their minds and mouths were committed to stability and deception while their bodies were urging eruption, violence, change. At last the little-Smiths, Harold prattling drunkenly, spilled from the lit porch into the night—a parting glance from Marcia, dark as a winter-killed rose—and the door was finally shut. Janet asked Frank, "Are you having an affair with Marcia?"

"Now there's a strange question."

"Never mind the question. What's the answer?"

"Obviously, no."

"You don't sound convincing. Convince me. Please convince me."

He shrugged. "I don't have the time or the stomach for it. She's not my type. She's tiny and jittery and has no tits. Lastly, you're my wife and you're great. Rare Egyptian! Royal wench! The holy priests bless you when you are riggish. Let's go to bed."

"We have to stack the dishwasher first. Anyway, don't think you've sold me. How does she know so much about Shakespeare all of a sudden?"

"I suppose she's been reading him."

"To please you. To get at me somehow."

"How does that get at you?"

"She knows I never read."

"But you find books in running brooks, sermons in stones, and good in everything."

"Ha ha. That busy little bitch, she keeps telling me she has a secret."

"She says this?"

"Her eyes say it. And her bottom. I used to think of her as so stringy and intellectual, but she's been doing a ton of hip-waggling lately."

"Maybe she's having an affair with Freddy Thorne."

"Take that expression off your face."

"What expression?"

"That amused look. Take it off! Take it off, Frank! I hate it!" And suddenly she was at him, after him with her fists, her struggling weight; he squeezed her against him, regretfully conscious that even now, as her pinned fists flailed his shoulders and her face crumpled into contorted weeping and the sharp smell of perfume was scalded from her, that the expression, of serene superiority, of a beautiful secret continually tasted, was still on his face.

Harold little-Smith could not immediately identify the woman who called him at his office one morning. He and Janet rarely talked on the telephone; it was Marcia and Janet, or Marcia and Frank, who arranged the many things—the tennis and sailing, the Friday-night plays and Saturday-night concerts—that the two couples had done together this summer. The woman's voice said, "I've been in town all morning shopping, the damn stores have *nothing,* and I'm hungry and cross and wondered if you'd like to split a lunch with me. *Not* fried clams, thank you." Just in time, he recognized Janet.

"Janet, really? It's a lovely idea, but this is the day I usually have lunch with Frank. Why don't the three of us have lunch together?"

"That's *not* the idea, Harold. Couldn't you call Frank and cancel it? Think of some good excuse. Tell him you have a girl friend. Don't be afraid of Frank, Harold."

"Who said I was?"

"Well, then. Please. I know it seems funny and pushy, but I must talk to you, and this was the only way I could think of. I knew Wednesday is your day with Frank and that you would be free otherwise."

Still Harold hesitated. He enjoyed a certain freedom of speech and thought because his life, from childhood up, had been outwardly orderly and obedient. Life was a kind of marathon you could run as you please as long as you touched all the checkpoints; his weekly lunch with Frank was one of the checkpoints. They discussed stocks and bonds and hardly ever spoke of their domestic life together in Tarbox.

Janet prompted, "You won't have to *pay* for my lunch, just *have* it with me."

This stung him; he considered himself something of a dandy, an old-fashioned elegant. Last spring, in St. Louis, he had given a girl two hundred dollars to spend the night with him. He told Janet the Ritz, upstairs, at one o'clock, and hung up.

It was strange she should have told him not to be afraid of Frank because it was she Harold had always been afraid of. Any vulgarity that could not be paid off and dismissed intimidated him. Meeting the Applebys the first time, he had wondered why Frank had married such a common girl—fine in bed, no doubt, but why marry her? Though she was from a respectable family (her father owned a pharmaceutical manufacturing firm in Buffalo, and her maiden name was on drugstore shelves across the country) Janet was one of the few women of Harold's social acquaintance who could have been, without any change in physical style, a waitress or a girl in a five and ten (in fact she had worked two summers behind a counter, selling men's jewelry, at Flint & Kent) or a dance-hall hostess. She would some day, some day soon, be fat. Already there was a crease at the front of her ankles, and the flesh of her upper arms was loose, and her hips had a girdled hardness. Not that Harold did not find her attractive. He did, and this went with his fright. Her beauty seemed a gift she would abuse, like a boy with a gun, or squander, like a fool with a fortune. She struck him as a bad investor who would buy high and sell after the drop and take everybody she could down with her. So he walked, up Milk, through the thick of Boston's large codger population, along Tremont, through the Common and the Public Garden, in a pinching mood of caution. The sidewalk was so hot it stung through the soles of his thin black Italianate shoes; yet scraps of velour and highlights of satiny white skin skated through his head, and it was somewhat romantic of him not to have taken a cab. Of the four Applesmiths, Harold was sexually the most experienced. He possessed that trivial air, trivial yet assured and complacent, that women feel free to experiment with, and before his marriage he had slept with enough to lose the exact count. After marriage (he had been old: twenty-six) there had been business trips, and call girls, generally doughy and sullen, with whiskeyish breaths and terrible voices; but he had never betrayed Marcia with a social equal.

After her second martini, Janet said, "Harold, it's about Marcia and Frank."

"They seem very amiable lately."

"I should hope so. I *know* they're seeing each other."

"You know? You have evidence? *Évidence?*"

"I don't need evidence, I *know*. There's a tone about them. He's always bringing her up, casually. 'Did Marcia seem irritable to you tonight?' 'What did you think, dear, of Marcia's dress?' What the fuck do I care about Marcia's dress?"

"But you have no evidence? There's been no confession from Frank? He hasn't asked to leave you?"

"Why should he want to leave me? He's happy. He's milking two cows."

"Janet, you don't put things very gracefully."

"I don't *feel* graceful about it. You evidently do. Evidently you're used to your wife sleeping around."

"I am not. The fact is, I don't believe this. I think there is an attraction between Frank and Marcia, yes. It's natural enough, considering how much we see each other. For that matter, there's an attraction between you and me. *Toi et moi*."

"This is the first I've heard of it."

"Oh, come on. You know what you are. You know how you look to men. I'd love to go to bed with you."

"You don't put things that gracefully yourself."

"Of course, we won't. We're married now and we've had our flings, our *escapades romantiques*. We have others beside our-selves to think about."

"Well it's the others I'm trying to talk about, Marcia and Frank. You keep talking about you and me going to bed. They *are* going to bed. What are you going to do about it, Harold?"

"Bring me some evidence, and I'll confront her with it."

"What kind of evidence do you expect? Dirty pictures? A notarized diaphragm?"

Ringlets of vibration, fine as watch springs, oscillated on the surface of his Gibson as he laughed; there was an unexpected poetry in the woman, face to face across a table for two, the cloth and the softness of her stirred forward by a passionate worry. Through the windows the trees of the Public Garden were hushed cascades, the great copper beech a glittering fall of lava. Janet said, "All right. How is Marcia in bed for you lately? Less or more?"

How common, really, this was; it smacked of midwifery, of witchery, of womanish cures and auguries, of stolen hairpins and menstrual napkins. The waiter, a gray man polished and bent by service like a spoon, came and Harold ordered without consulting Janet *potage à la reine, quiche Lorraine,* salad, a light dry Chablis. "You're putting me on a diet," she said.

He told her, "In answer to your question. I think more."

"See? She's aroused. She's full of it. Screwing."

He laughed; his Gibson glass was empty and no watchsprings materialized. "Come off it, Janet. You expected me to say less, didn't you?"

"Has it been less?"

"No, I was honest. She's been quite loving lately. Your thesis is that women are polygamous; the more they have the more they want?"

"I don't know, Harold. I've never been unfaithful to Frank, isn't that funny? But I would think, as a woman—"

As a woman: this plump soft phrase out of her mouth gave him the pleasure he felt when, after a party, drunkenly showering, to hear Marcia feign shock he would fasten her bra to his skinny wet chest.

"—that she would feel guilty toward you, and wants to prove to herself that this isn't taking away from her marriage, that she has enough for both; and that furthermore she wants to tell you about it, this wonderful thing about herself, about the whole business. I know that Frank has out of the blue started doing things that *I* never taught him."

The thin wedge of a headache entered Harold's right temple. He reflexively reached for his empty glass, uncertain if Marcia had changed or not, for of those conversations of tranced bodies there is little distinct to recall, only the companionable slow ascent to moon-blanched plateaus where pantomimes of eating and killing and dying are enacted, both sides taking all parts. He found Marcia kittenish, then tigerish, then curiously abstract and cool and mechanical, and finally, afterwards, very grateful and tender and talkative and sticky.

Janet smiled, tipping a little from her glass into his. "Poor Harold," she said. "He hates indiscreet conversations. It's too female, it threatens him. But you know," she went on, having realized he would be good to experiment with, "I can't talk to other women comfortably. I could only have said these things to a man." She stated this with an air of having produced a touching confession for him, but he found it presumptuous and offensive. He thought women should properly talk with women, and men with men, and that communication between the sexes should be a courtly and dangerous game, with understood rules, mostly financial, and strict time limits. Ninety minutes was usually quite enough, and this lunch lasted longer than that.

They agreed to have lunch again, next week, to compare notes. Harold went home to a house more transparent; its privacy had

been surrendered. While the Applebys lived in town, on a secluded lane on the far side of the Musquenomenee, in an ample
white house of nondescript style whose interior comfort was
essentially borrowed or inherited, the little-Smiths had built their
own, and designed it in every detail, a flat-roofed redwood modern oriented along a little sheltered ridge overlooking the marsh
to the south. The foyer was floored in flagstones; on the right an
open stairway went down to a basement level where the three
children (Jonathan, Julia, Henrietta) slept and the laundry was
done and the cars were parked. Above this, on the main level,
were the kitchen, the dining room, the master bedroom, a polished hall where hung reproductions of etchings by Rembrandt,
Dürer, Piranesi, and Picasso. To the left of the foyer a dramati-
cally long living room opened up, with a shaggy cerulean rug and
two facing white sofas and symmetrical hi-fi speakers and a
Baldwin grand and at the far end an elevated fireplace with a
great copper hood. The house bespoke money in the service of
taste. In the summer evenings he would drive back from the station through the livelong light hovering above the tawny marshes,
flooded or dry according to the tides, and find his little wife, her
black hair freshly combed and parted, waiting on the longer of
the sofas, which was not precisely white but rather a rough
Iranian wool bleached to the pallor of sand mixed with ash. A
record, Glenn Gould or Dino Lupati playing Bach or Schumann,
would be sending forth clear vines of sound from the invisible
root within the hi-fi closet. A pitcher of martinis would have been
mixed and held chilled within the refrigerator toward this precious moment of his daily homecoming; the tinge of green in the
vermouth was intensified by the leafy green, green upon green,
ivy and alder and hemlock and holly, crowding through their
walls of sliding plate glass. Outdoors on the sparkling lawn,
sparkling in the lowering light as the sun slowly approached the
distant radar station—exquisite silver disc, always fidgeting—
Jonathan, in bathing trunks and a candy-striped shirt, would be
playing catch with Julia, or some children of neighboring summer people, tossing a chewed sponge ball, a little pitted moon,
back and forth through the revolving liquid branches of the lawn
sprinkler. Henrietta, as neat and alert in feature as Marcia herself,

in her duckling nightie, bathed, would run toward Harold barefoot through the cerulean rug to be lifted and hugged and
twirled, and Marcia would pour two verdant martinis into glasses
that would suddenly sweat, and the ball would fall short and lie
crescented by sunlight, soaking, while the children noiselessly
argued which would retrieve it and get drenched, and his entire
household, even the stray milk butterfly perched on the copper
fireplace hood, felt about to spring into bliss, like a tightly wound
music box.

He detected small change in Marcia. They had met one summer on Long Island and married the next, and things, more or less,
had turned out as charmingly as had been predicted. They had
both been in their mid-twenties and were considered by their
contemporaries a bit intellectual and cool. They discovered each
other to be sensual, but allowed this coolness to characterize their
marriage. They never quarreled in public, rarely in private; each
expected the other to see clearly into the mechanism of their
union and to make without comment the allowances and adjustments needed. He excused his occasional call girls as hygienic; he
took them as he took, behind the closed bathroom door, without
complaint to Marcia, aspirins to relieve his headaches. He could
believe that Marcia might be unfaithful to him, but as some kind
of service to himself, to save him trouble, to accommodate him
with new subtlety. He had married her after most of her friends
had married. He had removed her from that crass monied Middle
Atlantic society where she had seemed stilted and fragile. He
trusted her to be always his. Smiling, she lifted the martini;
the gin and her earrings trembled. He sipped; the coolness was
delicious.

Without looking it, they were slightly older than most of their
friends in Tarbox; Harold was thirty-eight, Marcia was thirty-six.

She did seem, lately, more inventive and solicitous. A ram-
shackle boardwalk, in need of repair every spring, had come with
their land, with the old summer cottage they had torn down. It
led out to a small tidal creek too narrow for most powerboats;
here, at high tide, between banks tall with reeds, in water warmer
than the sea off the beach, they and their friends and their friends'
children could swim. At night, now, this summer, when the tide

was right, and the children were asleep, Marcia had taken to inviting him, Harold alone, for a swim before bed, without bathing suits. So they would walk down in moonlight through poison ivy and cut-back sumac, treading warily, and out the often-patched boardwalk, its slats of varied wood like the keys of a gigantic piano, and on the splintery soft dock take off their clothes and stand, husband and wife, naked together, gooseflesh rising, for an instant of nerve-gathering before plunging from the expectant summer air into the flat black water alive with reeds. Beside him her flitting breasts, arching arms, upturned face gashed by black licks of her hair bubbled through the blanched foam and slopping clammy slick. The water's million filaments sucked from his nerve ends the flecks of city filth. Our first love, our love of the elements, restored to him his youngest self. Sometimes, at high tide, like a laboring Cyclopean elephant a powerboat would come crowding up the channel with its searchlight and they would squat like aborigines under the dock in the root-riddled mud until the boat passed. And they would dry each other, Harold and Marcia, she toweling even his fumbly dripping genitals, thinking how innocently part of him they seemed, and not a harsh jutting second life parasitic upon him. As she ran ahead up the boardwalk, clutching her clothes to her breasts, her buttocks would be dancy in the steady moon. If in bed they made love, with salty bodies and damp hair, she praised his ardor—"so fierce"—and expertness—"oh, you know me so well"—as if a standard of comparison, someone gentle and clumsy, had appeared. And she would blurt "I love you" with a new emphasis, as if the "you" were darkened by the shadow of an unspoken "nevertheless."

At their next lunch Janet had nothing to offer but complaints about Marcia's constantly calling up and suggesting they do things together, as couples—sail, swim, play tennis, go to meetings. She was even trying to get her interested in the Tarbox Fair Housing Committee, which Irene Saltz and Bernadette Ong were organizing. "I said to her, 'But there isn't a single Negro in town,' and she said, 'That's the point. We're culturally deprived, our children don't know what a Negro looks like,' and I said, 'Don't they watch television?' and then I said, getting really mad, 'It seems to me awfully hard on the Negro, to bring him out here just so your children can look at him. Why don't they instead look at the Ongs on a dark day?' I shouldn't have said that, I think Bernadette's great; but there's something basically snotty about this committee. It's all because other towns have one. Like a drum-and-bugle corps."

Janet seemed old to Harold, though she was years younger than he, old and double-chinned and querulous, vexing herself with what he knew to be Marcia's simple gregariousness, her innocent need to be doing. He changed the subject. "What were you and Piet talking about so earnestly at the Thornes' party?"

Her valentine mouth, its lipstick flaking, frowned. "He was telling me his wife doesn't give him shit. He tells every woman."

"He's never told Marcia."

"She's never told you. Piet's been aching to break out for a long time and I don't know what's holding him back. Georgene's right there waiting."

It was fascinating, seeing his friends through a whole new set of windows. "And Freddy Thorne?" he asked delicately. He had long wondered if Janet had slept with Freddy.

Janet said, "Freddy's my friend. He understands women."

"And that's all you choose to say."

"That's all I have to say. We've never gone to bed, I'm fond of Freddy, he's harmless. Why are you men so mean to him?"

"Because you women are so nice to him."

Amused to discover himself jealous, Harold studied his fingers, which he set parallel to the table silver, and asked, "Do you think the Hanemas will get a divorce?" He liked Angela, one of the few women in town who could speak his language. He loved her upward-searching diffidence, her motherly presiding above their summer-evening gatherings. Everyone rather loved Angela.

"Never," Janet said flatly. "Piet's too tame. He's too thick in the conscience. He'll stick it out with those three, picking up whatever spare ass he can. The bad thing about a cockteaser like Angela is she turns her man loose on the world and lets a lot of other women in for trouble. Piet can be very winning."

"You speak as one who knows. *Elle qui sait.*"

"There've been overtures, nothing drastic. Among his other problems, he's shy."

"Poor Piet," Harold said, uncertain why, though Janet nodded in agreement.

That weekend, he asked Marcia, after a party, when both were drunk, "Do you love me?"

"I love you, Harold, but please not tonight. We're both too drunk and sleepy. Let's have a nap instead sometime tomorrow." Tomorrow was Sunday.

"I didn't mean to make love, I meant, honestly, *après douze années très heureuses*, aren't you pretty bored with me? Don't you ever think of what it would be like with other men?"

"Oh, maybe a little. Not very consciously." She was wearing a chiffon nightie the color of persimmon, and as she crawled into bed her dark limbs looked monkeyish. Getting into bed demanded nimbleness of her because the bed was high; also it was high and hard, because they found such a mattress best for lovemaking. The little-Smiths' bedroom, as they had designed it, was a shrine, a severe sacred space; its furniture consisted of little more than two teak bureaus, a reading lamp built into the headboard, a mirror on a closet door, a philodendron, and for a rug the hide of a zebra that Harold's grandfather had shot on safari with Teddy Roosevelt. When she was settled in, he turned off the light. The darkness was purple, and high in the window the marsh moon amid moving clouds seemed to swing back and forth like the bob of a pendulum.

"Tell me,' he said. "You won't hurt my feelings."

"OK. Ask me the men."

"Have you ever wanted to go to bed with Piet Hanema?"

"Not really. He reminds me too much of a fatherly elf. He's too paternal and sympathetic. Once at the Guerins we were left alone in the room with the bigger fireplace and he began to stroke my back and it felt as if he wanted to burp me. I think Piet likes bigger women. Georgene and Bea and I are too small for him."

"Freddy Thorne."

"Never, never. He's so slippery and womanish, I think sex is all talk with him anyway. Janet responds to him better than I do; ask her."

"You know I can't talk to Janet. Her vocabulary puts me off."

"It's getting worse lately, isn't it?"

"And Frank?"

Patterns of light—long lozenges of moonlight laid across the zebra rug and a corner of the bed; a rod of electric light coming from the hallway through the crack their door was left ajar, to comfort the children; a dim bluish smear on the ceiling from a carbon streetlight on the beach road, entering by the foyer transom—welled from the purple darkness as Harold held his breath, waiting for Marcia's answer.

It came very casually, in a voice half asleep. "Oh, Frank's been a friend too long to think about that way. Besides, he has whiskey breath and an ulcer. No, thanks." When, still studying their placid guests of light, he made no reply, she stirred and asked, "Why? Do you want Janet?"

He laughed quite loudly and said, "*Mon Dieu*, no! That girl's pure trouble."

"She's very hostile to me lately."

"I think," Harold said, snaking his arm around her and snuggling his genitals into the curved warmth of her backside, "we should make an effort to see less of the Applebys. Let's have the Guerins over sometime. Maybe with some new people like the Constantines. The wife seems pretty hip."

Marcia made no response, and he nudged her, and she said, "The Guerins are so depressing."

Janet was gayer at their next lunch, and looked five years younger. The day was one of those very hot days toward the end of August when to a woman summer seems a lover leaving, to be embraced with full abandon: appearances are past mattering; love disdains nothing. Sweat mars her makeup and mats her hairdo. Her arms swim freely in air. The steaming city streets crammed with secretaries have the voluptuousness of a seraglio. Janet wore an armless cotton dress printed with upside-down herons on a turquoise ground and swung herself along as if nothing in the natural world, no thrust of sun or thunderclap, could do her harm. Her feet, naked in sandals, were dusty, and Harold wondered, walking along Federal Street beside her in the heat, what it would be like to suck each dirty one of her ten toes clean. He took off his coat and swung it over his shoulder like a tough; they ate in a cafeteria whose glass doors were open at either end like sluice gates. Noise poured through him, backfiring trucks and the clatter of cutlery and the shouting of orders and the words of the girl across from him, with her sweating round face and eroded lipstick. She said, "How was *your* weekend?"

"Fine. You should know. We saw you every minute of it, except when somebody had to go to the bathroom."

"I know, isn't it boring? Frank and Marcia mooning at each other and exchanging ever so teeny-tiny little tender glances."

"You *do* exaggerate that."

"Balls, Harold. Frank absolutely gets choleric when he can't have Marcia as his tennis partner. And when they're across the net from each other, all those cute little pat shots, I could puke. He's always 'swinging by.' 'I'll swing by the Smith's to pick up Frankie.' 'I just swung by Smitty's to drop off the variorum Shakespeare, and they had me in for a drink.' It turns out 'they' was Marcia and you were off at a town Republican meeting. Harold, *why* are you a conservative?—it's such a pose."

He endured this tirade pleasurably, as if it were a massage or a shower. "But you still have nothing definite."

"How definite must definite be? Harold, he knows too much. He knew you were going to Symphony with the Gallaghers Saturday night. He knew Julia sprained her shoulder diving off the dock Thursday. When I talk to Marcia and tell him what she said he doesn't bother to listen because he's heard it all already. He knows you and she go skinny-dipping down by your dock and then fuck."

"Doesn't everybody know that? The dock part of it. The other doesn't invariably follow."

"How would everybody know? You think your friends have nothing better to do than splosh around the marshes with binoculars?"

"Marcia might tell Bea, or Georgene, or even Irene, in passing."

"Well she doesn't tell me and I'm her best friend supposedly. Frank tells me. Frank."

"I asked her the other night if she was having an affair with Frank."

Janet bit into her pastrami-on-a-roll and stared above the bun. "And she said?"

"I forget exactly what she said. We were both sleepy. She said he was too old a friend and had an ulcer."

"Two good reasons for it. Every woman has a nurse complex. And why not sleep with a friend? It's better than sleeping with an enemy. I've never understood why people are so shocked when somebody sleeps with his best friend's wife. Obviously, his best friend's wife is the one he sees most *of*."

"Well, she convinced me." He tried to state his heart's case. "We're not that unhappy, for her to do me dirt."

"Very well. She's as pure as Snow White and the stains in Frank's underpants are accidents of nature. Let's forget them. Let's talk about us. Why don't you like me, Harold? I like you. I like the way your nose comes to two points, like a very pale strawberry. Why don't you take the afternoon off and walk me through the Common over to Newbury Street and look at pictures? You understand pictures. What's this new gimmick of making things look like comic strips?"

She put her hand palm up on the tabletop; it was moist, a creased pink saucer of moisture on the silver-flecked formica. When he put his hand in hers, the gesture, amid the clatter and breeze of the cafeteria, felt hugely inflated: two immense white hands, like the mock-up of a beefburger, advertising love. With the other hand she was mopping up bits of pastrami with the final bite of the roll. "That's a delectable idea," he said, "but I can't. We're taking off Friday for Maine over Labor Day, so I have only one day left at the office. I need this afternoon. It's called Pop Art. It's also called hard-edge."

"So you'll be gone all weekend?" She withdrew her hand to wipe her fingertips, one by one, on a paper napkin. Her face seemed forlorn; her eye shadow had run, making her look theatrically tired.

Harold said, "Yes, and we're staying a few days past the holiday, so I'll miss next week's lunch with you. *Je regrette*."

"Do you?" In parting she told him, this blowzy stacked woman in upside-down herons, with a wave of her shapely swimmer's arm, "Have a *good* time with Marcia," the emphasis insolent. Then they went out of opposite ends of the cafeteria, she toward her maroon car in the Underground Garage, he toward his office on Post Office Square, glad to be released.

The family place in Maine overlooked a mottled blue harbor choked with glinting sails, swinging buoys, and surprising rocks that all jutted from the water at the same angle, testifying to a geological upheaval aeons ago. The largest rocks supported grass and shrubs and were therefore islands. The water was icy-cold and the beaches, far from the endless dunes of Tarbox, were niggardly arcs of shingle and brownish grit strewn with rack. Yet Harold, who visited Tarbox Beach only once or twice a summer, here swam before every breakfast. He was always happy in Maine. He ate the lobster and potato salad his mother set before him and read brittle paperback mysteries and old explorer's accounts in splotched bindings and sailed through the slapping spray and needled his sisters and brothers-in-law and slept soundly, having made love to Marcia like a sailor in from months at sea. She seemed his whore. She crouched and whimpered above him, her nipples teasing his lips. She went down on him purring; she was a minx. This was new, this quality of prostitution, of her frankly servicing him, and taking her own pleasure as a subdivision of his. Her slick firm body was shameless yet did not reveal, as her more virginal intercourse once had done, the inner petals drenched in helpless nectar. She remained slightly tight and dry. He did not wonder from whence this change in her chemistry had been derived, since he found it an improvement: less tact was demanded of him, and less self-control. Perhaps he abused her, for in the second half of their vacation, abruptly beginning on Labor Day night, she refused him. Afterwards she told Frank that suddenly she couldn't stand the confident touch of Harold's all-too-knowing hands. "He seemed a lewd little stranger who acted as if he had bought me." To have him inside her was distasteful: "like food in my mouth I couldn't swallow." Perhaps, in Maine, Marcia had experimented with corruption too successfully. Carrying within her like a contraceptive loop her knowledge of her lover, she had inflicted a stark sensuality upon her husband and then been dismayed by his eager submission to it. She realized she could serve several men in one bed, many men in one night—that this possibility was part of her nature; and she fled into an exclusive love for Frank. Making love to Harold suddenly lost seriousness. What they did with each other's bodies became as trivial as defecation, and it was not until months later, when his form was charged with the tense threat of his leaving her, that the curse of squeamishness was removed from their physical relations.

The little-Smiths returned to Tarbox Thursday night. Harold was conscious of having broken the string of appointments with Janet and doubted, without conscious regret, that there would be any more. Her theory had been wrong and may have never been more than a pretext. Growing up with three sisters had left him with little reverence for female minds. He had seen his sisters turn from comfortably shouting slugging animals into deceptive creatures condemned to assure their survival without overt aggression; their sensibilities were necessarily morbid. Janet was at best a poor reasoner and at worst a paranoid. About to go fat and lose her looks, stuck with a bilious and boring husband, she had turned desperately to a man in no way desperate. Brokers reaped in fair and foul weather, and Marcia had demonstrated a new versatility and violence in her love of him.

He did expect Janet to call him at his office Friday and, when no call came, was annoyed at the extent to which he permitted himself to listen for it. All day, as he rooted through the earth-bound stack of waiting mail and obsolete stock fluctuations, a signal from outer space kept tickling his inner ear. He remembered her strange way of wearing cloth, so that it came loose from her body and fluttered in the mind's eye. Perhaps they would see them this weekend. He hoped she wouldn't attempt a scene. Her indignation was so—fluffy. His secretary asked him why he was smiling.

Saturday morning, Marcia drove up to the center of Tarbox to talk to Irene Saltz about the Fair Housing group; Marcia had agreed to be on the education committee, whose chief accom-

plishment so far had been to give the high-school library a sub-
scription to *Ebony*. "It might take hours, you know how she
talks. Can you feed yourself and the children if I don't make it
back by noon? There's some pastrami in the freezer you can heat
up. The directions are on the package. The important thing is to
boil it with the cellophane *on*."

They had been up drinking with the Thornes and the Hanemas
the night before, and Harold was content to putter about gingerly, tucking away the props of high summer, folding the collapsed and torn plastic wading pool, coiling hose and detaching
the sprinkler. Jonathan rummaged the football from a closet and
he and Harold tossed it back and forth until a playmate, pudgy
Frankie Appleby, arrived, with his mother. Janet was wearing
snug blue denim slacks, an orange-striped boating jersey, and an
unbuttoned peach-colored cashmere sweater, hung on her shoulders like a cape. "Where's Marcia?" she asked, when the boys
were out of earshot on the lawn.

"In town conferring with Irene. Where's Frank?"

"He told me he was getting a haircut. But he didn't want to
take Franklin because he might go to the drugstore and have to
talk politics." She snorted, a sardonic equine noise, and stamped
her foot. She was caught beneath a bell of radiance; the mistless
sharp light of September was spread around them for miles, to the
rim of the marshes, to the bungalow-crowded peninsula of East
Mather and the ghostly radar dish, cocked toward the north.
Janet was hollow-eyed and pale and ripe with nervous agitation, a
soft-skinned ripeness careless of itself.

Harold said, "You think he's lying."

"Of course he's lying. Must we stand out here? The sun hurts."

"I thought you were a sun lover. *Une amoureuse du soleil*."

"Not today. I'm sick at what I have to do."

"To whom?"

"To youm."

Harold opened for her the door that entered from the lawn the
lower level of the house, where the children slept and the laundry
was done. The laundry room smelled of cement and soap and, this
morning, sourly, of unwashed clothes heaped around the dryer.

The gardening and carpentry tools and shelves of paint and grass seed and lime were ranged along the other wall, which reeked of gasoline from the power mower. Amid these fragrances Janet took a stance and said, "While you were away in Maine my car broke down, the transmission, so I had to go shopping in Frank's Corvair. I like the Lacetown IGA and on the way back that officious old Lacetown cop, the one with the gold teeth, stopped me for gliding through the stop sign, you know, just this side of the lace-making museum. What made me so mad, I was almost in Tarbox, where they never arrest you. Anyway, in looking through the glove compartment for the registration, underneath all the maps, I found this." She brought from her purse a piece of smudged white paper folded quarto. Harold recognized the indigo rim of Marcia's stationery. The notepaper had been given her as a wedding present, embossed with a monogram of her new initials, by a Southampton aunt, boxes of it; Marcia had laughed, thinking it hideously pretentious, the essence of everything she had married Harold to escape, and used it so seldom, once the thank-you notes were written, that after twelve years it was not used up. Indeed, he wondered if Janet had not somehow stolen a piece, it was so unlike Marcia to write on it. He reached and Janet held the folded paper back from him. "Are you sure you want to read it?"

"Of course."

"It's awfully conclusive."

"Damn you, give it to me."

She yielded it, saying, "You'll hate it."

The handwriting was Marcia's.

Dear Frank, whom I want to call dearest but can't—

Back from the beach, a quick note, for you to have while I'm in Maine. I drove home from our view of Nahant and took the children to the beach and as I lay there the sun baked a smell of you out of my skin and I thought, That's him. I smelled my palms and there you were again and I closed my eyes and pressed myself up against the sun while Irene and Bernadette chattered on and on and the children called from the ocean—there was ex-

traordinary surf today. I feel today left you sad. I'm sorry the
phone rang—like icy water being poured over us—and that I
teased you to stay longer. I do tease. Forgive me, and believe that
I cherish our times together however unsatisfactorily abbreviated,
and that you must take me as you can, without worry or self-
blame. Love satisfies not only technically. Think of me in Maine,
wishing you beside me and happy even in this wish, my "wan-
ton's bird."

> *In love and haste,*
> *M.*

The signature was hers, the angular "M" of three strokes emphatically overstruck; but the body of the letter was written with
a flowing smoothness not quite familiar, as if she had been drunk
or tranced—it had been years since he had examined her handwriting. He lifted his eyes from the paper, and Janet's face held
all the dismay he was still waiting to feel.

"Well," he said, "I've often wondered what women think about
while they're sunbathing."

"Oh Harold," she cried, "if you could see your *face*," and she
was upon him, had rushed into his unprepared embrace so swiftly
he had to pull Marcia's letter free from being crumpled between
them. The blue-bordered note fluttered to the cement floor. His
senses were forced open, admitting the scouring odors of cement
and *Tide;* along the far wall the sunburned lawn flooded the window with golden stitchwork, like a Wyeth. Janet's chest and hips,
pillows sodden with grief, pressed him against the enameled edge
of the dryer; he was trapped at the confluence of cold tears and hot
breath. He kissed her gaping mouth, the rutted powder of her
cheeks, the shying trembling bulges of her shut eyes. Her body his
height, they dragged each other down, into a heap of unwashed
clothes, fluffy ends of shirtsleeves and pajama pants, the hard floor
underneath them like a dank bone. Sobbing, she pulled up her
sweater and orange-striped jersey and, in a moment of angry
straining, uncoupled her bra, so her blue-white breasts came tumbling of their own loose weight, too big to hold, tumbled like
laundry from the uplifted basket of herself, nipples buttons, veins
seaweed green. He went under. Her cold nails contemplated the

tensed sides of his sucking mouth, and sometimes a finger curiously searched out his tongue. Harold opened his eyes to see that the great window giving on the lawn was solidly golden; no child's watching shadow cleft it; voices glinted from a safe distance, the dock. His face was half-pillowed in dirty clothes smelling mildly of his family, of Jonathan and Julia and Henrietta and Marcia. He was lying on ghosts that had innocently sweated. Janet's touch fumbled at his fly and he found the insect teeth of the zipper snug along her side. *Tszzzc:* he tugged and the small neat startled sound awoke them.

"No," she said. "We can't. Not here."

"One more kiss," he begged.

There was a wetness to her mouth, as her breasts overflowed his hands, whose horizon his tongue wished to swim to. She lifted away. "This is crazy." She kneeled on the cement and harnessed her bosom in cups of black lace that reminded him of the doilies in his grandmother's home in Tarrytown. It had been her side of the family that had known Teddy Roosevelt, who had taken Grandpa hunting. "The kids might barge in any second," Janet said, pulling down her jersey. "Marcia might come back."

"Not if she and Frank are copulating out by the dump."

"You think they'd do it to*day?*"

"Why not?" Harold said. "Big reunion, she's back from Maine with the horned monster. *Avec le coucou.* They've set us up for them to be gone for hours. Haircuts. Fair housing."

She adjusted her peach sweater so it again hung like a cape. Standing, she brushed the smudges on the knees of her slacks, from having kneeled. He remained sprawled on the laundry, and she studied him as if he were an acquisition that looks different in the home from in the store. She asked, "You really never suspected her until just now?"

"No. I didn't think she had the guts. When I married her she was a tight little mouse. My little girl is all growed up."

"You're not shocked?"

"I am desolate. But let's talk about you."

She adjusted her clothes with thoughtful firmness. "That was an instinctive thing. Don't count on me for anything."

"But I *do.* I adore you. *Ta poitrine, elle est magnifique.*"

As if the compliment had adhered, she removed a piece of lint from her jersey. "They're pretty saggy now. You should have known me when I was nineteen."

"They're grand. *Please* come upstairs with me." He felt it was correct, in asking her, to stand; and thus their moment of love was reduced to a flattened heap of laundry. Having surrendered all evidence, he was at her mercy.

Janet said, "It's impossible. The children." Lamely her hands sketched multiple considerations.

"Can't we ever get together?"

"What about Marcia and Frank?"

"What about them? Are they hurting us? Can we give them, honestly, what they give each other?"

"Harold, I'm not that cool. I have a very jealous moralistic nature. I want them to be punished."

"We'll all be punished no matter how it goes. That's a rule of life, people are punished. They're punished for being good, they're punished for being bad. A man in our office, been taking vitamin pills all his life, dropped dead in the elevator two weeks ago. He was surrounded by healthy drunks. People are even punished for doing nothing. Nuns get cancer of the uterus because they don't screw. What are you doing to me? I thought you were offering me something."

"I was, I did, but—"

"I accept."

"I felt sorry for you, I don't know what it was. Harold, it's too corrupt. What do we do? Tell them and make a schedule of swap nights?"

"You *do* de-romanticize. Why tell them anything? Let's get something to tell first. Let's see each other and see how it goes. Aren't you curious? You've *made* me want you, you know; it was you who chased me through all those hot Boston streets in your sexy summer dresses. Janet, don't you want me at all for myself? Am I only a way of getting back at Frank?" He glided the back of his hand down the slope of her left breast, then of the right. From the change in the set of her face he saw that this was the way. Touch her, keep touching her. Her breasts are saggy and want to be touched. Don't give her time to doubt, she hates what she knows and doesn't want the time. Don't pause.

She spoke slowly, testing the roof of her mouth with the tip of her tongue and fingering each button on the way down his shirt. "Frank," she told him, "is going to New York the first part of next week."

"*Quelle coïncidence!* Also next week Marcia was talking about going to Symphony Tuesday night and doing Junior League good deeds Wednesday morning and maybe spending the night in town. I think she should be encouraged to, don't you? Poor saint, that long hour in and out."

Janet gazed over his shoulder; her mouth, whose long out-turned upper lip was such a piquant mismatch with her brief plump lower, tightened sadly. "Has it really come to that? They spend whole nights together?"

"Don't bridle," he said, telling himself, *Don't pause.* "It's a luxury, to fall asleep beside the beloved. *Un luxe.* Don't begrudge them." He continued stroking.

"You know," Janet said, "I *like* Marcia. She's always cheerful, always has something to say; she's often got me out of the dumps. What I think I must mind is not Frank so much—we haven't been that great in bed for years, poor guy, let him run—as that *she* would do this to me."

"Did you hear what I said about Tuesday night?"

"I heard."

"Which of us should get the babysitter?"

So that fall Harold and Janet slept together without Frank and Marcia's knowing. Harold at first found his mistress to be slow; his climax, unmanageably urged by the visual wealth of her, was always premature. Not until their sixth time together, an hour stolen in the Applebys' guest room, beneath a shelf of Chinese-temple paraphernalia and scrolls inherited from Frank's father, did Janet come, pulling in her momentous turning Harold virtually loose from his roots, so that he laughed at the end in relief at having survived, having felt himself to be, for a perilous instant, nothing but a single thunderous heartbeat lost in her. He loved looking at her, her nude unity of so many shades of cream and pink and lilac, the soles of her feet yellow and her veins seaweed-green and her belly alabaster. He found an unexpected modesty and elusiveness in her, which nourished his affection, for he enjoyed the role of teacher, of connoisseur. It pleased him to sit beside her and study her body until, weary of cringing, she accepted his gaze serenely as an artist's model. He was instructing her, he felt, in her beauty, which she had grown to disparage, though her bluntness and forwardness had clearly once assumed it, her beauty of fifteen years ago, when she had been the age of his St. Louis mulatto. Harold believed that beauty was what happened between people, was in a sense the trace of what had happened, so he in truth found her, though minutely creased and puckered and sagging, more beautiful than the unused girl whose ruins she thought of herself as inhabiting. Such generosity of perception returned upon himself; as he lay with Janet, lost in praise, Harold felt as if a glowing tumor of eternal life were consuming the cells of his mortality.

The autumn of 1962, the two couples were ecstatically, scandalously close. Frank and Marcia were delighted to be thrown together so often without seeking it. Janet and Harold in private joked about the now transparent stratagems of the other two lovers. These jokes began to leak out into their four-sided conversations. To the Sunday-night ritual of fetched-in food had been added weekday parties, drinks prolonged into scrambled dinners, arranged on the pretext of driving the children (Frankie Jr. and Jonathan detested each other; Catharine was too much of a baby to respond to Julia's and Henrietta's clumsy mothering) back and forth to each other's houses. While the women cooked and fussed and preened around them, Frank and Harold with bottomless boozy searchingness would discuss Shakespeare, history, music, the bitchy market, monopolies, the tacit merger of business and government, the ubiquity of the federal government, Kennedy's fumblings with Cuba and steel, the similarity of JFK's background to their own, the differences, their pasts, their fathers, their resentment and eventual appreciation and final love of their fathers, their dislike and dread of their mothers, sex, their view of the world as a place where foolish work must be done to support fleeting pleasures. "Ripeness is all," Frank would sometimes say when silence would at last unfold its wings above the four spinning heads intoxicated by an intensity of friendship not known since childhood.

Or Janet would say, knowing they expected something outrageous from her, "I don't see what's so very wrong about incest. Why does everybody have a tabu about it? I often wanted to sleep with my brother and I'm sure he wouldn't have minded with me. We used to take baths together and I'd watch him get a hard on. He did something on my belly I thought was urination. Now he runs my father's antibiotic labs in Buffalo, and we can't."

"Sweetheart," Harold said to her, leaning forward above the round leather coffee table in the Applebys' lantern-hung living room, "that's the reason. That's why it's so tabu. Because everybody wants to do it. Except me. I had three sisters, and two of them would have stood there criticizing. *Trois sœurs est trop beaucoup.*"

Marcia sat up sharply, sensing a cause, and said, "I was just reading that the Ptolemies, you know, those pharaoh types, married brothers and sisters right and left and there were no pinheads produced. So I think all this fear of inbreeding is Puritanism." Her earrings scintillated.

"Cats do it," Frank said. "Sibling cats are always fucking."

"But are fucking cats," Janet asked, "always sibling?"

"I once talked," Harold said, determined to quarrel with Marcia, "to a banker who did a lot of financing for the Amish around Lancaster P-A, and he told me they're tiny. *Trés, trés petits.* They get smaller every generation. There's inbreeding for you, Marcia. They're no bigger than you are."

"She's a nice size," Frank said.

Marcia said to Janet, "I agree with *you*. I have a dreamy younger brother, he played the oboe and was a pacifist, and it would be *so* nice to be married to him and not have to explain all the time why you are the way you are, somebody who knew all the family jokes and would be sensitive to your *phases*. Not like these two clods."

"Vice versa," Harold persisted, "do you know why Americans

are getting bigger at such a phenomenal rate? Nutrition doesn't explain it. Exogamy. People marry outside the village. They fly clear across the continent, to Denver, to St. Louis, to marry."

Marcia asked, "Why on earth St. Louis? Denver I can see."

Harold continued, flushing at his slip (neither of the women knew of the mulatto, but Frank did), "The genes are fresh. It's cross-fertilization. So the advice 'Love thy neighbor' is terrible advice, biologically. Like so much of that Man's advice."

"He said love, He didn't say lay your neighbor," Janet said.

"I want my dreamy brother," Marcia said, pouring herself some more bourbon and twitteringly pretending to cry.

"Ripeness is all," Frank said, after a silence.

Or else they would sit around the rectangular tesselated coffee table in the little-Smiths' living room with its concealed rheostated lighting and watch Harold, bare-handed, gesticulating, conduct sides of Wagner's *Tristan*, or Mozart's *Magic Flute*, or Britten's *War Requiem*. Frank Appleby liked only baroque music and would sit stupefied, his eyeballs reddening and his aching belly protruding, while Harold, whirling like a Japanese traffic cop, plucked the *ting* of a triangle from the rear of the orchestra or with giant motions of embrace signaled in heaving oceans of strings. Janet hypnotically watched Harold do this and Marcia watched Janet curiously. What could she be seeing in this manic performance? How could a woman who nightly shared Frank's bed be even faintly amused by Harold's pathetic wish-fulfillment? One night, when the Applebys had gone, she asked Harold, "Are you sleeping with Janet?"

"Why? Are you sleeping with Frank?"

"Of course not."

"In that case, I'm not sleeping with Janet."

She tried a new tack. "Aren't you awfully tired of the Applebys? What ever happened to our other friends?"

"The big-Smiths moved to Newton."

"They were never our friends. I mean the Thornes and the Guerins and the Saltzes and the Gallaghers and the Hanemas. You know what Georgene told me the other day? She said Matt has had a nibble on the Robinson place, that Angela had wanted. A couple from Cambridge."

"How does Georgene come by all her information? She's become a real expert on the Hanemas. *Un spécialiste vrai*."

"Don't you think Freddy and Angela are fond of each other?"

"*Tu es comique*," Harold said. "Angela will be the last lady in town to fall. Next to yourself, of course."

"You think Georgene has Piet?"

"Well. She has a very indulgent smile on her face when she looks at him."

"You mean like Janet has when she looks at you?"

"*Tu es trop comique*. She's twice my size."

"Oh, you have big—"

"Parts?"

"Ideas of yourself, I was going to say."

The other couples began to call them the Applesmiths. Angela Hanema, who never dreamed, dreamed she went to the Applebys' house carrying a cake. On the front porch, with its six-sided stained-glass welcoming light, she realized she couldn't get in the front door because the house was full of wedding invitations. Marcia little-Smith came around the side of the house, in shorts and swinging a red croquet mallet, and said, "It's all right, my dear, we're going to be very happy." Then they were all, a crowd of them, walking along a country path, in some ways the path down to the dock, Angela still carrying the cake on upraised palms before her, and she said to Frank Appleby, "But can you get the insurance policies straightened out?" which was strange, because in waking life Angela never gave a thought to insurance. With a gargantuan wink he assured her, "I'm floating a bond issue," and that was all she could remember, except that both sides of the path were heavily banked with violets, hyacinth, and little blue lilies. She had coffee with Georgene the next morning after nursery school, and, feeling uneasy with Georgene lately, in nervousness told her the dream. Georgene told Bea and Irene, while Piet, who had heard the dream at breakfast, was telling Matt Gallagher at the office. So Bernadette Ong heard the dream from two directions, from Irene at a Fair Housing executive meeting and from Terry Gallagher after a rehearsal of the Tarbox–North Mather–Lacetown Choral Society; the thirsty singers commonly went back to the Ongs afterwards for a beer.

But it was Bea, Bea whose malice was inseparable from her flirtatiousness, in turn inseparable from her sterility and her tipsiness, Bea who told Marcia. Marcia was puzzled and not amused. She did not for a moment believe that Janet and Harold were sleeping together. She did not think Harold was up to it; a certain awe of Janet, as of all big women, had been heightened by falling in love with this woman's husband. She had not suspected that from outside the couples might appear equal in complicity. She was shocked, frightened. She told Harold; he laughed. They told the Applebys together, and it was Janet who laughed, Frank who showed annoyance. "Why can't people mind their own dirty business?"

"Instead of our dirty business?" Harold said gaily, the double tip of his nose lifted, Marcia thought, like a bee's behind.

"Our language!" she said, nettled.

"Come on, *mon petit chou*," he said to her, "Angela can't help what she dreams. She's the most sublimated woman we know. Bea can't help it that she had to tease you with it. Her husband beats her, she can't have children, she has to make her mark somehow."

Janet was in a lazy mood. "She must ask to be beaten," she said. "She picked Roger so he must have been what she wanted."

"But that's true of all of us," Harold said. "*Tout le monde.* We get what we unconsciously want."

Marcia protested, "But they must think we do *every*thing, which seems to me so sick of *them,* that they can't imagine simple friendship."

"It *is* hard to imagine," Harold said, wondering if to smile would be too much. They were all on the verge. He looked at Janet, sleepily leaning with a cigarette in the Applebys' yellow wing chair, her silk blouse veined by its shimmer and her skirt negligently exposing her stocking-tops and fasteners and bland known flesh, and thought how easy, how right, it would be to take her upstairs now, while these other two cleared away the glasses and went to their own bed.

Frank said, "They're starved. Their marriages have gone stale and anything that tickles their nose they think is champagne. We enjoy relaxing with each other and musn't let them make us self-conscious about it." He cleared his throat to quote. "The mutable, rank-scented many."

This speech conjured a malicious night all about them. Marcia's eyes, watching Frank, were dark, dark like stars too dense to let light escape, and she felt her being as a pit formed to receive this blood-slow soft-handed man whose own speech, more and more as she was his mistress, was acquiring Shakespearian color and dignity. *Tickles their nose is champagne.* He had called them back from the verge. The little-Smiths left at one-thirty and drove through the town whose burning lights, bared in November, seemed to be gossiping about them. From their bedroom window the marsh, rutted and tufted along the ebbed canals, appeared a surface of the moon and the onlooking moon an earth entire in space. Restless, apologetic, they made love, while miles away across the leafless town the other couple, also naked, mirrored them.

Full confession waited until winter. Snow fell early in New Hampshire, and during Christmas vacation the Hanemas, the Applebys, the Thornes, the Gallaghers, and the little-Smiths went north to ski with their older children. The lodge bulletin board was tacked thick with pictures of itself in summer, of canoes and couples pitching quoits and porch rails draped with wet bathing suits. Now packed snow squeaked on the porch steps, a sign forbade ski boots in the dining hall, the dinner was pea soup and baked ham and deep-dish apple pie, the children afterwards thumped and raced in the long hall upstairs, between the girls' bunk room and the boys', and downstairs their parents basked by the fireplace in the afterglow of exercise. Whiskey hurried to replace the calories fresh air had burned from their bodies. Georgene methodically turned the pages of *Ski*. Freddy murmured on the sofa to Janet, who looked discontented. Frank played Concentration with his son and Jonathan little-Smith, and was losing, because he was concentrating upon a rotating inner discomfort, perhaps the ham, which had had a thick raisin sauce. Gaily rattling ice cubes, Harold was mixing a drink for Angela, whose fine complexion had acquired on the bitter slopes an unearthly glow, had reached an altitude beyond decay; she looked more twenty-two than thirty-four. Marcia was listening to Matt Gallagher explain the Vatican's likely verdict, now that the ecumenical council was adjourned, on artificial birth control: "Nix. They won't give us sex, but they may give us meat on Fridays." Marcia nodded understandingly—having a lover deepened her understanding of everything, even of Matt Gallagher's adherence to the letter of an unloving church—and glanced toward Terry. Terry, sitting cross-legged on the floor in black stretch pants, carefully picked through a chord sequence on her lute; it was a gourd-shaped, sumptuous instrument, whose eight strings produced a threadbare distant tone. Matt had bought it for her for Christmas, in line with the policy of conspicuous consumption that had led to the Mercedes, and perhaps with a more symbolic intent, for its blond lustre and inlaid elegance seemed sacramental, like their marriage. Piet lay beside her on the rug gazing at the taut cloth of her crotch. The seam had lost one stitch. Conscious of Georgene sulking at his back, he rolled over and did a bicycling exercise in air, wondering if with Catholics it was different, remembering his long-ago love for Terry, unconsummated, when he and Matt were newly partners. Whitney and Martha Thorne, Ruth Hanema, Tommy Gallagher with his Gainsborough fragility, and Julia Smith in raven pigtails watched a World War II movie starring Brian Donlevy. The channel, from Manchester, was weakly received. The game of Concentration broke up. Frank needed more bourbon to soothe his stomach. In twos and threes the children were led upstairs or out to the gas-heated cottages beneath the bone-white birches. A bridge game among strangers beside the fireplace broke up. Georgene Thorne, a tidy woman with feather-cut graying hair and a boyish Donatello profile, nodded while leafing through *House & Garden* and followed her children out to their cabin to sleep. Freddy blew her a smirking kiss. Walking down the squeaking path alone, she thought angrily of Piet—his flirting, his acrobatics—yet knew it was in the bargain, she had got what she wanted. Her breath was white in the black air. The unseen lake gave a groan and crack, freezing harder. The black birch twigs rattled. Harold and Marcia tried to organize word games—

Botticelli, Ghosts—but everyone was too suffused with physical sensations to play. The television set, unwatched, excited itself with eleven-o'clock news about UN military action in the Katanga province of the Congo; and was switched off. Piet begged Terry Gallagher to give them a concert, and so she, watching as if from beyond her own will her white bewitched fingers assume each position on the frets, played the one melody she had mastered, "Greensleeves." They tried to sing with her but had forgotten the words. Her head was tilted; her long black hair fell straight from one side. She finished; Matt, with a military swiftness, stood; and the Gallaghers went outdoors to their cabin. In the momentary opening of the door, all heard a snowplow scraping along the upper road. High in a dusty corner a cuckoo clock, late, sounded eleven. Angela, stately, her fair cheeks flaming, now stood, and Piet, muscled like a loose-skinned dog that loves to be scratched, followed her upstairs to their room. This left the Applesmiths and Freddy Thorne.

The elderly young couple that ran the lodge came in from doing a mountain of dinner dishes and thriftily turned off all the lights but one and separated the fireplace logs so that the fire would die. Their smiles of good will as they faced their guests were wretchedly enfeebled by contempt. "Good night now."

"Good night."

"Night."

"*Bon soir.*"

Yet for an hour more, in semidarkness and the growing cold, Freddy held forth, unable to let go of a beauty he had felt, of a goodness the couples created simply by assembling. "You're all such beautiful women. Marcia, why do you laugh? Jesus Christ, every time I try to tell people something nice to their face they laugh. People hate love. It threatens them. It's like tooth decay, it smells and it hurts. I'm the only man alive it doesn't threaten, I wade right in with pick and mirror. I love you, all of you, men, women, neurotic children, crippled dogs, mangy cats, cockroaches. People are the only thing people have left since God packed up. By people I mean sex. Fucking. Hip, hip, hooray. Frank, do you believe in the difference between tragedy and comedy? Tell me, for fuck's sweet sake. This is a serious question."

Frank said carefully, rumbling from the slumped position that seemed to ease his stomach, "I believe in it as a formal distinction Shakespeare believed in. I wouldn't make anything absolute of it."

"Frankfurt, that is beautiful. That's just where any medium intelligent man of the world would come down. That's where you and I differ. Because I do. I believe there are tragic things and comic things. The trouble is, damn near everything, from the yellow stars on in to the yummy little saprophytes subdividing inside your mouth, are tragic. Now look at that fire our penny-pinching hosts broke up to save a nickel. Tragic. Listen to the wind. Very tragic. OK, so what's not tragic? In the western world there are only two comical things: the Christian church and naked women. We don't have Lenin so that's it. Everything else tells us we're dead. Think about it; think about those two boobies bounding up and down. Makes you want to laugh, doesn't it? Smile at least? Think of poor Marilyn Moronrow; her only good pictures were comedies, for Chrissake."

"And the Christian church?" Marcia asked, glancing sideways at Frank as if nervously to gauge his pain.

"Christ, I'd love to believe it," Freddy said. "Any of it. Just the littlest bit of it. Just one lousy barrel of water turned into wine. Just half a barrel. A quart. I'll even settle for a pint."

"Go ahead," Janet told him, lazily. "Believe it."

"I *can't*. Marcia, stop checking on Frank. He's hyperalgesic, he'll live. Come on, this is a real gut talk. This is what people are for. The great game of truth. Take you and that fuzzy big-throated purply sweater; you're terrific. You look like a tinted poodle, all nerves and toenails, a *champeen,* for Chrissake. If your grandfather hadn't been the Bishop of East Egg you'd have made a terrific whore. Janet, you're a funny case. Sometimes you have it, right up the alley, all ten pins, and other times you just miss. Something pruney happens around your mouth. Tonight, you're really on. You're sore as hell about some silly thing, maybe Harold's snubbing you, maybe you have the red flag out, but you're right there. You're not always right there. Where would you rather be? Jesus, you're in every drugstore, and people tell me it's a hell of a good laxative, though I've never needed one myself, frankly."

"We've diversified," Janet told him. "We do a lot with antibiotics now. Anyway it wasn't a laxative, it was mineral oil."

"More power to it. You've lost some weight, that's a shrewd move. For a while there you had something bunchy happening under your chin. You know, honey, you're a fantastic piece—I say this as a disinterested party, girl to girl—and you don't have to wear all those flashy clothes to prove anything. Just you, fat or skinny, Janet Applesauce, that's all we want for dessert; we *love* you, stop worrying. As I say, you're all gorgeous women. It killed me tonight, it really tumified me, seeing old Terry Tightcunt sitting there with her legs spread and her hair down jerking off that poor melon. Have you ever noticed her mouth? It's enormous. Her tongue is as big as a bed. Every time I work on her molars I want to curl up in there and go to sleep."

"Freddy, you're drunk," Marcia said.

"Let him alone, I like it," Harold said. "*Je l'aime.* Freddy's aria."

"Oh God," Frank said, "that men should put an enemy in their mouths to steal away their brains."

Janet said, "Freddy, enough of us. Tell us about Angela and Georgene."

"Beautiful girls. Beautiful. I'm not kidding. You all knock Angela—"

"We *don't*," Marcia protested.

"You all knock that saint, but she has absolutely the most eloquent ass I've ever seen except on an ostrich."

"Giraffes have beautiful behinds," Harold said.

"Out of your class, I would think," Frank told him.

Harold turned, nose upturned, and said, "You hippopotamus. You ox."

Janet said, "Boys."

Freddy went on, "And *didn't* she look lovely tonight? Angela."

Harold, who had a nasal bass voice of which he was proud, imitated the singing of an aria: "And didn't she, di-hi-hidn't she, look lovely, luh-hu-hovilee tonight. A-aaaaangela, lala!"

Freddy appealed to the two women. "Tell me straight. You're

women. You have nice clear Lesbian eyes. Didn't she look about twenty, a virginal twenty, those eyes full of sky, that fantastic skin all rosy, Jesus. I mean, you're both beauties, I'm telling you straight, but she's my ideal. I idolize her. I look at that ass and I think Heaven. Twenty miles of bluebirds and strawberry whip."

The two couples laughed in astonishment. Freddy blinked for orientation; the whiskey in his glass had magically replenished itself. Marcia said, "Freddy, and Georgene? You haven't mentioned your wife."

"A healthy child," Freddy said. "She cooks well, she plays tennis well. In bed"—he squinted estimatingly and wiggle-waggled his hand—"so-so. *Comme ci comme ça.* I like it to be long, to take forever, have a little wine, have some more wine, fool around, try it on backwards, you know, let it be a *human* thing. She comes too quick. She comes so she can get on with the housework. I gave her the *Kama Sutra* for Christmas and she wouldn't even look at the pictures. The bitch won't blow unless she's really looped. What did the Bard say? To fuck is human; to be blown, divine."

Freddy, as usual, had gone beyond all bounds of order; the Smiths and Applebys made restless motions of escape. Janet stood and tossed the contents of her ashtray into the smoldering fireplace. Frank collected the cards scattered by Concentration. Harold rested his ankles on the sofa arm and elaborately feigned sleep. Only Marcia, twiddling one of her earrings, retained an appearance of interest.

Freddy was staring at the far high corner of the lodge, where above the cuckoo clock hung a dusty mass of cobwebs with the spectral air of an inverted reflection in water. He said, "I've seen the light. You know why we're all put here on earth?"

From the depths of his spurious sleep, Harold asked, "Why?"

"It just came to me. A vision. We're all put here to *humanize* each other."

"Freddy, you're so stupid," Marcia said, "but you *do* care, don't you? That *is* your charm. You care."

"We're a subversive cell," Freddy went on. "Like in the catacombs. Only they were trying to break out of hedonism. We're trying to break back into it. It's not easy."

Janet giggled and put her hand across Frank's lips before they could pronounce, as they were going to, "Ripeness is all."

Then fatigue and defeat were among them unannounced. The room was cold. Silence stood sentry. Freddy rose sluggishly, said, "See you on the slopes," and took himself outdoors to his cabin. The black lake beyond the chalky birches seemed an open mouth waiting for attention. The liquorish sweat of his chest froze into a carapace; his bare scalp contracted. He hastened along the squeaking path to Georgene, her forgiveness a dismissal.

Still the two couples were slow to go upstairs. Freddy's sad lewdness had stirred them. Marcia and Janet rotated, picking up glasses and aligning magazines, and sat down again. Frank cleared his throat; his eyes burned red. Harold crossed and recrossed his legs, dartlike in stretch pants, and said, as if on Frank's behalf, "Freddy is very sick. *Très malade.*" Behind the fire screen the embers of the parted logs formed a constellation that seemed to be receding. The silence grew adhesive, impossible. Marcia pushed herself up from the sofa, and Janet, moving in her peach sweater and white slacks like a dancer intently gliding out of the wings toward her initial spring and pirouette, followed her to the stairs, and up. Both couples had rooms upstairs in the lodge. Frank and Harold listened below to the gush and shudder of activated plumbing, and switched off the remaining light. Again Frank cleared his throat, but said nothing.

In the upstairs hall, with its row of sleeping doors, Harold felt his arm touched. He had been expecting it. Frank whispered, mortified and hoarse, "Do you think we have the right rooms?"

Harold quickly said, "We're in nine, you're in eleven."

"I mean, do you think you and I should switch?"

From the elevation of his superior knowledge, Harold was tempted to pity this clumsy man groveling in lust. Daintily he considered, and proposed: "Shouldn't the ladies be consulted? I doubt if they'll concur."

A single bulb burned in the hallway and by this all-night light Frank's forward-thrust head looked loaded to bursting as he tried not to blurt. He wetly whispered, "It'll be all right. Janet's often said she's attracted to you. Take her. My blessing. What the hell. Let copulation thrive."

Harold feigned arch bemusement. "And Marcia? Does she want you?"

The other man nodded miserably, hastily. "It'll be all right."

The doors each of Rooms 9 and 11 were open a crack.

Harold remembered Janet's naked arms swinging moist along the gritty mica-starred streets of summer Boston, and could not resist tormenting his rival a moment longer. "Uh—do you and Janet work this"—he rotated his hands so the fingers and thumb reversed positions in air—"often?"

"Never. Never before. Come on, yes or no. Don't make a production of it. I'm sleepy and my stomach hurts."

In Frank's inflection there was a rising note of the bigger man whom Harold feared. There was also this, that from his desk at the bank Frank had thrown Harold, as broker, a wealth of commissions. The deposit of secrets Harold held in his head felt tenuous, no longer negotiable. Frank's big horned head was down. The two doors waited ajar. Behind one lay Marcia, with whom stretched side by side he shared every weary night; behind the other, Janet, whose body was a casket of perfume. He saw that the deceit he had worked with her would now lose all value. But there is always a time to sell; the trick of the market is to know when. Janet waited like a stack of certain profit. He carefully shrugged. "Why not? *Pourquoi non?* I'd love to. But be gentle." This last was strange to add, but here in the fragile wallboard and linoleum hall he had felt, as Frank's lifted head released a blast of muggy breath, the man's rank heaviness. Harold feared that his nervous lithe wife could not support such a burden; then remembered that she had sought it many times. The sight of Frank—his donkeyish outcurved teeth, his eyeballs packed with red fuses— became an affront; Harold turned to the door of Room 9, and touched it, and it swung open as if the darkness were expectant.

The latch clicked. A light from beyond the snow-heaped porch roof broke along the walls confusedly. Janet sat up in bed and her words, monosyllabic, seemed matches struck in a perilous inner space. "You. Why? Why now? Harold, it's wrong!"

He groped to the bed and sat on the edge and discovered she was wearing a sweater over her nightgown. "It was your husband's idea. I merely gave in. They'll think this is our first time."

"But now they'll *know*. They'll watch us. Don't you *see?* You should have acted shocked and said you wouldn't dream of any such thing. Frank knows when he's drunk, he wouldn't have minded. I'm sure it's what he expected. Oh God, Harold." She huddled tight against him sexlessly. His arms encircled her rounded back, sweatered like an invalid's.

"But I wanted you, Janet."

"But you can have me anytime."

"No, not anytime. When else could I be with you all night?"

"But how can you enjoy it, with those two a door away?"

"They're not hurting me. I like them both. Let them have what happiness they can."

"I can't stand it. I'm not as cool as you are, Harold. I'm going right in there and break it up."

"No."

"Don't take that bossy tone. Don't try to be my father. I'm all agitated."

"Just lie in my arms. We don't have to make love. Just lie in my arms and go to sleep."

"Don't you feel it? It's so *wrong*. Now we're really corrupt. All of us."

He lay down beside her, on top of the covers. The snow at the window had brightened. "Do you think it matters," he asked, "on the moon?"

"Somehow," Janet said, "it's *her*. She'll have this on me now."

"Marcia? No more than you have on her."

"But she completed college and I didn't."

He laughed in surprise. "I see. She completed college, therefore she knows more about erotic technique than you, therefore she's getting more out of Frank than you could get out of me. Right now she's doing the Fish Bite, followed by the astraddle position as recommended by the Bryn Mawr hygiene department."

Janet put her arms back beneath the covers and sniffed. "That's not it at all. But it seems to be what *you* think."

He supposed that, in his irritation at her lack of ardor, he had hopelessly offended her. All lost, he sighed through his nose.

After a pause she asked him, in the diffident voice of a salesgirl faced with an indecisive customer, "Why don't you get under the covers?"

So he did then travel through a palace of cloth and sliding stairways toward the casket of perfume that she spilled upon him from a dozen angles, all radiant. The radiator by the washstand purred in its seven parallel throats. She was, Janet, opaque, pale, powdery, heavy, sweet, cuffing, motherly; she roughly bid him rest with his narrow face between her breasts, his tongue outthrust like a paralyzed lizard's.

While for Frank, a space away, Marcia was transparent, gliding, elusive, one with the shadows of the room; he enlarged, enlarged until she vanished quite and the darkness was solid with himself, then receded, admitting her silvery breathless voice saying lightly, "How lovely. Oh. Fuck. How lovely. Fuck. Fuck."

Between the couples, in Room 10, Piet and Angela Hanema slept back to back, oblivious, Piet dreaming of mortised tenons unpleasantly confused with the interlocking leap and slide and dipped shoulder of a ski lesson he had had that afternoon, Angela dreaming of nothing, skippingly, of children without names, of snow falling in a mountainous place where she knew she had never been, of a great lion-legged table supporting an empty but perfect blue vase of *mei ping* form—dreams when she awoke she would not remember.

Harold would not forget the cool grandeur of Janet that night, or the crescent of light on her fat shoulders above him, or the graciousness of her submission to the long work of his second climax. Fatigue, and the distracting question posed by their open privacy, made him uncharacteristically slow. She lay beneath him with the passiveness of the slaughtered, her throat elongated, her shoulders in shadow.

"I'm sorry," he said. "I'm taking forever."

"It's all right. I like it."

"Shall I stop?"

"Oh no. No."

The mournful tranquillity of her voice so moved him he attained the edge, fell from suspense, and released her from bondage. She turned and slept. As if he and she were on a seesaw, her dead weight lifted him into insomnia. The snow beyond the window was insistently brilliant, a piece of overexposed film. The pillow supporting her tangled hair seemed a second snow. Each time Harold closed his eyes he saw again the mountainside, the stunted ice-burdened pines at the top beside the lift shed, the troughs of ice, the slewing powder, the moguls packed by many turnings; and felt tense effort twitch his legs. His shins ached. Music, translucent sheets of it as in Debussy, was trying to break through to him, in the gaps between her breaths. He turned and fitted his body to hers. With a child's voice she sighed, "Oh no, lover, not again."

Dozing, he woke toward dawn. A footstep snapped in the hall. Marcia. His forsaken wife, abused and near madness, was seeking him. Janet's unfamiliar corpulence curled unconscious beside him, making him sweat. Like a spy unsticking an envelope, he removed himself carefully from her bed. The fabric of the night itself was showing fragility, crumbling into the brown particles of distinct visual detail—dashes of dirt embedded in the floorcracks, his own narrow feet chafed across the instep by his ski boots, Janet's silk glove liners drying on the radiator like tiny octupi, a jar of hand lotion on her bare pine bureau cupping moonglow. Of the clothes he had entered this room in, he took time to put only his pants and sweater back on. The hall creaked again, nearer this door. He lightly pulled it open, his face a mask of tenderness.

There was Frank, coming from the lavatory, bug-eyed and mottled beneath the all-night bulb. At the sight of Harold his eyes underwent a painful metamorphosis, becoming evasive and yet defiant and yet ashamed and defenseless in sickness.

Harold whispered, "What's up?"

"Stomach. Too much booze."

"*Et ma femme? Dorme-elle?*"

"Like a rock. How about Jan-Jan?"

"*La même.*"

Frank pondered, revolving his condition through his mind. "It's like a ball of tar in there I can't break up. I finally threw up. It feels better. Maybe I'm nervous."

"Do you want to go back to your own room?"

"I suppose we should. The kids will soon be up and might come in."

"Good night, sweet prince. May flights of angels, et cetera."

"Thanks. See you on the slopes."

"*Oui*. See you on the slopes." Harold tried to think of the French for "slopes," couldn't, and laughed as if an irony had been belatedly uncloaked.

Janet had been stirred awake by Harold's leaving and the whispering in the hall and knew it was Frank returning to her bed, though she feigned sleep. Perhaps in this moment began her irritated certainty of being wronged. Janet was a woman in whom early beauty had bred high expectations. Their disappointment brought with it a soured idealism, an idealism capable only of finding the world faulty. She decided that with Harold's acquiescence in the end of deception she had been betrayed. Marcia had entered adultery freely whereas Janet had thrown herself upon Harold to assuage their despair. A cynical ménage cheated her of such justification. Each liaison with Harold had been an installment of vengeance; a pattern of justice was being traced in the dark. But her affair had proved to be not a revenge but a convenience, and Janet's idealism asked of life more than a rectangular administration of reassurance and sex. Deeper than her moral reservations lurked the suspicion that Marcia was more sensual than she, better in bed. Janet did not see why she should submit to two inadequate and annoying men so that Marcia could respectably be a nymphomaniac. The woman, whom Janet had always considered dry and dowdy, was really diabolical, and it irked Janet to know that, in the likely event of a scandal, she would get all the sympathy, and Janet all the blame.

The inadequacy and annoyingness of the men emerged as soon as Janet made resistance. They were sitting, the weekend after their swap, in the Applebys' living room, with its round leather coffee table and its shelves of inherited uniform sets: red Balzac, ochre Scott, D'Annunzio in gold-stamped white calfskin, Mann in the black Knopf editions, green Shaw by Dodd, Mead. This wall of books, never touched, absorbed their smoke and conversation. Snow, the first storm to visit Tarbox that winter, was sealing them in. Frank had made a hot rum punch and they were drunk. He said at midnight, "Let's go upstairs."

"No," Janet said.

"I don't mean with *me*," Frank explained. "You can have *him*."

"I find both of you distinctly resistible."

"Janet!" Harold said, not so surprised, since she had slept with him Wednesday and afterwards told him her feelings.

"I think it's too corrupt," she said. "Don't you, Marcia?"

Marcia pinched her left earring, as if it had chimed. "Not if we all respect each other."

"I'm sorry," Janet said. "I can't respect any of you. I especially can't respect a woman who has to have so many men."

"Only two," Frank protested.

"I'm sorry, Marcia. I honestly think you should put yourself in the hands of a doctor."

"That'll make *three* men," Harold said. He was inwardly betting that Janet's resistance was a kind of mist that seemed solid from a distance but proved negotiable as you moved into it: like golf in the fog.

"You're suggesting I should be *fixed?*" Marcia asked.

"I don't mean a physical doctor, I mean a therapist. An analyst. Frank has told me everything about your affair and I think the way you went after him was scarcely normal. I'm not speaking as the injured wife, I'd say the same if it was any man. In fact it probably could have *been* any man."

"Darling Janet," Marcia said, "I love your concern. But I didn't go after Frank. We came together because you were making him miserable. You were giving him an ulcer."

"His stomach has gotten ten times worse in these last months."

"So, I imagine, have you. From Harold's description of your strip-tease in the laundry room I'm amazed to discover you're so fastidious."

Janet turned to Harold. "You told her?"

He shrugged and touched his left earlobe. "She told *me* everything. I didn't want her to feel guilty."

Janet began to cry, stonily, without any concessive motions of her arms or hands.

Marcia lit a cigarette and stared at the other woman dry-eyed.

"Don't you worry," she said. "I wouldn't take Frank if you begged me. Tonight or any night. I want you to have him until you've ground him down to nothing. I've been keeping him afloat for half a year and frankly I'm tired to death of it. The *last* thing I expect is thanks from *you*."

Janet said nothing and both men pleaded for her.

"It was the bear market gave me the ulcer," Frank said, "not anything Jan-Jan did."

"She's *nice* in bed," Harold told his wife. "*Belle en lit.*"

Marcia told Frank, "Fuck her, then. Take her upstairs and fuck her and don't come creeping to me with your third-rate Shakespeare bits. I'm sick to tears of these big dumb women that don't do a damn thing except let the world lick their lovely derrières. Divorce me," she said to Harold. "Divorce me and marry her if she has such hot tits. Let me not to the blah blah blah admit impediments, isn't that it, Frank? This is the end. You, me, the whole rotten works." She stood, gauging the dismay in the faces suddenly beneath her.

"Marcia," Harold said. "Stop bullying Janet with your foul language."

"She's not bullying me," Janet said. "I agree with her."

"I'll heat up the punch," Frank said. "Or would anybody like a beer?"

"Frank, you're a prince," Harold said. "But if we're not going to bed I really could use the sleep. We have one of the Mills girls babysitting and she's having midyears at B.U."

Frank said, "That Exeter friend of mine who's buying the Robinson place teaches at B.U."

"I hear he's handsome," Janet said.

Marcia, feeling her scene slide away from her, said, "I can't stand any of you and I hate this dreary house." She went to the front hall for her coat, which was mousy and old. Harold followed, knowing that she had brought a diaphragm in her purse and wondering if now she would use it at home. But the little Smiths had waited too long to leave and both the Applebys, first Frank and then Janet too, had to wade through the snow and push Harold's Porsche to get it started down the driveway. The taillights slithered back and forth insolently in escaping and Janet said, "I hope that's the last we ever see of them. They're little and, I know they can't help it, they're poisonous. Isn't it a lovely night, Frank? I don't think I've noticed the weather once since we got involved with those people." In the spaces between the trees, dimly lit by their distant porchlight, flakes were hurrying to touch them, lightly, lightly, dying as they did. But in the hot front hall, as she bent over to tug off her galoshes, Frank patted her and she straightened, fierce, and said to him, "Don't you *dare* touch me. It's her you want. You go to her. Just go. *Go.*"

Janet wished powerfully not to be frigid. All her informal education, from Disney's *Snow White* to last week's *Life,* had taught her to place the highest value on love. Nothing but a kiss undid the wicked apple. We move from birth to death amid a crowd of others and the name of the parade is love. However unideal it was, she dreaded being left behind. Hence she could not stop flirting, could not stop reaching out, though something distrustful within her, a bitterness like a residue from her father's medicinal factory, had to be circumvented by each motion of her heart. Liquor aided the maneuver.

For some weeks the Applebys and little-Smiths stayed apart. Marcia and Janet each let it known there had been a fight. The other couples tactfully did not invite them to parties together. When Harold phoned Janet she said, "I'm sorry, Harold, I loved being with you, person to person, man and woman, you really know how to make a woman feel it. But I think doing it with couples is terribly messy, and I'll have to hang up the next time you call. Think of the children if of nobody else." When Frank called Marcia, she said, "I do want to be with you, Frank, just *with* you, anywhere. I want it worse than any man can imagine. But I'm not, simply *not,* going to give Janet any more ammunition. If I felt you loved me that would be one thing; but I realized that night in the lodge when you left my bed how committed you still are to her, and I must think now about protecting myself. She'd destroy me if she could. I don't mean to be melodramatic; that's her style, not mine. I'm not saying good-bye to you. When you and she get yourselves straightened out, I'd *adore*

to see you again. You're the love of my life, unfortunately."
Frank could not escape the impression that she was asking him to
get a divorce. Meanwhile, our advisory capacity in Vietnam was
beginning to stink and the market was frightened, frightened yet
excited by the chance of expanding war. Basically business was
uneasy with Kennedy; there was something unconvincing about
him.

One January Saturday all the Tarbox couples went into Boston
for dinner at the Athens Olympia and to see a hockey game:
Bruins vs. Red Wings. Both the little-Smiths and Applebys declined to go, under the mistaken impression that the other couple
was going. This left them alone in Tarbox together, and it naturally followed that since Jonathan and Frank Jr. had Saturday ski
lessons together at the hill in East Mather, under the radar station,
the fathers arrange for Frank Sr. to bring them both back at
four-thirty; and that, once at the little-Smiths, he accept the offer
of a drink, and then another, and then at six, egged on by the
giggling little-Smiths, he call Janet at home with the suggestion
that she get a sitter and pick up some pizza and come on down.
For much of what they took to be morality proved to be merely
consciousness of the other couples watching them.

Janet called back in ten minutes saying she couldn't find a
sitter; the hockey expedition had taken them all. Harold got on
the phone and told her to bring Catharine with her and they
would put her to sleep on the cot in Henrietta's room.

Holding the bulky baby in one arm and a steaming paper bag in
the other, Janet arrived at seven-thirty. She wore a knee-length
mink coat, a coat she had owned since early marriage but that,
pretentious and even comical in Tarbox, usually hung idle in a
mothproofed bag. Beneath the coat, she was wonderfully dressed:
in a poppy-orange silk blouse and blue jeans shrunk and
splotch-bleached like a teen-ager's and white calf-length boots she
pulled off to reveal bare feet. Seeing her pose thus clothed in his
long living room (on the shaggy cerulean rug her toes were rosy
from the cold, the insteps and sides of her feet lilac white, her
heels and the joints of her toes dusted with pollen), Harold felt
his entire frame relax and sweeten. Even Marcia was moved, to

think her husband had once possessed such a splendid mistress. Frank stepped toward her solicitously, as if toward an invalid, or a genie that might disappear.

From seven to eight they drank. Between eight and nine they put the children to bed. Franklin Jr., secretly afraid he would wet the sheets, refused to sleep in the same bed with scornful Jonathan. They gave him instead the cot in Henrietta's room. This left Catharine Appleby, her cheeks as red as permeated wineskins, to go into the great high square sacred marital bed, on top of a rubber sheet. Janet lay down and crooned to the baby while Marcia put the cooled-off pizzas in the oven. Harold read Frankie Junior a Little Golden Book entitled *Minerals*, while Frank watched Jonathan contemptuously settle himself under the covers with a Junior Detective Novel entitled *The Unwanted Visitor*. From nine to ten the grown-ups ate, from ten to eleven they talked, from eleven to midnight they danced. Harold put an old Ella record on their hi-fi and to the tunes of "These Foolish Things" and "You're the Top" and "I've Been Around the World" the pair of couples rotated, Harold and Janet sliding smoothly around the edges, Frank and Marcia holding to the center of the derugged floor. The sliding glass doors giving on the view of the marsh doubled their images, so that a symmetrical party seemed in progress, the two linked couples approaching and withdrawing from two others like blots on a folded paper, or like visitors to a violet aquarium who, seeing no fish, move closer to the glass and discover the watery shadows of women and men.

Marcia, almost motionless, watched Harold's hand confidently cup Janet's derrière as he waltzed her from corner to corner; Janet, whirling, glimpsed Marcia bending closer into Frank's static embrace as he rumbled at her ear. His face was glossy, suffused with drink. The hand of his not on her back was tucked in between her chin and his chest and Janet knew, while Harold's thighs slithered on her thighs, that a single finger of Frank's was hypnotically stroking the base of Marcia's throat, down to the tops of her breasts. It was a trick he had, one of the few. She whirled, and the hand of Frank's not at her throat was unzipping the back of Marcia's dowdy black dress. Then from another angle

Janet saw held between Marcia's lips like a cigarette the slitted drag of cruelty that came to her face, Janet had noticed, whenever she was very tired or very much at ease. To Marcia, Janet's eyes staring from across the room seemed immense, so dilated they contained the room in their circle of vision as a metal lawn ball contains, distorted and compressed, an entire neighborhood. Frank's delicate hand uncoupled her bra snaps; his single finger slipped further down her breasts. Her body slightly dissolved. She felt herself grow. "I've flown around the world in a plane," Ella, purple spirit, sang, "I've settled rev-o-lutions in Spain." Janet, dizzy from being whirled, felt tipped back by an insistent pressure, knoblike and zippered, amid a lizardly slithering, and thought it sad that Harold should appear a fool before these cruel two other people when she, alone with him, in an ideal seclusion, could have forgiven so well his conceited probing and insinuations of skin. As her image of herself expanded, milk and pollen and poppies, up to the parallel redwood boards of the ceiling inset with small round flush lights rheostated dim, it seemed to Janet that mothering had always been her specialty.

So it was she, when the music stopped, who said, "I'm sleepy and dizzy. Who's going to take me to bed?" Frank in the center of the room made no move, and Harold stayed at her side.

To make space for themselves the two couples had to rearrange the children. Catharine Appleby, her heavy flushed head lolling, was moved into bed with dainty six-year-old Julia Smith; and the door to Jonathan's room (he had fallen asleep with the light on and *The Unwanted Visitor* face down on the blanket) was closed, so no noise from the master bedroom would wake him. The two white sofas were pushed together to make a second bed. It seemed very strange to Janet, as strange as a visit to Sikkim or high Peru, to journey forth, between three and four that morning, toward their own home; to bundle their two oblivious children in borrowed blankets and carry them across the little-Smith's stone-hard lawn to their two dark cars; to hiss farewells and exchange last caresses through clothes that upon resumption felt like fake and stiff and makeshift costumes; to drive behind Frank's steady taillights through a threadbare landscape patched with pieces of dry half-melted snow; to enter a deserted house carrying children like thieves with sacks of booty; to fall asleep beside an unfamiliar gross man who was also her husband; to feel the semen of another man still moist between her thighs; to awaken and find it morning and the strangeness banished with no traces save a congested evasive something in Frank's grateful eyes and a painful jarring, perhaps inaccurate overlay printing, in the colors of the Sunday comics section.

This pattern, of quarrel and reunion, of revulsion and surrender, was repeated three or four times that winter, while airplanes collided in Turkey, and coups transpired in Iraq and Togo, and earthquakes in Libya, and a stampede in the Canary Islands, and in Ecuador a chapel collapsed, killing a hundred twenty girls and nuns. Janet had taken to reading the newspaper, as if this smudgy peek into other lives might show her the way out of her own. Why was she not content? The other three were, and there was little in her religious background—feebly Presbyterian; her father, though a generous pledger, had been rather too rich to go to church, like a man who would have embarrassed his servants by appearing at their party—to account for her inconvenient sense of evil. She suspected that Marcia and Harold and Frank, having completed college, knew secrets, and used her. She felt her flesh prized by them. She was their sullen treasure. Once, serving them scrambled eggs in her home after midnight, wearing a bathrobe over a nightie (she had gone to bed with a headache and a temper and had come back downstairs again after an hour of listening to their three-cornered laughter), Janet had leaned over the kitchen table with the frying pan and Frank had stroked her from one side and Harold from the other and Marcia, watching, had smiled. She had become their pet, their topic. They could not understand her claustrophobia and indignation, and discussed her "problem" with her as if it might lie anywhere but with them, the three of them.

"Did you ever see," Harold asked, as they sat around the round grease-stained leather table, "your parents making love?"

"Never. The nearest thing to it, some Sunday mornings the door to their bedroom would be locked."

"Dear Janet," Marcia said. "Poor dear Janet. Tiptoeing in her Sunday-school dress down that long silent hall and pushing, pushing at that locked door."

"Shit," Janet said. "I never pushed at anything. Speak for yourself."

"Dear me," Marcia said. "I suppose that should hurt."

"Bad girl, Janet," Harold said. "You pushed me into the laundry."

"Because you looked so *mis*erable." Janet tried not to cry, which she knew would encourage them.

"Let Jan-Jan alone," Frank said. "She's a lovely broad and the mother of my heirs."

"There's Frank," Marcia said to her husband, "giving himself heirs again." Their intimacy had forced upon each a rôle, and Marcia had taken it upon herself to be dry and witty, when in fact, Janet knew, she was earnest and conscientious, with humorless keen emotions. Janet looked at her and saw a nervous child innocently malicious.

"You don't have to defend Janet to me," Harold told Frank. "I love her."

"You desire her," Marcia corrected. "You've cathected in her direction."

Harold continued, shinily drunk, his twin-tipped nose glinting, "She is the loveliest goddam p—"

"Piece," Marcia completed, and scrabbled in her bent pack of Newports for a cigarette.

"*Pièce de non-résistance* I've ever had," Harold finished. He added, "Out of wedlock."

"The horn, the horn, the lusty horn," Frank said, "is not a thing to laugh to scorn," and Janet saw that the conversation was depressing him also.

Harold went on with Janet, "Were your first experiences with boys under bushes interesting or disagreeable? *Intéressant ou désagréable?*"

"Buffalo boys didn't take me under bushes," Janet said. "I was too fat and rich."

Marcia said, "*We* were never really *rich*. Just respectable. I thought of my father as a holy man."

"Saint Couch," Harold said, and then repronounced it, *"San' Coosh!"*

"I thought of mine," Janet said, growing interested, beginning to hope they could teach her something, "as a kind of pushover. I thought my mother pushed him around. She had been very beautiful and never bothered to watch her weight and even after she got quite large still thought of herself as beautiful. She called me her ugly duckling. She used to say to me, 'I can't understand you. Your father's such a handsome man.' "

"You should tell it to a psychiatrist," Marcia said, unintended sympathy lighting up her face.

"No need, with us here," Harold said. *"Pas de besoin, avec nous ici.* Clearly she was never allowed to work through homosexual mother-love into normal heterosexuality. Our first love-object is the mother's breast. Our first gifts to the beloved are turds, a baby's turds. Her father manufactures laxatives. Oh Janet, it's so obvious why you won't sleep with us."

"She sleeps with me," Frank said.

"Don't brag," Marcia said, and her plain warm caring, beneath the dryness, improved Frank's value in Janet's eyes. She saw him, across the small round raft crowded with empty glasses and decanters, as a fellow survivor, scorched by the sun and crazed by drinking salt water.

"Why must you ruin everything?" he suddenly called to her. "Can't you understand, we all love you?"

"I don't like messy games," Janet said.

"As a child," Harold asked, "did they let you play in the buffalo mud or did you have an anal nanny?"

"Anal nanny," Marcia said. "It sounds like a musical comedy."

"What's the harm?" Frank asked Janet, and his boozy dishevelment, his blood-red eyes and ponderous head rather frightened her, though she had lulled him to sleep, her Minotaur, for ten years' worth of nights. He shouted to all of them, "Let's do it! Let's do it all in the same room! Tup my white ewe, I want to see her whinny!"

Harold sighed daintily through his nose. "See," he told Janet. "You've driven your husband mad with your frigidity. I'm getting a headache."

"Let's humanize each other," Frank pleaded.

Marcia turned on him, possessive of his mind. "Frank, don't quote Freddy Thorne. I'd think you'd have more intellectual self-respect."

Yet it was Freddy Thorne who sensed the trouble, and who tried to turn it to his own advantage. "I hear there's a snake in Applesmithsville," he said to Janet.

"Where's that?" They were in her house, at the April party given to welcome the Whitmans to town. Janet was distracted by her duties as hostess; she imagined that people and couples needed her everywhere. Piet Hanema was lying all over the stairs and down came Foxy Whitman from the bathroom, with him looking up her skirt. She must take Foxy aside and explain about Piet.

"Oh," Freddy answered, demanding her attention, "here and there, everywhere. All the world is Applesmithsville." In the corner, by the wall of uniform sets, John Ong, his ageless face strained and courteous, was listening to Ben Saltz painstakingly jabber; Janet thought that a woman should go over and interpose herself, but with this alternative she turned herself a little closer into Freddy Thorne's murmur. Why does his mouth, she wondered, if he's himself such a dentist, look so toothlesss? "They're feasting off you, Jan-Jan," he told her. "You're serving two studs and Marcia's in the saddle."

"Spare me your vulgar fantasies, Freddy," Janet said, imitating Marcia. "Contrary to what seems to be the popular impression, Harold and I have never slept together. The possibility has been mentioned; but we decided it would be too messy."

"You're beautiful," Freddy told her. "The way you look me right in the eye handing out this crap is beautiful. Something you don't realize about yourself, you really have it. Not like these other cunts. Marcia doesn't have it, she's trying to jiggle herself into having it. Bea's trying to drink herself into it. Angela's trying to rise above it. You're right there. Do me a favor though and don't fib to jolly old Freddy."

Janet laughed; his words were like the candyish mouthwash by his porcelain dental chair—unswallowable but delicious. She asked, "And Georgene? Does she have it?"

"She's OK in a tennis dress, don't knock the kid. She fucks and she can cook, so what the hell. I'm not proposing marriage."

"Freddy, don't make me hurt your feelings."

"You want out, right?"

"In a way, in a way not. I'm, what's the word, not ambidextrous?"

"Ambivalent. Androgynous. Androdextrorogerogynous."

"We have *fun* with the Smiths, just sitting and talking, neither Frank or I have ever had really close friends before. You can't imagine just friendship, can you?"

He patted his bright bald head and in sudden exultation vigorously rubbed it. "Between you and me, yes. It's what a fish feels for the fish he's eating. You want out, I can get you out. Have a little affair with me and that circus you're supporting will pack up and leave town. You can be your own girl again."

"How little is little?"

"Oh"—his hands did one squeeze of an invisible accordion—"as much as suits. No tickee, no washee. If it doesn't take, it doesn't take. No deposit on the bottle, Myrtle."

"Why do you propose this? You aren't very fond of me. It's Angela you want."

"A, I don't, and B, I am, and C, I like to help people. I think you're about to panic and I hate to see it. You're too *schnapps* for that. You wear clothes too well. Terrific dress you have on, by the way. Are you pregnant?"

"Don't be silly. It's an Empire line."

"Now wouldn't it be awful to get knocked up and not know which was the father? Hey. Are you on the pills?"

"Freddy, I'm beginning to hate this conversation."

"Okey-doke-doke. Let it simmer. As Khrushchev said when he put the missiles on Cuba, nothing ventured, nothing gainski. I'm there if you think you can use me."

"Thank you, Freddy. You're a nice man." Janet's conscience pricked her; she added, "Yes."

"Yes how?"

"Yes, in answer to your question, I am on the pills. Marcia isn't yet. She's afraid of cancer."

Freddy smirked and made a ring with his thumb and forefinger. "You're golden," he told her. "You're the last of the golden girls." He put the ring to his mouth and fluttered his tongue through it.

Janet considered his offer seriously. As she picked her way through the tangle of her party it seemed not so implausible. Freddy would know his way around a woman. Marcia and Frank and Harold would be horrified. Harold's vanity would be unforgivably piqued. Love chases love. These things happen. Piet was making out with poor little Bea Guerin. Frank was grotesquely Twisting (his digestion!) opposite Carol Constantine. Eddie on the sofa was demonstrating with his circling hands to Bernadette Ong the holding pattern of air traffic over LaGuardia and Idlewild, and why the turboprops and private planes were brought down sooner than the pure jets, the beautiful new 707s and DC-8s, and why with every new type of commercial aircraft several hundred passengers will die through pilot error, and why the starlings and gulls at Logan are a special menace; and finally he brought his narrow curly-haired head down safely onto her silk shoulder and appeared to sleep. The guests of honor felt out of it. Foxy queasy, the Whitmans left early. When everyone had left except the little-Smiths, and they were sitting around the table having the dregs of the liqueurs, Janet asked Marcia, "Did Freddy Thorne seem attractive to you tonight?"

Marcia laughed; the glitter of her earrings clashed on the surface of her face. "Heavens, no. He asked me if I was happy in Applesmithsville."

"What did you say?"

"I was very frosty. He went away. Poor Georgene."

"He asked me, too. In fact"—Janet was not sure if this was a tactic, but the Benedictine made it seem one—"he offered to have an affair with me."

"He really is a fantastic oaf," Frank said. Brandy was the worst thing for him, and he was on his third glass.

Harold swirled his Grand Marnier thoughtfully. "Why are you telling us this?"

"I don't know. I was so surprised at myself, that it didn't seem like such a bad idea. Since he's lost all of his hair, he's rather handsome, in a sinister way."

"In a mealy-mouthed way," Marcia said. She sipped anisette.

"Janet, you disgust me," Harold said. "How can you unload this *merde* on three people who adore you?"

"I half-adore her," Marcia said.

"Two point five people who adore you," Harold said. "*Deux point cinq.*"

"I don't know," Janet said. "I guess I want to be talked out of it. I don't see why you men look so offended. It might bring Georgene in and don't we need some new blood? It seems to me we've said everything we have to say about sixty times. We know all about Frank's ulcer and Frank's father who avoided getting an ulcer by learning all about China and how Shakespeare doesn't work as well as China, maybe he's more acid; I *do* advise Maalox. We know all about what saints her father and grandfather the bishop were from Marcia, and how she hated Long Island and loves it up here away from all those dreary clubby types who kept playing badminton with martini olives. We know all about Harold's prostitutes, and the little colored girl in St. Louis, and how neither of us are quite as good . . ."

"Any funny business with Freddy," Frank said, bloating with menace, "and it's get thee to a nunnery. I'll divorce you."

"But then," Janet told him, "I'd have to drag all of us out into the open, and we'd look so funny in the newspapers. Things are so hard to explain that are perfectly obvious to friends."

"It's obvious to me," Freddy Thorne said to her the following weekend, when they were alone in the kitchen late at a dinner party given by the Guerins, "you never were in love with Harold, you went after him to even the score with Marcia." In the intervening week she had had a dental appointment, and in the gaps of prophylaxis he had wheedled from her her version of the full story.

"Freddy, how can you judge?" She helped herself to a piece of cream-cheese-laden celery left over from the hors d'oeuvres. "How can you hope to get inside people's lives this way? Harold when he and I are alone is something you can't imagine. He can be irresistible."

"We all can," was the answer. "Resistibility is a direct function of the female decision to resist or not to." He seemed to be sweating behind the thick eyeglasses that kept misplacing his eyes. Freddy had trouble seeing. He had recently installed a new drill with a water-spray attachment, and during her appointment his glasses had often needed to be wiped.

"Freddy," she told him, "I don't like being pried and poked at. You must make a woman your friend first."

"I've been your friend since you moved to town." He stroked her arm, left bare by the black-lace blouse. Candlelight shuddered in the other room, where the others were chattering. "On second thought," Freddy murmured on, "I think you took Harold on not to hurt the other two but to oblige them, to win their affection. For a magnificent piece who's also rich, you're damn unsure of yourself."

"For a near-sighted boob who's also a dentist, you're damn sure of yourself. Speaking of which, stop trying to make the Whitman girl. She's pregnant."

"Praise be. More men to man America's submarines. She doesn't know it yet, but she's a swinger. Women with that super-heated skin are usually fantastic in the sack. Their hearts beat harder."

"You're such a bastard," said Janet, whose skin, though strikingly pale, was rather grainy and opaque.

Freddy was right, she later reflected, in that obligingness had become a part of it; they had reached, the Applesmiths, the boundary of a condition wherein their needs were merged, and a general courtesy replaced individual desire. The women would sleep with the men out of pity, and each would permit the other her man out of an attenuated and hopeless graciousness. Already a ramifying tact and crossweave of concern were giving their homes an unhealthy hospital air. Frank and Harold had become paralyzed by the habit of lust; she and Marcia, between blow-ups, were as guarded and considerate with one another as two defaced patients in an accident ward.

In the following week she had a porcelain filling replaced, and Freddy called her on the phone every noon, always inviting her to sleep with him. But he never named a place where they could go, never suggested a definite time; and it dawned upon her that he had no serious physical intention: the verbal intimacy of gossip satisfied him. Meanwhile Harold, begging her to resume with him, had gone to the trouble of acquiring the key to a Beacon Street bachelors' apartment that was empty all day. Curious as to how bachelors live, she went there with him the Friday before the Sunday when Piet broke Freddy's little finger. At a glance she gathered that the inhabitants were homosexuals. The furnishings too beautifully harmonized; bent wicker and orange velvet prevailed. One of the men painted, or, rather, did collages juxtaposing magazine advertisements and war headlines, deodorized nudes with nacreous armpits and bombed peasants flecked with blood, green stamps and Robert McNamara and enraptured models in striated girdles, comic-strip cannons pasted at the crotch. It was quite ugly and malicious, yet the room was impossible to shock and the magnolias on the south of Beacon were about to flower. Harold was polite, timid, fatherly, reminiscent, touching. She allowed him to slide her from her clothes and, rising quickly, came with him and then, after a cigarette and wine, let him come again, let him gather himself into his groin and hurl himself painlessly into the dilated middle amplitudes of herself. Trembling as if whipped, he licked her eyelids and sucked her toes, one by one. The sensation felt hysterically funny. The next day, Saturday, she wrote Freddy a letter:

Freddy dear—

I am grateful for your caring. Truly. But my future, I am more than ever convinced, lies with Frank. So your phone calls must stop. After today I will hang up on your voice. May we continue to be pleasant, and friends? Please, I don't want to change dentists, you have all my records.

Fondly,
J.

She mailed it to his cottagelike office on Divinity Street. He received it Monday, read it smiling, was not disappointed, considered burning it on the gas flame in his lab but, the amorous keepsakes of his life having been few, instead crumpled the envelope into the wastebasket and tucked the letter into his coat pocket, where Georgene found it that evening, while he was at Lions. The next day she confessed her terror to Piet, and irrevocably offended him.

So Foxy was both right and wrong about Janet. She overestimated Janet's freedom, and had mistaken the quality of Freddy Thorne's sexuality. Though he seemed aggressive toward women, he really sought to make alliance with them. But then summer overwhelmed Foxy's speculations about the love life of others, and swept her as if out to sea, to a vantage where the couples on the shore of Tarbox looked like a string of colored beads.

Piet Hanema was sent out of the room and they decided he was Ho Chi Minh. Frank Appleby wanted him to be Casanova but Irene said the person couldn't be fictional. Frank told Irene that Casanova had been as real as you and I but everyone agreed they had no feeling for him. Irene suggested Vice-President Johnson. Everyone protested that he was much too dreary. Terry Gallagher came up with Ho Chi Minh and it seemed perfect. Good for Terry: ever since getting her lute, she was much more with it. More human. All spring she had been taking lute lessons from an old woman in Norwell. She had let her long black hair down; her wide lips were tucked up at the corners as if she were holding a coin or candy in her mouth. Looking at Terry, Eddie Constantine suggested that Piet be Joan Baez, but the rest voted to stick with Ho Chi Minh, and Georgene went to the foot of the Saltzes' stairs to call Piet down.

It was the last Sunday night in June. The tight wine-colored cones of the lilacs that Piet had noticed as he hesitated by Foxy Whitman's gate had loosened and expanded with the first hot week of May into papal miters of bloom, first the lavender and then the taller, holier, more ascetic white, ensconced amid heart-shaped leaves whose green was suddenly cheap. The lilacs faded and dried, and bridal wreath drooped, gathering dust, by every garage door and drive. Sagitta, most exquisite of constellations, flew unmoving between the Swan and Eagle, giant jeweled airplanes whose pilots are Deneb and Altair; the Milky Way wandered like a line of wash in the heat-bleached sky. Desultory parties, hardly organized, social weeds, sprang up to fill the pale nights bloated by Daylight Saving, parties mixed of tennis leftovers and sunburned half-couples and cold salami and fetched pizza and Bitter Lemon and sandy stray forgotten children lulled asleep by television's blue flicker. *President Kennedy's triumphal tour of Western Europe today subsided to quiet talks in Sussex, England . . .*

The Saltzes, great birdwatchers and walkers, as if Nature were a course they were cramming, had gone down late to the beach, to see the sandpipers and to swim. Irene suffered from sun poisoning and ventured out at midday protected in floppy hats and long-sleeved jerseys, and went swimming only toward evening. Up by the far rocks she and Ben had found the Hanemas, all four of them, with the Whitmans, the two of them. Ken liked to snorkel, and the Hanema children had been fascinated by his equipment. The beach here by the rocks dropped off steeply enough for diving. Piet was giving Ruth, in face mask and foot fins, a lesson while Nancy, anxious for her sister and envious, cried. Ken and Angela stood together, an almost godlike couple, untroubled, invulnerable, gazing at the horizon, where a sailboat race was suspended, gaudy spinnakers bellied. Foxy, in a skirted lemon-yellow maternity swimsuit, lay supine on a smooth rock, eyes shut, smiling. Irene was envious of everyone's happiness and ease beneath the same sun that gave her a painful rash. They had all been here since noon. Impulsively, yet with some small hope of inducing the Whitman woman, so complacently uncommitted, to work on one of her causes (pre-primary education, fair housing, soil conservation), she invited them back for a drink. The Saltzes lived near the green, in a narrow asbestos-shingled house visible from the Constantines. The Constantines saw the cars and came over. They brought Terry Gallagher with them. Carol, who had taken ballet and who sewed and wove and painted, also played the guitar, and that summer the two women sometimes met for duets. At Eddie's prompting, Ben Saltz phoned the Applebys, who were having the little-Smiths and Thornes over for a pick-up meal, and half of this party showed up—Frank, Marcia, and Georgene. By now it was after eight. Before the light died, Eddie took Angela, of all people, on his Vespa to the Italian place on Route 123 and they brought back five pizzas. Reëntering the Saltzes' narrow living room, Angela looked glorious, flushed from the wind and the fear and the effort of balancing the cardboard boxes. She wore a damp towel tucked around the waist of a wet black bathing suit, and when she bent forward to bite a point of pizza slice Piet could see her nipples. His wife. Where he had sucked. Not thinking it would be so long a party, they had brought their children along. Ruth, her wide eyes watering, watched streams of television with the older Saltz boy Bernard, and Nancy fell asleep in little Jeremiah's room. Irene loved word games. By eleven-thirty, when Ken Whitman was studying the laces of his sneakers and Frank Appleby's eyes had rolled inward upon his digestion and Janet had phoned twice to make sure that he and Marcia had not gone off alone somewhere and to ask him how ever were they supposed to get Freddy Thorne out of the house, the crowd at the Saltzes' had played four games of Ghosts, two of Truth, and three of Botticelli. This left Impressions. Eddie Constantine had gone out first and with only one wrong guess, Burl Ives, identified himself as the late Pope John. It took Georgene somewhat longer to discover that she was Althea Gibson. Then Piet volunteered because he wanted to go to the john and to check on Nancy (*I will never grow up and I will never ever in my whole life die.* Her hair was tangled and stiff; her aqua bathing suit, riding up in sleep, had exposed of her bottom half-moons sparkling with sand. Piet mourned the child's body but the tug of bright life down-stairs held him helpless here. *Sleep. Forgive us in your sleep.*) and they made him Ho Chi Minh.

At the foot of the stairs he tapped Georgene's flank with the side of his hand for old time's sake while gazing straight ahead. He came into the living room; he wore a sweater and plaid bath-ing trunks; his bare feet looked knobbed and splayed on the floor and in Foxy's eyes his naked legs wore a pale fur halo. "What kind of landscape am I?" he asked.

"Jungle," Georgene said.

"Rice paddies," said Marcia little-Smith.

Terry Gallagher said, "Torn."

Piet asked, "A torn landscape?"

"Maybe I mean pacified."

Angela closed her eyes. "I see a temple, with reddish pillars, and an idol with its head knocked off, overgrown with vines, and someone has been doing mathematical calculations with chalk on the broad part of one thigh."

"Sexy," Eddie Constantine said.

Georgene said, her chin hardening, "No fair couples using ESP."

Piet asked, "Anybody else? Foxy? Ken?"

Ken said, "I get Indiana, I don't know why."

Everyone laughed, except Foxy, who nodded. "He's right. Something quiet and gray and ordinary," she said. "Oregon? South Dakota?"

Frank Appleby said, "You mean North Dakota."

"No hints," Carol Constantine protested. She was sitting on the floor in the position of one weaving, or praying, or playing Monopoly. Her legs were folded under a green lily pad of a ballerina's skirt from which her torso rose like a stem. Her waist was remarkably thin and pliant and her nostrils, long slits, seemed always to be inhaling.

Piet asked, "What flower?"

"Poppy."

"Poppy."

"Nodding pogonia," Irene Saltz said. "Or maybe a fringed orchis."

"A fringed orchis in the shade of an enormous Chinese tulip tree," Frank Appleby said.

Carol said to Marcia, "I don't think Frank understands the game. He hints."

Foxy Whitman said, "I see something gray. Mistletoe."

"I keep getting gray out of you," Piet said to her, with strange edge, and asked Angela, "Flower? Ken?"

"Daisy fleabane," Ken said, perhaps antagonistically, staring at his feet. Did he mean it?

Angela said, "No flower or any flower. A single lily presented by a child to the major's wife on a fête day."

"A wilted gardenia in a busboy's lapel," Terry Gallagher said, and smiled broadly when they all burst into compliments. They felt her developing, coming to bloom.

Georgene said, "A thistle. From an official point of view."

Piet complained, "I can't even tell if you like this person or not."

"What sex are you getting?" Carol asked him. Her face, though composed and smooth, held contentious points of shadow—at the nostril wings, at the corners of her mouth, beneath her pouting lower lip, where there seemed to be a smudge. Piet saw that she lengthened the line of her lids with eye shadow, and realized that her eyes were small and rather close together, so close together that in certain flitting lights her stilted dignity of stance appeared that of a cross-eyed person. He felt better about her, less fascinated. Her hair was a dull brown nothing color done up in a pony tail she was too old for.

"Male," he answered. "But it doesn't seem to matter. His maleness isn't his claim to fame."

"Unlike who?" Carol coolly asked.

Piet obligingly blushed. "What—what period of painting?"

"Art Nouveau," Angela said promptly.

"Spanish cave," Foxy said, also prompt.

Frank Appleby rolled his eyes inward and groaned. "All I get is what Carol doesn't want me to get."

"What's that?" Carol asked.

"Soviet posters."

"No," Carol said, "I don't mind that. It's not very good, but I don't mind it."

Irene Saltz asked her, "Who appointed you referee?"

"Medical-textbook illustrations," Ken Whitman said firmly, "with a rice-paper overlay leaf."

"Good," someone said politely, after a pause.

"Terry and the Pirates," Eddie Constantine said.

Carol said, "I'm sorry, I think you're all horrible. He's definitely Yves Tanguy. And maybe Arshile Gorky."

"He's a playwright," Frank told her.

"That's Maxim," she told him.

Ken, remembering the success of some of his other puns, asked innocently, "Who was Maxim Ize?"

Foxy winced.

"A Jewish expansionist," Eddie said. "Whoops, no offense intended, Ben."

Patiently Piet asked, "Any other painters or periods of painting?"

"I don't think," Marcia said, "they ever work out very well. They're too literal. Stretch our minds, Piet."

Into this Piet read Frank's becoming bored, and asked him, "Frank, what play by Shakespeare am I?"

Frank revolved the question uncomfortably inside him, and after a swallow of brandy pronounced, "*Anthony and Cleopatra*, from the viewpoint of Octavius."

Marcia in a helpful wifely way prompted, "What about *Titus Andronicus?*"

"Too messy," Frank said. "This man is efficient."

Foxy Whitman—she had stopped off at her house to change from her tentlike maternity bathing suit into a more flattering shift, a canary-yellow muu-muu that tapped and hugged her hidden shape—was fighting for attention. "What about an *Othello* in which Iago is right?"

Frank said, "He's always right," and brayed.

Ben Saltz, looking tired, got to his feet and asked, "Who wants some more beer? Brandy? We have lots of gin but we're out of Bitter Lemon."

Georgene said, "Piet, you're taking much too long. We've given you beautiful answers and you spurn us."

"You've confused me, you're all so beautiful. I keeping thinking about Ken's medical textbook."

"Ignore it," Foxy said.

"All right: what beverage?"

"Tea."

"Tea."

"Souchong more than orange pekoe."

"Tea with nutmeg," Angela said.

"Angela, you really like this person, don't you?" It was Terry asking.

"I have to, he's my husband."

"I hate tea," Piet said. "I hate tea with nutmeg."

"You've never had it," Angela told him.

"Don't be too sure." The others hushed, to give them space to quarrel. Piet hastily moved on: "What kind of food?"

"Rice."

"Rice, but you want more," Ben said, returning with beer in two brown nonreturnable bottles.

Piet asked, "Boiled or fried?"

Angela said, "Boiled. It's purer."

Marcia said, "Delicately fried."

Terry closed her eyes and said, "A BLT on burnt toast."

Frank Appleby said, "To hell with you all. I'll say what comes to me. A monk barbecue."

Carol cried, all her lithe lines electric, her feet thrusting from under her skirt, "Frank, you're a pig! You've given it to him!"

Piet said in great relief, "I'm No-go Diem."

The voices of the others flocked: "Ngo, you're not." "Close, but no sitar." "Close? He couldn't be wronger." "Right church, wrong side of the aisle." This last was Georgene, reaching out to him; her help was accepted while she was spurned.

Piet arrived: "Ho Chi Minh." In a glad clatter the game collasped. The beer went around. Terry Gallagher and Ken Whitman stood with one motion and looked at each other, surprised by unison.

"It's treasonous," Piet was saying, "how affectionate your impressions were. This enemy of our democracy, all those flowers and delicate grays." His complaint was directed, Georgene felt, toward Angela and Foxy.

"*You* asked flowers."

"You never asked animals. A whiskery weasel."

"A very thin panda."

"Why hate him? He's what they want." This was Irene, who had been uncharacteristically silent.

"*Chacun à son goût,* as Harold would say if he were here," Marcia said with quaint loyalty.

"I thought that was good of me to remember him being a busboy in Paris," Terry said. "Thanks, people, but I must go. We went to early mass this morning and poor Matt's been showing houses all afternoon."

"I second that," Ken said. "Fox, come."

But the momentary impression, of Terry and Ken standing together as a handsome couple, tall and dark-haired and grave, led the others to tease Foxy.

"Oh please," Carol begged. "Stay for one more."

"We'll let Foxy be it."

"Foxy's it. It, Foxy."

"All pregnant women leave the room."

Foxy looked toward Ken; he read on her face a touching indecision. This boozy catty crowd tempted her; their own house was full of mosquitoes and uncompleted carpentry. Yet she was tired, and his wife, and faithful. She said, "No, I'd just be stupid. I don't really understand the game."

"Oh, but you do, you do."

"The game is to be yourself."

"Your impressions are lovely."

"We'll pick somebody simple. Margaret Truman. *Not* Jackie. It'll take ten minutes."

She wavered, and Ken spoke to her across the calling heads with perfect kindness, yet his voice frightened her; his appearance had no roundness. An immaculate cutout seemed wired for sound. "I'm dead, Fox, but you stay and play. Marcia can drop you off."

"Oh," she said, "but that's not right. Marcia has Harold to worry about. I'll go with you."

They all said, "You can't. You're it. Stay."

"Stay," Ken told her, and turned to leave, and she felt herself cut off, her roundness rejected; her shape offended him. She had asked him to rescue her from indecision and he had petulantly set her adrift. Angered, she agreed to stay, and went upstairs, where Piet had been. He had left no clues.

It did not take them long to decide, June having been so fertile of news: Pope John had died, Quang Duc had immolated himself, Valentina Tereshkova had become the first woman in space, John Profumo had resigned, the Lord's Prayer had been banned in the American public schools. Soon Georgene was at the foot of the stairs, calling, "E-liz-a-beth! Elizabeth Fox Whitman, come right down here!" It was the voice of her Wilmington aunt.

Like a rebuked child Foxy entered the living room; its human brightness seemed savage. The darkened rooms upstairs, rooms of pinned-up maps and scattered toy tracks, of silently sleeping children and docile plumbing fixtures, had been a better world. She thought of her bedroom and the moon that shared her insomnia. The blank pillow beside Ken's head was her. Here, Ken and Terry Gallagher were gone. Frank Appleby was asleep, his feet in sandals cocked up on the Saltzes' fake-colonial coffee table, his mouth ajar and raggedly snoring. Foxy also heard whispering in the kitchen and counted Eddie Constantine and Irene missing. The six survivors, four of them women, looked weary and forbearing and she realized she should have gone home with Ken. The game was exhausted, they were merely being polite, to make her feel loved and part of them. She must quickly guess and go.

"What—what kind of ocean am I?" Foxy wasn't sure if the rules forbad using associations others had used, and she wanted to be creative, sensitive, unique. On the nubbly sofa next to his wife, Piet Hanema gazed down into his glass.

"What kind of ocean?" Carol echoed. "How odd. Choppy, I guess."

"Sometimes choppy," Marcia said. "Sometimes very still and tranced. Sometimes even a big wave."

"Untracked," Piet said.

"Untracked?"

"Ships go back and forth across you and leave no trace. You accept them all. They don't impress you."

"A piece of ocean," Ben said, grinning, "with a mermaid in it."

Carol said, "No direct hints."

Suddenly immersed in timidity, Foxy asked, "Angela? Any ocean?"

"Not an ocean," Angela said. "A sad little pond."

"Sad?"

"Kind of scummy," Georgene said: a startling flat insult, but everyone, especially the men, laughed, agreeing.

"Well. What time of day?"

"Two in the morning."

"Eleven a.m., with rumpled sheets."

"Any time. All day."

Again, this unkind laughter. A slow blush caked Foxy's face. She wanted to like this person she was, in spite of them.

Angela tried to rescue her. "I see this person around nine at night, going out, into the city lights, kind of happy and brainless."

"Or maybe even," Marcia added, "at four-thirty in the afternoon, walking in a park, without a hat, smiling at the old men and the squirrels and the babies."

"And the bobbies," Piet said.

Carol sang, "We're getting too spe-ci-fic," and glanced toward the whispering kitchen with that abrupt head turn ballerinas use in pirouettes.

English, Piet's implication was. Queen Elizabeth, scummy? Virginia Woolf? *The Waves.* But those rumpled sheets. Perhaps an effeminate seedy man. Cecil Beaton. Alec Guinness, Piet's saying back and forth across an ocean, an actor's parts. But a scummy pond? How stupid she was being. Afraid to guess wrong, self-conscious, stuck. The furnishings of the Saltzes' living room pressed in upon her emptiness: velvety dark easy chairs wearing doilies on their forearms, maple magazine racks of *Scientific American* and *Newsweek* and *Look,* inquisitive bridge lamps leaning over the chairs' left shoulders, Van Gogh sunning on the walls, wedding pictures frozen on the top of an upright piano with yellow teeth, an evil-footed coat rack and speckled oblong mirror in the dark foyer, narrow stairs plunging upward perilously, children climbing each night in a fight with fear. Her mother's Delaware second cousins had lived in such houses, built narrow to the street and lined with hydrangea bushes where a child could urinate or hide from her third cousins. The Jews have inherited the middle class—nobody else wants it. "What social class?" Foxy asked.

"Too direct," Carol said.

"Lower," Georgene said.

"Middle lower," Piet said. "Some airs and graces."

"Transcending all classes," Angela told her. "Lower than low, higher than high."

"You sound," Ben Saltz said to Angela with a pedantic mannered twinkle, "like a Gnostic devotee."

"What a nosty suggestion," Marcia said.

"Oh, I *don't* understand how we *know* about this person, she seems so *common!*" Foxy cried.

"She has hidden talents," Piet said.

"He or she," Carol corrected.

Foxy asked, "What bird am I?"

"Of paradise," Angela said.

"Sparrow."

"Soiled dove."

"Soiled dove is good."

"I envision," Piet said, "a rather tall bird, with a shimmer on its breast. A cockatoo?"

"You're a cowbird," Georgene told Foxy.

Piet turned on Georgene. "How unfair!"

Georgene shrugged. "Using other people's nests."

It was like, Foxy felt, being naked and not knowing it, like being dead on the autopsy table and yet overhearing the remarks, the cold ribaldry. She wanted to be with Ken, to take the wakening presence within her and flee; she had sinned. "What figure am I in the Bible? I know you're going to say Delilah."

"No," Piet said, "you're too hard on yourself. Maybe you're Hagar."

"No," Ben said, "she's Abishag. Abishag was the girl who they brought in to David, when he was dying, to give him some heat. *Vecham leadoni hamelekh*, in the Hebrew."

"And what happened?" Marcia asked.

"*Vehamelekh loh yada-ah.* The king knew her not."

"Ben," Marcia said, "I think it's marvelous, the way you can rattle it off. Hebrew."

"I studied it for ten years. We were conservative."

"Even those little skullcaps?"

"Yarmulkes." His grin was leonine, thrilling, his teeth brilliant within his beard. "Summers I was sent to Camp Ramah."

Foxy asked, "Georgene?"

"I don't know the Bible. I would have said Delilah. Or Magdalen, except that seems presumptuous."

"I see her as one of those Jerusalemites who never got into the Bible," Angela said. "She just couldn't be bothered. She was flirting with a Roman soldier when the Cross went by."

"What a terrible woman," Foxy said. "A scummy pond, a cowbird."

"You've been listening only to Georgene," Piet said. "Georgene's being moralistic tonight."

"You don't like her either. Angela and Ben are the only ones who like her." Saying this made Foxy jealous, for she did not want Ben and Angela to be linked, she vaguely wanted Ben—not the real Ben, but the echoes he evoked—to be her own Jew.

The whispering from the kitchen had ceased.

"This is going on too long," Carol said, and stood up, stiff from long sitting, her throat and wrists stringy, tense. She did not quite dare go into the kitchen; she took a step toward the open doorway and sharply called, "Come help us, you two. She's stuck."

"I quit," Foxy said. "Who am I? I'm sure I've never heard of myself."

"You have, you have," Piet urged; he wanted her to do well, he was embarrassed for her.

"I'm some dreary little starlet and I never notice their names."

"At the moment," Piet told her, "you're a star."

"At the moment. Julie Andrews. Liz Taylor."

"No. You're on the wrong track."

"Phooey," Foxy said. "I was so proud of those. They're both English. I'm not Dame May Whitty?"

"You're being silly," Carol told her.

"Think big," Piet said. "Think world."

Ben said, "Ask some more questions."

They were all prompting, hissing at the balky child in the Christmas recitation. Georgene's hard eyes were plainly pleased. Marcia said, "Ask Frank what Shakespeare play you are. I'll wake

him up." Marcia glided to where Frank lay deflated and sunk in
the corner of the fat sofa and, wifely, whispered into his ear until
his lids parted and his eyes, open, stared sorely ahead. Foxy felt
his eyes, in mid-dream, gaze through her.

"Frank, help," she said. "What Shakespearian play am I?"

"*Troilus*," he said, and his eyes closed.

"I've never read it," Foxy said.

"I think you're the sonnets," Marcia said.

"In Russian and English *en face*," Piet said, and everybody,
everybody, laughed.

"Oh, you're all too clever," Foxy told them. "I'm totally lost
now. I was working on Princess Margaret." Their laughter renewed itself; she said, "I hate you all. I want to go home. I want
to give up."

"Don't give up," Piet said. "I know you know it. You're trying
too hard."

Ben asked her, "What's the opposite of a princess?"

"A ragpicker. Oh. A flowergirl. Eliza Doolittle. But I thought
you couldn't use fictional people."

"You can't. You're not Eliza," Georgene told her. "What's the
opposite of a virgin?"

Angela said, "I think Foxy should give up if she wants to."

"She's too close to give up," Carol said.

Irene Saltz, smoothing back her hair, returned to the living
room. Her black eyebrows were shapely as wingbeats. She told
Carol, "Eddie said to tell you he's gone home. He has to fly tomorrow and went out through the kitchen door."

"Typical," Carol said, and brightened. Her spine as she sat on
the floor became again a flower stem, slender, erect. She begged
Foxy, "Try one more impression."

With a surrendering sigh, Foxy asked, "What flower?"

The answers were elaborate, since they wanted her now to
guess, to know.

"A tiger lily," Carol said, "transplanted from a village garden to
a city street."

"Why would anyone bother to do that?" Georgene asked. "I
see something coarse but showy. A poppy."

"But Ho Chi Minh was a poppy," Piet told her.

"Yes. There may be an affinity," Georgene said, and turned on him those slightly bulging indignant eyes which, with her cultivated tan and graying hair, belonged to the caustic middle-aged woman she would become. Foxy remembered Georgene's silence during the candlelit dinner at the Guerins, a secretive and contented silence which had seemed, that uncomfortable night, to share, to be of the same chemical nature as, Foxy's pregnancy. Since then this woman had aged unkindly.

Irene said, "I don't know who it is." When Carol whispered the name into her ear, she snapped: "Eglantine."

"In Japan," Angela said, "after our bombs, wasn't there a flower that came out of nowhere and flourished in the radioactive area? I see this person like that, as turning our modern poison into a kind of sweetness."

Foxy said gratefully, "Angela, that's nice. I don't feel so badly now about being this person."

"Devil's paintbrush," Marcia said. "Or something hothousy."

"You know how sometimes," Ben Saltz said, "in weeding around the house, you come to a plant, such as Queen Anne's lace or those spindly wild asters, that is obviously a weed but you don't have the heart to pull because for the time being it's very ornamental?"

Angela said, "We're all like that."

Georgene said, "Speak for yourself, dollink."

"A geranium that's moved from sill to sill to catch the sun," Piet said. "A hyacinth that's sold in a plastic pot. Sometimes a Lady Palmerston rose. Foxy, have you ever noticed, in a greenhouse, how they put cut carnations in a bucket of ink to dye them? That's how they make those green ones for St. Patrick's Day. I think you're a yellow carnation they made drink purple ink, so you're this incredible black, and people keep touching you, thinking you must be artificial, and are amazed that you're an actual flower. As you die, you'll bleed back to yellow again." His flat taut-featured face became this much-touched flower fading.

Carol said, "There's a carefree toughness we're not suggesting."

"Let's do books," Marcia said, impatient. "*Moll Flanders*, by Ian Fleming."

"*Phineas Finn*," Angela said, "abridged for *Playboy*."

"*Little Red Riding Hood*," Ben said, "by the Marquis de Sade."

"*Stop*," Foxy begged. "I give up. I'm very stupid. Angela. Tell me."

"You're Christine Keeler," Piet told her.

In the silence, Foxy's stomach growled.

"That . . . tart? I am? Oh. I'm so *sorry*." Without willing it, without wanting it, not knowing at what instant she passed, averting her head, into tears, Foxy began in fatigue and confusion to cry; and it was clear to all of them, except Angela and Ben, that as they had suspected she was seeing Piet.

iii. *Thin Ice*

As in sleep we need to dream, so while waking we need to touch and talk, to be touched and talked to. *Foxy?*

Yes, Piet? Their simple names had a magic, the magic of a caress that searches out the something monstrous and tender in the genitals of another.

Do you think we're wrong?

Wrong? The concept seemed to swim toward her out of another cosmos of consideration. *I don't know. I don't think so.*

How good of you!

Not to think so?

Yes, yes, yes. Yes. Don't ever think so. Make it right for me. Hey. I dreamed about you last night. I never have before. It's funny, the people you dream about. It's a club with the stupidest rules. I'm always dreaming about Freddy Thorne and I can't stand him.

What did I do in your dream? Was I erotic?

Very chaste. It was in a department store, with a huge skylight overhead. You were a salesgirl. I stopped in front of your counter, without knowing what I wanted.

A salesgirl, am I? She had this mode, of contentious teasing, to vent a touchy pride. *And what do you suppose I am selling?*

It wasn't that atmosphere at all. You were very prim and distant and noncommittal, the way you can be; even though I couldn't say anything, you bent down behind the counter, out of sight, as if to find something, and I woke up with a killing erection.

Sometimes insomniac that summer, Piet, lying in bed beside sleeping Angela, would lift his hand and study its shape stamped black on the window of light-blue panes framed by cruciform mullions. His hand seemed one lifted out of the water in the instant before the final sinking. Angela's heedless slow breathing seemed a tide on the skin of the depths to which he could sink. He missed the squeaking, like glints of light, of the hamster's wheel. He had been shy and circumspect with Foxy, a hired man in her house, and had not intended to desire her. But she had moved with him through the redesign of this old wreck, outdoors to indoors, detail to detail, with a flirting breezy eagerness that had oddly confounded him with the naked wood, where she touched it.

Here there could be shelves.

Or cabinets.

Don't you like open shelves better? Doors are so self-righteous. Then they stick or stop shutting.

They make magnetic catches now that are pretty foolproof. Open shelves are a temptation. You have a cat, you're going to have children. You need spaces you can close. I have two old finish carpenters whose cabinets can be quite handsome.

Did they come from Finland together?

One "n" finish. Their names are Adams and Comeau.

And you want to make work for them.

Piet was taken aback; this woman seemed, as she moved this way and that in her antique kitchen, in her tapping billowing maternity smock, lighter than other women, quicker in exploring him, as if he appeared before her not as himself but as another, whom she had once known well, and still directed some emotion toward. He told her guardedly, *They care, I like them to do work for people who care.*

She turned and held up her arms to the view as if to an ikon and turned again and said urgently, *I want open shelves, and open doorways, and everything open to the sea and the sea air. I've lived my whole life in clever little rooms that were always saving space,* and swept from her narrow kitchen with her lemon-colored smock swinging coolly about her, the high fair color of her face burning. Piet saw she was going to be trouble.

Georgene asked him, "Why have you taken the job? You told me you had to build ranch houses."

They were beside the Ongs' tennis court on Sunday morning. Piet had given up church so that Angela could accept a challenge teasingly given by Freddy Thorne. Piet missed that hour of seated mulling and standing song. Also his head was pinched in tightened icy bands of last night's gin. The challenge, delivered loudly by Freddy at the Constantines' last night, had been for Angela to play him at singles; but then this morning Bernadette was already returning with her three sons from early mass, so the Ongs had to be invited to play, on their own court. The court had been carved from a sloping field adjoining their newly built house. The exotic and expensive house, all flat eaves and flagstones and suspended stairways, designed by an architect John knew in Cambridge, an associate of I. M. Pei, was a puzzling reminder, for the self-important young couples of Tarbox, of John Ong's incongruous prestige. John himself, a small bony butternut-colored man, in love with everything American from bubble chambers to filtered cigarettes, was a tennis enthusiast without aptitude; he invariably played in freshly pressed whites, complete to the wrist band, and a green eyeshade. His dainty popping strokes, accompanied by himself with a running comment of encouraging cries and disappointed coos, were rudely smashed away by his Occidental friends. Bernadette, however, was a walloper. She and Freddy, who stood comically flatfooted and served patball like a child, opposed John and Angela, whose game was graceful and well schooled and even, except at the net, where she had no sense of kill. Piet and Georgene, watching, talked. They spoke at what seemed normal pitch but took care not to be overheard.

He answered her, "Ranch houses are so boring. They all look alike."

There was in Georgene a store of clubwomanly indignation. "So do teeth," she said. "Teeth all look alike. Stocks and bonds all look alike. Every man works with things that look alike; what's so special about you? What makes you such a playboy? You don't even have any money."

Ever since childhood, being scolded had given Piet cerebral cramps; that the world was capable at any point of its immense surface of not loving him seemed a mathematical paradox it was torture to contemplate. He said, "The rest of you have money for me."

"That *is* your style, isn't it? You take. You take, and bow, and leave." Her face was in profile, one-eyed and prim, like the Jack of Diamonds. Sun-glisten salted her chin.

"It was *you*," he told her, having waited until a flurry of strokes and exclamations from the game concealed his voice, "who said we must be careful. Because of Janet's letter, remember? I needed you that day and you shut me out."

"That was months ago. I said to be careful, not to call it off."

"I don't like being told to be careful."

"No, of course you don't, you don't have to be. Angela knows damn well what you're up to but prefers not to see it."

Angela, hearing her name, turned her head. Piet called to her, "Georgene's admiring your style." To Georgene he said, smiling as if chatting, "And what about you and yours? Did you ever confront him with the letter?"

"Yes. Eventually."

"And what did the dear man say?"

She turned her tennis racket between her knees and studied the strings. Rough and smooth. Rough, smooth. "I forget. He wriggled out of it somehow. He said it was a purely paternal thing, that he had been trying to help Janet get out of the Applesmith mess, and she was too neurotic, she had turned on him. It was pretty plausible, from the way her note was worded."

"And then in relief you went to bed with him."

"Yes, as a matter of fact."

"And it was splendid."

"Not bad."

"You each had seven orgasms and read Henry Miller to each other between times."

"You see it very clearly."

"Working from your many vivid descriptions."

"Piet. Stop being a bastard. I'm tired of being a bitch. Come see me. Just for coffee."

"Just for coffee is as bad as for screwing if we're caught."

"I miss you."

"Here I am."

"You have somebody else, that's it, isn't it?"

"Dollink," he said, "you know me better than that."

"I can't believe it's that Whitman girl. She's just too stiff and pretty-pretty for you. She's not your type."

"You're right. It's not her. It's Julia little-Smith."

"Foxy's too tall for you, Piet. You make yourself ridiculous."

"Not only am I poor, I'm a midget. How did a high-class chick like you ever get mixed up with me?"

Georgene contemplated him coldly. Beyond her green eyes and high-bridged nose, wire mesh of the tennis court; beyond, the slope of summer grass whitening where wind touched it. Waves. Lattices. Combine and recombine. Dissolution. She whispered. "I wonder. It must have been purely chemical." The sadness of lust swept numbly up from below Piet's belt. They had come together. Time and again. Larches, tarpaper. Her purple turban.

A final point, and the game was over. Angela and John Ong, winners, walked to the sidelines shining with sweat. John spoke, and Piet didn't understand what he was saying; the vowels, all flattened toward "a," were strung together with clattering consonants. Piet, squinting upward, felt intelligence wildly straining toward him from behind that smooth golden mask. "He says he has no wind any more," Bernadette said for him. She was broad in the shoulders and pelvis and her face had the breadth of a smile even when she was not smiling. Piet loved the Ongs: they let him use their tennis court, they never patronized him, their presence in Tarbox was as contingent as his own. John lit a cigarette and suffered a fit of dry coughing, and Piet was surprised that the coughs were intelligible. An elemental vocabulary among all men. The cough, the laugh, the sob, the scream, the fart, the sigh. Amen.

John said, bent double by coughing, "Oo two now," meaning the other two couples must play. The Ongs walked together toward their house, amid their trio of petitioning boys.

The Hanemas faced the Thornes. Georgene had put on sunglasses; the rest of her face looked chiseled. The sun was high. Sheen skated on the green composition court. Angela served; her serves, though accurate, lacked pace and sat up pleasantly fat to hit. Georgene's return, one of her determined firm forehands, streaked toward Piet as he crouched at the net; anger had hurried her stroke slightly and the ball whacked the net at the height of his groin and fell dead on her side.

"Fifteen love," Angela called, and prepared, on tiptoe, to serve again.

Piet changed courts. Opposite him Freddy Thorne wore loud plaid shorts, a fairyish pink shirt, a duck bill hat for his bald head, fallen blue socks, and rubbery basketball sneakers that seemed too large. Freddy pointed his feet outward clownishly and hoisted his racket to his shoulder like a baseball bat. Angela, having laughed and lost rhythm, double-faulted.

"Fifteen all," she called, and Piet faced Georgene again. A fluid treacherous game. Advantages so swiftly shifted. Love became hate. *You give me my shape.* Georgene, eyeless, braced for the serve, gauged it for her forehand, took back the racket, set her chin, stepped forward, and Piet, gripping his handle so hard it sweated, bit down on a shout for mercy.

"Daddy. Am I pretty?"

Piet's jaw ached with a suppressed yawn. He had thought his job was done. He had watched Nancy brush her teeth and read with her for the twentieth time *Where the Wild Things Are* and recited with her, what they did more and more rarely, a goodnight prayer, a little litany of blessings into which Piet never knew whether or not to insert the names of his parents. He felt that they too, along with her maternal grandparents, should be remembered by the child; but their unalterable deadness disturbed her. So usually Jacobus and Marte Hanema went unblessed, and their unwatered ghosts in Heaven further withered. "Yes, Nancy, you are very pretty. When you grow up you will be as pretty as Mommy."

"Am I pretty now?"

"Aren't you being a silly? You are very pretty now."

"Are other girls pretty?"

"What other girls?"

"Martha and Julia." Topless little females shrieking in the icy water of Tarbox Bay. Round limbs sugared with sand. Squatting in sunset glaze to dam the tide.

Piet asked her, "What do *you* think?"

"They're ugly."

"They're pretty in their way and you're pretty in your way. Martha is pretty in a Thorne way and Julia is pretty in what way?"

"Smith way."

"Right. And Catharine in what way?"

"In an Applebay."

"In an Appleby way. And when Mrs. Whitman has her baby it will be pretty in a Whitman way." It was wrong to use the innocent ears of a child, but it gave Piet pleasure to say Foxy's name, to hold it in his mouth and feel his body suffused with remembrance of her. Angela, sensitive beyond her conscious understanding, showed irritation with his talk, so carefully casual, of the Whitmans, and the name had become subliminally forbidden in the house.

Nancy understood the game now. Her round face gleeful in the pillow, she said, "And when Jackie Kenneny has her baby it will be pretty in a Kenneny way."

"*Right.* Now go to sleep, pretty Nancy, or you will be grumpy and lumpy in the morning."

But there was in this child, more than in her blunt Dutch-blooded sister Ruth, that thing female which does not let go. "But am I the prettiest?"

"Baby, we just said, everybody is pretty in her own way and

nobody wants them to change because then everybody would be alike. Like turnips." He had left a martini-on-the-rocks beside his chair downstairs and the ice would be melting, spinning water into the jewel-clear gin.

Nancy's face was distorted by the effort not to cry. "But I'll *die*," she explained.

He groped for her thought. "You think if you're the prettiest God won't let you die?"

She wordlessly nodded. Her thumb had found its way to her mouth and her eyes darkened as if she were sucking from it ink.

"But pretty people must die too," Piet told her. "It wouldn't be fair to let only ugly ones die. And nobody looks ugly to people who love them."

"Like mommies and daddies," she said, removing and replacing her thumb in an instant.

"Right."

"And boy friends and girl friends."

"I suppose."

"I know your girl friend, Daddy."

"You do! Who?"

"Mommy."

Piet laughed. "And who's Mommy's boy friend?" Symmetry. The child said, "Martha's daddy."

"That awful man?"

"He's funny," Nancy explained. "He says poo."

"You mean if I said poo I'd be funny too?"

She laughed: the noise was pulled bubbling from deep near the door to the kingdom of sleep. "You said poo," she said. "Shame on Daddy."

A silence fell between them. The lilac leaves, flourishing, flowerless, had reached to the height of Nancy's window and, heartshaped, brushed her screen. Fear tapped, scraped. Piet did not dare leave. "Are you really worried about dying, baby?"

Solemnly Nancy nodded. "Mommy says I'll get to be an old, old lady, and then die."

"Isn't that nice? When you're a very old lady you can sit in your rocking chair and tell all your great-great-grandchildren how once you had a daddy who said poo."

The desired laugh rose toward the surface of the child's shadowed face, and without a sound submerged. She was gazing into the horror he had conjured up. "I don't want to be an old lady! I don't want to be big!"

"But already you're bigger than you were. Once you were no bigger than my two hands. You don't want to be that small again. You couldn't talk or walk or anything."

"I do too, Daddy. Go away, send Mommy."

"Nancy, listen. You won't die. That little thing inside you that says 'Nancy' won't ever ever die. God never lets anybody die; he lifts them up and takes them into Heaven. That old thing they put in the ground isn't you at all."

"I want Mommy!"

Piet, sickened, saw that Angela, in her simplicity, had made this doctrine of hope, the only hope, strange and frightful to the child. "Mommy's doing the dishes downstairs."

"I want her."

"She'll come and give you a kiss when you're fast asleep."

"I want her now."

"And you don't want Daddy?"

"*No.*"

Sometimes in these warm pale nights, as the air cooled and the cars on the road beyond the lilac hedge swished toward Nun's Bay trailing a phosphorescence of radio music, Angela would turn to Piet while he lay willing to yield himself to fatigue. It seemed crucial that he make no motion of desire toward her; then, speaking no word, as if a visitant from space had usurped his wife's body, Angela would press herself against him and with curved fingers curiously trace his sides and spine. Unspeaking also, lest the spell break, he would dare mirror her caress, discovering her nightgown, usually an opaque and entangling obstacle, transparent, rotten, sliding and falling from her flesh like deteriorated burial cloth from a body resurrected in its strength. She showed behind and between her legs a wealth of listening curves and damps. She tugged her gown to her throat and the bones of her fingers confided a glimmering breast to his mouth, shaped by an *ah* of apprehension; when with insistent symmetry she rolled onto her back to have him use the other, his hand discovered her mons Veneris swollen high, her whole fair floating flesh dilated outward toward a deity, an anyoneness, it was Piet's fortune to have localized, to have seized captive in his own dark form. The woman's beauty caressed the skin of his eyes; his shaggy head sank toward the ancient alleyway where, foul proud queen, she frothed most. His tongue searched her sour labia until it found them sweet. She pulled his hair, *Come up*. "Come inside me?" He realized, amazed, he who had entered Foxy Whitman the afternoon before, that there was no cunt like Angela's, none so liquorish and replete. He lost himself to the hilt unresisted. The keenness of her chemistry made him whimper. Always the problem with their sex had been that he found her too rich to manipulate. She touched his matted chest, *wait*, and touched her own self, and, mixed with her fluttering fingers, coming like a comet's dribble, he waited until her hand flew to his buttocks and, urging him to kill her, she gasped and absolved herself from tension.

He said, "My dear wife. What a nice surprise."

She shrugged, flat on her back on the sweated sheet, her bare shoulders polished by starlight. "I get hot too. Just like your other women."

"I have no other women." He stroked and smoothed the outflowing corona of her hair. "Your cunt is heavenly."

Angela motioned him off and rolled away to sleep; it was their custom since the start of their marriage to sleep nude after making love. "I'm sure," she said, "we're all alike down there."

"That's not true," Piet told her, "not true at all." She ignored his confession.

He had been shy and circumspect with Foxy and had not wanted to desire her. He would spend most of each day on Indian Hill with the three ranch houses, which rose in quick frames from the concrete foundations: an alphabet of two-by-fours, N and T and M and H, interlocked footings and girders and joists and flooring and studs and plates and sills. Piet, hammer in hand, liked to feel the bite taken into gravity. The upright weight-bearing was a thing his eye would see, and a house never looked as pretty again to him as it did in the framing, before bastard materials and bastard crafts eclipsed honest carpentry, and work was replaced by delays and finagling with subcontractors—electricians like weasels, grubby plumbers, obdurate motionless masons.

So, many days, it was not until three or four o'clock that he rattled down the beach road to the Robinson place. The worst problem, the lack of a basement, had been solved first. The servants' wing, four skimpy dormered bedrooms and a defunct kitchenette, had been torn down, enabling a back hoe to dig a hole ten feet deep to the edge of the kitchen, in two days. Four college boys with hand shovels had taken a week to dig under the length of the kitchen and hallway area and break through to the existing furnace hole beneath the living room. For a few days, while concrete was poured and spread (the operation coincided with an early-June heat wave; the scene in the cave beneath the house, boys stripped to the waist and ankle-deep in sludge, was infernal), half of Foxy's home rested on a few cedar posts and Lally columns footed on cinder block. Then, above the basement where the wing had been, Piet built a modified annex of one story, two rooms one of which could be a nursery and one a playroom, with a screened-in sunporch overlooking the marsh, connected to the kitchen by a passageway where gardening tools could be kept. Before June's end Foxy had ordered six rose bushes from Vos & Sons' greenhouses, and had had them set along the butt end of the new wing, and was trying with Bovung and peat moss to nurse them to health in a clayey earth still littered with splinters and scarred by tractor-tire tracks.

In five July days, a roofer's crew stripped the lumpy leaky accumulation of shingles and hammered down a flat snug roof.

The old sagging porch was torn away. Light flooded the living room, whose walls, as the hot-air ducts from the new furnace were installed, were covered with wire lath and plastered by an old Czech from Lacetown, with his crippled nephew: the last plasterers south of Mather. These major renovations, substantially completed by August, cost Ken Whitman eleven thousand dollars, of which only twenty-eight hundred came to Piet's firm, and only a few hundred adhered as profit. The rest went for material, for rough labor, for the skilled labor of Adams and Comeau, to the heating contractor, the concrete supplier, the plumbing subcontractor. Kitchen improvement—new appliances, additional plumbing, cabinets, linoleum—came to another three thousand, and Piet, pitying Whitman (who never asked for pity, who comprehended the necessities and expenses with a series of remote nods, as the house at each transformation became less his and more Foxy's), held his own charges close to cost. As everyone, especially Gallagher, had foreseen, the job was a loser.

But it gave Piet pleasure to see Foxy, pregnant, reading a letter beside a wall of virgin plaster, her shadow subtly golden. And he wanted her to be pleased by his work. Each change he wrought established more firmly an essential propriety. At night, and in the long daytime hours when he was not yet with her, he envisioned her as protected and claimed by sentinels he had posted: steel columns standing slim and strong in the basement, plaster surfaces of a staring blankness, alert doors cleverly planed to hang lightly in old frames slumped from plumb, a resecured skylight, now of double thickness and freshly flashed, above her sleeping head. He saw her as always sleeping when he was not there, her long body latent, ripening in unconsciousness. Sometimes, when he came in midafternoon, she would be having a nap. The sea sparkled dark in the twisting channels. Lacetown lighthouse trembled in the distance and heat. High summer's hay smell lay thick upon the slope, full of goldenrod and field mice, down to the marsh. Beside the doorway there were lilac stumps. No workmen's cars were parked in the driveway, only her secondhand Plymouth station wagon, hymnal blue.

He lifted the aluminum gate latch. He examined the unfinished framing of the annex, noted two misnailed and split pieces of cross-bridging between joists, walked around the front of the house where the porch had been and an unconcluded rubble of mud and hardened concrete splotches and dusty hundredweight paper bags and scraps of polyethylene film and insulation wool now was, and, continuing, tapped on the side door, a door that seemed to press outward with the silence it contained. Within, something made the house slightly tremble. It was Cotton, the

Whitmans' heavy-footed caramel tom. Piet entered, and the cat, bowing and stretching and purring in anticipation of being picked up, greeted him amid the holy odor of shavings.

Foxy was above him. With a stealth meant to wake her slowly, Piet moved through the unfinished rooms, testing joints with his pocket knife, opening and shutting cabinet doors that closed with a delicate magnetic suck. Above him, a footstep heavier than a cat's sounded. Furiously Piet focused on the details of the copper plumbing installed beneath the old slate sink, suspended in mid-connection, where the plumbers had left it, open like a cry. She was beside him, wearing a loosely tied bathrobe over a slip, her face blurred by sleep, her blond hair moist on the pillowed side of her head. *They said they'd be back.*

I was trying to figure out why they had quit.

They explained it to me. Something about a male threader and a coupling.

Plumbers are the banes of this business. Plumbers and masons.

They're a vanishing breed?

Even vanishing they do slowly. You and Ken must be tired to death of living in the middle of a mess.

Oh, Ken's never here in the day and it's fun for me, to have men bringing me presents all day long. Adams and Comeau and I sit around the coffee table talking about the good old days in Tarbox.

What good old days?

Apparently it's always been a salty town. Look, would you like something to drink? I've woken up with a terrible thirst, I could make lemonade. That only needs cold water.

I ought to get back to the office and give the plumbers a blast.

They promised they'd be back so I'd have hot water. Do you mind if it's pink?

Pink lemonade? I prefer it. My mother used to make it. With strawberries.

In the good old days, Adams and Comeau tell me, the trolley car ran along Divinity Street and all the drunks would pile out because this was the only un-dry town between Boston and Plymouth. Even in the middle of a blizzard this would happen.

Funny about the trolley cars. How they came and went.

They used to make me sick. That awful smell, and the motorman's cigars.

Speaking of messes, what about where your porch was? Do you see that as lawn, or a patio, or what?

I'd love a grape arbor. Why is that funny?

You'd lose all the light you've gained. You'd lose your view from those windows.

The view bores me. The view is Ken's thing. He's always looking outward. Let me tell you about grape arbors.

Tell me.

When I was growing up one summer, the summer before Pearl Harbor, my parents wanted to get out of Bethesda and for a month we rented a brick house in Virginia with an enormous grape arbor over bricks where the ants made little hills. I must have been, what? '41, seven. Forgive me, I'm not usually so talkative.

I know.

I remember the little offshoots of the vines had letters in them, formed letters, you know. She made an A with her fingers. *I tried to make a complete collection. From A to Z.*

How far did you get?

I think to D. I never could find a perfect E. You'd think in all those vines there would have been one.

You should have skipped to F.

I was superstitious and I thought I couldn't. I inhibited myself all the time.

Piet grimaced and considered. The lemonade needed sugar. *It seems to be going out. Inhibition. In a way, I miss it.*

What a sad thing to say. Why? I don't miss it at all. Ever since I got pregnant I've become a real slob. Look at me, in a bathrobe. I love it. Her lips, in her clear pink complexion, looked whitish, as if rubbed with a chapstick. *Shall I tell you a secret?*

Better not. Tell me, what shade of white do you want your living-room woodwork? Flat white, glossy, ivory, or eggshell?

My secret is really so innocent. For years I wanted to be pregnant, but also I was afraid of it. Not just losing my figure,

*which was too skinny to care about anyway, but my body being
somehow an embarrassment to other people. For months I didn't
tell anybody except Bea Guerin.*

Who told everybody else.

*Yes, and I'm glad. Because it turns out not to matter. People
just don't care. I was so conceited to think that people would
care. In fact they like you a little better if you look beat-up. If
you look used.*

You don't look very used to me.

Or you to me.

Do men get used? They just use.

*Oh, you're so wrong. We use you all the time. It's all we know
how to do. But your saying that fits with your missing inhibition.
You're very Puritan. You're quite hard on yourself. At first I
thought you fell down stairs and did acrobatics to show off. But
really you do it to hurt yourself. In the hope that you will. Now
why are you laughing?*

Because you're so clever.

*I'm not. Tell me about your childhood. Mine was dreary. My
parents finally got a divorce. I was amazed.*

*We had a greenhouse. My parents had Dutch accents I've
worked quite hard not to inherit. They were both killed years
ago in an automobile accident.*

Yes, of course. Freddy Thorne calls you our orphan.

How much do you see of Freddy Thorne?

No more than I must. He comes up to me at parties.

He comes up to everybody at parties.

I know that. You don't have to tell me.

*Sorry. I don't mean to tell you anything. I'm sure you know
quite enough. I just want to get this job done for you so you and
your baby can be comfortable this winter.*

Her lips, stunned a moment, froze, bloodless, measuring a space
of air like calipers. She said, *It's not even July.*

Time flies, he said. It was not even July, and he had never
touched her, except in the conventions of greeting and while
dancing. In dancing, though at least his height, she had proved
submissive to his lead, her arm weightless on his back, her hard

belly softly bumping. He felt her now expectant, sitting composed in a careless bathrobe on a kitchen chair, aggressive even, unattractive, so full of the gassy waitingness and pallor of pregnancy.

He said casually, *Good lemonade*, in the same moment as she sharply asked, *Why do you go to church?*

Well, why do you?

I asked first.

The usual reasons. I'm a coward. I'm a conservative. Republican, religious. My parents' ghosts are there, and my older girl sings in the choir. She's so brave.

I'm sorry you're a Republican. My parents worshipped Roosevelt.

Mine were offended because he was Dutch, they didn't think the Dutch had any business trying to run the country. I think they thought power was sin. I don't have any serious opinions. No, I do have one. I think America now is like an unloved child smothered in candy. Like a middle-aged wife whose husband brings home a present after every trip because he's been unfaithful to her. When they were newly married he never had to give presents.

Who is this husband?

God. Obviously. God doesn't love us any more. He loves Russia. He loves Uganda. We're fat and full of pimples and always whining for more candy. We've fallen from grace.

You think a lot about love, don't you?

More than other people?

I think so.

Actually, I never think about love. I've left that to your friend Freddy Thorne.

Would you like to kiss me?

Very much, yes.

Why don't you?

It doesn't seem right. I don't have the nerve. You're carrying another man's child.

Foxy impatiently stood, exclaiming, *Ken's frightened of my baby. I frighten him. I frighten you.* Piet had risen from his chair and she stood beside him, asking in a voice as small as the distance between them, *Aren't we in our house? Aren't you building this house for me?*

Before kissing her, yet after all alternatives had been closed to him, Piet saw her face to be perfectly steady and clean of feeling, like a candleflame motionless in a dying of wind, or a road straight without strategies, like the roads of his native state, or the canals of Holland, and his hands on her body beneath the loose robe found this same quality, a texture almost wooden yet alive and already his; so quickly familiar did her body feel that there was no question, no necessity, of his taking her that afternoon— as a husband and wife, embracing in the kitchen, will back off because they will soon have an entire night, when the children are asleep, and no mailman can knock.

Outdoors again, amid the tracked clay, the splinters, the stacked bundles of raw shingles, the lilac stumps, Piet remembered how her hair, made more golden by the Tarbox sun, had been matted, a few damp strands, to her temple. She had averted her blushing face from his kiss as if to breathe, exhaling a sigh and gazing past his shoulder at a far corner of the unfinished room. Her lips, visually thin, had felt wide and warm and slippery; the memory, outdoors, as if chemically transformed by contact with oxygen, drugged Piet with a penetrating dullness.

His life with Angela suffered under a languor, a numbness that Georgene had never imposed. His blood brooded on Foxy; he dwelled endlessly upon the bits of her revealed to him—her delicate pubic fleece, her high-pitched coital cries, the prolonged and tender and unhoped-for meditations of her mouth upon his phallus. He became an obsessed inward housekeeper, a secret gardener.

I didn't know you'd be blond here too.

What would I be? You're red.

But you're so delicate. Transparent. Like the fuzz on a rose.

She laughed. *Well I've learned to live with it, and so must you.*

He lived dimly, groping, between those brilliant glimpses when they quickly slipped each other from their clothes and she lay down beside him, her stretched belly shining, and like a lens he opened, and like a blinded skier lost himself on the slopes of her presence. July was her fifth month; her condition forced upon their intercourse homely accommodations. Since bending was awkward, she would slide down in the bed to kiss him. *Do you really like that?*

Love it.

Is there a taste?

A good taste. Salty and strong. A bit of something bitter, like lemon.

I'm afraid of abusing you.

Don't be. Do.

She never came. However gladly she greeted him, and with however much skill he turned her body on the lathe of the light, shaping her with his hands and tongue, finally they skidded separate ways. *Come in me.*

Are you ready?

I want you in me.

He felt her inner music stall. Her cunt was young, snug. A kind of exasperation swept him forward toward the edge, and as she whimpered he ejaculated, and sighing she receded. But in her forgiving him and his forgiving her, in her blaming herself and his disagreeing, in their accepting the blame together, their love had exercise and grew larger. Her brown eyes, gazing, each held in miniature the square skylight above him. She apologized, *I'm sorry. I can't quite forget that it's you.*

Who should I be?

Nobody. Just a man. I think of your personality and it throws me off the track.

Does this happen with Ken?

No. Sometimes I come first. We've known each other so long we're rather detached, and just use each other. Anyway, as I guess I've told you, we don't make much love since I've gotten big.

That seems strange. You're lovely this way. Your skin is glossy, even your shape seems right. I can't imagine making love to you with a flat tummy. It wouldn't be you. You'd lack grandeur.

Ken is strange. He wants sex to stay in a compartment. He married me, and that solved the problem, as far as he was concerned. He never wanted me to have a baby. We had enough money, it was just his selfishness. I was never his wife, I was his once-a-week whore for all those years.

I'm jealous.

Don't be. Piet, don't feel bad about my not coming. I feel love too much with you, is the problem.

You're kind, but I honestly fear I'm second-rate at this. Like my skiing and my golf. I began too late.

Horrible man. I hate you when you fish for compliments. As all the ladies must tell you, you're incredible. You're incredibly affectionate.

Any man you took to bed with all his clothes off would be affectionate.

No. At least, I've only known three men, and the other two weren't especially.

Not the Jew? She had told him about the Jew.

He laughed at me. Sometimes he hurt me. But then I had been a virgin and probably he couldn't help hurting me. Probably he wouldn't hurt me now.

Do you want him now?

I have him now. Is that awful to say? I have him in you, and you besides. It's better. He was perverse, Piet.

But you're perverse too.

Her brown eyes childishly widened. *How? You mean*—her fingertips touched her lips, then his penis—*that? But why is that perverse? Don't you like it?*

I love it. It binds us so close, though, I'm frightened.

Are you? I'm glad. I was afraid only I was. Piet. What will the world do to us?

Is it God or the world you care about?

You think of them as different? I think of them as the same.

Maybe that's what I mean when I say you're perverse. Her face so close to his seemed a paradigm, a pattern of all the female faces that had ever been close to him. Her blank brow, her breathing might have belonged to Angela; then Foxy turned her head on the pillow so her pink face took the light from above, the cold blue light of the sky, and was clearly not Angela, was the Whitman woman, the young adulteress.

She was frightened, brazen, timid, wanton, appalled by herself, unrepentant. Adultery lit her from within, like the ashen mantle of a lamp, or as if an entire house of gauzy hangings and partitions were ignited but refused to be consumed and, rather, billowed and glowed, its structure incandescent. That she had courted him; that she was simultaneously proud and careless of her pregnancy; that she would sleep with him; that her father had been an inflexible family-proud minor navy deskman; that her mother had married a laundromat entrepreneur; that by both birth and marriage she was above him in the social scale; that she would take his blood-stuffed prick into the floral surfaces of her mouth; that there had been a Jew she had refound in him; that her mind in the midst of love's throes could be as dry and straight-seeking as a man's; that her fabric was delicate and fragile and burned with another life; that she was his slave; that he was her hired man; that she was frightened—compared to these shifting and luminous transparencies, Angela was a lump, a barrier, a boarded door. Her ignorance of the affair, though all the other couples guessed it, was the core of her maddening opacity. She did not share what had become the central issue of their lives. She was maimed, mute; and in the eggshell-painted rooms of their graceful colonial house she blundered and rasped against Piet's taut nerves. He was so full of Foxy, so pregnant with her body and body scents and her cries and remorses and retreats and fragrant returnings, so full of their love, that his mind felt like thin ice. He begged Angela to guess, and her refusal seemed willful, and his gratitude to her for permitting herself to be deceived turned, as his secret churned in sealed darkness, to a rage that would burst forth irrationally.

"Wake up!"

She had been sitting reading a book in lamplight, and blinked. Her eyes, lifted from the bright page, could not see him. "I am awake."

"You're *not*. You're drifting through life in a trance. Don't you feel what's happening to us?"

"I feel you getting meaner every day."

Bruised moths bumped and clung to the lampshade above her shoulder. "I'm upset," he said.

"What about?"

"About everything. About that pinchy-mouthed gouger Gallagher. About the crappy ranch houses on the hill. About Jazinski: he thinks I'm a drunk. About the Whitman job. I'm losing my shirt for the bastard and he isn't even grateful."

"I thought you enjoyed it, tripping down there every day to visit the little princess."

He laughed gratefully. "Is that what you think of her?"

"I think she's young. I also think she's arrogant. I think she'll be mellowed eventually, I think having a baby will do her good. I don't think she needs your paternal attentions especially."

"Why do you think my attentions are paternal?"

"Whatever they are. Can I go back to my book? I don't find Foxy Whitman or this conversation that interesting."

"God, you are smug. You are so fantastically above it all you stink."

"Listen, I promise I'll make love to you tonight, just let me get to the end of this chapter."

"Finish the fucking book for all I care. Stuff it. Give yourself a real literary thrill."

She heard the appeal in his violence and tried to lift her head, but the hooked print held her gaze. Absent-mindedly she asked, "Can't you relax ten minutes? I have five more pages."

He jumped to his feet, strode two steps to the mirror above the telephone, strode back. "I need to go out. I need a party. I wonder what the Applesmiths are doing. Or the Saltines."

"It's eleven o'clock. Please hush."

"I'm dying. I'm a thirty-four-year-old fly-by-night contractor. I have no sons, my wife snubs me, my employees despise me, my friends are all my wife's friends, I'm an orphan, a pariah."

"You're a caged animal."

"Yes." He took an aggressive stance, presenting himself before her with fists on hips, a bouncy close-set red-haired man whose rolled-up shirtsleeves revealed forearms dipped in freckles. "But Angel, who made the cage, huh? Who? *Who?*"

He meant her to fling him open and discover his secret, to be awed and enchanted by it, to decipher and nurture with him its intricate life. But, enclosed in the alternative world—a world exotic yet strict, mixing a lover's shamelessness and a father's compassion—arising from her lap, she did not respond. The book was an old college text, little appreciated at the time, stained by girlish annotations and translucent blots of the oil she and her roommates had used under their sunlamp, the Modern Library edition of *The Interpretation of Dreams*.

Janet Appleby had confessed to Angela on the beach that she was seeing a psychiatrist. Angela explained it to Piet: "It's just twice a week, for therapy, as opposed to real analysis. Frank's all for it, though it was her idea. She described coming home about three a.m. from the little-Smiths after a terrible scene with Marcia and suddenly knowing that she needed help, help from somebody who isn't a friend or a lover or has any reason to care about her at all. She's only been a few times but already she's convinced she doesn't know why she does what she does. She never loved Harold, so why did she go to bed with him? She told herself it was because she felt sorry for him but he didn't feel sorry for himself especially so who was she kidding? And why now, even though they've all stopped sleeping with each other, or at least she and Harold have, can't they stay away from the other couple every weekend? She says now they've somehow acquired the Thornes, too, especially Freddy—"

"That jerk," Piet said.

"—and it's a real mess. Onion rings and gin. The Thornes never go home, apparently. Georgene just sits and drinks, which she never used to do, and Freddy writes an endless pornographic play on his knee."

"So Janet has to go to a psychiatrist because Georgene drinks?"

"Of course not. Because she thinks she, Janet, is neurotic."

"Define neurotic."

Janet had a variety of bikinis and semi-bikinis and Piet pictured her making her confession while lying belly down on the sand, her top untied to give her back an unbroken ·tan, her cheek pillowed on a folded towel, her breasts showing white when she lifted up on her elbows to explain better or to survey her children.

Angela said, "You know what neurotic is. You do things you know not why. You sleep with women when you're really trying to murder your mother."

"Suppose your mother's already been murdered?"

"Then maybe you're trying to bring her back to life. The ego tries to mediate between external reality and the id, which is our appetites. The ego carries all this bad news back and forth, but the id refuses to listen, and keeps trying to do whatever it wanted to do, even though the ego has turned its back. I don't explain it very well, because I don't understand it, but dreams are a way of letting out these suppressions, which mostly have to do with sex, which mostly has to do with your parents, who have become a superego and keep tormenting the ego from the *other* side. You know all this, everybody does."

"Well, do you see anything unnatural about Janet sleeping with Harold now and then? Frank can be a real boor; would you like to go to bed with him for the rest of your life, night after night?"

"It's not a question of natural or unnatural or right or wrong. It's understanding why you do things so you can stop doing them. Or enjoy doing them. Certainly Janet does not make herself happy. I don't think she enjoys her children very much, or sex, or even her money. She could be great, you know. She has everything."

"But it's just those people who are unhappy. The people with everything are the ones who panic. The rest of us are too busy scrambling."

"Piet, that's a very primitive attitude. You're saying the rich can't get through the needle's eye. The first shall be last."

"Don't poke fun of the Bible. What's your stake in all this hocus-pocus with egos and ids? Why are you so defensive? I suppose you want to go to a psychiatrist too."

"Yes."

"The hell you will. Not as long as you're my wife."

"Oh? You're thinking of getting another wife."

"Of course not. But it's very insulting. It implies I don't give you enough sex."

"There is no such implication."

"I give you more than you want."

"Exactly. Maybe a psychiatrist could tell me why I don't want more. I do and I don't. I hate myself the way I am. It's doing awful things to both of us."

Piet was taken aback; he had inwardly assumed that Angela knew best, that the amount of sex she permitted was the proper amount, and the surplus was his own problem, his own fault. He asked her, "You don't think our sex life is right?"

"It's awful. Dreadful. You know that."

He tried to pin this estimate down. "How would you rate it on a scale of one to ten?"

"Two."

"Oh come *on*, it's not *that* bad. You can be gorgeous."

"But so rarely. And I don't use my hands or mouth or anything. I'm sick. I need help, Piet. I'm turning you into a bully and a cheat and myself into one of those old maids everybody says you wouldn't believe how beautiful she once was." Blue-eyed, she began to cry. When she cried, it made her face look fat, like Nancy's. Piet was touched. They were in the kitchen, she with vermouth and he with gin-and-Bitter-Lemon, after putting the girls to bed. Against the tiny red florets of the kitchen wallpaper Angela's head, nicely oval, with summer braids and bun, did have a noble neatness that was maidenly. He then realized that in a sociable way she was preparing him for another night without lovemaking. Confessing her frigidity sanctioned it.

He protested, "But everybody loves you. Any man in town would love to go to bed with you. Even Eddie Constantine flirts with you. Even John Ong adores you, if you could understand him."

"I know. But I don't en*joy* knowing it. I don't want to go to bed with *any*body. I don't feel I'm a woman really. I'm a kind of cheerful neuter with this sex appeal tacked on as a kind of joke."

"My poor Angel. Like having Kick Me on your back."

"Exactly. I really thought, listening to Janet, how much we're alike. A lot of coziness and being nice to creeps and this disgusted emptiness at heart. We both come from good families and have big bottoms and try to be witty and get pushed around. Do you know she keeps sleeping pills by her bed and some nights doesn't bother to count how many she takes?"

"Well you don't do that."

"But I could. It sounded very familiar, the way she described it. I love sleep, just delicious nothing sleep. I'd love not to wake up."

"Angela! That's sinful."

"The big difference between Janet and me is, I repress and she tries to express. No?"

"Don't ask *me*."

"I'm sure you've had an affair with her and know just what I mean. Tell me about us, Piet."

"You are a scandalous wife. I have never slept with Janet."

"In a way, I want you to. In a Lesbian way. I felt very drawn, lying beside her on the beach. I think I must be Sapphic. I'd love to have a girls' school, where we'd all wear chitons and play field hockey and sit around listening to poetry after warm baths."

"If you have it all analyzed, you don't need an analyst."

"I don't. I'm just guessing. He'd probably say the reverse was true. I can't stand being touched by other women, for instance. Carol Constantine is always patting, and so does Bea. He might say I'm *too* heterosexual, for America the way it is now. Why did nobody marry me, for example, until you came along? I must have frightened them away."

"Or your father frightened them away."

"Do you want to know something else sick? Can you take it?"

"I'll try."

"I masturbate."

"Sweetie. When?"

"More in the summer than in the winter. I wake up some mornings between four and five, when the birds are just beginning, or a trailer truck goes by on the road, and the sheets feel terribly sensitive on my skin, and I do it to myself."

"That sounds pretty normal. Do you imagine anybody, any particular man?"

"Not very clearly. It's mostly sensation. You're the only man

I've ever known, so if I picture anyone it's you. Now why don't I wake the real you up?"

"You're too considerate and shy."

"Oh balls, Piet. Just balls."

"You must stop talking to Freddy Thorne at parties. Your language is deteriorating."

"*I'm* deteriorating. I don't know how to act in this sexpot."

"Sexpot?"

"Tarbox."

"A sexpot is a person, not a place."

"This one's a place. Get me out or get me to a doctor."

"Don't be silly. The town is like every other town in the country. What you're saying is you're too good for this world. You're too fucking good for any of us."

"Don't raise your voice. I hate that high voice you put on."

"Of course you hate it, you're supposed to hate it. You hate me, why not hate my voice?"

"I don't hate you."

"You must, because I'm beginning to hate you."

"Ah. Now you're saying it."

"Well, I don't quite mean it. You're gorgeous. But you're *so* self-centered. You have no idea what I'm like inside—"

"You mean you're having an affair and you want me to guess the woman?"

"No I don't mean that."

"Foxy Whitman."

"Don't be grotesque. She's pregnant and adores her icy husband and gives me a professional pain in the neck besides."

"Of course—but why do I imagine it? I know it's neurotic but every time you go down there and come back so affectionate to me and the children I think you've been sleeping with her. I watch her face and feel she has a secret. She's so tender and gay talking to me. She knows me all too well, they've only been in town since March."

"She likes you. Maybe she's a Lesbian too."

"And it's not just Foxy, it can be Janet or Marcia or even Georgene—I'm madly jealous. And the more jealous I get the less

I can bring myself to make love to you. It's sad. It's miserable. Your telephone was busy for half an hour yesterday and I made myself a martini at eleven in the morning, imagining it was some woman."

Her oval face yearned to cry some more but a sophisticated mechanism produced a half-laugh instead. Painfully Piet looked toward the floor, at her bare feet; neither of her little toes touched the linoleum. His dear poor blind betrayed Angel: by what right had he torn her from her omnipotent father? Each afternoon, an hour before quitting, old man Hamilton would walk down his lawn between his tabletop hedges, trailing pipesmoke, bringing a quart bottle of Heineken's and Dixie cups for the workmen. Piet told her, "I don't have Appleby's money. I can't afford it."

She asked, "Isn't there some way I can earn it? I could go into Boston this fall and get enough education credits to teach at least at a private school. Nancy will be away all day in the first grade; I must do *some*thing with my time. I can begin therapy, just twice a week, with the education courses. Oh, Piet, I'll be a wonderful wife; I'll know *every*thing."

It grieved Piet to see her beg, to see her plan ahead. She was considering herself as useful, still useful to him, exploring herself bravely toward a new exploitation when to him she was exhausted, a stale labyrinth whose turnings must be negotiated to reach fresh air and Foxy. Foxy asleep, moonlight lying light along her bones and diagonally stroking the down of her brow: at this vision his stomach slipped, his skin moistened, numbness stung his fingertips and tongue. There was a silver path beneath the stars. Obliviously Angela barred his way. "No," broke from him, panicked as he felt time sliding, houses, trees, lifetimes dumped like rubble, chances lost, nebulae turning, *"no;* sweetie, don't you see what you're doing to me? Let me *go!"*

At his high voice her face paled; its eager flush and the offer of its eyes withdrew. "Very well," she said, "go. What are you going to, may I ask?"

Piet opened his mouth to tell her, but the ice shelling his secret held.

Angela diffidently turned her back. "Your routines," she told him, "are getting less and less funny."

"Daddy, wake up! Jackie Kenneny's baby died because it was born too tiny!"

Nancy's face was a moon risen on the horizon of his sleep. Her eyes were greatly clear, skyey in astonishment. Red tear ducts the tone of a chicken's wattle. Slaughter. The premature Kennedy had been near death for two days. Nancy must have heard the news over television. "I'm sorry," he said. His voice was thick, stuffed and cracked. August was Piet's hay-fever season. Strange, he thought, how pain seeks that couple out. Not wealth nor beauty nor homage shelters them. Suffering tugging at a king's robe. Our fragile gods.

"Daddy?"

"Mm."

"Was the baby scared?" Fear, a scent penetrating as cat musk, radiated through the flannel perfume of her infant skin. He had been dreaming. His brother. His brother frozen under glass, a Pope's remains, Piet apologetic about not having stayed and helped him, been his partner, in the greenhouse. *Is het koud, Joop?* Frozen by overwork, gathering edelweiss. He turned and explained, to the others, *Mijn broeder is dood.* Yet also Foxy was in the dream, though not visibly; her presence, like the onflow of grace, like a buried stream singing from well to well, ran beneath the skin of dreaming as beneath reality, a living fragility continually threatened.

"The baby was too little to be scared. The baby never knew anything, Nancy. It had no mind yet."

"He wants his mommy!" Nancy said, stamping her foot. "He cries and he cries and nobody listens. Everybody is *happy* he hurt hisself."

"Nobody is happy," Piet told her, returning his cheek to the pillow, knowing the child was right, nobody listens. The window against whose panes his upheld hand was silhouetted at night as a monstrous many-horned shape now, at dawn, gave on the plain sweet green of leaves, heart-shaped lilac and feathery, distant elm. Space, it seemed, redeems. Piet reached outwards and pulled Nancy toward him, into the mediating warmth that remained of his sleep. She fought his embrace, feeling its attempt to dissolve and smother the problem. Her wide face studied him angrily, cheated. Freckles small as flyspecks had come to her nose this summer, though they had thought she had inherited her mother's oily brunette skin. Angela's serene form pricked by his own uneasy nature. Flecks of lead in the condensed blue smoke of her irises. Sea creatures. Vague light becomes form becomes thought becomes soul and dies. The retina retains nothing. Piet asked, "Where's Mommy?"

"Up. Get up, Daddy."

"Go talk to Mommy about the Kennedy baby while Daddy gets dressed." Last night he had attempted to make love and though Angela had refused him he had slept nude. He did not wish his body to frighten the child. "Go downstairs," he said. "Daddy feels funny."

"Are you drunk?" She had learned the word and felt threatened by it; once Frank Appleby had crawled into her playpen and shattered a plastic floating duck, and the next day they had explained to her that he had been drunk.

"No. I *was* drunk, and now I wish I hadn't been. My head hurts. I feel sad about the Kennedy baby."

"Mommy said I would never die until I was an old old lady wearing earrings."

"That's absolutely right."

But— It was unspoken. Impatiently needing to urinate, he threw back the covers; his body filled her eyes and they overflowed into tears. He said, "But the little baby was even smaller than you?"

She nodded helplessly.

Piet kneeled and hugged her and recognized in his arms the mute tepid timbre he had often struck from Angela's larger form. He said urgently, "But the baby came out too soon, it was a mistake, God never meant it to live, like a big strong chubby girl like you." His nakedness in air, the stir of her skin in his arms, was gently leading his penis to lift. A cleft or shaft of sun.

Nancy pulled from his arms and shouted from the head of the stairs, "God should have teached the baby not to come out!"

Angela called, "Piet, are you up?"

"Be down in three minutes," he answered. He half dressed and shaved and finished dressing. Today was to be a deskwork day. From the bedroom windows his square lawn looked parched. A droughty summer. Prevailing winds shifting. Icecaps melting. The great forests thinning. On Indian Hill clouds of dust coated the constructions, seeped into the unfinished frames cluttered by leaning plywood and loose electric cable. Here and there in the woods a starved maple turning early. The crickets louder at night. But from Foxy Whitman's windows the marshes, needing no rain, sucking water from the mother sea, spread lush and young, green as spring and carved like plush by the salt creeks' windings. Some afternoons, the tide high, the marshes were all but submerged, and Piet felt the earth reaching for the moon. Atlantis. Ararat.

The narrow farmhouse stairs descended through two landings and stopped a step from the front door, in a hall so cramped the opening door banged the newel post. On Piet's right, in a living room which the crowding lilacs left rather dark and where like sentinels in castellar gloom the empty glasses used last night by the little-Smiths and Saltzes and Guerins were still posted on arms and edges of furniture, Nancy and Ruth were watching television. A British postal official, relayed by satellite, supercilious and blurred, was discussing yesterday's seven-million-dollar robbery of a London mail train, the biggest haul in history—"not counting, of course, raids and confiscations which should properly be termed political acts, if you follow me. As far as we can determine, there was nothing political about these chaps." Television brought them the outer world. The little screen's icy brilliance implied a universe of profound cold beyond the warm encirclement of Tarbox, friends, and family. Mirrors established in New York and Los Angeles observed the uninhabitable surface between them and beamed reports that bathed the children's faces in a poisonous, flickering blue. This poison was their national life. Not since Korea had Piet cared about news. News happened to other people.

On his left, in the already sun-flooded kitchen, Angela laid out breakfast plates on four rectangular mats. Dish, glass, spoon, knife. Her nipples darkly tapped her nightie from within. Her hair was down, swung in sun as she moved, blithe. She seemed to Piet to be growing ever more beautiful, to be receding from him into abstract realms of beauty.

He said to her, "Poor Nancy. She's all shook up."

Angela said, "She asked me if the Kennedy baby was up in Heaven with the hamster going round and round in the wheel. Honestly I wonder, Piet, if religion's worth it, if it wouldn't be healthier to tell them the truth, we go into the ground and don't know anything and come back as grass."

"And are eaten by cows. I don't know why all you stoics think death is so damn healthy. Next thing you'll get into a warm bath with your wrists slit to prove it."

"Oh, you do like that idea."

Nancy came into the kitchen sobbing. "Ruthie says—Ruthie says—"

Ruth followed, flouncing. "I said God is retarded." She sneered at Nancy, *"Baaby."*

"Ruth!" Angela said.

"Retarded?" Piet asked. It was an adjective her generation applied to everything uncooperative. *The retarded teacher kept us all after class. This retarded pen won't write. Frankie is a re-tard.*

"Well He is," Ruth said. "He lets little babies die and He makes cats eat birds and all that stuff. I don't want to sing in the choir next fall."

"I'm sure that'll make God shape up," Piet said.

"I don't see why the child should be forced to sing in the choir every Sunday," Angela told him, standing bent as Nancy cried into her lap. Her hair overhung the child. Mothering. Seeking the smothering she had fled from in Piet. Loves her more than me. Each to each. Symbiosis.

"For the same fucking reason," Piet told Angela, "that I must spend my life surrounded by complaining females." He ate breakfast surrounded by wounded silence. He felt nevertheless he had done a good deed, had rescued Nancy from the grip of death.

Better anger than fear. Better kill than be killed.

He drove to the office, rattling down Charity, parking on
Hope. A space today, lately often not. Talk of the need for a
stoplight at the corner where Divinity turned. Confusing to out-
of-towners. Too many cars. Too many people. Homosexuality
the answer? The pill. Gallagher was talking on his phone, Irish
accent emergent. "We've got thirty-three rooms, Sister, and removing a lone partition would give us a grand refectory." Piet
heated water on their electric coil and made instant coffee. Max-
well. Faraday. He settled at his desk to concentrate on deskwork.
Lumber $769.82, total, overdue, if has escaped your previous
notice please remit, since a sound credit rating, etc. His nasal
passages itched and his eyes watered. Another scratchy August
day. Foxy far. Hours away. Her laughter, her fur. *To visit the
little princess. Too pretty-pretty for you.* His own phone rang.

"Allo, dollink." It had been a month since they had talked.

"Hello." He used his flat contractor's voice.

"Are you surrounded? Is Matt there?"

"No. Yes." They had recently installed in their crowded space
a corrugated-glass divider (ASG mfg., 1" thickness overall)
which set Gallagher apart and made him appear, subtly, the head
of the office. But the partition was thin and without a client in his
cubbyhole Gallagher kept the door open, to create a breeze. He
needed a breeze, or his shirt would wrinkle. He had walled
himself in without a window. In there with him were an electric
clock, a Ford-agency calendar, a colored zoning map of Tarbox,
an aerial photograph of the downtown and beach area, an overall
map of Plymouth County, a Mandarin-orange street directory of
Tarbox, the pale-blue annual town reports back to 1958, a thin
red textbook entitled *Property Valuation*, a thumbed fat squat
black missal. While Piet worked, when he did, at a yellow oak
desk salvaged from a high school and littered with molding samples and manufacturers' catalogs, Gallagher's desk was military
gray steel and clean except for a pen set socketed in polished
serpentine, a blotter, framed photographs of Terry and Tommy,
and two telephones. Behind his head hung framed his license
from the Board of Registration of Real Estate Brokers and Sales-

men. He had just purchased for their firm the fifty-odd acres and
the thirty-odd rooms of an estate in Lacetown with iron deer on
the lawn. He had intended to develop the grounds piecemeal but
had since got wind of an order of nuns who were seeking to
relocate a novitiate. As he exultantly told Piet, the Church doesn't
haggle. In the meantime their tiny office supported among its
debts a hundred-thousand-dollar mortgage; it felt precarious. But
gambling was Gallagher's meat, and having dared the deal increased the amount of psychic space he occupied. Piet feared
Georgene's voice was coming through too strong; he huddled the
receiver tight against his ear.

"Don't worry, I'll hang up in a minute," she said. "I just had a
crazy impulse to call and find out how you were doing. Is that
presumptuous? I still have some rights, don't I? I mean you and
me, we *were* something real, weren't we?

"I understand you," Piet said.

"You can't really talk, can you?"

"That sounds correct."

"Well, if you'd call me once in a while this wouldn't happen.
We hear you had a little party last night and I felt very hurt we
weren't invited. The way Irene let it slip out was positively
malicious."

"The orders," Piet said uncertainly, "are slow coming through
this time of year. The government's buying up a lot of west-coast
fir."

"Piet, I miss you so much, it's killing me. Couldn't you just
come for coffee on your way to somewhere else sometime? Like
this morning? It's perfectly safe. Whitney's off at camp and Irene
took Martha and Judy down to the beach. I told her I had a
plumber coming. It's true, our pressure's down to nothing. Don't
ever live on a hill. Can't you come, please? Just to talk a *little*
bit? I promise I won't be pushy. I was *such* a bitch at the Ongs'."

"The estimate looks discouraging."

"I'm *mis*erable, Piet. I can't stand living with that man much
longer. He gets worse and worse. I'm losing all sense of myself as
a woman."

"I thought he did good work."

Georgene laughed, a brisk, slightly formal noise. "I'm sure Matt isn't fooled at all. The games you two play down there. No, if you must know, he does lousy work. Freddy's lousy in bed, that's what you want to hear, isn't it? That's what you always wanted to hear. I lied to you. I protected him. He can't manage anything until he's drunk and then he's sloppy and falls asleep. He wilts. Do you understand what I'm saying?"

"We're speaking of upright supports."

"It's *so* sad. It makes me so *ashamed*. I have no self-confidence at anything any more, Terry and I lost six-two, six-three to Bernadette and Angela yesterday, I suppose she told you, crowing about it."

"No."

"*Please* come over. I'm *so* blue, so *blue*. I won't pry, I promise. I know you have somebody else but I don't care any more. Was I ever that demanding? Was I? Didn't I just take you as you came?"

"Yes." Gallagher loudly rustled papers and tapped shut a steel desk drawer.

"God, I hate the sound of my voice. I hate it, Piet. I hate to beg. It's taken me weeks to bring myself to make this call. You don't have to go to bed with me, I promise. I just need to have you to myself for half an hour. For fifteen minutes."

"We're behind schedule now, I'm afraid."

"Come, or I'll tell Freddy about us. I'll tell Freddy and Angela everything. No. Forget Angela. I'll tell Foxy. I'll waltz right down there and plump myself down and tell her the kind of bastard she's mixed herself up with."

"Let me call you back. I'll look at my schedule again."

She began to cry; Georgene's crying, rare, was an unlovely and unintelligent sound, and Piet feared it would fill the little office as it filled his skull. "I didn't know," she sobbed, "I'd miss you this much, I didn't know . . . you were into me . . . so deep. You knew. You knew just what you were doing to me, you bastard, you marvelous poor bastard. You're making me suffer because your parents were killed. Piet, I didn't kill your parents. I was in Philadelphia when it happened, I didn't know them, I didn't

know you . . . oh, forgive me, I have no idea what I'm saying . . ."

"In the meantime," Piet said, "watch out for seepage," and
hung up.

There was an inquisitive silence behind him. He responded,
"Bea Guerin. She thinks her house might be settling. She doesn't
trust those cedar posts I put in because we used metal in the
Whitman renovation. I think she's hysterical. It's too bad, all she
needs is a baby. Which reminds me, Matt, something I wanted
your opinion on. Angela thinks she needs to go to a psychiatrist."

As Piet had hoped, the second statement caught Matt's attention; the truth is always more interesting than the lie. "Angela's
the sanest woman I know," Matt said.

"Ah, Matt," Piet answered, "in this fallen world, being sane and
being well aren't the same thing." Gallagher uncomfortably
frowned; it was part of his Catholicism to believe that all theolog-
ical references in private conversation must be facetious. Piet had
developed with Gallagher a kidding pose, a blarneyish tone, useful in both acknowledging and somewhat bridging the widening
gap between them. Gradually they were finding each other impossible. Without an act, a routine, Piet would hardly have been
able to talk to Gallagher at all. "And surely she's no saner than
Terry," he said.

"Terry. She's gone gaga over the lute. She's in Norwell twice
a week and now she wants to take pottery lessons from the
woman's husband."

"Terry is very creative."

"I suppose. She won't play for *me*. I don't know how to treat
Terry these days."

Piet abruptly volunteered, "Actually, what Angela needs is a
lover, not a psychiatrist."

Matt's brittle face, his jaw so smooth-shaven it seemed bur-
nished, hardened at this; his mouth tightened. He felt in Piet's
train of association possible news for himself. Yet he was curious;
he was human, Freddy Thorne would have pointed out. He
asked, "You'd let her?"

"Well, I'd expect her out of decency to try to conceal it. I'd simply not pry. If it came into the open, I'd of course have to be sore."

They were talking through the doorway; Matt was framed by corrugated glass. The office was so small there was no need to raise their voices. Matt said, "Piet, if I may say so—"

"You may, my good fellow. An honest man's the noblest work of God."

"You seem quite jealous of her. Terry and I have always been struck by you two as a couple, how protective and fond you are of each other, while pretending the opposite."

"Do we pretend the opposite?" Piet was offended, but Matt was too intent to notice.

"Terry and I," he said, "don't have your room for maneuver. Fidelity can't be a question. Do you know that, in the view of the Church, marriage is a sacrament administered by the couple themselves?"

"Maybe some of the sacrament should be giving the other some freedom. Why all this fuss about bodies?" Piet asked. "In fifty years we'll all be grass. You know what would seem like a sacrament to me? Angela and another man screwing and me standing above them sprinkling rose petals on his back." Piet held up his hand and rubbed thumb and forefinger. "Sprinkling blessings on his hairy back."

Gallagher said, "Mother and father."

"Whose?"

"Yours. As you described that I pictured a child beside his parents' bed. He loves his mother but knows he can't handle her so he lets the old man do the banging while he does the blessing."

Again offended, Piet said, "Everybody's so damn psychoanalytical all of a sudden. Let me ask you something. Suppose you discovered Terry wasn't going off for music lessons."

"I'd refuse to discover it," Gallagher answered with catechetical swiftness, and smiled. The smiles of the Irish never fail to strike a spark; they have the bite in their eyes of the long oppressed. The flint of irony. He told Piet, "You have a kind of freedom I don't have. You can be an adventurer where I can't. I have to have my adventures here." He laid his hand flat on the steel desk. His hand was hair-backed. Big pores. Coarse dogma.

Piet said, "And they make me damn nervous. What the hell are we going to do with that rotten old castle in Lacetown? That partition you were telling the sister about can't just be knocked out. It's weight-bearing."

Matt told him, "You shouldn't be in this business, you're too conservative. You don't have the nerves for it. What you got to realize, Piet, is that land can't lose. There's only so much of it, and there are more and more people."

"Thanks to the Pope."

"You have more children than I do."

"I don't know how you do it, it's a miracle."

"Self-control. Try it."

This was Piet's day to fight. That Gallagher, with his wife off with some old potter, felt able to deliver instruction so angered Piet that he rose from his creaky swivel chair and said, "Which reminds me, I better get over to the hill and see if they're using wood on the houses or cardboard like you tell them to."

Matt's face was a crystal widening toward the points of the jaws, his shaved cheeks and flat temples facets. He said, "And check on Mrs. Whitman while you're at it."

"Thanks for reminding me. I will."

Stepping outdoors onto treeless Hope Street, Piet was struck by the summer light so hard that his eyes winced and the world looked liquid. It was all, he saw, television aerials and curbstone grits, abortive—friendships, marriages, conversations, all aborted, all blasted by seeking the light too soon.

On Indian Hill the three ranch houses had reached a dismal state of incompletion. The frames, sheathed in four-by-eight sheets of plywood, were complete but the rooms within were waiting for electricians and plumbers and plasterers. Cedar shingles lay on the damp earth in costly unbroken stacks. Jazinski was watching two trade-school boys nail shingles and Piet was annoyed by his idle supervision. He told him, "Get a hammer," and spent the morning beside him, aligning and nailing cedar shingles over insulating foil. The cedar had an ancient fragrance; the method of aligning the shingles, by snapping a string rubbed with chalk, was agreeably primitive. Sun baked Piet's shoulders and steamed worry from him. It was good to work, to make weatherproof, to fashion overlapping fishscales. He was Noah; the skinny-armed young Polack swinging his hammer in unison beside him perhaps was a son. Piet tried to converse with Leon, but between hammer blows the boy responded with pronouncements that, sullen yet definite, were complete in themselves, and led nowhere.

On the death of the Kennedy baby: "That crowd has everything but luck. Old Joe can't buy them luck." On the Catholic religion: "I believe in some kind of Supreme Being but none of the rest of it. My wife agrees, I was surprised." On the progress of the job: "It's waiting on the plumbers now. I guess two have been already sold. The families want to move in by the start of school. Do you want to give the plumbers a ring, or shall I?" On the colored Construction King operator, whom Piet remembered fondly, for having shown him cheerfulness on a day of death: "I feel this way about it. If they measure up they should be treated like everybody else. That don't mean I want to live next door to them." On the future: "I may not be here next summer. I'm looking around. I have responsibilities to myself."

"Well, Leon, maybe next summer I won't be here, and you can be me."

The boy said nothing, and Piet, glancing over, wondered how his arms could remain so stringy and pale, like those of a deskworker, though he worked all summer in the sun.

In the rhythmic silence Piet began to talk with Foxy in his head. He would take her a flower from the roadside—a stalk of chicory, with flowers as blue as the eyes of a nymphomaniac. *For me?*

Who else?

You're so tender. When you're not with me I remember the passion but I forget the affection.

He would laugh. *How could I not be affectionate?*

Other men could. I guess. I've not had much experience.

You've had enough, I'd say.

What can you see in me? I'm getting huge, and I never come for you, and I'm not good, or witty, like Angela.

I find you quite witty.

Should we go up to bed?

Just for a moment. To rest.

Yes. To rest.

I love your maternity clothes. The way they billow and float. I love the way your belly is so hard and pushes at me. In another month it'll start kicking.

Do you really like me this way? Look, I'm getting veins in my legs.

Beautiful blue. Blue blond furry rosy Foxy.

Oh Piet. Take these awful Paisley things off. I want to kiss you.

As you like.

Leonine he would lie back. Eyelids lowered, her dusty-rose cheek dented by the forcing apart of her jaws, her sleeping face would eclipse that gnarled choked part of him a Calvinist whisper by his cradle had taught him to consider vile. Touch of teeth like glints of light. Her fluttered tongue and lips' encirclement. Her hair spun air between his lifted thighs, nipples and fingernails, muddled echoes of blood. He would seek the light with one thrust and she would gag; penitent he would beg *Come up* and her tranced drained face swim to his and her cold limp lips as he kissed them wear a moony melted stale smell whose vileness she had taken into herself. All innocent they would lock loins, her belly gleaming great upon his, and though short of breath and self-forsaken she would not quite come; this had happened and would happen again that summer of the solar eclipse.

Three weeks ago, it had been ninety per cent at their latitude. An invisible eater moved through the sun's disc amid a struggle of witnessing clouds. The dapples of light beneath the elm became crescent-shaped; the birds sang as in the evening. Seen through smoked glass the sun was a shaving, a sideways eyebrow, a kindergarten boat riding a tumult of contorted cumulus. The false dusk reversed; the horns of the crescents beneath the trees pointed in the opposite direction; the birds sang to greet the day. Not a month before, he had first slept with Foxy.

Only one other time had been so ominous: the Wednesday in

October of 1962 when Kennedy had faced Khrushchev over Cuba. Piet had had a golf date with Roger Guerin. They agreed not to cancel. "As good a way to go as any," Roger had said over the phone. Stern occasions suited him. As Piet drove north to the course, the Bay View, he heard on the radio that the first Russian ship was approaching the blockade. They teed off into an utterly clear afternoon and between shots glanced at the sky for the Russian bombers. Chicago and Detroit would go first and probably there would be shouts from the clubhouse when the bulletins began coming in. There was almost nobody else on the course. It felt like the great rolling green deck of a ship, sunshine glinting on the turning foliage. As Americans they had enjoyed their nation's luxurious ride and now they shared the privilege of going down with her. Roger, with his tight angry swing, concentrating with knit brows on every shot, finished the day under ninety. Piet had played less well. He had been too happy. He played best, swung easiest, with a hangover or a cold. He had been distracted by the heavensent glisten of things—of fairway grass and fallen leaves and leaning flags—seen against the onyx immanence of death, against the vivid transparence of the sky in which planes might materialize. Swinging, he gave thanks that, a month earlier, he had ceased to be faithful to Angela and had slept with Georgene. It had been a going from indoors to outdoors; they met at beaches, on porches, beneath translucent trees. Happy remembering her, picturing her straight limbs, Piet sprayed shots, three-putted, played each hole on the edge of an imaginary cliff. Driving home, he heard on the car radio that the Russians had submitted to inspection and been allowed to pass. He had felt dismay, knowing that they must go on, all of them, Georgene and Angela and Freddy and himself, toward an untangling less involuntary and fateful. He had been fresh in love then.

Leon said: "That sun is brutal. I like winter myself. My wife and I thought we'd try skiing this year."

Noon passed, and one. The connective skin between thumb and palm, where the hammer rubbed, smarted as if to blister. Piet left Leon and drove into town, through town, on down the beach road. Dusty flowers, chicory and goldenrod, a stand of late daisies, flickered at the roadside, but he was in too much of a hurry to stop. *I wanted to bring you a flower but it seemed too urgent so I just brought you myself.*

Of course. What a nice present.

Her house was empty. No Plymouth station wagon, no workman's truck, was in the driveway. The door was unlocked. The hall rug awry. Cotton slept in the blue sling chair. The work was nearly done, the plastering completed even to the sweeping up. A round thermostat and square light switch on the smooth wall side by side. Rough edges. Books of wallpaper samples lay face up on the sanded and sealed floor. A folder of paint shades was propped against a pine baseboard. In the kitchen all that was needed was white paint and for the dishwasher on order to arrive. Sawdust and earth smells still lived in the house. Salt air would wipe them away. She had promised to invite Piet and Angela down when the house was finished. The wallpaper books were open to samples that were not Angela's taste. Big pastel splashes. Vulgar passion.

Where was she? She never shopped at this hour, her nap hour. Had he only dreamed of possessing her? The tide was low and the channels seen from the kitchen windows were ribbons glittering deep between banks of velvet clay. Three red deer were bounding across the dry marsh to the uninhabited shrub island. The days to hunting season were finite. The crystalline sky showed streaks of cirrus wispy at one end, like the marks of skates braking. Miscarriage. Doctors, workmen returning. Without her here he felt the house hostile, the walls of their own will rejecting him. Too soon, too soon. He became anxious to leave and, driving back toward town, turned on an impulse up the Thornes' long driveway.

The Saltzes and the Constantines, maliciously called the Saltines by the other couples, had jointly bought a boat, the Applebys' catboat, with a six-horsepower motor, and after a Saturday or Sunday of sailing would drink beer and California sauterne in their damp bathing suits and have other couples over. The Sunday night before Labor Day a crowd collected in the Constantines' messy Victorian manse. The couples were excited and wearied by tennis; this was the weekend of the North Mather Court Club Open Tournament. Annually the North Mather men, rangy automobile salesmen and insurance claims agents who exerted themselves all winter long on two domed courts grassed with plastic fiber, easily eliminated even the best of the Tarbox men, such as Matt Gallagher; but, contrariwise, the North Mather wives wilted under the assault of their Tarbox counterparts. Invariably Georgene and Angela, Terry and Bernadette dominated the female finals, and for weeks before Labor Day their telephones jangled as the men of North Mather, centaurs in search of Amazons, beseeched the fabulous Tarbox women to be their partners in mixed doubles.

None of the Saltines played. A delicate social line had early hardened and not been crossed. Instead, today they had taken Freddy Thorne, who played terribly, out into the Bay for skin diving. It amused him to keep his wetsuit on. His appearance in the tight shiny skin of black rubber was disturbingly androgynous: he was revealed to have hips soft as a woman's and with the obscene delicacy of a hydra's predatory petals his long hands flitted bare from his sleeves' flexible carapace. This curvaceous rubber man had arisen from another element. Like a giant monocle his Cyclopean snorkeling mask jutted from his naked skull, and his spatulate foot flippers flopped grotesquely on the Constantines' threadbare Oriental rugs. When he sat in a doilied armchair and, twiddling a cigarette, jauntily crossed his legs, the effect was so outrageous and droll, monstrous and regal that even Piet Hanema laughed, feeling in Freddy's act life's bad dreams subdued.

"Read us your play," Carol Constantine begged him. She wore a man's shirt over an orange bikini. Something had nerved her up tonight; a week ago, she had dyed her hair orange. "Let's all take parts."

All summer it had been rumored that Freddy was writing a pornographic play. Now he pretended not to understand. "What play?" he asked. Beneath the misted snorkel mask he missed his customary spectacles. His eyes were blind and furry; his lipless mouth bent in upon itself in a pleased yet baffled way.

"Freddy, I've *seen* it," Janet Appleby said. "I've seen the cast of characters."

With the dignity of a senile monarch Freddy slowly stared toward her. "Who are you? Oh, I know. You're Jan-jan Applesauce. I didn't recognize you out of context. Where are your little friends?"

"They're in Maine, thank God."

"Don't be your usual shitty self, Freddy," Carol said, sitting on the arm of the chair and draping her gaunt arms around his rubber shoulders. The action tugged open her shirt. Piet, sitting cross-legged on the floor, saw her navel: a thick-lidded eye. Carol caressed Freddy's air hose, hung loose around his neck. "We want to do your play," she insisted.

"We can make a movie of it," Eddie Constantine said. He flew in spells; he had been home three days. His growth of beard suggested a commando, cruel and sleepless. He held a beer can in each hand. Seeing his wife draped across Freddy, he had forgotten who he was fetching them for, his vacant eyes the tone of the same aluminum. Abruptly, as if tossing a grenade, he handed a can to Ben Saltz, who sat in the corner.

"I want to be the one who answers the door," Carol said. "Don't all dirty movies begin with a woman answering the door?"

Ben sat staring, his dark eyes moist with disquiet. He had recently shaved, and looked enfeebled, slack-chinned, mockingly costumed in sailing clothes—a boat-neck jersey, a windbreaker, a white officer's cap, and suntans cut down to make shorts, fringed with loose threads. Ben's calves were heavily, mournfully hairy. Piet glimpsed himself in that old-fashioned male shagginess but his own body hair was reddish, lighter, gayer, springy. Ben's lank hairs ran together to make black seams, like sores downrunning into the tops of his comically new topsiders, cup-soled, spandy-bright. Except for his sunburned nose, Ben's skin was pasty and nauseated. He had pockmarks. His wounded love of Carol weighed on the air of the room and gave the couples an agitated importance, like children in safe from a thunderstorm.

"What's a dirty movie?" Freddy asked, blinking, pretending to be confused.

"*Tom Jones*," Terry Gallagher said.

Angela rose up unexpectedly and said, "Come on Carol, let's undress him. I know he has the play in his pocket."

"You think he takes it underwater with him?" Piet asked mildly, exchanging with Foxy a quizzical look over Angela's uncharacteristic display of flirtatious energy. They had become, these two, the parents of their spouses, whose faults they forgave and whose helplessness they cherished from the omniscient height of their adultery.

Foxy had come to the party without Ken, but with Terry Gallagher. Ken and Matt, having been easily beaten in North Mather, had played consolation singles together all afternoon on the Ongs' court. The two men, uncomfortable among the couples, were comfortable with each other. Foxy and Terry shared tallness and an elusive quality of reluctance, of faintly forbidding enchantment, reflected, perhaps, from their similar husbands. But Foxy was Snow White and Terry Rose Red—something Celtic strummed her full lips, her musical hands, the big muscles knitting her hips to her thighs. She stood tall and joined in the rape, asking Janet, "Where are his pants? You told me he always carries it in his pants."

"Upstairs," Carol said brokenly, wrestling with Freddy's flailing arms, struggling to undo his jacket's rusty snaps. "In Kevin's room. Don't wake him up."

Janet, who had been in therapy two months now, watched the struggle and pronounced, "This is childish."

Angela tried to pin Freddy's ankles as he slid from the chair. One of his flippers kicked over a tabouret holding a crammed ashtray and a small vase of asters. Angela brushed up the ashes and butts with two copies of *Art News,* Eddie carefully poured beer over Freddy's head, and Ben Saltz sat dazed by the sight of Carol, her hair a color no hair in nature ever was, writhing nearly nude in the man's black embrace. The rubber of his suit squeaked as her bare skin slid across his lap. Her shirt had ridden up to her armpits; her orange top twisted, and a slim breast flipped free. Crouching on the carpet, Carol quickly readjusted herself, but kneeled a while panting, daring to look nowhere. All these people had seen her nipple. It had been orangish.

In the front parlor, reached through a doorway hung with a

beaded curtain, Irene Saltz's voice was saying, "I can't believe you know what you're saying. Frank, I *know* you, and I *know* that you're a human being." She was drunk.

His voice responded, heated and pained. "It's *you* who want to keep them down, to give them on a platter everything everybody else in this country has had to work for."

"Work! What honest work have you ever done?"

Janet Appleby shouted toward them, "He's worked himself into an ulcer, Irene. Come on in here and take your husband home, he looks sick."

The Constantines' house was large, but much of its space was consumed by magniloquent oak stairways and wide halls and cavernous closets, so that no single room was big enough to hold a party, which then overflowed into several, creating problems of traffic and acoustics. Janet was not heard, but Frank's voice came to them from the parlor clearly. "The federal government was never meant to be a big mama every crybaby could run to. Minimal government was the founders' ideal. States' rights. Individual rights."

Irene's voice in argument was slurred and even affectionate. "Frank, suppose you were Mrs. Medgar Evers. Would you want to cry or not?"

"Ask any intelligent Negro what the welfare check has done to his race. They hate it. It castrates. I agree with Malcolm X."

"You're not answering me, Frank. What about Medgar Evers? What about the six Birmingham Sunday-school children?"

"They should have the protection of the law like everybody else, like everybody else," Frank said, "no more and no less. I don't approve of discriminatory legislation and that's what the Massachusetts Fair Housing Bill is. It deprives the homeowner of his right to chose. The constitution, my dear Irene, tries to guarantee equality of *opportunity*, not equality of status."

Irene said, "Status and opportunity are inseparable."

"Can't we shut them up?" Eddie Constantine asked.

"It's sex for Irene," Carol told him, standing and buttoning her shirt. "Irene loves arguing with right-wing men. She thinks they have bigger pricks."

Janet's lips opened but, eyes flicking from Carol to Freddy to

Ben, she said nothing. Self-knowledge was turning her into a watcher, a hesitater.

Terry Gallagher came down the Constantines' grand staircase holding a single often-folded sheet of paper. "It's nothing," she said. "It's not even begun. It's a cast of characters. Freddy, you're a fake."

Freddy protested, "But they're beautiful characters."

Amid laughter and beer and white wine, through the odors of brine and tennis sweat, the play was passed around. It bore no title. The writing, beginning at the top as a careful ornamental print, degenerated into Freddy's formless hand, with no decided slant and a tendency for the terminal strokes to swing down depressively.

DRAMATIS PERSONÆ

Eric Shun, *hero*
Ora Fiss, *heroine*

Cunny Lingus, *a tricksome Irish lass*
Testy Cull, *a cranky old discard*

Anna L. Violation ⎫
Ona Nism   ⎬ *nymphs*
Labia Minoris   ⎭

Auntie Climax, *a rich and meaningful relation*

ACT I

Eric *(entering):* !
Ora *(entered):* O!

"That's not fair," Janet said. "Nobody is really called Ora or Ona."

"Maybe the problem," Piet said, "is that Eric enters too soon."

"I was saving Auntie Climax for the third act," Freddy said.

Terry said, "I'm so glad Matt isn't here."

Foxy said, "Ken loves word games."

"Good job, Freddy," Eddie Constantine said. "I'll buy it." He clapped Ben Saltz on the back and held the paper in front of Ben's eyes. Ben's face had become white, whiter than his wife's sun-sensitive skin. Foxy went and, awkwardly pregnant, knelt beside him, tent-shaped, whispering.

Piet was busy improvising. The crude energy the others loved in him had been summoned. "We need more plot," he said. "Maybe Ora Fiss should have a half-brother, P. Niss. Peter Niss. They did filthy things in the cradle together, and now he's returned from overseas."

"From Titty City," Eddie said. He was of all the men the least educated, the least removed in mentality from elementary school. Yet he had lifted and hurled thousands of lives safely across the continent. They accepted him.

Janet said, "You're all fantastically disgusting. What infuriates me, I'm going to have to waste a whole twenty-dollar session on this grotesque evening."

"Leave," Carol told her.

Piet was continuing, gesturing expansively, red hair spinning from his broad arms. "Ora is frightened by his return. Will the old magic still be there? Dear God, pray not! She takes one look. Alas! It is. 'Ora!' he ejaculates. 'Mrs. Nism now,' she responds coldly, yet trembling within."

"You're mixing up my beautiful characters," Freddy complained.

"Let's play some new game," Carol said; she squatted down to gather the residue of the spilled ashes. Her slim breasts swung loose in Piet's eyes. Welcome to Titty, somber city of unmockable suckableness: his heart surged forward and swamped Carol as she squatted. Love for her licked the serial bumps of her diapered crotch. Her bare feet, long-toed, stank like razor clams. Her painted hair downhung sticking drifting to her mouth. She stood, ashes and aster petals in her lily palm, and glared toward the corner where, beneath a Miró print, Foxy was ministering with words to the immobilized Ben Saltz.

"Let's not," Freddy Thorne said to her. "It's good. It's good for people to act out their fantasies."

Angela leaped up, warm with wine, calling Freddy's bluff, and announced, "I want to take off all my clothes!"

"Good, good," Freddy said, nodding calmly. He stubbed out his cigarette on his own forehead, on the Cyclopean glass mask. It sizzled. His wise old woman's face with its inbent lips streamed with sweat.

Piet asked him, "Shouldn't you take that outfit off? Don't you eventually die if the skin can't breathe?"

"It's me. Piet baby, this suit *is* my skin. I'm a monster from the deep."

Angela's hand had halted halfway down the zipper at the back of her pleated white tennis dress. "No one is watching," she said. Piet touched her hand and redid the zipper, which made a quick kissing sound.

"Let her go, it's good," Freddy said. "She wants to share the glory. I've always wanted to see Angela undressed."

"She's beautiful," Piet told him.

"Jesu, I don't doubt it for a sec. Let her strip. She wants to, you don't understand your own wife. She's an exhibitionist. She's not this shy violet you think you're stuck with."

"He's sick," Foxy told Carol, of Ben, in self-defense.

"Maybe," Carol said, "he'd like to be left alone."

"He says you all gave him lobster and rum for supper."

Ben groaned. "Don't mention." Piet recognized a maneuvering for attention, an economical use of misery. But Ben would play the game, Piet saw, too hard in his desire to succeed, and the game would end by playing him. The Jew's fierce face was waxen: dead Esau. Where his beard had been it was doubly pale.

"Shellfish," Eddie explained to all of them. "Not kosher."

Carol said sharply, "Foxy, let him sit it out. He can go upstairs to a bed if he has to."

"Does he know where the beds are?" Freddy asked.

"Freddy, why don't you put that mask over your mouth?" Carol's skin was shivering as if each nerve were irritated. The holiday eve was turning chilly and the furnace had been shut off for the summer. Her lips were forced apart over clenched teeth like a child's after swimming and, touched and needing to touch her, Piet asked, "Why are you being such a bitch tonight?"

"Because Braque just died." Her walls were full of paintings, classic prints and her own humorless mediocre canvases, coarse in their coloring, modishly broad in their brushwork, showing her children on chairs, the Tarbox wharf and boatyard, Eddie in a turtleneck shirt, the graceless back view of the Congregational Church, houses, and trees seen from her studio windows and made garish, unreal, petulant. Cézanne and John Marin, Utrillo and Ben Shahn—her styles muddled theirs, and Piet thought how provincial, how mediocre and lost we all are.

Carol sensed that he thought this and turned on him. "There's something I've been meaning to ask you for a long time, Piet, and now I've had just enough wine to do it. Why do you build such ugly houses? You're clever enough, you wouldn't have to."

His eyes sought Foxy's seeking his. She would know that, hurt, he would seek her eyes. Their glances met, locked, burned, unlocked. He answered Carol, "They're not ugly. They're just ordinary."

"They're hideous. I think what you're doing to Indian Hill is a disgrace."

She had, slim Carol, deliberately formed around her a ring of astonishment. For one of their unspoken rules was that professions were not criticized; one's job was a pact with the meaningless world beyond the ring of couples.

Terry Gallagher said, "He builds what he and Matt think people want to buy."

Freddy said, "I *like* Piet's houses. They have a Dutch something, a fittingness. They remind me of teeth. Don't laugh, everybody, I mean it. Piet and I are spiritual brothers. I put silver in my cavities, he puts people in his. Jesus, you try to be serious in this crowd, everybody laughs."

Angela said, "Carol, you're absurd."

Piet said, "No, she's right. I hate my houses. God, I hate them."

Janet Appleby said, "Somebody else died last month. A poet, Marcia was very upset. She said he was America's greatest, and not that old."

"Frost died last January," Terry said.

"*Not* Frost. A German name. *Oh*. Marcia and Harold would know it. None of us *know* anything."

"I thought you'd start to miss them," Freddy said to her.

Janet, sitting on the floor, sleepily rested her head on a hassock. She had switched from twice-a-week therapy to analysis, and drove into Brookline at seven-thirty every weekday morning. It was rumored that Frank had commenced therapy. "We need a new game," she said.

"Freddy, let's play Impressions," Terry said.

"Let's think up more names for my play," he said. "They don't have to be dirty." He squinted blindly into space, and came up with, "Donovan U. Era."

"You had that prepared," Janet said. "But Harold the other night did think of a good one. What was it, Frank?" With a rattle of wooden beads, the couple had returned from the political parlor. Frank looked sheepish, Irene's eyebrows and lips seemed heavily inked.

"León MacDouffe," Frank pronounced, glancing toward Janet, wanting to go home.

Carol said, in the tone of a greatly removed observer, "Irene, your husband looks less and less well. I think he should go upstairs but nobody else has bothered to agree. It makes no difference to me but we can't afford to have our rug ruined."

Irene's expression as she studied Ben was strange. Maternal concern had become impatient and offended. Delilah gazed upon the Samson she had shorn. In the room's center Eddie Constantine, a small effective man without religion or second thoughts, wiry and tanned and neatly muscled, vied in his health for her attention; a beer can glinted in his hand and his gray eyes could find the path through boiling Himalayas of cloud. As he gazed at her it dawned on the room that she was worth destroying for. Though pale and heavy, she had a dove's breasted grace. Irene asked, "Why can't he go upstairs in his own house a few doors away?"

"I'll take him," Eddie said and, going and thrusting his head under Ben's arm, expertly hoisted him up from the chair.

The sudden motion, like a loud noise to the sleeping, led Ben's conversational faculty to roll over. "I'm very interested in this," he said distinctly. "What should the aesthetics of modern housing be? Should there be any beyond utility and cost?"

Gleefully Freddy Thorne chimed in, "Did the peasants who put up thatched huts worry about aesthetics? Yet now we all love the Christ out of thatched huts."

"Exactly," Ben said. He sounded like himself, and was reasoning well, but the sounds floated from his ghostly mouth at half-speed. "But perhaps a more oral and sacramental culture has an instinctive sense of beauty that capitalism with its assembly-line method of operation destroys. *Commentary* this month has a fascinating—"

"Greed," Carol said vehemently, "modern houses stink of greed, greed and shame and plumbing. Why should the bathroom be a dirty secret? We all do it. I'd as soon take a crap in front of all of you as not."

"Carol!" Angela said. "That's even more wonderful than my wanting to take off my clothes."

"Let's play Wonderful," Freddy Thorne announced, adding, "I'm dying in this fucking suit. Can't I take it off?"

"Wear it," Piet told him. "It's you."

Foxy asked, "How do you play Wonderful?"

"You," Freddy told her, "you don't even have to try."

Terry asked, "Is it at all like Impressions?"

Ben said, his weight full on Eddie now, his colorless face turned to the floor, "I'd like to discuss this seriously some time. Super-cities, for example, and the desalinization of seawater. I think the construction industry in this country is badly missing the boat."

"Toot, toot," Eddie said, pulling on an imaginary whistle cord and hauling Ben toward the doorway.

Irene asked, "Shall I come along?" Her expression was again indecisive. To be with her husband was to be with her lover. The romantic Semitic shadowiness of her lower lids contended with pragmatic points in her eyes and lips seeking their good opinion, these heirs of the Puritans.

Eddie looked at her acutely, estimated her ripeness, chose his path, and said decisively, "Yes. I'll get him over there and you put him to bed." So all three made exodus from the musty room, through the huge space-wasting hallway smelling in all weathers of old umbrellas, into the leaf-crowded night splashed by blue streetlamps.

Carol swung her arms, relieved and seething. The Applebys exchanged solicitous confidences—Frank's stomach, Janet's head—and also left, reluctantly; their manner of leaving suggested that this was an end, an end to this summer of many games, that they were conscious of entering now an autumn of responsibilities, of sobered mutuality and duty. Only Freddy Thorne begged them not to go. He had peeled himself out of his skin-diving suit and stood revealed in a soaked T-shirt and crumpled bathing trunks. The skin of his legs and arms had been softened and creased by long enclosure like a washerwoman's palms. The Applebys' leaving left Freddy and Piet alone with many women.

Foxy rose, stately in yards of ivory linen, seven months gone, and said, "I should go too."

"Sweetheart, you can't," Freddy told her. "We're going to play Wonderful."

Foxy glanced at Piet's face and he knew that whatever was written there she would read, *Don't go*. He said, "Don't go."

Terry asked Freddy, "How do you play?" Piet pictured Gallagher, grim as a mother, waiting up for her, and wondered how she dare not go, dare sit there serene. Women have no conscience. Never their fault. The serpent beguiled me.

Freddy licked his lips, then answered weakly, "Each of us names the most wonderful thing he or she can think of. Carol, where's the fucking furnace? I'm freezing."

She fetched from another room an Afghan blanket; he wrapped it around himself like a shawl. "Freddy," she said, "you're getting old."

"Thank you. Now please sit down and stop swishing, Carollino. Eddie and Irene are just putting Ben to bed. They'll be back in a minute. And what if they aren't? The world won't stop grinding. Imagine Eddie's off on a flight to Miami. *Che sarà, sarà*, I keep telling everybody."

"Explain," Terry said, "the point of Wonderful."

"The point is, Terrycloth, at the end of the game we'll all know each other better."

Angela said, "I don't *want* to know any of you better."

Foxy said, "I don't want any of you to know *me* better."

Piet asked, "Where's the competitive element? How can you win or lose?"

Freddy answered Piet with oracular care. He still wore the giant monocle and was drunk, drunker than anyone except Angela, white-wine-drunk, a translucent warm drunkenness whose truth lifts the mind. "You can't lose, Piet. I'd think you'd like that for a change. You know, Peterkins—may I speak my heart?—"

"Oh do, brother, do!" Piet holy-rolled on the floor. "Say it, brother, say it!"

Freddy spoke solemnly, trying to be precise. "You are a paradox. You're a funny fellow. A long time ago, when I was a little boy studying my mommy and my daddy, I decided there are two kinds of people in the world: A, those who fuck, and, B, those who get fucked. Now the funny thing about you, Petrov, is you think you're A but you're really B."

"And the funny thing about you," Piet said, "is you're really neither."

Before he began sleeping with Foxy, when Freddy, however unknowingly, held Georgene as hostage, Piet would not have been so quick to answer, so defiant. Freddy blinked, baffled by feeling Piet free, and more openly an enemy.

"If you two prima donnas," Terry said, "would stop being hateful to each other, we could play Wonderful."

"I think more wine would be wonderful," Carol said. "Who else?"

"Me," Angela said, extending a shapely arm and an empty glass. "I must face Georgene in the finals tomorrow."

"Where *is* Georgene?" Piet asked Freddy politely, afraid he had overstepped a moment before, saying "neither."

"Resting up for the big match," Freddy answered, apparently forgiving.

"We really must go soon," Foxy said to Terry.

"Us too," Piet told Angela. In her rare moods of liberation she held for him the danger that she would disclose great riches within herself, showing him the depths of loss frozen over by their marriage.

Carol poured from the Almadén jug, making of it a dancer's routine. Six glasses were refilled. "OK," Freddy said. "Carol has begun by saying that more wine is wonderful."

"I didn't say it was the most wonderful thing I could think of. I still have my turn."

"All reet-o, take it. You're the hostess; begin."

"Must I start?"

All agreed yes, she must, she must. As Carol stood barefoot in silence, Angela asked of the air, "Isn't this exciting?"

Carol decided, "A baby's fingernails."

Gasps, *ah*, awed, then parodies of gasps, *aaah*, greeted this.

Freddy had provided himself with a pencil and wrote on a small piece of paper, the back of his folded play. "A baby's fingernails. Very well. Please explain."

"I must explain?"

"Well. I mean the whole process, all the chemistry. I don't understand it, which may be why it seems wonderful. You know," she went on, speaking to Foxy, who alone of the women did not absolutely know, "the way it produces out of nothing, no matter almost what we do, smoke or drink or fall downstairs, even when we don't want it, this living *baby*, with perfect little fingernails. I mean," she went on, having scanned all their faces and guessed she was not giving enough, "what a lot of *work*, somehow, ingenuity, *love* even, goes into making each one of us, no matter what a lousy job we make of it afterwards."

Piet said, "Carol, how sweet you are. How can anyone so sweet hate me and my nice little houses?" He felt she had taken the opportunity to repair her image; she was aware of having appeared a hennaed bitch and, deserted by the Saltzes and her husband, needed love from those left around her, and perhaps especially from him, who like her had been born lower in the middle class than these others.

She said, "I *don't* hate you. On the contrary, I think you have too much to give people to waste it the way you do."

After a mild silence Angela said, "I can't tell if that's an insult or a come-on."

"We have a baby's fingernails," Freddy Thorne said. "Who's next?"

"Let's have a man," Terry Gallagher said.

Piet felt singled out, touched, by her saying this. Let's. She reposed on the floor, a tall woman, legs bent under her broadened haunches and the knit of her hips. Her lips held a coin. Her dark hair's harp-curve hung down. Once he loved her, too shy then to know they are waiting. Vessels shaped before they are filled. He drank more of the wine of a whiteness like that of the sun seen through fog, a perfect circle smaller than the moon. The eclipse. Love doomed? Foxy was watching him sip, her pink face framed by pale hair fluffed wide by seabathing. Sometimes her belly tasted of salt. Bright drum taut as the curve of the ocean above the massed watchsprings of blond hair. Her navel inverted. Their lovemaking lunar, revolving frictionless around the planet of her womb. The crescent bits of ass his tongue could touch below her cunt's petals. Her far-off cries, eclipsed.

"Piet, you go," Angela said.

His mind skimmed the world, cities and fields and steeples and seas, mud and money, cut timbers, sweet shavings, blue hymnals, and the fuzz on a rose. Ass. His mind plunged unresisted into this truth: nothing matters but ass. Nothing is so good. He said, "A sleeping woman." Why sleeping? "Because when she is sleeping," he added, "she becomes all women."

"Piet, you're drunk," Carol said, and he guessed he had spoken too simply from himself, had offended her. The world hates the light.

Freddy's mouth and eyes slitted. "Maybe sleeping," he said, "because awake she threatens you."

"Speak for yourself," Piet said, abruptly bored with this game and wanting to be with his sleeping children; maybe they, Ruth and Nancy, were the women he meant, drenched and heavy with sleep like lumps of Turkish delight drenched in sugar. "A sleeping woman," he insisted.

"Containing a baby's fingernails," Freddy Thorne added. "My, we're certainly very domestic. Horizonwise, that is. Terry?"

She was ready, had been ever since her smile became complacent. "The works of J. S. Bach."

Piet asked jealously, "Arranged for the lute?"

"Arranged for anything. Played anyhow. That's what's so wonderful about Bach. He didn't know how great he was. He was just trying to support his seventeen children with an honest day's work."

"More domesticity," Angela murmured.

"Don't you believe it," Piet told Terry. "He wanted to be great. He was mad to be immortal." In saying this he was still involved with Carol, arguing about his houses, her paintings, apologizing, confessing to despair.

Terry said serenely, "He feels very unself-conscious and— ordinary to me. Full of plain daylight. It's wonderful to have him in your fingers."

"Keep it clean," Freddy said, writing. "The works of J. S. Bach, not necessarily for stringed instruments. Angela."

"I'm about to cry," Angela said, "you're all so sure of what's good. I can't think of anything wonderful enough to name. The children, I suppose, but do I mean *my* children or the fact of having children, which is what Carol already said? Please come back to me, Freddy. Please. I'm not ready."

Foxy said, "The Eucharist. I can't explain."

"Now it's Freddy's turn," Piet said. It had been a double rescue: Foxy Angela, he Foxy. Exposure was, in the games Freddy invented, the danger. The danger and the fruit.

Freddy rested his pencil and with a groping mouth, as if the words were being read from a magic text materializing in air, said, "The most wonderful thing I know is the human capacity for self-deception. It keeps everything else going."

"Only in the human world," Carol interjected. "Which is just a conceited little crust on the real world. Animals don't deceive themselves. Stones don't."

Angela sat up: "Oh! You mean the world is *everything?* Then I say the stars. Of course. The stars."

Surprised, frightened—he seemed to sink in the spaces of her clear face—Piet asked her, "Why?"

She shrugged: "Oh. They're so fixed. So above it all. As if somebody threw a handful of salt and that's how it stays for billions of years. I know they move but not relative to us, we're too small. We die too soon. Also, they *are* beautiful—Vega on a summer night, Sirius in winter. Am I the only person who ever looks at them any more? One of my uncles was an astronomer, on my mother's side, Lansing Gibbs. I think there's an effect named after him—the Gibbs effect. Maybe it's a galaxy. Imagine a galaxy, all those worlds and suns, named after one man. He was very short, some childhood disease, with pointed teeth and bow legs. He liked me, even when I got taller than him. He taught me the first-magnitude stars—Vega, Deneb, Antares, Arcturus . . . I've forgotten some. As a girl I'd lie on the porch of our summer place in Vermont and imagine myself wandering among them, from life to life, forever. They're wonderful."

"Angela," Foxy said. "You're lovely."

"Angela can be lovely," Piet admitted to them all, and sighed. It was past time to go.

"Freddy, tell us about self-deception," Terry said. Freddy looked elderly and absurd, huddled in his shawl. In the slots of his flippers his toenails were hideous: ingrown, gangrenous, twisted toward each other by the daily constriction of shoes.

Freddy told them, "People come to me all the time with teeth past saving, with abscesses they've been telling themselves are neuralgia. The pain has clearly been terrific. They've been going around with it for months, unable to chew or even close their jaws, because subconsciously they don't want to lose a tooth. Losing a tooth means death to people; it's a classic castration symbol. They'd rather have a prick that hurts than no prick at all. They're scared to death of me because I might tell the truth. When they get their dentures, I tell 'em it looks better than ever, and they fall all over me believing it. It's horseshit. You never get your own smile back when you lose your teeth. Imagine the horseshit a doctor handling cancer has to hand out. Jesus, the year I was in med school, I saw skeletons talking about getting better. I saw women without faces putting their hair up in curlers. The funny fact is, you don't get better, and nobody gives a cruddy crap in hell. You're born to get laid and die, and the sooner the better. Carol, you're right about that nifty machine we begin with; the trouble is, it runs only one way. Downhill."

Foxy asked, "Isn't there something we gain? Compassion? Wisdom?"

"If we didn't rot," Freddy said, "who'd need wisdom? Wisdom is what you use to wave the smell away."

"Freddy," Piet said, tenderly, wanting to save something of himself, for he felt Freddy as a vortex sucking them all down with him, "I think you're professionally obsessed with decay. Things grow as well as rot. Life isn't downhill; it has ups and downs. Maybe the last second is up. Imagine being inside the womb—you couldn't imagine this world. Isn't anything's existing wonderfully strange? What impresses me isn't so much human self-deception as human ingenuity in creating unhappiness. We believe in it. Unhappiness is us. From Eden on, we've voted for it. We manufacture misery, and feed ourselves on poison. That doesn't mean the world isn't wonderful."

Freddy said, "Stop fighting it, Piet baby. We're losers. To live is to lose." He passed the sheet of paper over. "Here it is. Here is your wonderful world." The list read:

> Baby's fingernails
> woman (zzzz)
> Bach
> Euch.
> ☆ ☆ ☆
> capac. for self-decep.

Foxy said sharply, "I won't believe it. Everything people have ever built up, Freddy, you'd let slide and fall apart."

"I do my job," he answered. "It's not the job I would have chosen, but every day I put on that white coat and do it."

White coat. The antiseptic truth. He has learned to live in it. I have not. Better man than I. Piet felt himself falling in a frozen ridged abyss, Freddy's mind. Foxy silently held out her hand toward him; Terry turned to him and recited, "Hope isn't something you reason yourself into. It's a virtue, like obedience. It's given. We're free only to accept or reject."

Angela stood and said, "I think we're all pretty much alike, no matter what we think we believe. Husband, I'm drunk. Take me home."

In the hall, with its elephantine scent of umbrellas, Piet playfully poked Freddy in the stomach and said, "Tell Georgene we missed her."

Freddy's response was not playful; his blurred face menacingly bloated beneath the glare of his subaqueous mask. "She chose not to come. You have any message for her?" The cold fact of his knowing seemed to flow across Piet's face.

"No, just give her all our loves," Piet said nimbly, able to skim and dodge at this level, where actions counted, and no submission to death was asked. He doubted that Freddy knew anything. Georgene had wept after sleeping with him again after her long hiatus of innocence, but Piet had tested her strength before and knew she could withstand all pressure of grief, all temptation to confess. Freddy's tone of menace was a bluff, a typical groping gesture in the murk. His element. Piet jabbed again: "Shouldn't you be going home to her now?" Freddy was making no show of leaving with the four others.

"She's asleep," he said. A woman asleep. As ominous as wonderful. Rather than come to a gathering where her lover might be, she had chosen to sleep. Nursing her misery. Piet felt her captive within the murk of this man, her husband, and regretted having visited her again.

Carol had fallen silent, listening for Eddie's return. Now she roused herself to say good night. She and Freddy, both dressed to swim, waved together from the sallowly lit side porch. Down the side street the Saltzes' narrow house was dark but for a bulb left burning at the rear of the downstairs. Tarbox was settled to sleep. The waterfall by the toy factory faintly roared. A car screeched its tires by the rocks at the base of the green. A jet rattled invisibly among the stars. Its sound was a scratch on glass. A final flurry of good nights. Foxy and Terry, limping shadows on the blue September street, went to the Gallaghers' Mercedes. Without glancing backward she twiddled the fingers of her left hand: farewell until I touch you. Angela said softly, "Poor Foxy, why didn't Terry have the sense to take her home hours ago?"

Insulted, Piet asked, "You thought she wanted to go?"

"Of course, she was exhausted. Isn't she due next month?"

"Don't ask me. How should I know?"

"Once in the middle of that endless game—and by the way you and Freddy should *not* work out your private difficulties in front of us ladies; it's *not* that fascinating or delightful—I happened to glance over at her and she looked completely desolated."

"I didn't notice."

"She was so beautiful when she came to this town and we're turning her into a hag."

The shade of the brick pavement under the streetlamps was the purple of wine dregs. Piet noticed a small round bug scurrying along in a crevice: a citizen out late, seen from a steeple. No voice to call him home. Motherless, fatherless. *Onvoldaan.* Too much wine had unfocused the camera of Piet's head; he lifted his eyes and saw beyond the backstop screen his church bulking great, broad and featureless from the rear, a stately hollow blur.

Piet heard about Ben's losing his job from three directions. Angela was told after nursery school, where she had agreed to teach Tuesdays and Fridays, though Nancy now went to the public first grade. Irene herself told her; it came out flat, handed to Angela in a voice like a printed card. "I suppose you've already heard. Ben's changing jobs."

"No! I hadn't heard at all. How exciting! Where is his new job? I hope it won't mean you're leaving Tarbox."

"Well, that part of it is still a bit up in the air. But he has definitely given them his resignation."

"Good for him," Angela said, having been forced into inanity by the constraint of Irene's manner; the impulse of condolence had to be forcefully suppressed. Angela told Piet, "She looked ghastly. Ravished. All of a sudden, you know how pretty she's been looking this summer, she was a weighed-down Jewish middle-aged woman. Her eyes were absolutely black telling me and, you know, *too* steady. Quite hard. I felt she was *bargaining* with me."

"I never knew," Piet said, unable to feign much surprise, for he had already been told the news, "exactly what Ben did anyway."

"He miniaturized, sweetie. For the space program. It was secret exactly what." She was setting out the places for the girls' supper; she was at her most companionable while making meals. They themselves were to have dinner at the Guerins tonight.

"I meant," Piet said, "how good was he at it? Was he just a technician, or was his work more theoretical?"

"He loves theory in conversation."

"Which makes me wonder. From what Irene used to imply, the whole Mariner Venus probe belonged to Ben. At the least he was in the same league with John Ong. Now it turns out his company can can him virtually the minute the poor bastard wanders from the straight and narrow."

"Oh, you think the Saltine business had something to do with it?"

"Obviously. Everything to do with it. The Constantines ran him ragged. Neither one of them ever sleeps and Eddie only flies forty hours a month, by regulation. Even Irene was letting slip that Ben was missing the early train." Piet was putting forward as conjecture what Georgene had passed on to him as fact, as reported by Freddy.

"I can't believe it was that bad."

"You're so *god*dam innocent, Angel. You can't believe that anybody has more sexual energy than you. These four would stay up all night swapping off. Carol loves having two men at the same time; before Ben she was sleeping with that kid Eddie used to bring to basketball."

"How do you know all this?"

He said quickly, "Everybody knows it."

Angela thought, pausing in ladling chicken soup into two chaste bowls. "But would she *take* both at once?—I mean, is there

room? And where would it happen? In her studio, with all those
messy tubes of paint? What would Irene do while this acrobatic
act was going on?" Her blue eyes flickered with the attempted
vision; Piet was pleased to see her interested. But he could not
locate, among all the males they knew, the man with whom he
would share her. Thorne was too awful, and Whitman too pure.

The next Tuesday, Angela came back from nursery school late,
the sky of her eyes scintillating, and said, "You were right. It was
the Constantines. Irene took me home for a cup of tea, only it
turned out to be bourbon, and told me everything. She's extremely bitter about it. She refuses to see the Constantines at all,
though Carol keeps coming over and wants to talk it out. Irene
admits it was partly her fault, and Ben should have known enough
to control it himself, but she says it was just terribly exciting for
them, they had always been so serious about everything, and had
never really been close friends with another couple before. She
and Ben just thought it was *wonderful*, the way the Constantines
lived by a wholly different philosophy, and were always so relaxed and game for everything, and ate whenever it occurred to
them, and would stay up all night if they felt like it. She says, to
give them credit, that Carol and Eddie can be terribly charming,
and in a way they're not to blame, it's how they are, amoral. In a
way, she says, she's even grateful for the summer, it was an
experience she's glad she's had, even though it nearly wrecked her
marriage and they apparently are really strapped for money now.
She admitted she lied to me about changing jobs. Ben has no other
job."

"Of course not. Did she go into the mechanics of it at all? I
mean, what was the effect on Ben so bad they had to fire him?"

"She didn't really, except to admit he wasn't merely late, some
days evidently he wouldn't go in at all, especially after they got
the boat, when they'd go for these long all-day cruises. Once they
actually made it to Provincetown, can you imagine, in this old
catboat made for playing around the marshes in. Irene said she
was terrified half the time, but Eddie apparently is a very clever
sailor. I love the picture—Irene in that huge floppy purple hat
and long-sleeved blouse, and Ben fighting seasickness all the way.
Like two owls and two pussycats in a beautiful pea-green boat.

To Provincetown! My father and uncle used to take a crew of six, and even then the children weren't allowed along. And of course Ben doesn't really have any stomach for alcohol either, so even when he did go in to work he'd be too sick to work often, and he doesn't have a private office, just a glass cubicle, so there was no hiding it."

"What about the sex? Did she go into that?"

"She got very cagey, and I didn't want to press her; I felt so flattered and bewildered by it all, just sitting there and getting this torrent. I wonder why she decided to tell *me*?"

"You're our town conscience. Everybody must placate you."

"Don't be sarcastic. She did imply it wasn't what I may have heard from other sources. She said that Eddie could be very appealing—as if she had felt this appeal but hadn't of course succumbed. If you've succumbed, it's no longer an appeal, is it?"

"You're the expert," Piet told her. He was offended by how fully vicarious experience seemed to satisfy her.

"The evenings they all spent together she described as being all *talk*. Freddy Thorne and sometimes Terry were there. She went out of her way, I thought, to let me know that the night she and Eddie put Ben to bed and all the lights in their house looked out she and Eddie were really in the kitchen talking about Ben's job; even by then he had gotten a pretty drastic warning."

"But no sex. Booze and boats undid him."

"Irene didn't precisely *say*, but the suggestion was certainly *not*. She even—I was dumbfounded, it coming from Irene—called Carol a cockteaser. As if she *should* have gone to bed with Ben, and didn't, or didn't often enough, I don't know. It's pretty messy and sad. When you think of the children especially. Most of it apparently happened at the Constantines' house because it was easier for the Saltzes to leave Bernard, who stays up forever reading anyway, to sit for his brother, but after midnight Irene would sometimes feel guilty enough to go home, leaving Ben talking with Eddie. They would talk everything—space, computers, public versus private schools, religion. Eddie is so lapsed he begins to scream whenever he thinks at all about the Church."

"And then Carol would lay them both."

"Piet, I don't want to diminish your high estimate of Carol but I really think that's unlikely. Maybe in Okinawa whorehouses, but in somebody's home who we know . . . it's grotesque."

"Love, she's human. She could take one in her mouth."

The sky of Angela's eyes flashed. "That's what you want me to do, isn't it?"

"No, no, no," he said. "Good heavens, no. That's sodomy."

Foxy had a rather different story, Carol's as confided to Terry Gallagher. Terry and Carol shared music; Foxy and Carol once in a while drew together, with one of the exquisite Constantine girls, Laura or Patrice, posing in leotards. "She says," she said, "that the Saltzes just moved in on them. That they were outcasts in the town, and terribly lonely, and when they saw that she and Eddie would accept them, there was just no moderation. That Ben had had a *very* sheltered and old-fashioned upbringing, in a Hebrew ghetto in Brooklyn—"

Piet laughed. "I can just see Carol saying 'Hebrew.' " Foxy was a fair mimic and unconsciously colored her retellings with something of the lilt of the telling. Piet's head lay on her lap, and the heartbeat of her unborn infant was next to his ear.

"—a Hebrew ghetto, and was just *starved* for, well, a little swinging. Carol's point, and she's very convinced about this, is that until the Constantines came to town the Saltzes had been excluded by the 'nice' couples, the Guerins who live just a block away on Prudence Street, and the darling Thornes, and the extremely lovely Applesmiths, and the ever-fashionable Hanemas, not to mention the delightfully up-and-coming Gall—"

"Not true. We always asked Ben to basketball. They don't ski or play tennis, whose fault is that? They were always at large parties. The Dutch are more of a minority in this town than Jews."

"Well, this is what Carol's impression was, presumably from Irene." Absent-mindedly as she talked Foxy was stroking Piet's hair. "Your hair is quite unsmoothable."

"Is it thinning out? Will I get bald like Freddy? Red-haired men do. It's Jehovah's rebuke to our vigor. Don't stop. I am *very* hurt that Irene, whom I've always adored, thought we were all anti-Semitic."

"Well evidently she did. Does. She was furious when the elementary school put Bernard in a Christmas pageant. As Joseph yet. According to Terry, Carol is positive that Irene was the real moving spirit behind the couples' getting together. The Saltzes' marriage has been on the rocks for years. They were staying together because of Bernard, and then Jeremiah was a mistake. Irene had a kind of nervous breakdown over it."

"I remember her as so lovely, pregnant. I do love pregnant women."

"So I see."

"According to Carol according to Terry, what is or was Irene's complaint about Ben?"

"She feels he has no ambition, no drive. Her father came up the hard way in the garment business. Anyway, Piet, who knows why women like some men and don't like others? Chemistry? Carol's story is that Irene took a fancy to Eddie and lit out after him the way she lights into everything—Fair Housing, or the nursery school, or conservation. He became a cause."

"I love the way you say 'cozz.' Honeh chile, ah loves it."

"How do you say it? Cawss. Like the way you say 'haas' for 'house.' "

"OK, I'm an immigrant. Anyway, your description sounds more like Terry than Carol. Carol would say 'She wanted him' or something with the same awesome simplicity and then look daggers. 'She vowed to *have* him.' 'She thenceforth consecrated herself to sharing his pallet.' "

"She wouldn't at all. She'd say, 'The bitch went into heat and got herself screwed.' "

"Oh, my mistress. Your language. Skeerooed."

"Don't jiggle your head like that. You'll induce me."

"It's true, Irene has been promoted by all this to full-fledged bitch status. She used to be somebody you talked to early at cocktail parties to get her out of the way."

"Carol says she and Eddie used to sit after the Saltzes had left and laugh, Irene was being so blatant."

"Then he'd go down the street and laugh out of the other side of his mouth. I love the idea of Eddie Constantine being a worthy project like school integration or the whooping crane. The most worthless man I know. To think we all entrust our lives to him. What did Carol say she and Ben did to combat this assault on the young aviator's virtue?"

"She says she pitied Ben but, frankly, never found him attractive."

"She excluded him. One more Wasp."

"Yes," Foxy said, "she did mention that, that she was the only Wasp in the ménage. Eddie apparently hates Wasps, and is always testing her. Scaring her when he drives the car, and things like that."

"I thought she was a lapsed R.C."

"*He* is. *She* was a Presbyterian." Her fingers had trespassed from his hair to the sensitive terrain of his face, taut planes she explored as if blind. "Furthermore," she said, in a voice whose musical shadows and steeps had become, like the flowing sight of her and her perfumed weight, a body his love inhabited, "furthermore, and stop looking at me like that, she doesn't think what he did with them has anything to do with Ben's losing his job. Carol thinks he was just poor at it, which in a way I can believe, since the times he's talked to Ken—"

"Ken and Ben, they don't know when," Piet said.

"—the times he talked to Ken, after expressing all this interest in biochemistry, and the secret of life and whatnot, Ken says he shows no real comprehension or much interest beyond the superficial sort of thing that appears in *Newsweek*. He's really looking for religious significance, and nothing could bore Ken more. What was his word?—eclectic. Ben has a thoroughly eclectic mind."

"*My* theory is," Piet said, closing his eyes the more keenly to sense Foxy's circumambient presence, her belly beside his ear, her fingers on his brow, her thighs pillowing his skull, "that the Saltzes went into it so Ben could learn about aviation from Eddie and improve his job in the aerospace complex. That once they got into that smelly old house, Carol being a nymphomaniac, she had to get laid, and rather than stand around watching, Eddie gave Irene a bang, and she said to herself, 'What the hell! This is fun!' "

"Well, without everything being spelled out, that's more or less Carol's story too."

"Carol and I, we think alike."

"Oh, don't *say* that!" Foxy urgently begged, touching his lips, recalling them to the incomparable solemnity of their sin.

Angela brought home new refinements of Irene's version. "She took me aside after nursery school almost in tears and said Carol's been spreading around the story that she, Irene, felt ostracized in town because she was Jewish. She wanted me to know this was perfectly untrue, that she and Ben agree they've always been very warmly treated, and they'd be very upset to have their friends think they thought otherwise. She says Carol is *extremely* neurotic, that Kevin is the way he is because of how she's treated him. Whenever she wants to paint she locks him in his room and some mornings he screams so much the neighbors have complained. Irene also said her point about Bernard's being in the Christmas play has been deliberately misunderstood. She never said they shouldn't put on a Christmas pageant; she just thinks to be fair they should have some kind of Hanukkah observance too."

"Yeah," Piet said, "and why not make the kids celebrate Ramadan by not eating their box lunches?"

Angela, who had been considering Irene's cause seriously, from the standpoint of an hereditary liberal, told Piet, "I don't know why you bother to go to church, it seems to do you less and less good."

Georgene threw a lurid borrowed light upon the mystery. Over the phone, she told Piet, "Freddy's been talking to Eddie—"

"Freddy and Eddie, they're always ready," Piet said. Gallagher was off talking to the nuns who were about to buy the mortgaged estate in Lacetown, and Piet was alone in the office.

"Don't interrupt. Eddie told him that Ben late at night used to talk about the work he was doing on these rockets—is there a thing called the Titan?—and the ridiculous waste and backbiting between the different departments and government representatives, and some of the ideas they were working on with solid propellants and self-correcting guidance systems, which I guess Ben helped with, and Eddie was shocked, that Ben would be telling him all this. He thinks if he told *him* he must have told others, and the government got wind of it, and had him released."

"Don't you think Ben would put any spy to sleep that tried to listen to him?"

"Freddy thinks that Eddie might have been the one to turn Ben in. I mean, he *is* in aeronautics, so he would know who to report him to."

"Why would he want to ruin his wife's lover? You think Eddie minds?"

"Of course he minds. That woman has put him through hell. She's insane. She's an utter egotist."

"More hell than vice versa?"

"Oh, much more. Eddie's just a little boy who likes to play with engines."

"Huh. I distrust all little-boy theories of male behavior. They rob us of our sinful dignity."

"Hey. When are you coming to see me again?"

"I just did."

"That was a month ago."

"Time flies."

"God this is humiliating. The hell with you, Piet Hanema."

"What have I done?"

"Nothing. Forget it. Good-bye. I'll see you at parties."

"Wait."

She had hung up.

The next day she called again, imitating a secretary. "I just wanted to report, sir, in regard to our conversation as of yesterday a.m., that two men in suits and hats were seen surveying and then entering the Saltz residence on West Prudence Street, Tarbox."

"Who told you this?"

"A patient of Freddy's told him, very excited. Who would wear hats in Tarbox but FBI agents? Apparently the entire town knows about Ben."

"Do you think he'll be electrocuted like the Greenbergs or traded to Russia for Gary Powers?"

"Ha ha. Ever since you've been sleeping with Foxy you've been high as a kite. You're riding for a fall, Piet. This time I am *not* going to catch you."

"I have not been sleeping with that extremely pregnant and very chaste lady. Hey. I dreamed about you last night."

"Oh. A nice dream?"

"Not bad. It was in a kind of wine cellar. Freddy was running for selectman this fall and you took me down into the cellar to show me the champagne you were going to use if he won. Then down there, surrounded by old wicker furniture, you asked me to smell the new perfume you were wearing behind the ear. You said, very proudly, you had bought it at Cogswell's Drug Store. I put my face deep into your hair and you gently put your arms around me and I realized you wanted to make love and woke up. Somehow you had much longer hair than yours. You had dyed it red."

"It wasn't me at all. You bastard."

"It was, Georgene. You talked just like yourself, in that reedy indifferent voice, about Freddy's chances of winning."

"Come see me, Piet."

"Soon," he promised.

That evening, Angela said, "Irene was almost funny today. She said that Ben with nothing to do keeps entertaining these two young Mormons. They think they're a lost tribe of Israel, so it's really like a family reunion with Ben."

"What Mormons?"

"You must have noticed them walking around town, what do you *do* all day? Two young men with suits and broad-brimmed Western-style hats on. Apparently it's part of every Mormon's life to go out and proselytize some benighted area. That's us. We're Hottentots as far as they're concerned."

"I heard they were FBI men."

"Irene says that's what everybody thinks. She says Carol has been spreading it all around that Ben betrayed government secrets."

"That woman is losing her marbles. Carol."

"I saw her in the A & P today and she couldn't have been sweeter. She said Eddie wants to take me for another ride on his Vespa."

At the center of this storm of gossip, the destroyed man raked leaves, made repairs and painted within his house, took his sons to the beach on clear weekend afternoons. Summer over, the beach was restored to the natives, who ran their dogs along the running surf and tried to raise kites above the sea of dunes. The clouds changed quality, changed from the puffy schooners of hot weather to grayer, longer bodies, with more metal in them. The horse trailers of North Mather stables parked in the Tarbox lot and teen-age girls galloped across the dun-colored flats of low tide. Here one Sunday morning in mid-October, Piet, walking with Ruth—since he had not gone to church today she had not sung in the choir—saw Ben Saltz at a distance, holding little Jeremiah by the hand, stopping with Bernard to examine shells and instructive rubbish in the wrack. Piet wanted to approach Ben, to express fellow-feeling, but he dreaded the man as he dreaded the mortally diseased. His own life felt too precarious to be drawn into proximity with a life that had truly broken through. Angela thought they should have the Saltzes over, just the two couples, for a relaxed dinner. Piet resisted, then consented; but Irene coolly refused. She and Ben had agreed that, since they were not in a financial position to repay hospitality, they would not accept any. By tacit agreement among the other couples the Saltzes were no longer invited to parties, which would have been painful for them and have embarrassed the Constantines. Still Piet yearned to peer into the chasm, to spy out the face of catastrophe. He went out of his way at all hours to drive by their house. The Saltzes' lights went dark early at night; the Constantines' defiantly blazed. They were seeing a lot of the Guerins, the Thornes, and the Gallaghers. In the mornings, the older children—Bernard, Laura—of each household set off to school along parallel paths across the much-traversed green; before evening they returned together, talking more seriously than children should have to.

One windy weekday afternoon Piet, rounding the green in his pick-up truck, saw Ben putting up storm windows. They were stacked, a leaning deck of great glass cards, at the side of the house, and Ben was puzzling over the numbers. Wanting to hail him, yet afraid to slow down and be caught, Piet gave himself only a glimpse; but it was a glimpse, shockingly, of happiness. Ben was letting his beard grow back. His archaic profile as it bent to the Roman numerals chiseled on the upper edges of the storm windows seemed asleep and smiling. His air was of a man who deserved a holiday like any other, who had done something necessary and was now busy surviving, who—Piet's impression was—had touched bottom and found himself at rest, safe.

Piet dreamed, at this same time of his life, that he was in an airplane, a big new jet. The appointments, in beige and aqua, of the immense tubular interior were vivid to his eyes, though he had never ridden in such a plane. Since the army, he had flown rarely; the last time had been two years ago, to visit his brother in Michigan. The plane to Detroit had been a sooty-engined Electra, shivering in flight like an old hound. Now the luxurious plane of his dream was gliding as if motionless through the sky; the backs of heads and hands receded tranquilly down the length of aqua-carpeted aisle. The pilot's voice, too musical and southern to be Eddie Constantine's, jubilantly announced over the loudspeaking system, "I think we've slipped it, folks!" and through his little rubber-sealed porthole Piet saw a wall of gray cloud, tendrilous and writhing, slowly drift backward, revealing blue sky. They had evaded a storm. Then the plane rocked and jerked in the bumpy air currents; it sank flatly through a gap in atmosphere, grabbed for something, missed, slipped, and tilted. The angle of tilt increased; the plane began to plunge. The huge hull rushed toward the earth. The delicately engineered details—the luminous stenciled seat numbers, the chrome rivets holding the tinted head napkins—stayed weirdly static amid the rising scream of the dive. Far down the aisle, a stewardess, her ginger hair in a high stiff coiffure, gripped the seats for support, and the curtains hiding the first-class section billowed. Otherwise there was no acknowledgment of the horror, no outcry. Piet thought, *The waste*. Such ingenious fragility utterly betrayed. The cost. The plane streamed straight down. The liquid in Piet's inner ear surged, froze. He knew there could be no pulling from this dive and awoke in darkness, convinced of his death.

Angela's breathing was moist and regular beside him. Her body tilted the mattress toward the middle. Her honeyish pungent female smell monopolized the warm bed. Vague light limned the ridges of the pleated linen shade of the lamp on the bureau by the window. His house. A trim ship motionless on the swell of the night. He raised his hand from beside his cheek. Its black silhouette showed cornute against the cruciform mullions and blue panes. His hand. He made the fingers twiddle. He was alive. Yet, having faced the full plausibility of his death—the screaming air of the dream had been so willing to swallow him, so voraciously passive—he was unable to reënter the illusion of security that is life's antechamber. Heavy as lead he lay on the thinnest of ice. He began to sweat. A ponderous creeping moisture coated his skin and, like a loose chain dangling from his stomach, nausea, the clumsy adrenal nausea of panic, threatened to wrench him inside out. Nimbly he turned and lay on his back.

He had experienced this panic before. Antidotes existed. Picture snow. Picture a curved tent secure against the rain. Pretend the blankets are shelter. Think of skin. Piet tried to lull himself with bodies of women he knew. Foxy's powdery armpits and petaled cleft simpler than a rose. The freckled boniness below Georgene's throat. Her factual nakedness and feather-cut hair full of gray, dulled his lust to see it, perhaps lovelessness let them come always together. Unlike Angela's ambrosial unsearchable. Carol's lissome waist and nerved-up dancer's legs. Bea Guerin's swarmy drunken breasts, nectar sweat between. The rank elastic crotch of the step-ins of Annabelle Vojt who, though both were virgins, would allow him, in that rain-pattered cavity of a car parked amid nodding weedy hay, to kiss there, and exploringly tongue, applying mind to matter, his face upside-down between her thighs, his broad back aching, crickets trilling, her tranced fingers combing his uncombable hair. Of pious family, in the hamburger heat, the radio down but glowing, she would sometimes wordlessly remove the secret wall of silk, heaving with a motion that disturbed him by being expert her pelvis up free from the car seat and tugging her pants down from behind; to that mute silver flicking and heave, leaping arched from memory like a fish, he held tight a second, then it too, with the other pale bodies, proved too slippery to ride into sleep. He was too agitated to sink. Nerves and atoms whirled and scintillated within him. Hollow-boned like a bird, he would forever hover, retasting the same sourness.

Angela's even breathing broke pace; she turned with a slithering turmoil of sheets, and the stride of her unconscious sighing resumed.

Horribly awake, Piet tried to pray. His up-pouring thoughts touched nothing. An onyx dust of gas above his face. Something once solid had been atomized. *Thou shalt not covet. Whosoever lusteth in his heart.* Pedrick's foolish twisting. A dour desert tribe: Dead Sea. Pots broken by a shepherd boy. Orange dust. One more dismal sect. Mormons. Salt Lake. Hymnals unopened all week stink of moldy paper: unwrapping a fish. Forgive me. Reach down and touch. He had patronized his faith and lost it. God will not be used. Death stretched endless under him. Life a scum, consciousness its scum. Piet lay as a shimmering upon an unfounded mineral imperviousness. His parents were twin flecks of mica squeezed in granite. No light touched them into light. The eternal loss of light: in the plane's plunge, not knowing he was dreaming, honest to his bones, he had phrased it so to himself, like any unchurched commuter whose day takes a bad turn. Why tease God longer? Busy old fellow has widows and orphans to interview, grieving Tehranese, still benighted. Bite down on death. Bite down. No screaming within the plane. All still in falling. Stoic grace learned from movies. Hope of heaven drains the sky. No Hottentot he. Away with the blindfold. Matter mostly nothing, a titter skinning a vacuum. Angela sleeps in the cradle of the stars, her uncle's web. Nothing sacred. Triune like cock and balls: Freddy Thorne. Oh Lord, this steepness of sickness, this sliding. Patient parents thumbing home seeds in peat had planted a tree whose fruit he had fed to women. The voracious despair of women had swallowed God.

From his height of fear Piet saw his life dwindled small, distinct. The three new houses, sold, on Indian Hill as from a helicopter. Now Gallagher wanted acres more, saw himself a developer, a builder of cities. Gallagherville. Terrytown. Hanema Plaza. Angela Place. Maps, prospecti, underground garages, a grateful Commonwealth votes its thanks. Sir Matthew Galleyslave, having given employment to thousands, true prince of the Church, dinner at the White House starring Pablo Casals and Ruby Newman. *And Mr. President, this is my partner.* That flinty Irish smile, stiff-backed, wall-eyed. Jack: *This cunning little fellow? May I pet him?* Another voice, more musical: *Does he bite?*

Feeling his thoughts expand into nonsense, Piet went tense with gratitude, with eager anticipation of sleeping, and snapped wide awake again, his heart churning. He needed to touch something. He could never rise with Gallagher because he needed to touch a tool. Grab the earth. The plane had plunged and he had been without resources, unchurched, unmanned. He needed to touch Foxy, her nipples, her belly, in oblique moonlight. Her head was full of braid and crosses. She believed. She adored his prick. With billowing gauzy width she had flung herself onto him, was his, his woman given to him.

Angela obliviously stirred, faintly moaned. Piet got out of bed and went downstairs for a glass of milk. Whenever he was most lovesick for Foxy, that summer, he would go to the refrigerator, the cool pale box full of illuminated food, and feed something to the void within. He leaned his cheek against the machine's cold cheek and thought of her voice, its southern shadows, its playful dryness, its musical remembrance of his genitals. He spelled her name with the magnetized alphabet the girls played with on the tall blank door. FOXY. PIET L VES FOXY. He scrambled the letters and traveled to bed again through a house whose familiar furniture and wallpaper were runes charged with malevolent magic. Beside Angela, he thought that if he were beside Foxy he could fall asleep on broken glass. Insomnia a failure of alignment. A rumbling truck passed, vanishing.

The weight of this stagnant night. Fear scurried inside him, seeking a place to stop. How Annabelle would spread her legs as if imperiously to seize his entire face in the lips of her young swamp. Foxy's delicately questioning sideways glint: a dry mind that sized him up through veils of rapture. His daughters' anxious great eyes: in a sense what a mercy to die and no longer torment his children with the apparition of their father. The death of another always a secret relief. Tides of life swing up to God for slaughter. Slum clearance. Dearest Lord do shelter Foxy my shyest candleflame from this holocaust Thy breath. Amen. Revolving terror scooped the shell of him thin. A translucent husk emptied of seed, Piet waited to be shattered.

The Chinese knife across the eye. The electric chair dustless in the tiled room. The earthquake that snaps cathedral rafters. The engorged mineral ocean. The knotted silk cord. The commando's piano wire. The crab in the intestine. The chicken bone in the windpipe. The slippery winter road. The misread altimeter. The firing squad crushing out its Spanish cigarettes in the baked clay courtyard, another dull dawn, exhaling philosophically. The boy from Ionia. The limp-limbed infant smothered in his crib. The rotting kidney turning the skin golden. The shotgun blast purging the skull of brains. The massive coronary. The guillotine. The frayed elevator cable. The booming crack and quick collapse of ice: in Michigan on the lakes the fishermen would ride their jalopies to the bottom in the air bubble and with held breaths ascend to the jagged light. The threshing machine. The random shark. Puffy-tongued dehydration. Black-faced asphyxia. Gentle leprosy. Crucifixion. Disembowelment. Fire. Gas in the shower room. The scalper's hurried adze. The torturer's intent watchmaker's face. The pull of the rack. The suck of the sea. The lion's kittenish gnawing. The loose rock, the slipping boot, the dreamlike fall. The anger of kings. The bullet, the bomb, the plague, the wreck, the neglected infection, the mistaken reaction. The splintered windshield. The drunken doctor's blunder shrugged away. The shadow of fragility on the ice, beneath the implacably frozen stars: the muffled collapse, the opaque gasp, the unresisted plunge.

"Angela?" His voice sounded alien, dragged from a distance. "Could you wake up a little and put your arm round me? I've had a nightmare."

She half-woke and half-obeyed, turning toward him but sinking into sleep again on her stomach; her arm tried to reach him but lapsed at her side. He listened for the glinting of the hamster's wheel and instead heard the refrigerator shudder and break into purring.

Dear Piet—

The tide is coming in high and so blue it seems ink. A little boy in a red shirt has been anchored in a rowboat off the island ever since my second cup of coffee. I have been thinking about us and there seems a lot to say until I sit down and try to write it. When we were together yesterday I tried to explain about Ken and me and "coming" but you chose to be haughty and hurt—my lover, don't be. How timid I feel writing that odd word "lover." And ridiculous too. But you must have a name and what else are you of mine?

Ken is my husband. I love him as such. I feel right, is what I tried to say, making love to him. There is no barrier between us except boredom which is not so serious since life is such a daily thing anyway. With you there are many barriers—my guilt of course, a true shyness and fear of seeming inadequate compared with the other women you've had, our fear of being discovered, a sometimes (I suggest) needless impatience and hurry in you, your annoying habit of mocking yourself and waiting to be contradicted, and even your extreme lovingness toward me, which I find sometimes dismaying, let me confess. To all this add the libidinous vagaries of the pregnant state. These barriers are piled high, so my not coming, dear Piet, does not mean I do not go high with you. I go very high. Do not ask me to say more. Do not ask me to deny my pledge to Ken—which I felt at the time and still feel is sacred above and beyond all discomfort and discontent—or try to compete. There is no competition. I do not understand why I have taken you into my life at this time of all times but the place you occupy is one you have created and you must not be insecure in it.

I have brought this letter outside to the sun, me in my under-wear, casually enough, since none of my bathing suits fit. I trust the plumbers not to suddenly arrive. The boy in red has gone away. I don't think he caught anything. Rereading this, it seems so poorly expressed, so self-protective and hedgy, I wonder if I will give it to you. Your sleepy but fond

Foxy

Undated and not always signed, Foxy's letters accumulated in the back of a Gallagher & Hanema office filing cabinet, under the carbon paper, where Gallagher would never look. They were of varying shapes and sizes. Some consisted of as many as four sheets smoothly covered on both sides with a swift upright script. Others, holding a few hurried words, were mere scraps passed wadded into Piet's hand at parties. Orderly, superstitious, Piet saved them all, and fitfully read them through in the numb days following his night of dread. He read them as an insignificant person seeks himself in a fable whose hero is a remote ancestor.

My lover!—

My whole house breathes of you—the smell of planed wood is you, and the salt wind is you, and the rumpled sheets whose scent is sweetest and subtlest—of us—is you. I have been all open windows and blowing curtains and blue view these last hours—so much yours I must write and tell you, though Ken is downstairs waiting to go to the little-Smiths. In a few minutes I will see you. But surrounded by others. Accept this kiss.

Other letters were more expansive and discursive, even didactic. Piet felt in them an itch to shape him, to rectify and justify.

Holy Firecracker Day

My dear lover—

I have gone far down the beach, the public end, past the holiday crowds (Italian grandmothers with aluminum chairs sit-

ting right in the surf, skirts up to their knees and knitting in their laps) to where none of our mutual friends might ambush me. It is curiously different down here, cliffy and pebbly, and windier and the water choppier than the sheltered stretch where our lovely Tarbox matrons and their offspring dabble. Lacetown lighthouse seems very close in the haze. Now and then a pair of Boston or Cape fairies go by in their skimpy trunks—Freddy calls them ball-huggers—holding hands. Otherwise I am alone, a pregnant and therefore pass-proof lass with a crinkled New Yorker on her knees for a writing pad, coining funny phrases for her lover, who thinks he is a Jew.

I explained badly about Peter. You are not he, the coincidence of your names notwithstanding. For years he has ceased to be a name for me, just a shadow, a shadow between me and my parents, between me and Ken. He didn't love me—I amused him, awkward and innocent shiksa as I was. I was a toy for him (toy/goy), and the frightening thing I discovered, I liked it. I loved being used/abused. There was nothing he could do that did not intensify my love for him, even his terrible mood of coldness, the scorn that wished me away. He needed to be alone more than I could let him be alone. It was all very young and uncontrolled and must have been influenced for each of us by how our parents had behaved. My father's absences had been cruel for my mother and as long as Peter was not absent from me, even if his language was foul, I was grateful. Or perhaps I was attracted to just that pride, a kind of mechanical selfishness, in which he resembled my father. Do you know, he has become famous? His picture was in Time a year or so ago, with a junk sculpture he had welded. He still lives in Detroit. With his mother, unmarried. So I had years when I could have flown to him, years of being childless with Ken, and I didn't. It would have been like eating chocolate sundaes again.

You and I are different, surely. With you I feel for the first time what it is like _not_ to be young. With you I feel that I at last have exercised my right of _choice_—free of habit or command or compulsion. In a sense you are my first _companion_. Our sweet sin is strangely mixed with the sweetness of pregnancy—perhaps Ken

*waited too long to make me pregnant and now that it is here I
have turned toward someone else with the gratitude. I trust you
and fear you. I feared Peter, and trust Ken. The conjunction is
uniquely yours.*

*Am I proposing marriage? Scheming woman!! Nothing of the
kind—I am so securely tied to Ken I dare open myself to you as I
might to a stranger in a dream, knowing I was all the time
securely asleep beside my husband. Please do not fear I will try to
take you from Angela. I know even better than you how precious
she is to you, she and the home you have made together, how
well, truly, you are wed. Isn't it our utter captivity that makes us,
in our few stolen afternoons together, so free? My hand is tired
and shakes. Please don't leave me yet. My flying Dutchman—
contradiction in terms?*

Later.

*I went down to swim—delicious, like being inside a diamond,
the water at Woods Hole was much warmer—and examined the
pebbles. Did you know, I once took a term of geology? I recognized basalt and quartz, the easy ones, black and white, God and
the Devil, and then a lot of speckly candyish stones I mentally
lumped as "granite." So much variety! And what a wealth of time
we hold in our hands in the smoothness of these stones! I wanted
to kiss them. Remembering your smoothness. I do love the beach.
I wonder if I was ever myself until Ken moved me into sight of
the sea.*

*Then, to my horror, who should come along but Janet and
Harold! Damn!! It was I who was embarrassed, and they who
should have been. They were brazen as always—they had left
Frank and Marcia back with the children and what was I doing
way up here in Fairyland? I told them the walk was necessary
exercise and that I wanted to sketch the Lacetown lighthouse.
They noticed that I had been writing a letter and were very
twinkly and jolly and I think genuinely like me but seemed
depressingly corrupt. Who am I to pass judgment? Yet I seem
very righteous within myself still and virtually cried, as you saw,
when I turned out to be Christine Keeler.*

Still later.

I fell asleep. So strange to wake in floods of light, mouth bloated and hair full of sand. I must go home. Ken is tennising with Gallagher and Guerin and I don't know who the fourth is. You? Answer to a riddle: the fourth of July.

Piet, have I explained anything? I think I wanted somehow to untangle us from those others, to spare you that woeful wild look that comes into your eye when it's time to be back on the job or you imagine the phone in your office ringing. In a way, because you suspect a Heaven somewhere else (like Harold's French: a constant appeal to above), you live in Hell, and I have become one of the demons. I don't want this, I want to be healing—to be white and anonymous and wisecracking for you, the nurse I suppose my father said I was too good to be. I worry that you'll do something extravagant and wasteful to please your funny prickly conscience. Don't. Have me without remorse. Remorse is boring to women. Your seducing me is fine. I wouldn't have missed it for the world. Better you than Freddy Thorne.

Which is a way of concealing that falling asleep on the sand has sexed me up. I crave your strength and length, and remain,

Your mistress

Oh blessed, blessed Piet—

How tactless, how worse than tactless wrong I was to use you today as an audience for my feelings about Ken. How comic your anger was—you seemed amazed that I had feelings about him—and how sad, in the end, your effort to turn your anger into a joke. It is one of your charms that you make both too much and too little of yourself, with a swiftness of alternation that is quite hypnotic. But your departure left me depressed and with a need to try again.

When I said that he and I had been married seven years whereas you and I had known each other a few months it was not a criticism—clearly your newness in many ways works to your advantage. But in the mysterious (as much to me as to anyone) matter of my sexual response, it is an advantage in Stage I, a dis- in Stage II. Maybe men like new women while women perform best with men they know. There is something of trust in this—there really is, whenever you spread your legs, the flitting fear you are going to be <u>hurt</u>—*and something of the sad (why do I find it sad?) fact that with women personality counts for less in sex than with men. In actual sex as opposed to all the preamble. A dull familiar trustworthy tool is all we ask. Female genitalia are extremely* <u>stupid,</u> *which gets us into many a fix our heads would get us out of.*

Why must I apologize to you for continuing to enjoy my husband? You have woken me from my seven years' sleep and Ken benefits. Isn't it enough for your ego to promise you that you exist in dimensions where Ken is blank? And that his ignorance of our affair, of what consumes my inner life, makes him seem a child, a child behind glass, a child <u>willfully</u> *behind glass. He has never been very curious about life, above the molecular level. He is a masked man who climbs a balcony to be with me at night. I discover in myself a deep coldness toward him. In this coldness I manipulate our bodies and release the tension you have built in me.*

Yet <u>do</u> *let me love him as I can. He is my man, after all. Whereas you are only* <u>a</u> *man. Maybe* <u>the</u> *man. But not mine.*

I suppose I am confused. Having decided, long before we slept together, to have you, I determined to keep you each in place, in watertight compartments. Instead, the two of you are using my body to hold a conversation in. I want to tell you each about the other. I live in fear of calling out the wrong name. I want to confide you to Ken, and Ken to you—he is unhappy about his career, and apprehensive about our unborn child, and turns to me more often now than since our first year of marriage. Of course, I am so safe. He pierces me saying, You can't impregnate the pregnant. You can't kill the dead. Compared to you it is mechanical but then Ken's career is to demonstrate how mechanical life is.

Yours is to build and blessed lover you have built wonderfully in me. I breathe your name and in writing this I miss your voice, your helpful face. Do you really think we bore God? You once told me God was bored with America. Sometimes I think you underestimate God—which is to say, you despise the faith your fear of death thrusts upon you. You have struck a bad bargain and

keep whittling away at your half. You should be a woman. The
woman in the newspaper holding a dead child in her arms knows
God has struck her. I feel Him as above me and around me and in
you and in spite of you and because of you. Life is a game of lost
and found. I must start Ken's supper. Unapologetic love. Love.

Piet turned with relief from these narcissistic long letters to a
small scrap asking: *Are you still sleeping with Georgene?*

After she had told him about the Jew, he had told her about
Georgene. In September her instinct, or gossip, informed her that
he had resumed. In truth, there had been the unplanned lapse on
the day the Kennedy infant died, and in the month and a half
since, only three visits, and these largely spent in tentative exploration of the new way out. He found Georgene sulky, passive,
flat-stomached, and sexually unadventurous. Whether in Freddy's
bed or outdoors under the sun, Piet was so nervous and watchful
he had difficulty maintaining an erection. Foxy's note seemed a
warning, a loud snap in the dark. He saw Georgene once more,
early in October: the shedding larch needles pattered steadily on
the tarpaper, the sun was wan, her chin trembled, her eyes in tears
refused to confront his. He left her with no doubt that he would
not come soon again, blaming Angela's suspiciously *gemütlich*
intimacy with Freddy, Freddy's threatening manner lately, Piet's
strained relations with Gallagher and increased work load, Georgene's own well-being—surely the essence of an affair was mutual
independence, and Georgene had sinned, endangering herself, by
becoming dependent. Her firm chin nodded but still her green
eyes, though he seized her naked shoulders in his hands, refused to
gaze into his. To Foxy's question he answered No, he had not
slept with Georgene since soon after the Whitmans came to town
and he had first glimpsed Foxy slamming her car door after
church. He retrospectively dated his love from this glimpse. He
admitted that Georgene remained his friend, and—with such a
husband, who could blame her?—now and then called him at his
office; Piet admitted this on the chance that Foxy already knew,
via Matt and Terry. Thus, in being deceived, Foxy closer approached the condition of a wife.

RIDDLES

1. What is five feet nine, Episcopalian, and about to burst?
2. What is smaller than a box car but bigger than mortality?
3. What is five feet ?, clever with its hands, has red hair, big feet, and foreign origins?
4. What is smaller than a breadbox but gives satisfaction anyway?

4. Right. Where are you, lover?
3. An auburn kangaroo doing needlepoint. Hah!
2. A bed.
1. Foxy Whitman.

As they aged in their affair her notes became briefer and more playful; as fall progressed he was able to see her less. The renovations within her home were completed, and Gallagher had obtained a lucrative rush contract, the enlargement of a local restaurant in antique style. So Piet was compelled to spend long days rough-hewing factory-planed beams and fabricating seventeenth-century effects in green lumber. The owners of the Tarbox Inne, a pair of pushing Greek brothers, wanted the new wing ready for operation by November. The trips were tedious and frequent to Mather for old bricks, to Brockton for handwrought iron, to Plymouth for research into details of colonial carpentry: *the side bearers for the second story being to be loaden with corne, &tc., must not be pinned on, but rather eyther lett in to the studds, or borne up with false studds, & soe tenented in at the ends. In this story over the first, I would have a particion, whether in the middest or over the particion vnder, I leave it to the carpenters. I desire to have the sparrs reach downe pretty deep at the eves to preserve the walls the better from the wether. I would have the howse strong in timber, though plaine & well brased. I would have it covered with very good oake-hart inch board . . .* Trying to turn these ethical old specifications into modern quaintness demoralized Piet. The fraudulent antiquation of the job seemed prophetic of the architectural embalming destined for his beloved unself-conscious town, whose beauty had been a by-product of neglect. Maddeningly, he could not get to Foxy, and absurdly he hoped for her unmistakable silhouette to bloom on the streets of strange towns, in the drab alleyways leading to construction-supply yards. Every blue station wagon stopped his heart; every blond blur in a window became a broken promise. Now and then they did meet in spots away from Tarbox—in a Mather bar where fluorescent beer advertisements described repetitive parabolas, in a forest preserve west of Lacetown where huge mosquitoes clustered thick as hair on her arms whenever they paused in walking to embrace, on a wild beach north of Duxbury where the unsoftened Atlantic surf pounded wrathfully and the high dunes were littered with rusting cans, shards of green glass, and abandoned underpants. The danger of being discovered seemed greater out of town than in it, within the maze of routines and visiting patterns they could predict; and as Foxy's time drew near she became reluctant to drive far. Outside of Tarbox they seemed to themselves merely another furtive illicit couple, compelled toward shabby seclusion, her pregnancy grotesque. Within her breezy home they seemed glorious nudes, symphonic vessels of passion. Their dream was of a night together.

Piet—Ken has to go to a conference—in New York, Columbia—this Tuesday/Thursday. Could you possibly get free to see me, or shall I go to Cambridge and stay with friends— with Ned and Gretchen—for these days? Ken wants the latter— doesn't want me left alone—but I can argue him down if there's a reason—is there? I ache and need to be praised by you. My bigness is either horrible or a new form of beauty—which?

He could not get free. The restaurant wing was in the finish stage and he and Adams and Comeau had to be there ten hours a day. And now that the foliage was down, the beach road seemed transparent. He was timid of driving his truck past the Thornes' watching hill to the Whitmans' house, visible in fall from the little-Smiths'. At night, also, he was barred from seeing her, by a new turn in their social life: Angela in her fascination with psychiatry had taken up with the Applebys and Freddy Thorne, which involved both the Thornes. Georgene's brittle, slightly hyperthyroid eyes, when it emerged in conversation that Ken Whitman was going to be away, flicked toward Piet with the narrowing that appeared on her face when set point was deuced. Piet told Foxy to go to Cambridge, to place herself above gossip and to remove his temptation to do something desperate, revealing, and fatal.

Damn! My mother has decided to come hold my hand through "the adventure" so she will be in the house from Monday on. Could you go to church tomorrow?

After church, on the hill, beneath the penny eye of the weathercock, Piet walked down the gray path past the iron pavilion toward the reddish rocks by which Foxy had parked. Standing waiting with an alert appearance of politeness, she was vast, a full sail in pale wool, one of the high tight turbans fashionable that fall covering her hair and making her face appear stripped and sleek. He felt pulled into her orbit; he yearned to embrace, to possess forever, this luxurious ball, this swollen woman whose apparition here recalled his first impression, of wealth and an arrogant return home.

"Hi."

"Hi. Why the solemn face?"

"You look so good. You look grand."

"So do you, Mr. Hanema. Is that a new suit?"

"New last fall. You didn't know me then. Is that a new hat?"

"It's called 'a hat to meet your mother at the airport in, to show her you're doing all right.' "

"It's very successful."

"Is it too severe? I'd take it off but it's pinned."

"It's great. It brings out the pampered pink of your face."

"God, you're hostile."

"I may be hostile, but I adore you. Let's go to bed."

"Wouldn't that be a relief? Do you know how many days it's been since we made love?"

"Many."

"Nineteen. Two Tuesdays ago."

"Can we elude your mother?" Piet's palms and the area of his lips had gone cold; he felt here at the town's center that he was leaning inwards like a man on the edge of a carrousel.

Foxy said, "I can if you can get away from Angela and Gallagher."

"They're a vigilant pair these days. Jesus, I hate not seeing you. I find myself—"

"Say it." Perhaps she thought he was going to confess another woman.

"Terrified of death lately."

"Oh, Piet. Why? Are you sick?"

"It's not practical death I'm worried about, it's death anytime, at all, ever."

She asked, "Does it have to do with me?"

He had not thought so, but now he said, "Maybe. Maybe I'm frightened of you having your baby and everything changing."

"Why should it?"

He shrugged. "You'll be a mother. It won't be my child. It just won't work, you'll be too torn."

She was blank, still. Sunday was gathered around them, the sky a rung bell, cars in all colors hurrying home. Against her silence he suddenly pleaded, "I need to see you, woman. I need to see your belly."

They were exposed in sunlight and traffic, and she decided to turn to her car. "Call me," she said. "Can you call tomorrow before nine? Mother's plane comes in at ten-thirty." She thought. "No. You can't. Ken is going into Boston with me, so he'll be at the house." She thought again. "I'll try to call your office when I go shopping in the afternoon. But you'll be at the Inne." She paused a third time, having been listening to herself. "Damn, this is shitty," she said. "I *want* you to see me. I want to be with you all the time. I want to own you."

As if this last admission had confirmed and justified him in his sense of certain loss, Piet waved his hand generously, meaning it couldn't be helped. "Your wanting it," he told her, "is what matters to me. We'll keep in touch. Be nice to your Mom."

Her white-gloved hand appeared to flinch on the car-door handle. "I must go," broke from her. In full view of the town, he comically bowed, and saw she was wearing, for the good of her legs, elastic stockings dusty rose in color.

"Charrming," he said, "to be seeing ye sae fair on so fair a morrning, Mrs. Whitman."

"Likewise, I'm sure, Mr. Hanema," she replied, her brown eyes alive in the trap of their plight.

The brilliant October days brimmed for him with her absence. On the evenings when there was no party, no gathering, Piet and Angela sat at home in the stifling atmosphere of his longing. "Stop sighing."

Piet looked up surprised from a page of *Life:* saffron-robed monks protesting. "I'm not, am I?"

"Well, your breathing is unpleasant."

"Sorry. I'll try to stop breathing."

"What's bothering you? The Tarbox Inne?"

"Nothing. I just feel restless. What's in the refrigerator?"

"You've already looked. You'll get fat, the way you nibble. Why don't you go out and look at the stars? I can't stand that sighing."

"Will you come out with me?"

"In a minute." She was absorbed in her book, the new Salinger, with an endless title and a mustard jacket whose front and back were identical. "They're about to have a revelation." At what point in their courtship was it, years ago, on the Nun's Bay cliffs, that she had astonished him by knowing the stars, her uncle having been an astronomer? Her cheek to his so he could follow her pointing hand, she had taught him. Find the bright stars first. Then travel between them. Imagine straight lines. The dew touching them through the blanket. Her father's windowlights marching across the grass but dying among the shrubs trimmed like table tops. Her warm breath telling of legends above them.

He left her beneath the lamp and ventured across the crunching driveway into the yard's darkness, green-veined like black marble. The high-pitched thrum of cicadas encircled him. The clear night threatened frost. The rigid cascade of stars had been dealt a sideways blow: Vega the queen of the summer sky no longer reigned at the zenith, having yielded to paler Deneb and to a faint house-shaped constellation. Cepheus. In Andromeda Piet searched for the very dim stir of light that Angela had once pointed out to him as another galaxy altogether, two million light years distant. Through oceans of onyx its light had traveled to him. Mirrorwise his gaze, followed shortly by his death, would travel outward in an eternal straight line. Vertigo afflicted him. Amid these impervious shining multitudes he felt a gigantic slipping; sinking upwards, he gripped the dim earth with his eyes. The leaves of a broken lilac branch, dead and unable to girdle their stems and fall, hung unstirring in windowlight. He pictured Foxy, a vapor, a fur, a memory of powdery armpits, lips dry then wet, the downy small of her back where his thumbs would massage the ache of carrying a child, her erect coral nipples teased by his fingernails, the guarded blur of her gaze. She became formless and undefended beneath the sorrowful confiding of his seed. *I abuse you.*

No. Don't stop.

I'll come.

Do. I can't this time. Do, Piet.

Truly? You like it? She nodded, silent, her mouth full. Her tongue fluttered him into heat; her hand helped. *Oh. Sweet. Swallow me.* She swallowed him.

The leaves of the broken lilac branch, dead and unable to girdle their stems and fall, hung unstirring in windowlight. Behind glass Angela calmly turned a page. Above his square yard the burning dome seemed splintered by a violent fleeing. Give me now her by whom You have fled.

Piet that night fell asleep promptly, but awoke in the early morning, hours before dawn, feeling cheated, having been unable to dream. Angela lay oblivious beside him. He brought her hand to his penis but it slipped away. With his own skilled hand he lightened himself of desire; yet still he could not relax and sink. He remembered from childhood a curling warm darkness he could snuggle backwards into, at the touch of a soft blanket, of a furry toy, of rain overhead, of voices below. Now, at midpoint of his life's arc, this first darkness had receded beyond recovery and the second, the one awaiting him, was not yet comfortable. Sudden faces, totally unknown, malevolent, flicked through his mind as it sought to erase itself into sleep. Detailed drawings of unbuilt buildings, clear in every pinion and cornice, were momentarily laid flat upon his unsteady inner surface. Again and again his racing heart checked his mind's intended dissolution. He itched to thump Angela awake; the desire to confess, to confess his misery, his fornication with Foxy, rose burning in his throat like the premonition of vomit. After many turnings and futile resettlings he crept downstairs, outdoors.

The stars had wheeled out of all recognition. They were as if seen from another earth, beyond the Milky Way, rich in silence and strangeness. Treading lightly upon the rime-whitened grass, ice to his bare soles, he finally located, southward above the barn ridge with its twin scrolled lightning rods, a constellation gigantic and familiar: Orion. The giant of winter, surprised in his bed. So the future is in the sky after all. Everything already exists. Piet returned to his snug house satisfied that a crisis in his love for Foxy had passed, that henceforth he would love her less.

iv. *Breakthrough*

Foxy felt that her mother's presence in the house formed a dreadful, heavensent opportunity to confess that she had a lover. No practical benefit could follow from such a confession, and her mother, in the blithe, efficient complacence bestowed upon her by remarriage and middle age, exerted no pressure to confess; rather, she assumed that the marriage she had chosen for her daughter was going all the smoother now that its one blemish, childlessness, was about to be removed. This assumption annoyed Foxy; the world's downward skid seemed to her greased by such assumptions. Confession to the contrary ballooned against the roof of her mouth. Foxy had carried her secret alone too long. Her two hidden burdens had grown parallel, and now the guilty one also demanded to emerge, to show itself, to be satisfied by a wider environment, a sunlit hemisphere of consultation and sympathy.

Yet her mother was in the house two weeks, and Foxy proved awkwardly retentive. Her delicate flush masked an inconvenient toughness. The baby was late. There were jokes, too many, about the possibility of quintuplets like those born in South Dakota the previous month. Ken and Foxy's mother—Constance Price Fox

Roth, she begged them to call her Connie—got along all too nicely. They dressed in the same way: in costumes rather than clothes. Ken had outfits for every occasion, for going to work, for being at work, for being at home casually, for being at home less casually, for walking on the beach, for playing tennis, for playing touch football with the other young husbands of Tarbox on fall Sunday afternoons; he owned a closet of suits graded by sobriety, madras and linen and tweedy sports jackets, sweaters of many weights, chinos and jeans in all degrees of wear, several types of sneakers, even a foulard and a smoking jacket for the at-home occasion pitched to just this formality. In the same style, Foxy's mother, now wealthy, changed at every turn of the day. Between five-thirty and six, when the two women could make themselves a drink and settle to waiting for Ken's arrival from Boston, Connie would slip into one of her quieter cocktail dresses and Foxy in her exhausted maternity tent would be obliged to covet her mother's figure; though thickening at the waist and shrinking at the hips, it was still more compact and orthodoxly sexy than Foxy's languorous, flat-footed, overall own. Too keenly Connie would await Ken. He had grown handsomer in the years since Foxy's parents had approved him, the same years in which Foxy had grown numb to his handsomeness. The elegant height held so uprightly, the shapely long skull now becomingly touched at the temples with gray, the gray gaze bold as a child's. Connie was impressed by Ken's professional distinction, which Foxy had come to see as an anticlimax to their long student wait, a cheat. Mrs. Roth was intrigued by what Foxy dismissed as aspects of Ken's essential coldness—the dash and abruptness with which he performed some actions, such as driving his car, ending a conversation, or acquiring this house. "I *love* the house, Liz," she told her daughter. "The view is *so* New England." Her accent sounded exaggeratedly southern to Foxy; her ceaseless emphases suggested a climacteric society where politeness has absorbed the deeper passions and become a charade. Yet beneath this flossy alien creature with teased and skillfully tinted hair, this second wife chosen to reign over mountains of laundromat quarters, there was the prior woman, the war wife and young mother, with her straggling dull bun, her serge dresses and low-heeled shoes, her scorched ironing board and her varnished Philco crackling with news from both oceans, her air of brave fatigue, her way of suddenly dropping her hands and revealing dread. Foxy thought she could find this woman if she needed her.

Mrs. Roth continued with proprietary enthusiasm: "It's a *castle*. How sweet and ambitious of Ken to have wanted it just for the two of you."

"And the baby."

"Oh, of course, for the baby, *how* could I forget the *ba*by? The cherub is why I'm here!"

Foxy said, of the house, "It was a wreck of an old summer place when we moved in. We got a rather cute local contractor to make it livable. The walls, the porch, the kitchen and the little wing beyond are all new. We had to excavate a cellar."

Foxy's mother, squinting through the smoke of the red-filtered cigarette, the aged skin of her throat betrayed by the lifting of her head, surveyed Piet's work. Foxy's heart felt displaced upward by an inward kicking. "I don't know, Liz. It seems a bit fussy. All this old-fashioned blank plaster just *isn't* you and Ken."

"You need something solid on the marshes," Foxy said defensively, "to keep out the wind."

Wishing to be tactful, and sensing a sudden need for tact, Mrs. Roth said, "I'm sure as you live here you'll make it more cozy," and changed the subject. "Speaking of the wind, Libby, do you know—it's fresh on my mind, my book circle has been reading Greek mythology, it seems to be the literary rage this year—the ancient Greeks and all those people apparently thought women were *fertilized* by it? The *wind!*"

Foxy laughed. "Do you remember, Mother, in Bethesda, old Miss Ravenel always sitting rocking in her breezeway?" Every day, she steered the conversation to reminiscence of Bethesda.

"*Do* I?" Connie cried. "Of course, That's what she was waiting for, to be fertilized!" The laughter in the big bare-walled room sounded thin; each woman had proved fertile but once.

Ken liked his mother-in-law's presence in the house because it kept Foxy entertained at home, away from the gatherings of the couples he had taken to describing to her as "your friends."

When they did go out, it was the three of them together, and Foxy's mother, in crackling purples, with a white silk stole she kept flicking and adjusting, was a social success, half-chaperon, half-fool. Freddy Thorne and she hit it off especially well. After the little-Smiths' Halloween party, held the night after the holiday and without masks, she said to Foxy, "I must say, he seems terribly *up* on things, to be only a *den*tist. He was fascinating on modern psychology and myths. Don't you, among your gay friends, find him one of the most sympatico?"

"Frankly, Mother, no. I find him insidious and odious."

"Truly? Of course, his mouth is unfortunate, but then no man will truly seem handsome set against Ken." She spoke gropingly, for in two weeks she had begun to sense Ken's curious absence, the deadening in Foxy that his presence caused. He was off this morning playing tennis, having served breakfast to himself and set his dishes nicely rinsed, as a kind of rebuke, in the slate sink. "Who *do* you like?" she asked.

"Well," Foxy said, "mostly the women, sad to say. Terry Gallagher, she's the tall one with straight dark hair who couldn't be coaxed into playing her lute even though she brought it, and in a way Janet Appleby. She's the plump one who toward the end got quite drunk and did the impersonation of her psychiatrist."

"I thought she should be happier than she is."

"She thinks that too. And of the couples, I quite like the Hanemas and don't mind the Guerins. I can't communicate with Roger but Bea, even though she's a show-off about it, I think is genuinely affectionate. *Their* tragedy is, they can't have any children."

"The Hanemas. Not that horrid little redheaded man who ran around slapping everyone's behind and doing handstands?"

"That is Piet, yes. His wife is lovely. Very kind and serene and amused."

"I didn't notice her. But I must say, as a group, you all seemed *very* sympatico with each other. You're fortunate to have found friends you can have *fun* with. Your father and I had no such circle. We were alone; alone with you. It's good, to be able to let off steam."

"Ken thinks we *make* steam. Ken thinks we know each other

too well. It's true, one man of a couple we know has lost his job because of their involvement with another couple."

"Which was he?"

"They don't come any more. His name was Ben Saltz. They were Jewish." Helplessly, incriminatingly, Foxy blushed.

Her mother gave no sign of remembering, with her, Peter. Rather, she said, tidily dousing her cigarette in her slopped coffee saucer, "It must have been a combination of circumstances."

"The woman he was in love with was there last night. Carol Constantine. Piled red hair with dark roots and a very thin waist. She paints. I've been thinking of buying a painting from her, after your chilling remarks about our bare walls."

"I noticed her. Stunning now, but she'll soon go brassy. She knows it, too. And she can expect precious little mercy from that dandy little husband of hers."

"Eddie? We don't take him very seriously."

"You should. He is a very vain and ruthless young Italian. I told him to his face, I'd be happy to ride in any airplane he was piloting; he was too conceited to crash."

"Mother! Aren't you wicked, flirting with these men young enough to be your sons?"

"I wasn't flirting, I was alarmed. And so is his poor emaciated wife."

"Speaking of couples," Foxy asked, homesick for Washington, "how are the Kennedys?"

"People say, better than they used to be. He used to be notorious, of course."

"She looks less anxious in the newspapers lately. At her Greek beach."

"A *dreadful* misfortune, their premature child. But I suppose being Catholics they have some way of turning it all to the good. One more angel up there, tra la."

"You don't think we Episcopalians have these ways."

"Dear good Elizabeth." Her mother's hand reached tentatively to touch hers, and their wedding rings lightly clashed, gold to gold. "I must confess I've stopped thinking of myself as anything. Roth scorns it all, of course. It was mostly a navy thing with your father."

"Does he still go to church?"

"I've never thought to ask him, and now it's been years since I've seen him. He's in San Diego, I may never see him again. Think of that."

Foxy refused to think of it. Carefully she asked, "Is it true, what everybody said, they almost got divorced?"

"The Kennedys. We don't see many government people, but yes, you do hear that sort of thing. Not divorced, of course; they'd have to buy an annulment, I suppose from Cardinal Spellman. Of course, with his back, he's *not* as active as apparently he was." Mrs. Roth rested her elbows on the table edge and wearily smoothed the skin beneath her eyes. "Why do you ask?"

Foxy said, "I'm curious about divorce." In turning her head to mute this admission she read the banner headline of the newspaper left neatly folded at Ken's empty place: DIEM OVERTHROWN. Diem. *Dies, diei, diei, diem.* "I wonder sometimes if Ken and I shouldn't get one."

The planet turned while Foxy waited to hear which woman would respond, her mother or Mrs. Roth. "Seriously?" Which was it?

Foxy sought cover. "Not very," she said very lightly. "The thought comes and goes. Since coming out here I have too much time to myself. Once the baby arrives I'll be all right."

"Well I *won*der," her mother said. "But if you're not happy why didn't you end things when there was no one else involved? You lived alone with Ken how many years was it? Seven?"

"I didn't *know* I wasn't happy till I moved here. Oh mother, it's such a mess—so *sad*. He's everything I could want but we don't make *con*tact."

"Oh, child. Cry, yes. I'm so sorry."

"He's so good, Mother, he's so goddam *good*. He doesn't *see* me, he doesn't *know* me."

"Are you sure?"

"Oh, yes, yes. I've been seeing another man and Ken doesn't have a clue. A *clue*."

"What other man?" Mrs. Roth asked sharply. "Truly seeing?"

"It doesn't *matter* what other man. A man. Oh, God, yes, seeing to sleep with."

"The child is his?"

"No, Mother, the child is *Ken's*."

This admission was the worst; as Foxy sobbed into crumpled whiteness, sobbed toward her own lap beyond the pinkness of her fingers supporting her face, she saw that this was the worst, that had the child been Piet's there would be a rationale, she would not be so purely beyond the pale.

"Well," the other woman at last found tongue to say, "it must stop."

Foxy felt the power of tears; behind the silver shield of them she advanced against her mother, refusing her an easy victory, demanding to be rescued. "But if I could *stop* I wouldn't have started. It was so wrong in the first place. It wasn't his idea it was *mine*. What I'm most afraid of isn't hurting Ken it's hurting *him*, of using his love for me to make him *marry* me."

"The man, I take it, is married also?"

"Of course he is, we're all married out here."

"Has he expressed a wish to marry you?"

"No. Yes. I don't know. It's not possible."

"Well, my advice is certainly to break it off. But I'd be the last person to say that divorce is always catastrophic."

"Oh, but it would be. He loves his wife."

"He says this?"

"He loves us both. He loves us all. I don't want to be the bitch who took advantage of him."

"Such elevated morality. In my day it was the woman who was taken advantage of. If it's the man I think it is, he'll land on his feet."

"Who do you think it is?"

"The contractor. The tall Irishman, I forget his name, who danced with you last night."

"Matt Gallagher?" Foxy laughed. "He's a good dancer but, Mother, he's just like Ken, only not as bright."

Connie blushed, hearing in her daughter's laugh how wrong her guess had been. She said, weakly, "He's the only one tall enough for you," and then, stronger, having found the right line, "Sweetheart, I don't *want* to know who the man is. If I knew the man, I'd be obliged to tell Ken. I'd rather know what dissatisfies you. To me, Ken seems perfect."

"I know he seems that to you. You've made that clear."

"And he a*dores* you. Is it the sex?"

"The sex is all right."

"You have climaxes?"

"Mother. Of course."

"Don't be so short. I didn't begin to enjoy my body until I was past thirty."

"Well I must say I don't much enjoy my body in this condition. I can't bend in the middle and my legs hurt." She abruptly stood and swept back and forth carrying plates and cups, making her mother call to her on the fly.

"How can this other man have continued with you when you are carrying this child?"

Foxy shrugged. "He never knew me when I wasn't carrying this child. It didn't seem to matter that much. He's very tender about it. His wife has stopped having children. She believes in overpopulation."

"Oh, Liz, he sounds *so* unstable to me. You have *such* unfortunate taste."

"You ask me about Ken. I think what's wrong with him is that I didn't choose him. You chose him. Daddy chose him. Radcliffe and Harvard chose him. All the world agreed he was right for me, and that's why he's not. Nobody *knew* me. Nobody *cared*. I was just something to be bundled up and got out of the way so you and Daddy could have your wonderful divorce." The accusation was so grave she sat down at the table again. Beneath her crowded heart there was an unaccustomed burning.

Her mother massaged the moist red spaces below her eyes, and answered huskily, "Is that how it looked to you? It wasn't that way, we didn't think, but I'm so sorry, Liz, so sorry. We both loved you so, you had always been so brave for us, all those dull years your bright voice, your prettiness, we were terrified over what you were doing to yourself with Peter."

"But, Mother"—their hands on the table avoided touching, remembering the grotesque click of wedding rings—"I knew that. I knew Peter. I knew it would end of itself, you shouldn't have stepped in. I lost all dignity. This other man and I. I know it will end. He'll leave me. He'll move on. Don't tell Ken about it. Please."

"I never *thought* to tell Ken. He wouldn't know what to do with it; he might panic. You know, Liz, I'm not totally a garish old fool. I can see Ken's limits. He's like your father, he needs a form for everything. But within the rules, I think he's remarkable. He's worth treasuring."

"He is, I do treasure him. It's just so devastating, to have a husband whose job is to probe the secrets of life, and to feel yourself dying beside him, and he doesn't know it or seem to care."

"He cares, I'm sure."

"He cares about his equipment and I'm part of it."

Mrs. Roth came to attention again. "You honestly believe," she said, "that you and this other man can end it? It hasn't gone too far?"

The breakfast debris on the table, orange rinds and eggshells and newspaper, seemed to Foxy to epitomize the contents of the world. Small wonder the child was reluctant to emerge. Its weight within her—the fetus had dropped over a week ago, and its movements, once a faint fluttering, had grown tumultuous—felt leaden, panicked, betrayed. Foxy answered her mother. "It may be ended already. We've hardly talked since you came. We haven't—been together really, for five weeks."

Mrs. Roth's fingertips crept up her face and now stroked, as if treasuringly, the shape of her eyeballs beneath shut lids. "Dear Libby," she said, not looking. "What I most remember from that terrible Bethesda house was the radio dial glowing, and your lovely flaxen hair, that I combed, and combed."

"Gone, Mother, gone," Foxy airily stated, rising and startling in the small of her back an untypical, musical phrase of pain.

Just ten now, still stocky yet dawningly comely, Ruth was given to placid self-communings in her room, which she kept extremely neat. For her birthday Piet had given her a full-length mirror, a doorway to vanity, a father's doting and perhaps intrusive gift. He had grown shy, wary of intruding on her. When he ventured into Ruth's room, he glanced at the mirror to detect signs of its use and surprised his own sharp reflection, looking pouchy and thievish. Surrounded by her mirror, by the splashy flowers of the wallpaper she had chosen herself, by collections, each to its shelf, of books, seashells, bottlecaps, and the foreign dolls sent to her by Angela's parents from the harbors of their winter cruises, by a turquoise-oceaned map of the world and a green-and-white Tarbox High football banner, by Scotch-taped Brownie snapshots she had taken herself of her parents arm-in-arm, of the hamster who had died, of the lilac hedge in bloom, of her friends at the beach but none of her sister—so surrounded, Ruth would sit at the fold-down desk Piet had built for her and do her homework, or make entries in her laconic diary of weather and excursions, or maintain her scrapbook of figures carefully scissored from *Life* and the *National Geographic*, an assortment including Sophia Loren, Queen Elizabeth II of England, a Russian spacedog, a huge stone Pharaoh threatened with immersion by the Aswan Dam, a naked Nigerian bride, a Pakistani mother bewailing the death of her child by earthquake, Jacqueline Kennedy, a vocal group called the Beatles.

On days like this Monday when Piet returned home before Angela, he felt his daughter busy above him; she was bused back from school by four. The silence behind her closed door, broken when she rearranged objects or crooned to herself hymns learned at choir, intimidated him; he had scrubbed her diapers and warmed her bottles and now his only function was to safeguard her privacy, to make himself unobtrusive. He reread the newspaper and considered replacing the rotten boards of his own barn and instead made himself an early gin-and-Bitter-Lemon. Now that the tavern addition was completed, and christened with a formal banquet attended by all three selectman and fire chief Kappiotis, who fell asleep, there was not enough for Piet to do. Gallagher had sold the estate in Lacetown to the nuns, but a Watertown firm whose director's brother was a priest had been awarded the fat reconstruction contract. They were told the bids had been considered blind; all Gallagher's charm with the sisters had been wasted. They were down to a single job, converting the old Tarbox house on Divinity into offices and apartments suitable for rental. Old Gertrude Tarbox, having constructed for herself a paradise of hoarded paper and tin, was in September carted off to a nursing home, at the command of cousins living in Palo Alto, through the agency of a New Bedford bank. Piet's job—replacing clapboards, removing partitions, sanding floors, dressing up ratty surfaces with decorator panels of vinyl surfaced to counterfeit wood—was scarcely enough to occupy Adams and Comeau and Jazinski, who, being employees paid by the hour, were entitled to work first. So Piet was often idle. He drank deep of the sweetened gin and tried not to think of Foxy; since she had hidden behind her mother she was in his mind like a canker that memory's tongue kept touching. The summer seemed dreamlike and distant. She had vanished—the slam of a car door after church. He missed the thrift of a double life, the defiant conservation. Faithful, he was going to waste. Attenuated hours spread lifeless around him. He drank to kill time.

Angela came home brimful of Irene. "You know what that woman has done? She's gotten a paying job at the Lacetown Academy for Girls, starting next Monday, today a week, which means I have to do the whole kindergarten by myself."

"Tell her you can't do it."

"Who said I can't? If I can't go to a psychiatrist at least I can run a dozen children by myself, without Irene's kibbutzy theories getting in my way."

"You *want* to do it."

"What's so surprising about that? I don't want to very much. I don't think children this small are my meat really, but I do want to see how teaching after all these years strikes me. I mean, wouldn't you like it if I could bring home a little money?"

"You're afraid I can't support you."

Angela bent and rubbed her cheek against his temple softly, yet hastily, the brush of a wing about to fly. "Of course you can. But I'm a person too. My children are growing up." She whispered:

"Nancy goes all morning without sucking her thumb, unless something happens to remind her." She whispered because she had brought the child home, and Nancy was on the stairs, wondering if she dared go bother Ruth.

"What else did Irene say? You've been gone forever. Has Ben found a job yet?"

"No, I'm not even sure he's looking. But she was full of news. She keeps a beady black eye on the Constantines across the way and says they've taken up with the Guerins. Roger and Bea are over there every night, and what Irene thinks, you have to hear it from her to get the humor of it, is that the attraction is between the like halves of the couples." She drew a box in air with her fingers to explain. "Carol and Bea are attracted to each other, and Roger and Eddie."

"Well does she think they're putting this attraction into practice? I'm having another drink. Would you like one?"

"Bourbon, not gin. Piet, summer's over. She doesn't quite dare say so. But she thinks Carol is capable of anything physically and Bea *does* have this very passive streak. She's always been a kind of a woman's woman, in a way; she *flirts* with women, and gives them little pats."

"But it must be a huge step," Piet said, though knowing that heterosexually it was not so, "between that kind of current and taking off your clothes and doing the stuff."

Angela took her musky gold drink from his hand; as she sipped her eyes went bluer, gazing toward scenes she had been told of. "But," she said, "we're none of us getting younger and if it's something you've always wanted aren't the inhibitions less and less? Things keep getting less sacred."

Piet said, pouring lucid gin for himself, "Roger *is* homosexual, sure, but his charm has always been his refusal to admit it. Except in his manner to women, which is either rude or excessively polite."

"I think there's a difference," Angela said, "between being homosexual and being angry at females. Has Roger ever, on the golf course say, made a pass at you?"

"No. But he *is* very comfortable, and can't *stand* being stuck behind a female foursome. But I think Eddie's the mystery. How can Irene accuse her lover of a few months ago of being a working fairy?"

"Well, for one thing, she didn't exactly, and for another she is quite hurt and bitter. When I sort of asked her this, all she'd say was that Eddie could be very *persuasive*. I don't know what it meant, but she said it three or four times."

Piet asked her, "Where does your friend Freddy Thorne fit in this new arrangement?"

"Oh, well Freddy's the one who brought them together; the Guerins and Constantines had almost nothing to do with each other until Freddy. I guess he's over there pretty much, stirring the brew."

"Poor Georgene."

Angela asked, alert, her upper lip lifted, her wet teeth aglint, "Why poor Georgene?"

"On general principles. Married to that evil jerk."

"You can't really think he's evil. He just loves a mess. Anyway, Georgene's been *very* frosty to me ever since school started. Once Irene goes, it wouldn't surprise me if Georgene stopped doing her day."

"What else did Irene have on her teeming mind?"

"Let me remember. John Ong is apparently sick. Something with his chest; the doctors have told him to quit smoking and he won't. He can't."

"My Lord. Cancer?"

"Nobody knows. Of course, he's older than any of us, it just hasn't showed, because he's Asiatic."

"Is he in the hospital?"

"Not yet. And, oh yes, of course. This will please you. Foxy Whitman has had her baby."

The air compressed; a sense of suffocation was followed by a carefree falling independent of space. Piet asked, "When?"

"Sometime this weekend. I think on Sunday. You saw her Friday night at the little-Smiths'. Maybe dancing with Matt Gallagher brought it on. He's awfully bouncy."

"Why hasn't anybody told us before?"

"Piet, you're taking it so *per*sonally. You're not exactly the next of kin. I *am* surprised that Matt didn't mention it at work. Terry must have heard, if she's Foxy's best friend."

"Matt and I don't communicate much at work these days. He's sulking because we lost the nunnery. But that's very nice. She had gotten enormous. Boy or girl?"

"Boy. Seven pounds something. Should we send flowers? I like Foxy, but we don't seem quite at the flower-sending stage."

"Oh, send her some. Loosen up. You can't take them with you, Angel. Flowers don't grow in Heaven, they only spring from dung."

Angela grimaced, puzzled by his hostile patter, and left the kitchen, calling, "Ru-uth! Come down and be sociable. Nancy wants to play Fish."

Alone, Piet tried to grasp the happiness distinct yet unsteady within him. She was safe. The child had been a boy. Foxy's luck had held. He wanted to be very close to her, to creep into the antiseptic white room where she lay, deflated and pink, invisibly bleeding, breathing in unconsciousness, her pale mouth askew, her hair adrift. He saw hothouse flowers—lush gladiolas, display dahlias, beribboned hyacinths fragrant of greenhouse earth packed tight by mossy thumbs, red cut roses leaning heavy-headed and coolly rank. He glimpsed the glass of water standing stale-beaded beyond her blurred face, and the cartoon cards of congratulation, and a candy bar concealed half-eaten in an enameled drawer. And in a chamber beyond this possessive daydreaming waited the realization that, in giving birth without notifying him, she had been guilty of an affront and in that guilt promised him freedom. Once, uncoming, she had masturbated against his thigh squeezed between hers. *Is this too awful for you?*

No, of course not, no. Youth must be served.

Don't tease. I'm shy enough with you as is.

With me, your lover? Shy?

Just am.

It's so touching, how hard women must work.

Touch my nipples.

Gladly.

More gently. I'm almost there.

Come. His thigh was beginning to ache and tingle, the circulation hampered. *Oh come. Good. Terrific. Wow.*

On top of the refrigerator was a wooden salad bowl brimming with Halloween candy that Ruth and Nancy had begged. To celebrate, to lend substance to, his happiness Piet took down the bowl and gobbled a handful of imitation corn; he rarely ate candy, out of fear for his teeth.

Though Foxy had made the appointment three weeks ago, while still in the hospital, for this Friday at one, Freddy Thorne seemed startled by her appearance in his office. Until now she had kept her Cambridge dentist, but toward the end of her pregnancy her teeth had begun to twinge, and with the baby nursing her mobility was lessened. No one, not even Piet, denied that Freddy was a competent dentist. Yet she could not escape the feeling, entering his inner office, that by coming to him, in his absurd cottage tucked beside the post office on Divinity Street, when there were other competent dentists in town, she was, emboldened by motherhood, playing the game that Tarbox had taught her, the game of tempting her fate.

He wore a white jacket and, an inch or more in front of his regular glasses, a pair of rectangular magnifying lenses. The sanctum was fanatically clean, from the circular napkin on the swinging tool tray to the scrubbed blush of Freddy's palms, uplifted in surprise or blessing, in front of his backwards white jacket. A square black clock said twelve after one. His first appointment after lunch. She had nibbled around ten; the baby had scattered her habits of sleep and eating. It reassured her that like all normal dentists Freddy ran behind schedule. "Well look who's here!" he said when she entered. "Lovely day," he murmured while he adjusted her into the chair. Now he asked, as her mouth obediently opened, "Which is the area of discomfort?" Three persons had spoken: the first a frivolous prying man she knew, the second a polite bored acquaintance, the third a wholly alien technician.

"Here," she said. She pointed with her finger from outside her cheek and with her tongue from within. Freddy held the pick and mirror crossed at his chest as she explained. "The upper, molar I suppose it is. I get a twinge when I eat candy. And over here, on the other side, I can feel a hole where a filling used to be. Also all the books say, and my mother in*si*sted, my teeth would fall out because the calcium went into the baby."

"Did you take calcium pills?"

"Iron, I know. I took whatever Doc Allen gave me."

Freddy said, "With a modern diet calcium displacement isn't usually a problem. Primitive women *do* tend to lose their smiles. Shall we have us a look?" His touch with the exploratory picks was delicate. A steel point touched a nerve once, and tactfully feathered off. Mint on his breath masked the odor of whatever he had eaten for lunch, perhaps veal. His perfumed fingers were in her mouth, and, like many things she had abstractly dreaded, like childbirth, like adultery, the reality was more mixed than she had imagined, and not so bad.

"You have strong teeth," he said. He made precise pencil marks on one of those dental charts that to Foxy as a child had seemed a wide-open scream. Curious, his choice of "strong" over "nice" or "good."

She counted the marks and said, *"Four* cavities!" Always in dental chairs she wanted to talk too much, to fend the drill away from her mouth.

"You're in respectable shape," he told her. "Let's begin with the upper right, the one you've been feeling."

He removed an injecting needle from a tray of blue sterilizer. She told him, "I don't usually bother with Novocain."

"I want you to today." His manner was mild and irresistible; where was that sloppy troll she knew from parties? With the secondary lenses in place, his eyes were totally elusive. Freddy became a voice and a touch. He said, "This is a new gadget," and his fingers exposed a spot on her upper gum where, with a tiny hiss, something icy was sprayed. Thus numbed, she did not feel the stab of the needle.

They waited for the Novocain to take effect. Freddy busied

himself behind her back. She yawned; Toby had been fed at two and awakened again at five. Her feet on the raised metal tread looked big and flat and pale in ballet slippers. Above her feet a large window curtained in dun sacking framed an abstract view: the slate roof of the Tarbox post office descended in courses of smaller to greater from a ridge of copper flashing set smack, it seemed, against the sky. The day was balmy for this late in November. Small tugging clouds darkened Tarbox with incongruous intensity when they crossed the sun. She wondered why Piet had sent no flowers. Freddy shuffled tinkling metal and his receptionist, a pug-nosed girl with skunk-striped bangs, passed back and forth between the anteroom and a nether room in which Foxy could glimpse a table, a Bunsen burner, a tattered chart dramatizing dental hygiene for children, and the end of a cot. Nearer, on a chest of enameled drawers, a small blond radio played colorless music interrupted now and then by a characterless male voice, a voice without a trace of an accent or an emotion. Foxy wondered where such music originated, whether in men or machines, and who supplied it so inexhaustibly to dentists' offices, hotel lobbies, and landing airplanes. Ken called it toothpaste music.

Freddy cleared his throat and asked, "Is your mother still here? Will she be coming tonight?" The Thornes were giving a black-tie party tonight. To Foxy it meant that after weeks of seclusion she would at last again see Piet.

"No, we put her on a plane Tuesday. At last."

"Did Ken not enjoy having his mother-in-law in the house?"

"He minded it less than I did. I'm used to being a hermit."

"She seemed jolly."

"She is. But I haven't really had much to do with her since college. I'm too old to have a mother."

"She enjoyed the baby." It was not quite a question.

"She made the noises. But people that age, I discover, aren't very flexible, and it took a lot of my energy to keep the baby off of her nerves. She kept changing clothes and trying to reminisce while I wobbled up and down stairs." As the moment for Freddy to use the drill neared, Foxy's mouth watered, fairly bubbled with the wish to tell him everything—the musical first pains, the narrowing intermittences, the dreamlike unconcern of the doctors and nurses, the anesthesia like a rustling roaring wing enfolding her, the newborn infant's astonishingly searching gaze, her wild drugged thought that he more resembled Piet than Ken, and the miraculous present fact that she, slim Foxy, was a good nurser, a tall tree of food.

Freddy said, "She seemed in no hurry to go back to her husband."

"Yes, I wondered about that. She spoke very loyally of 'Roth,' when she thought of him. I think she sees her life as a kind of Cinderella story, rescued at the end, and now that she's living happily ever after, she's bored."

"She found Ken congenial." Again, it was not quite interrogative.

"Very."

Freddy had not expected so curt a response; delicately balked, he licked his lips and volunteered, "She also seemed attracted to me."

"Oh, Freddy, we all are."

The receptionist, who had been tinkling in the corner with the sterilizer, flashed a naughty smile behind Freddy's back. Sensing teasing, he became dryer in manner. "We discussed fertility; did she tell you?" The receptionist left the room.

"Breathlessly. All about myths."

"In part. We concluded, as I remember, that women could as easily be fertilized by the wind as by men, if they believed in it. That all conception is immaculate, on the handiest excuse." That blurred smirk: what was she supposed to imagine it implied?

Foxy said, "How silly. We're obviously helpless."

"Are you?"

"Otherwise why would there be so many only children? I *hated* being an only child. My father just wasn't there. We had plenty of electric fans."

"Did you?" He had lost track of the joke, the wind.

"One in every room. I know I certainly don't intend my child to be only." There it was: just when Foxy had decided for the hundredth time that Freddy was contemptible, she found she had been drawn out.

He asked, "Numb yet?"

She said, "Almost. What's that cot for?" She gestured toward the nether room, to fling the conversation from herself. A small cloud crossed the sun and dipped them into momentary shadow as if into intimacy. The music was mechanically doing "Tea for Two." She was suddenly hungry for English muffins.

"Not what you think," Freddy said.

"I don't think anything. I'm just asking."

"Instead of lunch sometimes I take a nap."

"I've wondered how you keep going with all those parties. But what did you think I thought?" She made silent motions indicating the young receptionist, doing her doll stare and touching her forehead for the skunk bangs, and, folding her hands beside her face, sleep. She formed a kissing mouth to cement her meaning.

"No," Freddy whispered. "That I give abortions."

Shocked, stifled by shock, Foxy wanted to flee the chair. "I *never* thought that."

"Oh, but dentists do. It's a perfect set-up. They have everything, the chair, anesthetic, instruments . . ."

She judged he was saying these things to enlarge himself in her eyes, to inflame with innuendo her idea of him. If he had gone to medical school, he had aspired to power over life and death; having failed, having settled for dentistry, a gingerly meddling at the mouth of life, he still aspired. She put him down: "I don't want to hear about it."

He answered, "You must be numb now," and began to drill. Upside down, his warm cheek close against her head, Freddy resolved into a pair of hairy nostrils, a dance of probing fingers, and glinting crescents of curved glass. His aura was maternal, soapy. Foxy relaxed. Her breasts began to sting and she anticipated release, leaving this office, collecting the baby in his vanilla Carry-Cot at Bea Guerin's, driving down the winding beach road to her empty house, undoing her upper clothes, and giving her accumulated richness over to that tiny blind mouth so avid to suck. He had begun on the right breast this morning, so it would be the left this noon. Twenty minutes, and the Novocain would be wearing off, and she could make a lunch of leftover salad and a tuna sandwich. How innocently life ate the days. How silly she was, how Christianly neurotic, to feel beneath the mild mixed surface of aging and growing, of nursing and eating and sleeping, of love feigned and stolen and actual, a terror, a tipping wrongness, a guilt gathering toward discharge. Poor Freddy, their ringleader, was revealed as a competent dentist. "Lady Be Good" was played. Beneath the red blanket of her closed eyelids Foxy saw that she must soon break with Piet, and felt no pain.

In mid-melody the radio music stopped.

The characterless male voice, winded, hurried, as if called back to the microphone from a distance, pronounced, "A special bulletin. Shots have been heard in Dallas in the vicinity of the Presidential motorcade. We repeat. Gunshots have been reported in Dallas in the vicinity of President Kennedy's motorcade."

There was a second of sharp silence. Then the needle was returned to the groove and the toothpaste music smoothly resumed "Lady Be Good." The black clock said 1:36.

Freddy held the drill away from her mouth. "You hear that?"

She asked him, "What does it mean?"

"Some crazy Texan." He resumed drilling. The pitch of speed lifted impatiently. The star of heat pricked its cloud of spray, and hurt. Freddy sighed mint. "You may spit."

The receptionist, wide-eyed from having overheard the radio, came in from the anteroom to whip the silver and to listen. "Do you think it was Communists?" the girl asked. The music halted again. She signed herself with the cross. On the slates opposite, a small flock of pigeons, having settled near the post office chimney for warmth, clumsily swirled and lifted. The bulletin was repeated, with the additional information that the motorcade had definitely been fired *at*. Three shots had been counted. The pigeons gripped flight in their dirty wings and beat away, out of Foxy's sight. The girl brought a pellet of silver in a chamois pad and set it on the impeccable circular napkin of Freddy's tool tray. Freddy rolled it tighter with his fingertips. The blunder of resuming the music was not repeated. Words spaced by silence filled in the solid truth. The President had been shot at, the President had been hit, he had been hit in the head, his condition was critical, a priest had been summoned, the President was dead. By two o'clock, all of this was known. Amid medicinal whiffs, Freddy had swabbed Foxy's cavity and flanked the tooth with cotton and clamps and pressed the silver filling tight. Foxy had waited in the chair ten additional minutes to hear the worst. Kennedy dead, she left. The nurse was crying, her eyes still held wide, as if like a doll's unable to close unless she lay down. Foxy, grateful to her for showing emotion, patted her hand, a cool tap in passing. Living skin seeks skin. The girl blurted, "We didn't even vote for him, my family, but would have the next time."

Freddy seemed distended and titillated by this confirmation of chaos. Escorting Foxy out through the anteroom, he said in the hall, "This fucks up our party, doesn't it?"

"You must cancel," Foxy told him. She would not see Piet tonight.

"But I've bought all the *booze*," Freddy protested.

Foxy went out into Freddy's tiny front yard, which held a crabapple tree skeletal and spidery without leaves. The post office flag was already at half-mast. Divinity Street was so silent she heard an electric sander working well down the block. Through the plate-glass windows of the pizza shop and the Tarbox *Star* and the shoe-repair haven that was also a bookie joint, she saw shadows huddled around radios. She thought of the little blond radio's embarrassed fall from its empyrean of bland music, of the receptionist's navy-blue eyes lacquered by tears, of Freddy's stupid refusal to mourn, mistaken and contemptible, yet—what was better in herself? She tried to picture the dead man, this young man almost of her generation, with whom she could have slept. A distant husband had died and his death less left an emptiness than revealed one already there. Where grief should have dwelt there was a reflex tenderness, a personal cringing. At Cogswell's corner she glanced up toward the Congregational Church and her heart, blind lamb, beat faster. The Plymouth was parked by the rocks; she must hurry to the baby. Striding uphill through the spotty blowing sunlight, Foxy imagined her son's avid toothless mouth. Her left breast eagerly ached. She tested the right side of her mouth and found it still numb. Would her lopsided smile frighten him? Then it seemed to her that the cocky pouchy-eyed corpse had been Piet and the floor of her stomach fell and the town around her gripped guilt in its dirty white gables and tried to rise, to become a prayer.

The Thornes decided to have their party after all. In the late afternoon, after Oswald had been apprehended and Johnson sworn in, and the engines of national perpetuity had demonstrated their strength, Georgene called all the houses of the invited and explained that the food and liquor had been purchased, that the guests had bought their dresses and had their tuxedos cleaned, that she and Freddy would feel lonely tonight and the children would be *so* disappointed, that on this terrible day she saw nothing wrong in the couples who knew each other feeling terrible together. In a way, Georgene explained to Angela, it would be a wake, an Irish wake, and a formal dinner-dance was very fitting for the dead man, who had had such style. Do come. Please. Freddy will be very hurt, you know how vulnerable he is.

The fashion that fall was for deep décolletage; Piet, arriving at nine, was overwhelmed by bared breasts. He had been reluctant to come. His superstitious nature had groped for some religious observance, some ceremony of acknowledgment to gallant dead Kennedy, though he was a Republican. He knew Freddy would be blasphemous. Further, he felt unwell: his tongue and gums had developed a rash of cankers, and since Foxy had become inaccessible Angela had also ceased to make love to him, and his tuxedo was old, a hand-me-down from his father-in-law, and unfashionably wide-lapelled, and the black shoulders showed his dandruff. Entering the Thornes' living room he saw naked shoulders and flaringly bared bosoms floating through the candlelight, haunting the African masks, the gaudy toss pillows, the wickerwork hassocks and strap-hinged Spanish chests and faded wing chairs. Logs burned in the fieldstone fireplace. The bar table of linen and glasses and bottles formed an undulant field of reflected fire. Janet

Appleby wore an acid-green gown whose shoelace straps seemed unequal to the weight squeezed to a sharp dark cleavage like the vertical crease of a frowning brow. Marcia little-Smith, in a braless orange bodice, displayed, as she reached forward, earrings shuddering, to tap a cigarette into a copper ashtray each dent of which was crescental in the candlelight, conical tits hanging in shadow like tubular roots loose in water. Georgene wore white, two filmy breadths of cloth crossed to form an athletic and Attic binder, her breasts flattened boyishly, as if she were on her back. Carol Constantine had stitched herself a blue silk sheath severely narrow at the ankles and chastely high in front but scooped in the back down to her sacral vertebrae. Irene Saltz—for the Saltzes had come, partly renewed confidence brought on by Irene's job, partly impish insistence on Freddy's part—had put on a simple cocktail dress of black velvet; its oval neckline inverted the two startled arcs of her eyebrows as she jealously, anxiously surveyed the room for the whereabouts of Ben and Carol and Eddie. Piet was touched by her. Like him, she felt it was wrong to have come. She had lost weight. Humiliation flattered her.

Bea Guerin drifted toward him with uplifted face; her bosom, sprinkled with sweat, was held forward in a stiff scarlet carapace like two soft sugared buns being offered warm in the metal vessel of their baking. "Oh Piet," she said, "isn't it awful, that we're all here, that we couldn't stay away, couldn't stay home and mourn decently?" With lowered lids he fumbled out a concurrence, hungering for the breasts that had risen to such a roundness their upper rims made a dimpled angle with Bea's chest-wall. *Why don't you want to fuck me?* Her lifted upper lip revealed the little gap between her front teeth; she laid a trembling hand on his arm, for balance, or as a warning. *You're surrounded by unkind people.* Embarrassed, he sipped his martini, and the cankers lining his mouth burned.

He said, "I hear you're seeing a lot of the Constantines."

"They're bores, Piet. Roger enjoys them, but they're self-centered bores. After a while one minds their not having gone to college."

"Who does Roger enjoy most, Eddie or Carol?"

"Don't be wicked, Piet. I don't mind it from these others, but I hate it from you. You're not wicked, why pretend?"

"Answer my question."

"Carol can be fun," Bea said, "but she's *so* cold. Cold and crude. I think—this is terribly sad—I think she was honestly in love with Ben, terribly in love, and never let herself know it, and now she can't admit it, it's too un*dig*nified, and does the *cruelest* imitations of him."

"But Ben is so boring."

"Piet, I don't think they noticed, they're such bores themselves. Oh, it's awful, everybody is so boring. Roger is so ex*treme*ly boring."

"You think I wouldn't be?"

"Not for a while, sweet Piet. Not for a long while. But you don't like short women, it's *so* Napoleonic of you."

Piet laughed and gazed over Bea's head. Where was Foxy? He searched the flickering room in vain. He felt that in her staying away she had achieved over him a moral ascendancy that completed the triumph, the royal disregard, of her giving birth to a son. Pity sucked at him; he felt abandoned, small. He asked Bea, "Where are the Gallaghers?"

"Matt told Georgene they were going with their children to a special mass. She said he was polite over the phone but just barely."

"Matt is getting very independent. And the Ongs?"

"John was too sick."

"How sick is he?"

"Freddy says he's dying," Bea said, the curve of her cheek a Diana's bow in candlelight. Dying. Before coming to the party Piet and his daughters had watched, on television, the casket being hauled from the plane amid the spotlights of the air field: a long gleam on the polished wood as sudden as a bullet, the imagined airless privacy within, the flooding lights without, the widow blanched amid rapid shadows, the eclipsing shoulders of military attachés. The casket had tipped, bumped. Bea said to Piet, "You haven't asked where are the Whitmans."

"Oh, aren't they here?"

: COUPLES

"Piet, you're *so* obvious. I have *no* idea where they are, but you've been looking over my head *all* this time. It's not very flattering."

"I was thinking I should get another drink." To quench panic. The refrigerator. The stars.

"Piet," Bea said swiftly, softly, seeing he was pulling away. "I could love you, if you'd let me."

At the drinks table Carol was flirting simultaneously with Harold and Frank. "Frank," she said loudly in a voice that did not quite dare call the party to attention, to make an occasion, "give us a Shakespeare quote. Nobody knows quite what to say."

"Good night, sweet prince?" Angela offered. It startled Piet to see her there, her fine oval skull and throat suspended in the hovering light, shadows fluctuating on her white shoulders, the scalloped neckline, the discreet parabola of pearls.

Frank Appleby, red-eyed, considered and said, "Ambition's debt is paid."

Carol asked, "Is that a quote?"

"From *Julius Caesar*. What a dumb floozy." He gave Carol a crunching shoulder hug that Piet feared would shatter her brittle blue sheath.

"What about"—Harold little-Smith interrupted himself with a giggle—"For Oswald is an honorable man?" Enjoying the laughter of the others, he went on, "I *really* had to laugh, the news came in just as I was having dessert, *gâteau avec des fraises*, with three of my most Republican associates, including, Frank—this will amuse you—young Ed Foster, who as Frank knows thinks Bob Taft was turning pink at the end. *Un peu de rose au fin.* Naturally everybody's first assumption, including the broadcasters, who are all liberals of course—"

Carol interrupted, "Harold, are you *really* a conservative?"

Janet spoke up. "Harold and Frank are different. Frank's a Federalist; he honestly *loves* the Founding Fathers. Harold's an ultramontane; with him it's just a form of swank."

"*Merci pour votre mots très incisifs.* May I please continue? Well, naturally everybody assumed that a *right*-wing crackpot had done it. You remember at first there was a lot of melancholy fill-in about Dallas the Birchers' paradise, et cetera; we were all very pious and tut-tutty."

"Is that French?" Carol asked.

"But then, around two-thirty, when I'd got back to the office and the stuff on Oswald had begun to filter through, young Ed called up absolutely ec*stat*ic and said, 'Did you hear? It wasn't one of ours, it was one of *theirs!*'" Perhaps because all those listening had experienced the same reversal of prejudice, there was less laughter than Harold had expected.

Frank offered, "Ever since McCarthy cracked up, all the real wolves have been on the left."

Freddy said, "One thing I'm absolutely certain of, he wasn't in it alone. There were too many shots. The whole fucking thing was too successful."

He was unanimously pooh-poohed. Janet said, "Freddy, you see conspiracies in everything."

"He thinks," Angela stated, "we're all a conspiracy to protect each other from death."

"To shut out the night, I think I said."

Piet was impressed that Freddy remembered anything of what he said. Shapelessness was growing bones. Feeding on calcium stolen from Piet's own slack and aimless life. Lately Freddy had taken to staring at Piet too hard, meaningfully.

"One conspiracy I'll let you all in on is," Harold little-Smith said, "when the market opens again, buy. Business was *not* happy with Kennedy, and it's going to *love* Johnson. He's just the kind of old bastard business is happy under."

Carol with her long bare back shivered. "That gross sad man. It was like the high-school shot putter accepting the class presidency, all humility and rotten grammar. Freddy, are you going to let us dance?"

"Whatever my guests think is proper. I don't know how to act, frankly. I've never had my President assassinated before. I was a baby when they did Lincoln in. Honest Abyface."

Ben Saltz overheard and came up to them. His face above his beard appeared to Piet shell-white, a grinning fragment from an exploded past. "And yet," he informed Freddy, "this country since 1865 has an unenviable record for political violence. *Four* presidents, plus the attempts on Truman and both Roosevelts— as you know, Teddy was actually wounded, in his unsuccessful campaign in 1912—not to mention Huey Long. There isn't a country west of the Balkans with any kind of the same record. The Prime Ministers of England go everywhere with a single body-guard."

"We fought for the right to bear arms," Frank said.

Carol was saying, "Ben will dance with me, won't you, Ben? Wouldn't you like to dance with me?"

His carved lion's smile appeared, but his eyes remained dubious, frightened, human. Carol twitchily seized Harold's arm and said, "If Ben's scared to, Harold will, won't you, Harold? Dance with me. After Janet's been so mean about your elegant politics. Freddy, put on music." She turned the chill pallor of her back on Piet.

Ben too, in a trim tuxedo that looked rented, turned his back, and spoke to Angela. Piet heard his wife ask, ". . . like her teaching by now?"

Ben's voice, doleful and clear, responded, ". . . gratifying to me to see her using her mind after all these years, being at least to some extent intellectually challenged."

Georgene was standing in the middle of the room with the air of a hostess undecided between duties. Piet approached her and let her sip his drink. "Carol is terribly high," he said.

"Well, take her to bed. You know where it is."

"I wouldn't dream of it. She'd scratch. But I wonder whose inspiration it was to have the Saltzes and Constantines together."

"Freddy's, of course."

"But you made it stick. Freddy has a lot of ideas that you let wither."

Georgene's righteous clubwoman's temper flared. "Well really Piet, it's too tedious, if people aren't going to have their affairs in private." We were different, she was saying, we were secret, and brave, and better than these corrupt couples. She went on aloud, roughly pushing her fingers through her graying hair, as if comb-ing out larch needles, "I seem to be the only person I know left who has any sense of privacy."

"Oh. That's an interesting remark."

"It's not meant to be."

"Sweet Georgene, what *are* you doing with all this privacy, now that I'm not around?"

"Oh," she said, "men come and go. I can't keep track of them all. They've worn a path through the woods." She asked, "Do you care?"

"Of course. You were wonderful for me."

"What happened then?"

"It began to frighten me. I felt Freddy knew."

"What if he did? I was handling Freddy."

"Maybe I'm not being entirely honest."

"I know you're not," Georgene said, "you never are," and, like a playing card being snapped, showed him her edge and dealt herself away. Let women in, Piet thought, and they never stop lecturing. Pedagogy since the apple. Be as gods.

Roger Guerin came up to him. His brows were knit tight and he was wearing a frilled and pleated dress shirt, with ruby studs and a floppy bow tie in the newest fey fashion. He asked, "Put your golf clubs away yet?"

Piet said, "There may be one more warm weekend."

Eddie Constantine came up to them crouching. "Hey Jesus," he said, "have either of you looked down Marcia's dress yet? She's nose cones down to her navel."

"You've always known they were there," Piet told him.

"Believing isn't seeing. God, we were in the kitchen talking about some cruddy thing, air pollution, and I kept looking down and they kept bobbling around, I got such a hard-on I had to dive in here to level off."

Roger laughed, too loudly out of his tiny mouth, like one who has learned about laughing late in life, and Piet realized he was standing here as an excuse, that the point of Eddie's anecdote had been to amuse and excite Roger. My cock, he had been secretly saying, is big as a fuselage. Women, he had been saying, are dirt.

"How about Janet?" Roger asked him. "Held by those two little shoestrings."

Eddie drew closer, still in his scuttling position, to the other man, stiff-standing. "It looks to me the way they're squeezed she's carrying a second backside, in case the first wears out." The beauty of duality. A universe of twos. "Hey Roger, do you want to know what crazy Carol did the other night? We were . . . you know . . . in my lap . . . up . . . and what does the bitch do but swing her leg way the hell back and stick her foot in my mouth! It was great, I damn near puked. Get Bea to try it."

Piet moved off and gently, by standing expectant, detached Janet from the little-Smiths and Freddy Thorne. The glass in her hand held a few melted ice cubes; he touched it to take it from her. She did not resist, her head was bowed. In the hushed space walled by their bodies Piet asked, "How goes it, Jan-Jan? How's your beautiful shrink?"

"That bastard," she said, without looking up, "that son of a bitch. He won't tell me to stop seeing Harold."

"We all thought you'd stopped seeing Harold ages ago. Ever since your goodness and health regime."

Now she did look up. "You're nice, Piet. Naïve but nice."

He asked her, "Why is it your psychiatrist's job to tell you to stop seeing Harold?"

"That's what *he* says," she said. "Because I love him, that's why. He's a fat old Kraut with a brace on one leg and I love him, he's a total fink but I adore him, and if he gave even the simplest kind of a fart about me he'd tell me to stop sleeping with Harold. But he won't. He doesn't. The old re-tard."

"What *does* the man tell you?"

"I've been going now five months and the only hint he's ever dropped is that because of the pharmaceutical business every time I take a pill I'm having intercourse with my father, it's his seed. I said to him, What am I supposed to do when I get a headache and need two aspirin, dial a prayer?"

"Dear lovely Janet, don't cry. Tell me instead, should Angela go? Ever since you started, she's wanted to go. What's my duty as a husband?"

"Don't let her. Get her a lover, send her to Yugoslavia, anything but this. God, it's degrading. It'll get her all mixed up and she's so serene. She doesn't know how neurotic she is."

"She's beginning to. She tells me she feels too detached, as if she's already dead."

"Mm, I know that feeling. Angela and I are somewhat alike."

"Yes, that's what she says too. She says you both have big bosoms and it makes you both melancholy."

"Let Angela speak for herself. I'm not sure I like being somebody's twin. Are you going to get me another bourbon or not?"

While Piet was at the drink table, Freddy Thorne sidled up to him and said, "Could we talk a moment? Alone."

"Freddy, how exciting! Just little old me and big old you?"

"Notice I'm not smiling."

"But I can see your skull smiling through, behind those poodgy lips."

"How much have you had to drink?"

"Never ask an Irishman that question at a wake. Eh cup quaffed fer sorree's sake isn't nae cup at all. Stop standing there looking portentous. I have to take Janet her drink. I think I'm falling in love with Janet."

But by his return with the drink, Janet was deep in conversation with Harold, and Piet let himself be led to a corner by Freddy, the corner behind the unstrung harpframe.

"Piet," Freddy said, biting the word short. "I'll give you this cold turkey. I know about you and Georgene."

"Cold turkey? I thought that was how dope addicts broke the habit. Or am I thinking of the day after Thanksgiving?"

"I told you that night at the Constantines to lay off. Remember?"

"Was that the night you were Chiang Kai-shek?"

"And just now I see you and she having a cozy-type talk in the middle of the room. Righty-right?

"I don't care what they say at the State Department, I think we should let you invade. Unleash Freddy Thorne, I'm always saying, as our many mutual friends will testify."

Freddy said nothing. Piet found the lack of any answer a frightening void. He asked, "How do you think you know this?" When again no answer came, he asked, "What do you think you know?"

"She told me herself. You and she were lovers."

"Georgene?"

"Well, did she lie?"

"She might have, to get back at you for something else. Or you might be lying to me. When is this supposed to have happened?"

"Don't play games. You know when."

"All right. I confess. It happened last summer. We were tennis partners. I lost my head, her pretty white dress and freckles and all, I flung her right down on the service line and we conceded the set six-love. I'm sorry. I'm sorry, I'm sorry, I'm sorry." His mouth felt very dry, though his third martini was light in his hand: empty, flown, the olive a tame green egg.

Freddy tried, with some success, to gather himself into a menacing mass, a squinting cloud, his narrow hairless skull majestic. When he frowned, forked wrinkles spread back on his pate. "I'm going to hurt you," he told Piet, and stalked toward the kitchen, for more ice.

Angela, seeing Piet shaken, left Ben lecturing to air and came to her husband and asked, "What were you and Freddy saying? You're pale as a ghost."

"He was telling me I must have my teeth straightened. Ow. My mouth hurts."

"You won't tell me. Was it about me?"

"Angel, you've got it. He asked me for the honor of your hand. He said he's been in love with you for years."

"Oh, he always says that."

"He does?"

"It's his way of bugging me."

"But you like it. I can tell by your face that you like hearing crap like that."

"Why not? Why are you so mean about Freddy? What has he ever done to you?"

"He threatens my primitive faith," Piet told his wife.

Foxy came into the room with Ken. She wore a strapless silver gown. Her breasts were milk-proud. There was a slow luminous preening of her upper body as she turned, searching for Piet in the mad shadows. The Whitmans' entrance at the front door had disturbed the air of the house, for the candleflames now underwent a struggle and the furniture and walls seemed to stagger and billow. She had come for him. She had abandoned her house and warm baby on this tragic night solely to seek him out, to save him from harm amid this foul crowd. He heard her explain to Georgene: "We had the sitter all lined up and thought we'd come for a little while just to make it worthwhile for her—she's Doc Allen's daughter and we don't want to discourage her when we're just beginning, we've never *needed* sitters before. Then after she came we sat around for the longest while unable to tear ourselves away from the television."

"What's happening now?" Roger's deep voice inquired.

"Oh," Foxy said, "mostly old film clips. What are really heartbreaking are the press conferences. He was so quick and sassy and, I don't know, attentive. He somehow brought back the *fun* in being an American." Piet saw that as she spoke she held close to her husband's arm, sheltering. Ken stood erect and pale in impeccable black. His studs were onyx.

"I loved him," Bea Guerin cried, in a flung voice whose woe seemed distant within it, a woe calling from an underworld, "I could never have voted for him, I really don't believe in all those wishy-washy socialist things he wanted, I think people must be themselves even if it's only to suffer, but I *loved* the way he held himself, and dressed, never wearing a hat or an overcoat, I mean."

"The terrible sadness," Frank Appleby said, "of those strange wall eyes."

Marcia asked, "Were they really wall? I thought it was just he was always reading a Teleprompter."

Music translucently flooded the room. Doris Day, "Stars Fell on Alabama." Freddy loved Doris Day. Freddy was all heart and as American as apple pie and Swapsies.

"Freddy!" Carol cried. "You angel! Where's Roger?" The Thornes' rug of interwoven rush rosettes was rolled to the legs of the satin chaise longue, and Carol and Roger, she lithely, he stiffly, danced. "Oh," she cried, "your hand is icy!"

"From holding a drink," he muttered, scowling, embarrassed, and on the bony stem of her naked back set his hand edgewise, curled in a limp half-fist like a sleeping child's.

The others watched uneasily. In moving to get his wife and himself a drink, Ken Whitman fastidiously skirted the bare floor and, waiting for Freddy to bring ice from the kitchen, talked softly with Janet. Ben Saltz moved to be beside Foxy. Her ges-

tures expressed pleasure at seeing him again, after his long absence
from parties; then, in response to words of his, she looked down
at her flat soft stomach and obligingly, not displeased, enjoying in
his Jewishness the ghost of Peter, blushed. Angela touched Piet's
arm and asked, "Shall we dance?"

"Do you want to? It seems blasphemous, waltzing on the poor
guy's grave."

"It does, it is, but we must. It's terrible taste, but we can't let
Roger and Carol do it alone. They're getting too embarrassed."

She was familiar and thick and pliant in his arms; he had never
learned proper steps and in the course of their marriage she had
learned to follow his vague stridings lightly, as if they made a
pattern, her thighs and pelvis gently cushioned against his. Their
heights were equal. She rarely wore perfume, so her hair and skin
released a scent unspecific but absolutely good, like water, or life,
or existence itself, considered in contrast to the predominant
vacuum between the stars.

"Where," he asked her, "are Irene and Eddie?"

"In the kitchen talking about air pollution."

"They are the *smuggest* couple," Piet said. "After all that fuss. I
hope you take Irene's injured confidences henceforth with a lick
of salt." He meant a saltlick, a large cake such as were mounted in
the barnyards of Michigan dairy farms, but it came out sounding
like a tiny amount, less than a grain.

"Well Ben," Angela said, "is talking to your ex-pregnant girl
friend, so Irene *had* to go back to Eddie."

"That's too complicated," Piet said, trying to match his feet to
the change of tempo as "Stars Fell on Alabama" became "Soft as
the Starlight." "And the other lady is surely ex-pregnant but she
was never my girl friend."

"I was kidding. Don't resist me like that. Relax. Glide."

"I hate this party, frankly. When can we go home?"

"Piet, it's the sort of party you love."

"I feel we're insulting Kennedy."

"Not at all. Yesterday, he was just our President way down in
Washington, and now he belongs to all of us. He's right here.
Don't you feel him?"

He looked into her blue eyes amazed. There was an enduring strangeness to Angela that continued through all disillusions to enchant him. Perceiving this, he resented his subtle bondage, and burned to tear Foxy from Ben, to trample on his bushy face with boots. Ineptly he stepped on Angela's toe.

Now Ken and Janet joined them on the dance floor, and Freddy and Irene. Above his black shoulder the twin circumflex of her perfect eyebrows seemed a lifted wingbeat. Her hair was parted precisely in the middle. Eddie Constantine came as if to capture her but at the last moment veered off and cut in to dance with Angela. Piet went and asked Georgene, standing gazing by the table of lightened bottles and dirtied glasses.

In his arms she asked him, "Do you think it's too early for the ham? We bought some salmon but no Catholics have come."

He accused her: "You and your noble privacy. Your husband just lowered the boom on me."

"Freddy? What on earth for?"

"For having an affair with you."

"Don't tease. Our times together were very precious, at least to me."

"Tease! He said you yourself told him everything. Postures, dates, phases of the moon."

"That's such a lie. I've *never* admitted anything about us, though he's tried to get me to often enough. It's the way he works. I hope *you* didn't admit anything."

"I didn't, but it was sheer perversity. I assumed he had me cold."

"He talks to Carol and Janet all the time; maybe one of them has made him think he knows something."

"Are you sure he doesn't? Are you sure you didn't tell him some night before dropping off to sleep, figuring I was a lost cause anyway, and needing something to even some score with, like an affair he'd had with Carol."

"Carol? Do you know this?" He loved feeling her experience fear in his arms; there was a dissolution of the bodily knit indistinguishable from sexual willingness.

"No. But he's over there all the time, and Carol's not too fussy.

Not," he added hastily, "that Freddy isn't a gorgeous hunk of man."

She ignored his unkind parody of tact, asking instead, "And you? *Are* you a lost cause?"

"Soft as the Starlight" became "It Must Have Been Moonglow." "Well," Piet said carefully, "more and more, as Freddy acts as if he knows."

"Oh, Freddy. He doesn't want to know *any*thing, he just wants people to *think* he knows *every*thing. But if I'm not worth the trouble to you, there's no use talking, is there, Piet?" With her quick athletic firmness she put her hands on his arms and pushed herself out of his embrace. "Only don't come running to *me* the next time you need a little change of ass." Watching her retreat, he realized that all these months, all through Foxy, he had been considering Georgene still his mistress.

Foxy was across the room dancing with Frank Appleby. They moved together placidly, without reference to the beat, silver locked in lead's grip. "Wrap Your Troubles in Dreams" became the song. Marcia was at hand and, slithery quick, she nestled against his damp shirtfront, asking, "Piet, what's happened to you? You're not funny like you used to be."

"I never was trying to be funny."

"You were too. You were so delighted to be with us, at the beach, skiing, anywhere. Now you've stopped caring. You think we're ugly, silly people."

"Marcia, I love you. I bet you were class secretary in school."

"Is it your work? What are you doing now that it's too cold to put up any more cozy little horrors on Indian Hill?"

"We've been saved by the bell. Just the other week we got a big inside job on Divinity. They hauled off Gertrude Tarbox to a nursing home and the bank in New Bedford that held the mortgage is turning the house into offices. We've taken out three truckloads of *National Geographic*s." Telling Marcia this troubled him, for he had been working in this house all day, alone, operating a big sander on the floors of what had once been a chandeliered dining room. Lost in the hypnotic whine and snarl of the machine, fascinated by the disappearance of decades of dirt and paint, by this reversal into clean wood, he had been ignorant of the President's assassination until Jazinski returned at three from a mysteriously long lunch hour. Deafened by the sander, Piet had let the bullet pass painlessly through him.

Marcia asked irritably, "Why does anyone need office space in Tarbox?"

"Oh, you'd be surprised. There's a crying shortage downtown. Insurance companies, chiropractors. AA wants to set up a branch here. This isn't the idyllic retreat you moved to, Marcia. We're sadly suburban. There's going to be a big shopping center between here and Lacetown. Isn't Frank on the committee to squeeze more train service out of the poor old New Haven, or the MBTA, or the Lionel Company, or somebody?"

"Piet, when are you going to get away from Gallagher? Frank and Harold were talking at lunch in Boston to a man who knows the South Shore and he expects Gallagher to go bankrupt. The banks own him twice over and he keeps gambling. If the nuns hadn't bailed him out last summer he couldn't have met another payment."

"No, sweetie, you don't understand. Matt can't lose. We live in an expanding universe." To quiet her, to quell her critical spirit, he dipped his hand to her buttocks; they were narrow and nipped-in like the responsive little wheels at the front of a tractor. At a guiding touch from him she brought her body closer, so close his lips shrank from the cold aura of her dangling earring. He murmured, "How *is* Frank, speaking of the MBTA?"

"The same. Maybe worse. Simply going to bed doesn't soothe him any more. He needs to get out from under that heavy neurotic bitch."

"Oh hell, we all need to get out from under."

"Not me. I need Harold. To hurt me. He's beautifully cruel, don't you think?"

"Beautifully?"

"And yet gallant, in an old-fashioned way. I'm his, but he respects my independence. I think we're a very nice old-fashioned couple, don't you?"

"Antique. Victoria and Prince Albert. But let's talk about me.

Don't I need to get out from under Angela?"

"Oh Piet," Marcia said impatiently, "without Angela, you'd die."

Struck empty by this, unable to answer, he sang with the gauze-voiced record into the curled cool shell of her ear, "*Cast*les may *tum*ble, that's *fate* after *all*, life's really *fun*ny that *way.*"

She mistook his mood and flattened her body more sinuously against his. Her fingertips found the small hairs at the back of his neck, her pelvis lifted an inch. This a woman twice spoken for: he glanced around the room for rescue. Ken was still dancing with Janet. His temples looked gray as they circled near a candle. Freddy had replaced Eddie with Angela. Eddie and Irene had gone to stand against the wall, talking. Frank Appleby was making himself another drink. Foxy had fled. Doris Day's song became "Moonglow." Harold, catching Piet's eyes, came over, dug his fingers into Marcia's sleeping arm so cruelly her olive skin leaped white between his nails, and said, "Now on the idiot box they're talking about giving him an eternal flame. *Une flamme éternelle.* For Christ's sake, he wasn't the Unknown Soldier, he was a cleverly manufactured politician who happened to catch a nobody's bullet. *Chérie, es-tu ivre?*"

Marcia said huskily, having slept against Piet's body, now awoken, "Yes."

"Then come with me. *Pardonnez-nous,* Piet."

"Gladly. I'll go catch a bullet." Piet made his fourth martini, silvery. Foxy. Was she in the woods? Where was Ben? Not among the men dancing. Like a moth to flame was she to Jews. Abram over Lot. Ben's fingers, deft from miniaturizing, gliding down the tawny long insides of her stocking-topped thighs to fumble in the nigger-lipped pale fur there. Her clitoris welling through a milky film slowly, ruby rosy, watchsprings in a pansy shape. All shadowy smiling distances, Foxy would stretch and guide. Ben leonine, in the concealing shade of a Thorne-owned bush. Beyond these black windows she had opened to another lover.

Piet turned in pain from the window and it seemed that the couples were gliding on the polished top of Kennedy's casket. An island of light in a mourning nation. "Close Your Eyes." "Cuhlozzz yur eyeszz": the velvet voice from Hollywood whispered an inch inside Piet's ear. The olive egg in his martini had been abandoned by its mother high and dry. His cankers hurt, especially the one his tongue had to stretch to reach, low and left on the front gum, at the root of his lip. A maze of membranes, never could have evolved from algae unassisted. God gave us a boost. He felt he shouldn't have another drink. No supper, empty stomach. Marcia's slithering had stirred him. Half-mast, subsided, lumpy. His kidneys signaled: the sweetness pealing of a silent bell: relieve me. The Thornes' bathroom. There Georgene would wash herself before and after. Said his jizz ran down her leg, too much of it, should screw Angela more. Hexagonal little floor tiles, robin's-egg toilet paper, posh purple towels. *Welcome to the post-pill* . . . Sashaying from the shower nude, her pussy of a ferny freshness. The grateful lumpiness following love. Well done, thou good and faithful. Turning up the familiar stairs, his black foot firm on the swaying treads, he glanced into the dark side room, where a few obscure heads were watching a weary flickering rerun of the casket's removal from the belly of the airplane. Ben was there, bent forward, his profile silvered as in Sunday-school oleographs, facing Sinai. Roger and Carol, sharing a hassock. Frank sucked a cigar whose smoke was charged with the dartings of light as casket became widow, widow became Johnson, Johnson became commentator. Ghouls. Foxy must be in the kitchen. The paneled bathroom door was closed. Tactfully he tapped. Her musical voice called, "Just a min-ute."

Piet said, "It's me," and pushed. The door gave. She was sitting on the toilet in her uplifted silver gown, startled, a patch of blue paper like a wisp of sky in her hand. The pressure of the oval seat widened her garter-rigged and pallid thighs; she was perched forward; her toes but not her heels touched the hexagonal tiles of the floor. "I love you" was pulled from him like a tooth. The mirror above the basin threw him back at himself. His flat taut face looked flushed and astonished, his mouth agape, his black tie askew.

Foxy said in a whisper reverberant in the bright tiled space, "You're mad to be in here." Then with incongruous deliberation she patted herself, let the paper drop into the oval of water below, and, half-turning on the seat, depressed the silver handle. Sluggishly the toilet flushed: Georgene used to complain about the low water pressure on the hill. Foxy rose from the vortex and smoothed her gown downward. Facing him, she seemed tall, faintly challenging and hostile, her closed lips strangely bleached by pale pink lipstick, newly chic. He made sure the door behind them was shut, and moved past her to urinate standing. With a pang, initially reluctant, his golden arc occurred. "God," he said, "it's a relief to see you alone. When the hell can we meet?"

She spoke hurriedly, above his splashing. "I wasn't sure you wanted to. You've been very distant."

"Ever since you've had the baby I've been frightened to death of you. I assumed it was the end of us."

"That's not true. Unless you want it to be true."

"The fact is, all fall I've been frightened of everything. Death, my work, Gallagher, my children, the stars. It's been hideous." A concluding spurt, somewhat rhetorical, and a dismissive drying shake. He tucked himself in. "My whole life seems just a long falling."

"But it's *not*. You have a good life. Your lovely family, your nice square house, me if you want me. We can't talk here. Call me Monday. I'm alone again."

He flushed, but the water closet had not filled. "Wait. Please. Let me see your breasts."

"They're all milky."

"I know. Just for a moment. Please. I do need it."

They listened for steps on the stairs; there were none. Music below, and the television monologue. Her mouth opened and her tongue, red as sturgeon, touched her upper lip as she reached behind her to undo snaps. Her gown and bra peeled down in a piece. Fruit.

"Oh. God."

She blushed in answer. "I feel so gross."

"So veiny and full. So hard at the tops, here."

"Don't get them started. I must go home in an hour."

"And nurse."

"Yes. What funny sad lines you're getting here, and here. Don't frown, Piet. And gray hairs. They're new."

"Nurse me."

"Oh darling. No."

"Nurse me."

She covered one breast, alarmed, but he had knelt, and his broad mouth fastened on the other. The thick slow flow was at first suck sickeningly sweet. The bright bathroom light burned on his eyelids and seemed to dye his insides a deep flowing rose, down to the pained points of his knees on the icy tile. Foxy's hand lightly cupped the curve of the back of his skull and now guided him closer into the flood of her, now warned by touching his ear that he was giving her pain. He opened his eyes; the nipple of her other breast jutted cherry-red between ivory fingers curled in protection; he closed his eyes. Pulses of stolen food scoured his tongue, his gums; she toyed with his hair, he caressed her clothed buttocks. She was near drowning him in rose.

Knocks struck rocklike at the unlocked door inches behind them. Harsh light flooded him. He saw Foxy's free hand, ringed, grope and cup the sympathetic lactation of the breast jutting unmouthed. She called out, as musically as before, "One moment, please."

Angela's lucid polite voice answered, "Oops, sorry, Foxy. Take your time."

"All ri-ight," Foxy sang back, giving Piet a frantic look of interrogation. Her bare breasts giant circles. A Christian slave stripped to be tortured.

His body thundered with fear. His hands were jerking like puppets on strings but his brain took perspective from the well-lit room in which he was trapped. There was no other door. The shower curtain was translucent glass, two sliding panels; his shape would show. There was a little window. Its sill came up to his chest. Realizing the raising of the sash would make noise, he motioned Foxy to flush the toilet. As she bent to touch the silver handle the shape of her breasts changed, hanging forward, long-tipped udders dripping cloudy drops. He undid the brash catch and shoved up the sash as the water closet again, feebly, drained. Setting one black dancing slipper on the lip of the tub, he hoisted himself into the black square of air headfirst. Trees on this side of the house, elms, but none near enough to grasp. His hands could touch only vertical wood and freezing air pricked by stars. Too late he knew he should have gone feet first; he must drop. This the shady rural side of the house. Soft grass. The toilet had quieted and left no noise to cover the sounds of his scrambling as he changed position. Foxy thought to turn both faucets on full. By logic she must next open the door to Angela. Piet backed out of the window. Foxy was standing by the roaring faucets staring at him and mopping herself with a purple washcloth and resecuring the bodice of her silver gown. He imagined she smiled. No time to think about it. He stood on the slick tub lip and got a leg through the little window and doing a kind of handstand on the radiator cover maneuvered the other leg through also. Button. Caught. Ah. There. He slid out on his chest and dangled his weight by his hands along Thorne's undulate shingles. Loose nails, might catch on a nostril, tear his face like a fish being reamed. Air dangled under his shoes. Ten feet. Eleven, twelve. Old houses, high ceilings. Something feathery brushed his fingers gripping the sill inside the bathroom. Foxy begging him not to dare it? Angela saying it was all right, she knew? Too late. Fall. No apologies. Pushing off lightly from the wall with his slippers and trying to coil himself loosely against the shock, he let go. Falling was first a hum, then concussion: a harpstring in reverse. His heels hit the frost-baked turf; he took a somersault backwards and worried about grass stains on his tuxedo before he thought to praise God for breaking no bones. Above him, a pink face vanished and a golden window whispered shut. They were safe. He was sitting on the brittle grass, his feet in their papery slippers stinging.

The silhouette of the trunk of the elm nearest him wavered; a female voice giggled. "Piet, you're such a show-off," Bea Guerin said.

Ben Saltz's orotund voice pronounced, "That was quite a tumble. I'm impressed."

Piet stood and brushed dirt from his clothes. "What are you two doing out here?"

"Oh," Bea said, and her offhand accents seemed, out of doors, disembodied, "Ben brought me out here to watch a satellite he miniaturized something in go by overhead."

"A tiny component," Ben said. "My old outfit developed it, with maybe one or two of my bright ideas. I thought it might be passing right about now, but all we've seen is a shooting star."

"So lovely," Bea said, and to Piet, still dizzy, the tree was talking, though the scarlet of her dress was growing distinct, "the way it fell, flaring all greeny-blue, like a match being struck, then nothing. I hadn't seen a comet since a child."

"That wasn't a comet," Ben said. "That was a meteor, an inert chunk of matter, of space dust you might say, burning up with friction upon contact with our atmosphere. Comets are incandescent and have elliptical orbits."

"Oh Ben, you're wonderful, you know everything, doesn't he, Piet? But now tell us, whatever were you and Foxy *doing?*"

"Why do you say Foxy?"

"We saw her close the window. Didn't you?"

"Are you sure it was Foxy? I thought it was Angela."

"Angela, poo. Of course it was Foxy, that lovely honey hair. Were you making love? In the bathroom?"

"Boy, that takes nerves of iron," Ben said. "Not to mention pretty well-padded bodies. I've tried it in a boat and it just wasn't my style, very frankly."

"Don't be silly," Piet said. "Of course we weren't. You two are grotesque." Perhaps anger could dissolve this unexpected couple.

"Why is that *silly?*" Bea cried in a soft raising wail, as when she had mourned Kennedy. "Everyone knows about you and Foxy. Your truck is parked down there all the time. We think it's *nice.*"

"My truck hasn't been there for months."

"Well my dear, she's hardly been in a condition to."

"You know," Ben said, "I wonder about that. Forbidding intercourse during pregnancy. I suspect it will turn out to be one more pseudo-medical superstition, like not breast-feeding because it wasn't sanitary, which they sincerely believed in the Thirties. I *made* Irene breast-feed, and she's grateful."

"You're a wonderful husband, Ben," Piet said. "Now you're making her work and she's grateful again."

Bea put her hand, trembling, on his forearm. "Now don't be

sarcastic to Ben, just because you yourself are embarrassed. We won't tell anybody we saw you jump. Except Roger and Irene."

"Well, who shall I tell about you and Ben necking out here?"

"You may tell one person," Bea said, "those are the rules, but you mayn't tell Angela, because she'll tell Freddy Thorne, and then everybody will know. I'm freezing."

All three, they went back into the house together. Doris Day was singing "Stardust." Angela was coming downstairs from the bathroom. She asked, "Where have *you* all been?"

Piet told her, "Ben says he made one of the stars out there, but we couldn't find it."

"Why were you looking under the trees? I *won*dered who was mumbling outside; I could hear you from the bathroom." Suspended halfway up the stairs, she shimmered like a chandelier. Now that he had safely rejoined the party, Piet was piqued by Bea's assumption that Angela told Freddy Thorne everything. Wanting to ask his wife if this were true, he asked her instead, "How much have you drunk?"

"Just enough," she answered, descending. Parting an invisible curtain with her hands, she floated past him.

Piet hurried on; he had questions to ask of every woman. He kept tasting cloying milk. Foxy was in the kitchen, talking to Janet, who turned her back, so the lovers could talk. He asked Foxy hoarsely, "Make it OK?"

"Of course," she whispered.

He went on, "Did I imagine it, or were you standing there smiling at me?"

She glanced about to see they were not being overheard. "You were so manic, it was like a silent comedy. I wanted to tell you not to be silly and kill yourself, but we couldn't make any talking noises, and anyway you were clearly in love with the idea of jumping."

"In love! I was terrified, and now my right knee is beginning to hurt."

"You were terrified of Angela. Why? After all, so your husband is in the bathroom with another woman. It's not the end of the world. Maybe you were helping me get something out of my eye."

Piet drew on his impoverished reserves of moral indignation. "I'm shocked," he said, "that you would laugh. With all our love in the balance."

"I tried to catch your hand at the last minute; but you let go." Her smile became artificial, feral. "We better stop talking. Freddy Thorne has a fishy eye on us and here comes Harold Little."

Harold, petitely storming, his slicked-down hair mussed in pinfeathers in back, said, continuing a conversation begun elsewhere, "If I believed in the omnipotent Lord Jesus, I'd say this was punishment for his letting our one staunch ally in Southeast Asia get nailed to please the pansy left in this country. *La gauche efféminée.*"

"Oh Harold," Foxy said, mothering, "in," "don't talk like that, you're imitating somebody else. Cardinal Richelieu. You think we'll think you're cute if you go right-wing. We think you're cute now. Don't we, Piet?"

"Harold," Piet asked, "have you thought of asking the young widow for her hand? You and Madame Nhu would make a lovely couple. You both have a fiery way of expressing yourselves."

"You both speak French," Foxy added.

"The trouble with this *merde*-heap of a country," Harold said, sullenly flattered by their teasing, "there's no respectable way to not be a liberal."

Piet said, "Why, look at me. I'm not a liberal. Look at all your fellow brokers. They swindle the poor and pimp for the rich. Nothing liberal about that."

"They're idiots." In French: "*Idiots.*" Harold told Piet, "You never venture outside of this bucolic paradise, so you don't know what imbeciles there are. They really *care*," he said, "about the difference between driving a Buick and a Cadillac."

"That's too hideous to believe," Piet said and, seeing Carol alone by the harpframe, went over to her. "What have you been telling that jerk Freddy Thorne?"

"I don't know," she said, "but I'll tell you this, Piet Hanema. He was about the only person who kept coming around when the rest of you were ostracizing Eddie and me because of poor old Irene. Poor old Irene my ass. Did you see her take Eddie into the kitchen as soon as they got here?"

"You beauty. Let's dance." Doris Day was now singing "Under a Blanket of Blue." Carol's back beneath his hand was extensively naked, bony and supple and expressive of the immense ease with which in bed his hairy long arms could encircle and sooth her slender nerved-up dancer's nakedness. His thumb grazed the edge of one shoulder blade; his palm lay moist across her spine's raised ridge; his fingertips knew the fatty beginnings of her sides. Pliant sides that would downslip, gain muscle, and become the world's wide pivot and counterthrusting throne, which in even a brittle woman is ample and strong. With a clothy liquidity Carol was yielding herself up, grazing easily the length of him. The bodies of women are puzzle pieces that can fit or not, as they decide. Imperceptibly Carol shaded the tilt of her pelvis so his penis felt caressed. She rubbed herself lightly from side to side, bent her neck so he could see her breasts, blew into his ear. The music stopped. She backed off, her face frowningly dilated, and sighed. She told him, "You're such a bastard," and walked away, naked from nape to waist. Mermaid. Slip from his hands like a piece of squeezed soap.

Such a bastard. When he had been told, at college, coming in late from a date that had left his mouth dry and his fly wet and his fingertips alive with the low-tide smell of cunt, about his parents' accident, his thought had been that had he been there, been there in Grand Rapids in any capacity, his presence would have altered the combination of events, deflected their confluence, enough to leave his mother and father alive. In the same way, he felt guilty about Kennedy's death, when Jazinski told him of it, in the silence of the sander.

Irene Saltz floated toward him, her eyebrows arched above bright tears, scintillant in candlelight. "Are you happy, Irene?" he asked her.

"I still love him, if that's what you're asking," she said.

"You want to be laughed at," Piet told her, "like me. We're scapegoat-types."

Triumphantly upheld by Freddy flanked by Georgene and Angela, the ham, the warm and fat and glistening ham, scotched and festooned with cloves, was fetched in from the kitchen. Bea Guerin, her washed-out hair, paler than wind, done up loosely in a psyche knot, followed holding a salad bowl heaped full of oily lettuce, cucumber slices, avocados, tomatoes, parsley, chives, chicory, escarole. Their blessings were beyond counting. With a cruciform clashing of silver Freddy began to sharpen the carving knife. Out of the gathering audience Frank Appleby boomed, "Upon what meat does this our Caesar feed, that he is grown so great?"

Georgene explained, "I had salmon for the Catholics but since none of them came I'll give it to the children for lunch."

Freddy's eyeglasses flickered blindly as he carved; he was expert. Nobody but Freddy could cut slices so thin. "Take, eat," he intoned, laying each slice on a fresh plate a woman held out to him. "This is his body, given for thee."

"Freddy!" Marcia little-Smith cried. "That's disgusting."

"Don't you think," Bea Guerin asked, her voice pure and plaintive and proud of sounding lost, "we should be fasting or something?"

"Fasting or fucking," Freddy Thorne said, with surgical delicacy laying on another slice.

Ken Whitman watched silent from near the wall, beneath an African mask. Ben Saltz, eagerly hunchbacked, fetched radishes and bread to the buffet table. Carol carried two bottles of burgundy black as tar in the candlelight. Piet, being passed a plate, chewed but without saliva; his mouth felt full of ashes that still burned. Suddenly old, he sought a chair. His knee did hurt.

Still limping, he visited Foxy the following Tuesday, when the nation resumed normal life. The three days of omnipresent mourning had passed for these couples of Tarbox as three tranced holidays each alike in pattern. The men each afternoon had played touch football on the field behind the Applebys, by Joy Creek, while the women and children stayed indoors watching television in the library. During dull stretches of the Washington ceremonies or the Dallas postmortems (Piet and his children, just back from church, were watching when Oswald was shot; Ruth calmly turned and asked him, "Was that real?" while Nancy silently stuck her thumb in her mouth) some of the women would

come outdoors and arrange themselves in Frank's hay and watch
their men race red-faced up and down the hummocky field,
shouting for the ball. These days on the verge of winter were
autumnally fair, struck through with warmth until the swift
lengthening of the shadows. At game's end, that long weekend,
the men and children would drink from paper cups the cider
someone (the Whitmans, the little-Smiths) had brought from the
orchard along the beach road, and then there would be a general
drift indoors, to cocktails and a long sitting around the television
set while the children grew cranky and raided Janet's supply of
crackers, peanut butter, raisins, and apples. Run and rerun as if on
the revolving drum of insomnia, Haile Selassie and General De
Gaulle bobbed together down Pennsylvania Avenue, Jack Ruby's
stripper drawlingly allowed that his temper could be mean, Lee
Oswald, smirking, was led down a crowded corridor toward a
lurching hat and wildly tipping cameras. The widow and one
of the brothers, passing so near the camera they blurred, bent
obliquely over an indeterminate tilted area of earth and flowers.
The dome was distant in the southern sunshine. Amid drumrolls,
the casket gleamed and was gone. The children came crying,
bullied by others. Another drink? It was time to go home, but not
yet, not quite yet. It was evening before they packed the children
into the cars. The space in the cars as they drove home was
stuffy with unasked questions, with the unsayable trouble of a
king's murder, a queasy earthquake for little children, a funny
stomach-gnawing only sleep eased. School and Tuesday came as
a relief.

Piet parked his truck in plain sight in the driveway. The
Whitmans' surviving lilacs were leafless and his eyes winced in
the unqualified light. Every season has a tone of light we forget
each year: a kitchen with frosted windows, a leaf-crowded side
porch, the chalky noons of spring, the chill increase, as leaves fall,
of neutral clarity. October's orange had ebbed in the marshes;
they stretched dun gray to the far rim of sand. The tide was low;
the sea lay sunken in the wider channels like iron being cast. Foxy
answered his second ring.

Opening the door, she looked delicate, as if recovered from an illness, or as if she had just chastised herself with a severely hot bath. "Oh. You. Wonderful."

"Is it? Are you alone? I've come to see the baby."

"But not me?"

Yet, once inside, on the loop rug, he embraced and held her as if there were no baby, as if there were no one alive in this sunken barren world but themselves. Beneath her coarse house smock, between her lifted breasts and bony pelvis, a defenseless hollow felt placed against his memory of her swollen belly. A snuffling aggrieved sound, less crying than a scratching at some portal of need, arose in the living room. Foxy clung to him in a pose of weeping, and reflexively he bent his head into her hair to kiss the side of her neck, and now her tongue and fingers, as if released from the timidity of long absence, tremblingly attempted to seize him, but blind as bees in a room of smoke they darted to absurd places—his unshaven chin, his jingling pockets, an eye that barely closed in time, a ticklish armpit her ardor could not unlock. He told her, "The baby's crying."

Together they went to where in the living room the baby lay breathing in a bassinet. A pearly quiet blessed its vicinity and the windows giving on the frost-charred marsh seemed to frame images thrown from within, by a magic lantern centered on the infant's untinted soul. Foxy asked, "Do you want to hold him?" and pulled the infant gently up and unceremoniously passed him to Piet's hands. Piet, cupping his broad palms under their sudden unsteady burden, let himself be astounded by, what he had forgotten, the narrowness of the buttocks, the feverish mauve skull. For a second the child appraised him with stern large eyes the color of basalt; then the irises crossed and the muscles in his forehead bulged like elastic levers to squeeze the eyebrows down. The baby began to cry. Fearing his noise would betray their secrecy, Piet returned him to Foxy. Brusquely, she jiggled the bundle against her bosom.

Piet asked, "What is his name?"

"You must know it."

"Angela told me but I've forgotten. An old-fashioned name, I thought. For such a modern couple."

"Tobias."

"That's not the cat?"

"Cotton is the cat. Tobias was Ken's grandfather."

"Why didn't you name him after Ken's father?"

"Ken apparently doesn't like his father."

"I thought his father was perfect, the perfect Hartford lawyer."

"He is. But Ken was very definite, I was surprised."

"Ken is full of surprises, now and then, isn't he? A fascinating fellow."

"Are you trying to sell him to me?"

Piet asked her, "Why are we fencing?"

Foxy said, "I don't know. The baby upsets you."

"I love the baby. I love you as a mother."

"But not as a mistress any more?"

"Well"—embarrassment gnawed his stomach—"you're not ready yet, are you?"

"I shouldn't make love for two more weeks but I think I could stand a little show of affection. Why are you so remote?"

"Am I?" How could he tell her, of the quietness he had found here, the sere marsh filling the windows, the serene room he had carved, its plaster walls spread wide like a wimple, of the pearly aura near the baby, of Foxy's own subdued dry grace, dry as if drained of sleep and self-concern—of this chaste charmed air and his superstitious reluctance to contaminate it? He confessed, "I just wonder if I have any business being here now."

"Why not now? What business did you ever have? I was never your wife. You came here for an extramarital screw, that was fine, I gave it to you, I loved it. Now what? I've made myself dirty by having a baby." Piet felt she too much enjoyed such tough talk, that it was something revived, on the excuse of him, from deeper in her experience. She stood with legs apart, bent forward a bit from the waist, Tobias held tight but unacknowledged in her arms. Her raised voice had lulled him to sleep. Piet loved her maternal clumsiness, her already careless confidence that the child was hers to handle.

He asked her, "How can you want me? You have this marvelous little package. You have Ken who gave it to you."

"He doesn't like it. He doesn't like the baby."

"Impossible."

Foxy began to cry. Her hair, lusterless in the dull late light, hung forward over the child. "It frightens him," she said. "I frighten him. I've always frightened him. I don't blame him, I'm a mess, Piet."

"Nonsense." His inner gnawing was transmuted into a drastic sunk feeling; he had no choice but to go to her, put his arms around her and the child, and say, "You're lovely."

Her sobbing would not stop. Her situation, including his concession and his sheltering arms, seemed to anger her increasingly. "Don't you like talking to me?"

"Of course I do."

"Don't you like talking to me at all? Don't you ever want to do anything with me except go to bed? Can't you wait a few more weeks to have me?"

"Please. Fox. Don't be so silly."

"I was afraid to take ether for fear I'd cry out your name. I go around the house saying 'Piet, Piet' to this innocent baby. I dragged poor Ken to that hideous party just to see you and you risked killing yourself rather than be found with me."

"You exaggerate. There was very little risk. I did it as much to protect you as myself."

"You're still limping from it."

"It was all that football."

"Oh, Piet. I'm beginning to nag. Don't leave me absolutely yet. You're the only thing real I have. Ken is unreal. This marsh is unreal. I'm unreal to myself, I just exist to keep this baby alive, that's all I was put here for, and it makes me *mad*."

"Don't be mad," he begged; but he himself felt anger, to be so pressed and sunk he could not spare breath to explain that for them to keep seeing each other now would be evil, all the more in that it had been good. They had been let into God's playroom, and been happy together on the floor all afternoon, but the time had come to return the toys to their boxes, and put the chairs back against the wall.

. . .

Ken came home from work looking more tired than she had seen him since graduate-student days. He carried a sheaf of mimeographed pre-prints and flopped them down on the hall table. "There's been a breakthrough in photosynthesis," he told her. "They've figured out something involving ferredoxin—it seems to be the point of transition between the light and dark reactions."

"What's ferredoxin?"

"A protein. An electron carrier with a very low redox potential."

"Who's figured it out?" He almost never talked to her about his work, so she was anxious to respond fruitfully. For his return she had put on a lemony cocktail dress, celebrative. Their child was six weeks old today.

"Oh," he sighed, "a couple of Japs. Actually, they're good men. Better than me. I've had it." He dropped himself into the armchair, the leather armchair they had steered up and down apartment-house stairs all over Cambridge. Feeling their life slip backwards, she panicked.

"Let *me* see," Foxy said, and went, all wifely bustle and peremptoriness, to the hall table to prove him wrong. The pamphlet on top was titled *Neurophysiological Mechanisms Underlying Behavior: Emotions and the Amygdala.* The one underneath was *Experimental Phenylketonuria: Pharmacogenetics of Seizures in Mice.* She looked no further.

To our Tarbox doppelgängers the "little" Smiths—

Another Yuletide finds us personally well and prosperous yet naturally saddened by the tragic and shocking events of this November. Man is truly "but as grass." A different sort of sadness entered our household when this September we saw young Tim, our precocious and precious baby of a few short years ago, off for his freshman year at St. Mark's. He has been home for weekends, very much the "young man," but it will be joyous to have him under the manse roof these holidays—even if he has, to our decibel's dismay, taken up the electric guitar. Meanwhile Pat, Audrey, and Gracelyn continue happily in the excellent Newton public schools. Pat, indeed, has been honored with (and that sound you hear is our buttons "popping" with pride)

"God," Marcia said, "the way she crawls right over poor Kennedy to tell us they can afford St. Mark's."

"To our decibel's dismay," Janet said, and both went helpless with laughter.

The evenings before Christmas are gloomy and exciting in downtown Tarbox: the tinfoil stars and wreaths hung from slack wires shivering audibly in the wind, the silent crêche figures kneeling in the iron pavilion, the schoolchildren shrieking home from school in darkness, the after-supper shoppers hurrying head-down as if out on illicit errands and fearful of being seen, the Woolworth's and Western Auto and hardware stores wide-awake with strained hopeful windows and doors that can't help yawning. This year the civic flags were at half-mast and some stores—the old jeweler's, the Swedish bakery—had forsaken the usual displays. In the brilliantly lit and remorselessly caroling five and ten, Piet, shopping with his daughters for their present to Angela, met Bea Guerin at the candle counter. At the sight of her small tipped head, considering, her hair stretched to shining, his heart quickened and his hands, heavily hanging, tingled. She turned and noticed him; her instinctive smile tightened as she gauged his disproportionate gladness at seeing her.

Ruth and Nancy wandered on uncertainly down an aisle of kitchen gadgets. Their faces looked dirty in the crass light; his daughters seemed waifs lost and sickened in this wilderness of trash. Their puzzled greed exasperated Piet. He let them go down the aisle and knew that they would settle on a package of cute Pop-pattern dish towels and a red-handled sharpener that would be lost by New Year's.

Innocent of children, Bea seemed strangely young, unsullied. She wore a green wool cape and elfish suède shoes. She held a box of long chartreuse tapers. More than young, she seemed unattached, a puckish interloper meditating theft. Piet approached her warily, accusing, "Candles?"

"Roger likes them," she said. "I find them eerie, really. I'm afraid of fire."

"Because you live in a wooden house? We all do."

"He even likes real candles on the tree, because his family had them. He's such an old fogey." Her face, upturned toward him in the claustrophobic brightness, was grave, tense, homely, frightened. Her hairdo pulled her forehead glossily tight. His parents' house had held prints of Dutch paintings of girls with such high shining brows.

"Speaking of your house—"

Nancy had returned to him and pulled at his thumb with an irritating hand tacky from candy. "Daddy, come look with us."

"In a second, sweet."

"Come look with us *now*. Ruthie's teasing me, she won't let me *say* anything." Her face, round as a cookie, was flyspecked with freckles.

"I'll be right there," he told her. "You go back and tell Ruthie I said not to act like a big shot. You each are supposed to find your own present for Mommy. Maybe you can find some pretty dish towels."

Against her better judgment Nancy obeyed and wandered back to her sister. Piet said to Bea, "Poor child, she should be in bed. Christmas is cruel."

Having no children, she was blind to their domination, and her eyes expressed admiration of his patience, when in truth he had slighted an exhausted child. Bea prompted him, "Speaking of my house—"

"Yes," Piet said, and felt himself begin to blush, to become enormously red in this bath of plastic glare, "I've been wondering, would you mind, some morning or afternoon, if I came around and inspected the restoring job I did for you four years ago? I experimented, hanging the summer beam from an A-brace in the attic, and I'd like to see if it settled. Has your plaster cracked anywhere?"

Something by the side of his nose, some cruelly illuminated imperfection, held her gaze; she said slowly, "I haven't noticed any cracking, but you're welcome to come and look."

"But would you *like* me to?"

Bea's face, its almost lashless lids puffily framing her eyes at a slight slant, became even more of a child's, a child's piqued by Christmas greed yet hesitant, distrustful of gifts.

"Once," he prompted, "you would have liked me to."

"No, I would like you to; it's just"—she groped, and her eyes, a paler blue than Angela's, lifted to his—"a house, you know."

"I know it's a house. A lovely house. Tell me what would be a good morning?"

"Today's Thursday. Let's do it after the weekend. Monday?"

"Tuesday would be better for me. Monday's my catch-up day. Around ten?"

"Not before. I don't know what's the matter with me, I can't seem to get dressed in the mornings any more."

"Daddy. She is *being* a *pesty* crybaby and I am *not* being a *big shot.*" Ruth had stormed up to them, trailing tearful Nancy, and Piet was shocked to see that his elder daughter was, though not yet as tall as Bea, of a size that was comparable. While her father had been looking elsewhere she had abandoned the realm of the miniature. In this too strong light he also saw that her heated face, though still a child's, contained the smoky something, the guarded inwardness, of womanhood.

Bea beside him, as if licensed now to know his thoughts, said proprietarily, "She'll be large, like Angela."

At the New Year's Eve party the Hanemas gave, Foxy asked Piet, "Who is she?"

"Who is who?" They were dancing in the trim colonial living room, which was too small for the purpose. In pushing back the chairs and tables Frank Appleby and Eddie Constantine had scarred the eggshell-white wainscoting. The old pine floorboards creaked under the unaccustomed weight of the swaying couples, and Piet feared they would all be plunged into his cellar. Giving the party had been more Angela's idea than his; lately she, who used to be more aloof from their friends than he, seemed to enjoy them more. She had even persuaded poor Bernadette Ong to come, alone. John was still in the hospital.

"The woman who's taken my place," Foxy said. "Your present mistress."

"Sweet Fox, there isn't any."

"Come off it. I know you. Or has Angela turned into a hot ticket?"

"She *is* more amiable lately. Do you think she has a lover?"

"It's possible, but I'm not interested. The only person in Tarbox who interests me is you. Why don't you call me any more?"

"It's been Christmas. The children have all been home from school."

"Phooey to the children. They didn't bother you all summer."

"There's one more now." He feared he had hurt her, hit out roughly. He petted her wooden back and said teasingly, "Don't you really like any of our friends? You used to love Angela."

"That was on the way to loving you. Now I can't stand her. Why should she own you? She doesn't make you happy."

"You're a hard woman."

"Yes."

Demurely she lowered her lids and danced. Her body, its placid flats and awkward stiffness, was obscurely his, a possession difficult to value now that the bulge, the big jewel, of her belly was gone.

He said at last, "I think we *should* talk. It would be nice to see you." Betrayal upon betrayal. Dovetailing, rising like staging.

"I'm home all the time."

"Is Ken going back to work Monday?"

"He never stops working. He went to Boston every day of his vacation except Christmas."

"Maybe he's seeing a woman."

"I wish he would. I deserve it. But I'm afraid he's seeing a cell. He's beginning modestly."

He laughed and without bringing her visibly closer to him tightened the muscles of his arms for her to feel as an embrace. If Piet had a weakness, it was for feminine irony. "I'm dying to see you," he said, "but I'm afraid of being disappointing. Don't expect too much. We'll just talk."

"Of course, what else? You can't fuck a young mother."

"I think you enjoy misunderstanding me about that. I love your baby."

"I don't doubt it. It's me you don't love."

"But I do, I do, too much I do. I was in you so deep, loved you so terribly, I'm scared of getting back in. I think we were given it once and to do it all over again would be tempting fate. I think we've used up our luck. It's be*cause* I love you, be*cause* I don't want you to be hurt."

"All right, shut up for now. Freddy and Georgene are both looking."

The music, Della Reese, stopped. Piet pushed away from Foxy, relieved to be off, though she did look, standing deserted in a bouffant knee-length dress the milky green of cut flower stems, like the awkward proper girl from Maryland, leggy and young, she had often described to him, and he had never quite believed in.

He heard from the kitchen Bea's clear plaintive voice rising and falling within some anecdote, calling him. But in the narrow front hallway Bernadette Ong's broad shoulders blocked him. "Piet," she said plangently. "When do I get my duty dance?"

He took a grave tone. "Bernadette. How is John doing? When is he coming home?"

She was tipsy, for she took a step and her pelvis bumped him. Her breath smelled bronze. "Who knows? The doctors can't agree. One says soon, the other says maybe. With the government insurance covering, they may keep him there forever."

"How does he feel?"

"He doesn't care. He has his books. He talks to Cambridge on the phone now."

"That's good news, isn't it?" Piet edged toward the stairs.

She stepped again and barred him from touching the newel. "Maybe yes, maybe no. I don't want him back in the house the way he was, up all night fighting for breath and scaring the boys half to death."

"Jesus. Is that how it was?"

Bernadette, her body wrapped in silk, a toy gold cross pasted between her breasts, heard a frug record put on the phonograph and held wide her arms; Piet saw her dying husband in her like a larva in a cocoon. Nervously acrobatic, he slid past her and up a step of the stairs. "I'll be down in two seconds," he said, and needlessly lied, since she would assume he must go to the toilet, "I thought I heard a child cry."

Upstairs, captive to his lie, he turned away from the lit bathroom into the breathing darkness where his daughters lay asleep. Downstairs the voices of Angela and Bea alternated and chimed together. His wife and his mistress. In bed Bea had enraptured him, her skin sugary, granular, the soles of her feet cold, the grip of her vagina liquid and slim, a sly narrowness giving on a vastness where his drumming seed quite sank from sight. Her puffy eyelids shut, she sucked his fingers blindly, and was thus entered twice. She seemed to float on her bed at a level of bliss little altered by his coming and going and thus worked upon him a challenge; at last she confessed he was hurting her and curled one finger around the back of his ear to thank him. She was his smallest woman, his most passive, and his most remote, in these mournful throes, from speech or any question. He had felt himself as all answer. When the time for him to leave at last was acknowledged she wrapped herself quickly in a bathrobe showing, in the split second of standing, that her breasts and buttocks hung like liquid caught in too thin a skin. Ectoplasm.

He crouched where his two daughters' breathing intersected. Nancy's was moist and scarcely audible. Might fall through into silence. The frail web of atoms spinning. The hamster in his heavenly wheel. There. It. Is. Ruth's deeper, renewed itself with assurance, approached the powerful onward drag of an adult. The hauling of a boat upriver. Full steam. Boys soon. Bathroom jokes, Nancy Drew, drawings attempting bosoms: teen-age. The time she was Helen Keller for a school project, bumping through the bright house blindfold, couldn't get her to take it off. Frightening herself. Must do. So brave in choir, bored. Her breathing stuttered, doubled tempo. A dream. His leaving. He crouched deeper between their beds and held her damp square hand. Her breathing eased. Her head changed position. Sleeping beauty. Poison apple. I am your only lover. All who follow echo me. Shadows. Sleep.

The music downstairs stopped. Frug, nobody could do it yet, too old to learn. Nancy's breathing eluded his listening. Instead a most gentle of presences tapped at the window whose mullions were crosses. Snow. A few dry flakes, a flurry. This winter's shy first. The greenhouse at home banked deep in snow. A rusty warmth of happiness suffused him, joy in being rectangularly enclosed, alive with flowers growing, captive together, his mother at the far end tying ribbons tight with needling fingers, school vacation on, all need to adventure suspended.

Distantly, a gun was fired. Downstairs, his friends, voice by voice, launched "Auld Lang Syne." Though his place as host was with them, Piet remained where he was, crouching above the ascending din until it subsided, and he could again pick up the fragile thread of Nancy's breathing, and the witnessing whisper of the snow.

The visit to Foxy proved disappointing. It was a blowy earachy winter Monday; the truck rattled bitterly as he drove down the beach road and the radio through its static told of Pope Paul being nearly trampled in Jerusalem. The house was cold; Foxy was wearing a heavy sweater and a flannel nightie and furry slippers. She moved and spoke briskly, angrily, as if to keep warm. The offending marshes, which permitted the wind to sweep through the walls he had woven for her, were scarred by lines of salty gray ice rubble rimming the tidal channels. Gusts visibly walked on the water. She asked, "Would you like some hot coffee?"

"Yes, please."

"I'm freezing, aren't you?"

"Is the thermostat up?"

"The furnace is on all the time. Can't you hear it roaring? I'm scared it's going to explode."

"It won't."

"A friend of Ken's who's built his own house on the Cape thinks we were crazy not to excavate a full cellar under the living room."

"It would have meant at least another two thousand."

"It would have been worth it. Look at all the gas I burn buzzing around Tarbox visiting people to keep warm. Janet one day, Carol the next. I know all the dirt."

"What is the dirt?"

"There isn't much. I think we're all tired. Janet was very curious about Ken's boyhood and Carol thinks you're seeing Bea Guerin."

"How sweet of Carol."

"Come into the kitchen for the coffee. It's not so bad there."

"I wonder if wooden-framed storm windows on the marsh side wouldn't help. They have more substance than the aluminum combinations. Or what about shuttering them straight across with the boards that were there?"

"What would happen to Angela's view?"

This humorousness remembered the times she had lain in his arms remarking on her double theft, of Angela's man and Angela's house. In the less chilly kitchen, where the Whitmans had reinstated the electric heater, she said, "You'd laugh to see me at night, Ken on one side and Toby on the other. It's the only way I can keep warm."

Though he knew that her description was intended to pique his jealousy, he did feel jealous, picturing her asleep between her husband and son, her fanning spread of moonlit hair tangent to them both. Knowing that his interest in her child irked her, he asked, "How *is* the young master?"

"Strapping. He's two months old now and looks like Ken's father. That same judicial grimace."

"Two months," Piet said. He was wearing workboots and a lumberjack shirt underneath his apricot windbreaker. She gave him coffee in a mug, without a saucer, as if to a handyman. He felt tongue-tied and coarse, and found her large brown eyes uncomfortably alert. Listening for the phone, another lover? Of course not, she had a child. The mother in her den.

She looked at him intently. The unbiased winter light showed a small sty distorting the shape of her left eyelid. She said, "Two months is more than six weeks."

He groped for the significance of six weeks. "Oh. Terrific. But—do you want to? With me, I mean."

"Do you want to with me, is more the question."

"Of course. Of course I do, I love you. Obviously. But should we? Start everything up again. It frightens me, frankly. Haven't we paid our debt to society? Getting over you once was hard enough."

He feared she might mock him, but she nodded solemnly instead. Foxy's hair was not blond clear through like Bea's but blond in part, of many shades—oak, honey, ash, even amber—and darker with beach weather by. She lifted her head. There was a pink cold sore beneath one nostril. "I frighten you?"

"Not you. It. It would be *wrong* now."

"All right, then go. Go, Piet. Thanks for everything. It's been swell."

"Don't. Don't be hard." In waiting for her to begin to cry, he felt his own eyes warm. The scene must be played.

She seized the high, the haughty, rôle. "I don't know how a dismissed mistress should act. They didn't teach us at Radcliffe. Maybe I took the wrong courses. I'm sure I'll be better at it next time."

"Don't," he begged. Rays were being hurled from her dry eyes, and he hunched to dodge these spears.

"Don't what?" she asked. "Don't make a scene? Don't be a bitch? When all the poor little workingman has done is come into your house and charmed the pants off of you and let you fall in love with him, don't embarrass the poor baby, don't make yourself a nuisance. I won't, Piet love, I won't. Just go. Git. Go to Bea. Go back to Georgene. Go way back to Angela. I couldn't care less."

Her eyes, they wouldn't cry, and he must do something, anything, to smother their icy dry rays, that were annihilating him. He asked, "Can't we lie down together?"

"Oh," she said, and flounced herself, but her sweater and heavy nightie refused, amid the ghosts of summer's billowing, to fling, and the kitchen presences, stove, oven, sink, and windows, retained their precise shape, like unimpressed judges. "You'll make one more stab at it, as a favor. Forget it, I'm not that hard up."

But the integrity of her eyes had cracked, she had been brought to tears. He heard his voice grow wise and warm, reaching into the reserves of darkness he and Foxy had shared. "I want to rub your back, and hear about your baby."

She smoothed the skin beneath her eyes. "I think you're right about us," she confessed. "I just don't want to know exactly when it's happening."

This was, his release, of her many gifts to him the most gracious. In an hour, he knew, in good conscience he would be free. He asked, "Shall we go upstairs? We'll need covers over us."

She said, "We must leave the door open, to hear the baby. He's asleep in the nursery." Piet rejoiced that concern for her child was dovetailing with relinquishment of him.

The upstairs was even colder. In bed she kept her wool nightie on and he his underclothes; he rubbed the smooth planes of her back and backside until she seemed asleep. But when he stopped she rolled to face him, reached down to touch him, in Paisley underpants, and asked as if she could be refused, "Would you like to come inside me?"

"Terribly, actually."

"Gently."

Yes, she had been stretched by the child; the precious virginal tightness had fled. He offered to kiss her breasts, though a stale milky smell disturbed him; her fingers pushed his face away. She must save herself for the baby. Her long body beneath his felt companionable, unsupple, male. His mind moved through images of wood, patient pale widths waiting for the sander, intricate joints finished with steel wool and oil, rounded pieces fitted with dowels, solid yet soft with that placid suspended semblance of life wood retains.

A weight fell on the bed; Piet's heart leaped. Foxy's cheek against his stretched in a smile. It was the cat, Cotton. Purring, the animal nestled complacently into the hollow on top of the blankets between the lovers' spread legs. "I have two lovers," Foxy said softly, but fear had been touched off in Piet, and its flare illuminated the world—the Gallagher & Hanema office on Hope

Street, the colonial farmhouse on Nun's Bay Road, the unmistakable pick-up truck blatantly parked in the Whitmans' drive. He must hurry. He asked her, "Can you make it?"

"I don't think so. I've too many emotions."

"Then let me?"

She nodded stiffly and with a few unheeding, gay and forceful strokes he finished it off, holding her pinned through the distracting trembling with which she greeted his coming and which at first he had mistaken for her own climax. He left his lust as if on a chopping block miles within her soft machine. She looked at him with eyes each holding the rectangle of the skylight. "So quick?"

"I know. I'm lousy at love. I must go."

He dressed rapidly, to avoid the discussion and recapitulation he knew she desired. It was good, he thought, that the last time was bad for her. Her slowness to come, he saw now, had always been a kind of greed. As he carefully opened the door behind the lilacs, the baby began to cry in the nursery wing.

Outdoors was as still as a house in that interval after the last subcontractors have left and before the occupants have moved in and the heat is turned on. The woods toward the little-Smiths' house, purple diluted with rime, moved no more under the wind than frost-ferns on glass. No cars passed on the beach road. A single gull knifed across his vision, and he heard behind him Foxy begin to cry. His palms tingling against the wheel, he backed the truck around and headed toward the center of Tarbox. Through the leafless trees peeked a gold weathercock. As the cab warmed, he whistled along with the radio music, exhilarated once again at having not been caught.

Perhaps that day he discovered a treasure of cruelty in himself, for alone with Bea later that week, late in the afternoon, he struck her. She had been above him on all fours, a nursing mammal, her breasts pendulous, with a tulip sheen, and as if to mark an exclamatory limit to happiness he had cuffed her buttocks, her flaccid sides, and, rolling her beneath him, had slapped her face hard enough to leave a blotch. Seeing her eyes incredulous, he had slapped her again, to banish all doubt and establish them firmly on this new frontier. Already he had exploited her passivity in all positions; the slap distracted his penis and he felt he had found a method to prolong the length of time, never long enough, that he could inhabit a woman.

Bea's left eye slitted against a third blow and when it didn't come widened with the surprise of recognition. "That's what Roger does."

"So people say."

"I thought it was because he couldn't make love normally, because I didn't excite him otherwise. But that's not so of you."

"No, it's in you. You invite it. You're a lovely white hole to pour everything into. Jizz, fists, spit." He spat between her breasts and lifted his arm as if to club her.

Her eyes, so washed-out they were scarcely blue, widened in alarm and she turned her head sideways on the shadowy pillow. "It makes me wonder if I'm insane," she said. "That I do this to people. Eddie twists my wrist all the time. Please, Piet, I'd really rather you wouldn't. Use me but don't hurt me if you don't absolutely have to. I don't really like it. Maybe I should."

"Oh I know, I know, you must hate it, forgive me," Piet said, hiding his face in Bea's throat and hair. "Do forgive me." Yet he was pleased, for in abusing her he had strengthened the basis of his love, given his heart leverage to leap. He loved any woman he lay with, that was his strength, his appeal; but with each woman his heart was more intimidated by the counterthrust of time. Now, with Bea, he had made a ledge of guilt and hurled himself secure into the tranquil pool of her body and bed. High above the sound of children throwing snowballs as they returned from school in the dusk, Bea sucked his fingers, and her nether mouth widened until he was quite lost, and he experienced orgasm strangely, as a crisisless osmosis, an ebbing of light above the snow-shrouded roofs. Death no longer seemed dreadful.

The phone rang and surprised him by being Foxy. In the month since their unsatisfactory coitus in the cold house, she had not called, and had hardly spoken at parties. She had faded into the tapestry of friends. She asked, "Piet, is Gallagher there?"

"Yes he is," he cheerfully sang.

"Could you go out to a pay phone and call me?"

"Now?"

"Piet. Please. We must talk." Her voice had a distant chafed quality, and he pictured a handkerchief balled in her fingers.

"As you wish." He added a firm, man-to-man "Right." He felt Gallagher listening behind the corrugated glass partition, though his door was closed. Increasingly Gallagher's door was closed. Each morning, coming to his office, Piet found that the walls had been slightly narrowed in the night. Beside his desk hung a calendar, from Spiros Bros. Builders & Lumber Supply, showing a dripping golden retriever mouthing a green-headed mallard; as Piet worked at his desk he could feel the dog's breath pushing on his ear.

He went out into the valentine brightness of plow-heaped snow and entered an aluminum phone booth smelling of galoshes. A single dried-up child's mitten lay on the change shelf, unclaimed. The Whitmans' number rang three, four, five times unanswered. He pictured Foxy lying dead, a suicide, having called him in the clouded last moment of waking and then sinking in coma onto her bed, her long hair spilling, the child crying unheard. The phone was picked up; as if a window had been opened Piet saw, across the street, through the besmirched phone-booth glass, four men rocking a car, trying to push it free.

"Hello." Foxy's voice was cool, impersonal, unfocused.

"It's me. What took you so long to answer the phone?"

Her voice, relieved, collapsed—but not, he felt, all the way. "Oh. Piet. You're so quick to call back."

"You told me to be."

"I was with Toby."

"What's up?"

She hesitated. "I just wondered how you were. I had a spell of missing you, and realized that I'd been resisting calling you just to punish you and you weren't being punished, so what the hell."

He laughed, reassured yet suspicious, for he did not remember her as a waverer. "Well, I *was* being punished, but I figured unless we had something to tell each other it was right we didn't talk. I admired your tact." In her silence he hurried on. "I get your letters out and read them now and then." This was a lie; he had not done this for months; they seemed, all those blue barbs and squiggles, dead thorns the sharper for being dead.

As if sensing this, she laughed. "But I *do* have something to tell you. Good news, you'll be pleased. The house is warm now, and it wasn't your fault. When they installed the furnace the man had put the thermostat too near some hot-water pipes in the wall, so the thermostat thought the house was warm when only *it* was, and kept shutting off. Ken and Frank Appleby figured it out one drunken night. The Applesmiths have been coming over lately."

"Oh, sweet, but it *is* my fault. I was the general contractor, I should have noticed. But I was distracted by making love to you."

"Did you like making love to me? I was never sure, I'm awfully virginal somehow."

"Virginal and whorish together. I adored making love to you. It was somehow it. But don't you feel better now in a way? You can look Angela in the face, and me Ken."

"I never minded Angela. I had a mysterious feeling she approved."

The subject displeased him; he did not like Angela to be dismissed. He felt his mistresses owed it to him to venerate her, since he had taken it upon himself to mock her through their bodies. "And how is Toby? Are you enjoying him?"

"Pretty much. He lifts up his head and seems to listen to what I say. Unlike his father."

"Aren't you enjoying Ken?"

"Not much."

"And this is all you called me for? Got me out here in the snow for?"

"No." The syllable seemed a metallic sound the receiver had made purely by itself. When Foxy's voice resumed, it had collapsed all the way; he felt, listening, that he was skating on a crystal surface, the pure essence of her that God's hands had held before thrusting it into a body, her soul. "Piet. My period is two weeks late. And it would have to be you."

"Me what?" But of course he instantly knew. That cold house, that scared last piece. The chopping block. The hostage.

As she spoke, her voice made soft tearing noises, caused by the skating action of his listening. "It's not just the lateness, it's a whole chemical something, a burny feeling down low that I remember from carrying Toby."

"Would you feel it so soon?"

"It's been a month."

"So soon after giving birth, aren't your insides naturally mixed up?"

"But I had two periods."

"And it can't be Ken?"

"Not really, no." He thought her phrasing strange. She added, "He uses those things."

"Sometimes they break."

"Not Ken's. Anyway, it's not been that often. I depress him since the baby. And he's worried about his work. Not only Jews but now the Japanese are getting ahead of him."

"But *how* often?"

"Twice when it could have been, except for the thing, and once just recently, when I hoped it would bring my period on."

"And you *do* have the burny feeling?"

"Yes. And agitation. Insomnia. Piet, Piet, I'm so sorry, it's so stupid."

"Why did you let me that day, if—"

"I don't know, you didn't act like you were going to do it, and my old diaphragm doesn't fit, and—"

"I assumed you used pills. Everybody else does."

"Oh, *does* everybody else? You've taken a poll."

"Don't be petulant."

"Don't you be. About the pills, not that it matters, Ken doesn't trust them. He thinks it's all too intricate, they may trigger off something."

"Bang," Piet said. "Bang, bang."

Foxy was going on, "And if you must know, if you must know how naïve I am, I thought that I was nursing made me safe." Her tears crackled and rasped in the receiver cold against his ear.

He laughed. "That old wives' tale? I keep forgetting about you,

you're a Southern woman, raised on recipes learned at Aunt
Jemimah's knee."

"Oh," her wet pale voice gasped, "it's good to hear you laugh
at me. I've been in hell. I called you this morning to keep from
going crazy and then when you called back I was too frightened
to answer, and then I lied. I just lie and lie, Piet."

"It's something we all get good at," he said. The receiver was
such a little weight in his hand, chill and stiff and hollow, he
wondered why he could not hang it up and walk away free, why
it was clamped to him as the body is clamped to the soul.

Foxy was asking, "What shall we do?"

In the illusion of giving advice he found some shelter, right
angles and stress-beams of sense they could inhabit. "Wait a few
more days," he told her. "Take hot baths, as hot as you can stand
them. If it still doesn't come on, go to a doctor and take the rabbit
test. Then at least we'll know."

"But I *can't* go to Doc Allen. For one thing he'd be shocked
that I was pregnant again so soon. He might tell some of his
boatyard friends."

"Doctors never tell anything. But didn't you and Ken have a
doctor in Cambridge? Go to him if you'd rather. But not quite
yet. It might come on still. Angela is sometimes three weeks,
sometimes five; she's terribly casual. It's a miracle I haven't
knocked her up."

Though he had been serious, Foxy laughed. "Poor Piet and his
women," she teased, "picking his way through the phases of the
moon. I guess I turned out to be the dud."

"The opposite of dud, I'd say," and he glimpsed in himself amid
the terror pleasure that she had proved doubly fertile, that she
had shown him capable of bringing more life to bud upon the
earth.

She asked, "Will you call me? Please. You won't have to *do*
anything, I'll take care of it myself somehow—absolutely; no,
don't say anything. But it *is* lonely. Lonely, Piet."

He promised her, "I'll call you tomorrow." A last word felt
needed, a blessing to unclamp the receiver from his hand and ear.
He stammered in fear of sounding pompous as he unlocked to her

all the wisdom he possessed. "Foxy. After years of thought, I have come to this conclusion: there are two kinds of situation in the world, those we can do something about and those we can't, like the stars and death. And I decided it's a great waste, a sin in fact, to worry about what we can't help. So take a hot bath and relax. We're in the hands of Allah."

His not daring saying "God" disgusted him. But Foxy, lulled as if she had not listened, said singsong, "Call me tomorrow, Piet, and I bet it will have gone away like a silly dream, and we can go back to our nice comfortable estrangement."

So "estrangement" was the last word. He hung up and saw that the men had extricated the car from the white gutter, and all of Charity Street, alive with the rasping of shovels, seemed a sacred space, where one could build and run and choose, from which he was estranged.

Now began a nightmare of daily phoning, of small false hopes (the burning sensation seemed less distinct today, she had felt a uterine strangeness after this morning's scalding bath, a medical reference book at the Tarbox Library admitted of many postpartum menstrual irregularities) and of cumbersomely advancing certainty. The first rabbit test came back from the lab negative; but the Cambridge doctor explained that this early in the game there was only a ninety per cent accuracy, and implied disapproval of her haste. A curt, hawk-faced man with golfing trophies in his consulting room, he may have diagnosed at a glance her symptoms and recognized the plague, this not uncommon infection of decent society's computations with blind life's long odds, that to Foxy and Piet seemed so isolating. For a whole night of sleeplessness she lay trembling with the good news that she could not deliver to Piet until morning. But the one-in-ten chance dilated fascinatingly as Foxy refused to let go of her microscopic captive and surrender and bleed. Piet battered her over the phone, begged at her with his patience, his refusal to blame her: he had resigned from being her lover, he had lain with her to say good-bye, he was happy with his rare and remote wife, he had been gulled by Foxy's naïveté, she had no claim upon him—none of this he needed to say, it was assumed. She apologized, she ridiculed herself, she offered to take her child, her existing child, and vanish from the town; but for the time being he and he only knew her secret, only he could share with her the ordeal of these days. The sound of his voice was the one thing on earth not alien to her. They agreed to meet, out of pity for each other and a desire, like that of boxers clinching, to draw near to the presence, each to the other, that was giving them pain. In Lacetown there was an IGA whose large parking lot the plows would have cleared; behind the building, where the trucks unloaded, few cars parked. Of their friends only Janet sometimes shopped here. They would be safe.

Friday. A heavy mauve sky. A few dry flakes. His heart leaped at the sight, alone on the asphalt, beneath the close clouds, of the Whitmans' black MG. He parked his truck near the store incinerator barrel and walked across empty parking spaces. Foxy rolled down her window. A flake caught in her left eyebrow. He said, "I thought Ken took this car to Boston."

"He took the train today, because they forecast a storm. Get in."

Inside, having slammed the door, he said, "He's always thinking, Ken."

"Why do you dislike him? This isn't his fault."

"I don't dislike him. I admire him. I envy him. He has a college degree."

"I thought you were going to say he has *me*." They laughed, at her, at themselves, at them all. In leaving the limits of Tarbox they had acquired a perspective; their friends and their houses seemed small behind them. Only they, Foxy and Piet, were life-size. Only they had ceased flirting with life and had permitted themselves to be brought, through biology, to this intensity of definition. Their crisis flattered them like velvet backdrop. She sat awkwardly sideways in the bucket seat behind the wheel, her knees touching the gearshift, her legs long in yellow wool slacks, her hair loose over the shoulders of her Russian general's coat.

He said, "You look pretty good," and patted her thigh. "After our frantic phone conversations I thought you'd look more of a wreck."

She grinned; her nose and chin seemed whittled by the pressure of the coming storm. Snowflakes were making a thin white line along the rubber window sealer. On the loading platform of the IGA a solitary boy in a clerk's apron was stacking cardboard boxes, his breath a commotion of vapor. "Oh," she said, feinting. "We women can keep up appearances."

"I take it there's not much doubt left."

She nodded, as delicately as if a corsage were fastened near her chin. Dances. Girls in cars after dances. It had been a generation since he had sat like this. Foxy said, "Not in my mind. I'm driving in this afternoon to have another rabbit test. I was supposed to. The storm may cancel it."

"Not with you at the wheel." As if rationalizing his laugh, he added, "Funny how that one-in-ten chance didn't go away."

"You always said we'd press our luck too far."

"I'm sorry that the time that did it wasn't better for you."

"I remember it very clearly. How we moved from room to room, the cat jumping on the bed. It's all so silly, isn't it? Adultery. It's so much *trouble*."

He shrugged, reluctant to agree. "It's a way of giving yourself adventures. Of getting out in the world and seeking knowledge."

She asked, "What do we know now, Piet?"

He felt her, in the use of his name, drawing near, making of this desperate meeting an occasion of their being together, a date. He hardened his voice: "We know God is not mocked."

"I was never mocking God."

"No. Your God is right there, between your legs, all shapeless and shy and waiting to be touched. It's all right, Fox. I don't mean to complain. It's partly I suppose that I find you so attractive; I didn't expect to, it makes me crabby. It seems so much beside the point for me to still want you."

She adjusted her legs more comfortably; a knee touched his, and quickly pulled away. "You expected to hate me?"

"A bit. This has been hell, these ten days. Compared to your voice on the phone, you seem happy."

"That's the worst of it. I am happy. I'm happy to be carrying your child. My whole system wants to go ahead and have it."

"You may not have it. May not, may *not*."

"Oh of course. Absolutely. I agree."

But her face had withdrawn into sharpness. A moan caught in his throat; he lurched at her, fumbling, afraid of her face. Her breath was hot, her cheek cold with tears; her body within her massive coat sought to conform to his, but the bucket seats and floor shift prevented them. He backed off and read hastily in her distorted face absolution, permission to scour from her insides all traces of their love. "But how?" he asked. "Sweden? Japan? How do people *do* these things?" Beyond her mussed hair a lane of leafless maples made an embroidered edge upon the snowing sky.

"It's sad, isn't it?" she asked. "We don't seem to know the right people. I know there are abortionists *every*where, waiting for customers, and here am I, and there's no way to get us in touch."

"What about Ken? He knows doctors."

"I can't tell Ken."

"Are you sure? It would make things possible. You could fly to Japan even. He could give a guest lecture."

"He's not that good."

"I was joking."

"I know. Piet, I'll do anything to get rid of this except tell my husband about us. He couldn't handle it. He's too—complacent. And in a way I'm too complacent too. I knuckled under once and I won't again. I won't beg, or apologize for us when we were so *right*. I'd rather risk death. That sounds more arrogant than it is. You could tell Angela you slept with me and the two of you would absorb it, be better for it after a while, but our marriage just isn't built that way. We're not that close. We made a very distinct bargain, one that doesn't allow for either of us making mistakes this big. It would shatter Ken. Am I making any sense?"

He saw that she would not tell her husband, just as months ago she would not install closed cabinets. She was the customer; he must work with her whims. "Well, what about telling him it's his and going ahead and having another little Whitman? It might have red hair but there must be a red-haired gene in one of you."

She spoke with care, after biting the tip of her tongue. Women whose tongues won't stay in their mouths are the sexiest. "It's possible. But it seems to me, if you picture the little child, getting bigger day by day, me watching him as he looks less and less like Ken and more and more like Piet Hanema, as he starts swinging from banisters and nailing pieces of wood together, we'd be giving ourselves a lifetime of hell. I'd rather take the hell in a stronger dose and get it over with."

"My poor Fox." He leaned and kissed her nose. Her red hands lay inert in the lap of her greatcoat; possibly she shrugged.

A maroon Mercury coupe like Janet Appleby's slowly wheeled through the lot. But the driver was unknown, an elderly Lacetown citizen with grizzled jaws and a checked hunter's cap. He stared at them—white-ringed raccoon eyes—and continued his circling arc through the lot and out the other side. The apparition had given them both heartstop, and contaminated their hiding place. The boy stacking boxes was gone from the platform. "We better go," Piet said, "or they'll find us frozen in each other's arms."

At home, sheltered from the blizzard amid the sounds of Angela's cooking and his daughters' quarrelsome play, Piet struggled to see his predicament as relative, in any light but the absolute one that showed it to be a disaster identical with death. Pregnancy was life. Nature dangles sex to keep us walking toward the cliff. Slip-ups are genially regarded. Great men have bastards: Grover Cleveland, Charlemagne. Nobody cares, a merry joke, brown beer, the Lord of Norfolk salutes his natural son. One more soul: three billion plus one. Anyway she would probably move to Berkeley or Los Alamos and he'd never see it. Down the drain. Piet Hanema, father of a new nation. To your health. He sipped the double martini and a boiling soughing dread like pigswill welled up to meet the gin. Ken. His dread had to do with Ken's face, the strange trust its faintly rude blankness imposed, the righteousness of the vengeance it would seek. Sickened, slipping, Piet saw that he lived in a moral world of only men, that only men demanded justice, that like a baby held in a nest of pillows from falling he had fallen asleep amid women. He had been dumbstruck to hear Foxy speak slightingly of Ken. In Piet's mind there was no end of Ken, no limit to the ramifying offense of inflicting a child upon Ken's paternity. Paternity a man's cunt. Vulnerable. Gently. His father potting geraniums with stained thumbs, the perspective of the greenhouse implying an infinity of straight lines. He had preferred as a child the dead-ended warm room at the end where his mother sat broad-lapped among loop-ing ribbons. There was a mandate in his father's silences he had shied from. Straight man, his mouth strange from dentures. Ah God, how glad he was that they were gone, all things considered.

All things are relative. As a boy in trouble he would think of something worse. It would be worse than not making the football squad to get polio. It would be worse than not getting invited to Annabelle Vojt's party to accidentally shoot Joop in the eye and have him blind forever. It would be worse to be dead than to be in this box. Would it? In a manner analogous to dying he had trespassed into a large darkness. In Foxy's silken salty loins he had planted seed that bore his face and now he wished to be small and crawl through her slippery corridors and, a murderer, strike. God forgive. No: God do. God who kills so often, with so lordly a lightness, from diatoms to whales, kill once more, obliterate from above, a whip's flick, a finger down her throat, erase this mon-strous growth. For Thine is the kingdom.

Ken's face, barely polite. Pale from ambition and study. Piet's guts groveled again; he sipped silver to kill them. The bullet. The sleepy firing squad. The terrible realm where life leaps up from impeccable darkness. God's premeditated deed. Clay mixed with spit. Foxy's sly cunt, coral the petals, more purple within, her eyes like twin bells hung on a tree, tinkled by every wind. Yet she suffered, beneath the woman there was an animal, a man like him, an aged child rather, judging, guessing, hoping, itching. How monstrous to have a thing attach and fester upon you like a fungus. His balls sympathetically crawled. Poor soft Foxy. Erase. Pluck, Lord. Pluck me free.

He drank. The final sweetness of truly falling. Bea. Scared to call, she might guess. She knew some things. Had seen him leap from the window, Foxy's head golden in the bathroom light. In her bed he had left unconfessed only that last drab Monday visit when, trespassing unwittingly upon Ken's paternity, conjuring into the world another responsible soul, he had made himself legally liable. Disgrace, jail, death, incineration, extinction, eternal namelessness. The laughter of their friends. The maledictions of newspapers. He saw Bea smiling, her breasts melted, her body a still pool, his prick suspended in her like a sleeping eel, and knew why he loved her: she was sterile. His semen could dive forever in that white chasm and never snag.

His solitude became desolate. The blizzard crooned mournfully, a thing without existence, a stirring. He emptied his glass and went into the kitchen. His daughters and wife were arranging valentines. He had failed to get Angela one. Ruth and Nancy at school had received fuzzy hearts, mooning cows, giraffes with intertwined necks. Ruth was arranging the best on top of the refrigerator. Reaching up, her figure was strikingly lithe. His coming into the kitchen for more gin intruded upon a triangular female rapport especially precious to little Nancy. She turned her face, shaped like a rounded cartoon heart, upwards toward him, giggled at the approach of her own impudence, and said, "Daddy's ugly."

"No, Daddy not ugly," Ruth said, putting her arm about his waist. "Daddy pwetty."

"He has awful nostrils," Nancy said, moving closer and looking up.

Ruth continued the baby talk in which her impulse of love sought disguise. "Daddy has the beeyeutifullest nostwils," she said, "because he came from Howwand long ago."

Piet had to laugh. "What about my feet?" he asked Nancy.

"Acky feet," she said.

Ruth hugged him tighter and stroked his furry arm. "Loberly feet," she said. "Mommy has silly feet, her little toes don't touch the ground."

"That's considered," Angela said, "a sign of great beauty."

"You know something, Mommy?" Ruth said, abandoning Piet's

side and the baby voice. "Mrs. Whitman has *flat* feet, because at the beach this summer Frankie Appleby and Jonathan Smith were being detectives and following people and her footprints had no dent on the inside, you know, where the curvy place, whatever it's called—"

"Arch," Angela said.

"—where the arch is. It was like she was wearing sneakers only with toes." The child glanced over at her father. True, even so unkind an evocation of Foxy gave him pleasure. Slouching flat-footed broad, big with his baby. His tall cockpit.

"How fascinating," Angela said. Her hands busily sparkled amid the leaves of their supper salad. "What else have you noticed about feet?"

"Mr. Thorne has a green toenail," Ruth said.

"Daddy's toes," Nancy said, gazing up impudently from beneath Angela's protection, "are like Halloween teeth," and Piet saw that he represented death to this child: that what menaced and assaulted the fragility of life was being concentrated for her in his towering rank maleness; that this process would bring her in time to Ruth's stage, of daring to admire and tame this strangeness; and at last to Angela's, of seeking to salvage something of herself, her pure self, from the encounter with it. He loved them, his women, spaced around him like the stakes of a trap.

Ruth said, "Mommy, make Nancy stop insulting Daddy. Daddy's handsome, isn't he?"

Piet stooped and picked Nancy up; she shrieked and kicked in mixed pleasure and fear. A peppery whiff of red candy hearts was on her breath. Rotting her fine teeth. Angry, he squeezed her harder; she squealed and tried to fight down, all fear now.

"I don't know if Daddy's exactly *handsome*," Angela was saying. "He's what people call attractive." She added, "And nice, and good." He set Nancy down, pinching her unseen. She stared upward at him, now knowing something she would never forget, and could never express.

Perhaps as a sequitur of the tenderness of their being together with their children and their valentines, perhaps simply excited by their snugness within the blizzard, Angela led him to bed early and, like a warm cloud descending, made love to him sitting astride, in the classic position of Andromache consoling Hector.

Saturday morning their phone rang; Foxy spoke breathily, with her lips against the mouthpiece. "Is Angela right there?"

"No," Piet said, "she's out shoveling with the kids. What would you have said if she had answered?"

"I would have asked her if she was wearing a short or a long dress to the Heart Fund dance."

"It's really risky, you know. She's just beginning to be less suspicious of you."

"I had to talk to you, I'm sorry. I thought you'd be at the Gallaghers last night. Why didn't you come?"

"We weren't invited. Who was there?"

"Everybody. Except you and the Saltzes and the Ongs. There was a new couple who seemed stuffy and young."

"Matt didn't say anything to me. Anyway. What's up with you?"

"The test. It was positive. There's no doubt, Piet."

"Oof." He was fascinated, as he sank into this fact, by the delicacy of his furniture, the maple telephone table with tapering legs, the mirror in its acanthus frame of chipped gilt. These things had been fashioned by men without care, with no weight on their hands. He marveled at himself, that he had ever found the energy, the space, to set two sticks together.

Into his leaden silence she cried, "Oh Piet, I've become such a burden."

"No," he lied. "I still think of you as very light and kind."

"At any rate—hang up if Angela comes in—I think I've hit on something."

"What?"

"Freddy Thorne."

Piet laughed. "Freddy can bore it out of you. That's called an abortion."

"All right. I'll hang up. I won't bother you again. Thanks for everything."

"No. Wait," he shouted, fearing the receiver would already be away from her ear. "Tell me. Don't be so touchy."

"I'm in hell, darling, and I don't like being laughed at."

"That's what hell is like."

"Wait until you know."

He prompted her, "Freddy Thorne."

"Freddy Thorne once told me that dentists commit abortions. They have all the tools, the chair, anesthetic—"

"A likely story. And?"

"And last night at the Gallaghers, you know how he gets you into a corner to be cozy, I brought the subject around, and asked him if he knew any who did it."

"You told him you were pregnant."

"No. Heaven forbid. I told him I knew somebody who was, a perfectly nice girl from Cambridge who was desperate."

"True enough."

"And—are you sure Angela isn't listening?—"

"I'll go to the window and see where she is." He returned and reported, "She's down the driveway shoveling like a woman inspired. She's been in a very up mood lately. She was excited by the storm."

"*I* wasn't. I was driving in and out of Cambridge to donate my urine. Then we had to struggle over to the Gallaghers."

"And Freddy Thorne looked at you with that fuzzy squint and knew fucking damn well it was *you* who were pregnant."

"Yes. He did. But he didn't say so."

"What did he say? He consulted his abortion schedule and gave you an appointment."

"Not exactly. He said a very spooky thing. All this by the way was in the kitchen; the others were in the living room playing a new word game, with a dictionary. He said he'd have to meet the girl and the man."

"That *is* spooky. The girl *and* the man."

"Yes, and since if I'm the girl, he must guess you're the man, I could only conclude he wants to see *you*."

"You're concluding too much. Freddy just isn't that organized. He's playing games. Blind man's bluff."

"I didn't feel that. He seemed quite serious and definite. More his dentist self than his party self."

"You bring out the dentist in Freddy, don't you? I don't want to see him. I don't like him, I don't trust him. I have no intention of putting us at his mercy."

"Whose mercy do you suggest instead?"

The front door was pushed open. Deftly Piet replaced the receiver and faced the hall as if he had been just looking in the mirror. Nancy stood there, swaddled with snowy clothes. Her cheeks were aflame. Wide-eyed she held out to him on one wet leather mitten what he took to be a snowball; but it was half-gray. It was a frozen bird, with a gingery red head and a black spot on its chest, a tree sparrow caught by the blizzard. Crystals adhered to its open eye, round as the head of a hatpin. In a businesslike manner that anticipated his protests, the child explained, "Mommy found it in the snow all stiff and I'm going to put it on the radiator to get warm and come alive again even though I know it won't."

The Heart Fund dance was held annually at the Tarbox Amvets' Club, a gaunt cement-block building off Musquenomenee Street. The club contained a bar and two bowling alleys downstairs and a ballroom and subsidiary bar upstairs. A faceted rotating globe hurled colored dabs of light around and around the walls, speeding at the corners, slowing above the windows, crisscrossing in crazy traffic among the feet of those dancing. No matter how cold the weather, it was always hot in the Amvets'. Whenever the doors opened, steam, tinted pink and blue by neon light, rolled out to mix with the exhaust smoke pluming from parking cars.

This year the dance was indifferently attended by the couples Piet knew. Carol Constantine was a graceful Greek dancer, and while the patriarchs and wives benignly watched from card tables laden with *keftedes* and *dolmathes* and black olives and *baklava*, she would lead lines hand in hand with their sons—grocers, electronic technicians, stockbrokers. Carol had the taut style, the archaic hauteur, to carry it off. But Irene Saltz was on the board of this year's Heart Fund, and the Constantines had gone into Boston with the Thornes and Gallaghers to see the Celtics play. The Hanemas had come mostly out of loyalty to Irene, who had confided to them (don't tell *any*one, es*peci*ally not Terry Gallagher) that these might be their last months in Tarbox, that Ben had been offered a job in Cleveland. The Whitmans were at a table with the Applesmiths, and the Guerins had brought the new couple. Their name was Reinhardt. They looked smooth-faced and socially anxious and Piet barely glanced at them. He only wanted, as the colored dots swirled and the third-generation Greek girls formed their profiled friezes to the Oriental keening of the bouzouki, for the American dancing to begin, so he could dance with Bea. Angela was sluggish from all her shoveling, and Foxy looked rigid with the effort of ignoring him. Only Bea's presence, a circle like the mouth of a white bell of which her overheard voice was the chiming clapper, promised repose. He remembered her as a calm pool in which he could kneel to the depth of his navel. When the teen-aged musicians changed modes, and his arms offered to enclose her, and they had glided beyond earshot of their friends, she said, gazing away, "Piet, you're in some kind of trouble. I can feel it in your body."

"Maybe it's in your body." But she was not drunk, and held a little off from him, whereas he had had three martinis with dinner at the Tarbox Inne, and was sweating. He wanted to smear her breasts against his chest and salve his heart.

"No," she said, singsong, refusing to yield to the questioning pressure of his arms, "it's in you, you've lost your usual bounce. You don't even stand the same. Didn't I once tell you the unkind people would do you in?"

"Nobody's been unkind. You're all too kind. In that same conversation, which I'm surprised you remember, you asked me if I didn't want to—"

"I do remember. Then you did, and didn't come back. Didn't you like it?"

"God, I loved it. I love you. The last time was so lovely. There was no longer any other place to go."

"Is that why you haven't called?"

"I couldn't. You're right, there *is* something in my life right now, a knot, an awful knot. If it ever untangles, will you have me back?"

"Of course. Always." Yet she spoke from a distance; in sorrow he squeezed her against him, pressed her like a poultice against that crusty knot in his chest where betrayal had compounded betrayal. Frank Appleby, dancing with the Reinhardt girl, accidentally caught Piet's eye, and biliously smiled. Lost souls. Hello in hell. Frank, having no mistress pregnant, seemed infinitely fortunate: advantages of an Exeter education. Whitewash.

Bea backed off, broke their embrace, gazing at something over his shoulder. Piet turned, frightened. Foxy had come up behind them. "Bea, it isn't *fair* for you to mon*op*olize this a*dor*able man." She spoke past Piet's face and her touch felt dry and rigid on his arm. Maneuvering him to dance, she said, her voice sharp, her pale mouth bitter, "I've been commissioned by your wife to tell you she's sleepy and wants to go home. But hold me a minute." Yet her body felt angular and uneasy, and they danced as if linked by obligation. She was wearing, uncharacteristically, a cloying perfume, overripe, reminiscent of rotting iris; by the contrast Piet realized Bea's scent had been lemony. She had floated, a ghost, in his arms.

Freddy Thorne's office smelled of eugenol and carpet cleaner and lollypops; holding Nancy by her plump tugging hand, Piet remembered his own childhood dread of that dental odor—the clenched stomach, the awareness of sunlight and freedom outside, the prayer to sleep through the coming half-hour. In Freddy's walnut magazine rack old *Time* and *Newsweek* covers showed Charles De Gaulle and Marina Oswald. Both looked haggard. Freddy's pug-nosed receptionist smiled reassuringly at the nervous child, and Piet's heart, though tracked to run head-on into Freddy, was shunted by a flick of gratitude into love of this girl. A crisp piece, young. Like eating celery, salting each stalk as it parted. Had Freddy ever? He doubted it. He was full of doubt of Freddy; just to picture the man filled him with a hopeless wet heaviness, like wash in a short-circuited machine.

Piet's left palm tingled with shame. He envied little Nancy her fear of merely pain. As he tried to read a much-creased *Look,* his daughter rubbed against him. The wrong way. Two cats. Electricity is fear. Pedrick had once said you could picture God as electromagnetic waves. He missed the poor devil's struggling, ought to go again. Nancy whispered, and he could not hear. Exasperated by her numb bumping, he said "What?" loudly.

The child cried "Shh!" and her hand darted to his lips. He embarrassed her. She had come to trust only her mother. Angela would normally have taken her to this appointment but today there was a meeting after nursery school and Piet, faced with fate's challenge, reluctantly accepted. *Whose mercy do you suggest instead?* Now indecision and repugnance fluttered in him and only fatigue scaled his dilemma down to something that could be borne. Like waiting outside the principal's office. Old Orff, a fierce Lutheran. Despised the Dutch. Servile Calvinism. Sir, I'm sorry, just awfully sorry, I didn't know—*You didn't know anypody wutt be vatching?* Caught swinging on the banisters in the brick-and-steel stairwell. Nancy whispered more distinctly, "Will he use the busy thing?"

"It's called the drill. Only if you have any cavities."

"Can you see some?" She opened her mouth wide—a huge mouth, his mouth.

"Sweetie, I can't see any, but I'm not a dentist. If you do have any cavities, they will be little ones, because you have such little teeth, because you're such a little girl."

He tickled her, but her body was overheated and preoccupied and did not respond. "Tell him not to do it," she said.

"But he *must,* that's Dr. Thorne's job. If we don't let him fix things now, they will be much worse later." He put his face close to hers. Like a round white blotter she absorbed his refusal to rescue him; and, refusing in turn to cry, she imprinted him with courage. They went together into Freddy's inner office.

Once there, in the robin's-egg-blue reclining chair, with the water chuckling in the bowl beside her ear and Dr. Thorne joking overhead with her father, Nancy somewhat relaxed, and let the dentist pick his way along the reverberating paths of her teeth. "Two," he pronounced at last, and made the marks on his chart, and judged, "Not so bad."

"Two cavavies?" Nancy asked. "Will they hurt?"

"I don't think so," Freddy answered unctuously. "Let us see how quiet you can be. The quieter you are outside, the quieter you are inside, and the quieter you are inside, the less you'll notice the drill."

Piet remembered the dove-gray handbook on hypnotism by Freddy's bed, and would have made a jabbing joke about amateur psychology, but his need for mercy restrained him, and he instead asked humbly, "Should she have Novocain?"

Freddy looked down at him. "They're very little," he said.

Nancy withstood the first drilling in silence; but when Freddy began the second cavity without a pause a guttural protest arose in her throat. Piet moved to the other side of the chair and took her agitated hand in his. He saw into the child's mouth, where between two ridged molars the drill, motionless in its speed, stood upright like a potted flower. Her tongue arched against the point of intrusion and Piet had to restrain her hand from lifting to her mouth. Her guttural complaint struggled into a scream. Her eyes, squared in shape by agony, opened and confronted her father's. Piet burst into sweating; perspiration raced across his chest, armpit to armpit. The coral space of gum between Nancy's lower lip and lower incisors was a gorge of saliva and drill spray. Her back arched. Her free hand groped upwards; Piet caught it and held it, pleading with Freddy, "Let's stop."

Freddy leaned down upon the now convulsive child. His lips thinned, then opened fishily. He said "Ah," and let the drill lift itself away, done with. "There now," he told Nancy, "that wasn't worth all that fuss, was it?"

Her cheeks soaked, she spat into the chuckling bowl and complained, "I wanted only *one*."

"But now," her father told her, "they're both done with and now comes the fun part, when Dr. Thorne puts in the silver!"

"Not fun," Nancy said.

Freddy said, "She's not easily got around, is she? Her mother's daughter." His smirk appeared pleased.

"You shouldn't have plunged in so ruthlessly."

"They were *tiny*. Scratches on the enamel. She frightened herself. Is she apprehensive at home?"

"She has my distrustful nature. The older girl is more stoical, like Angela."

"Angela's not stoical, that's *your* theory. My theory is, she suffers." Freddy's smile implied he enjoyed access to mines of wisdom, to the secret stream running beneath reality. What a sad jerk, really. His skunk-striped assistant came in to spin the silver.

Nancy's ordeal was over. As Freddy inserted and smoothed her fillings, Piet brought himself to ask, "Could we talk afterwards for a moment, in private?"

Freddy looked up. His eyes were monstrously enlarged by the magnifying lenses that supplemented his ordinary glasses. "I'm running behind on my appointments today."

"OK, forget it." Piet was relieved. "It didn't matter. Maybe some other time."

"Now, Handyman. Don't be persnickety. I can fit a minute in."

"It might take two," Piet said, his escape denied.

Freddy said, "Allee allee done free, Nancy. You go with Jeannette and maybe she can find you a lollypop." He ushered Piet into the small side room where his old yellow porcelain chair and equipment were kept for emergency use and cleanings. The window here looked upward over back yards toward the tip of the Congregational Church, a dab of sunstruck gold. Freddy in his sacerdotal white seemed much taller than Piet. Piet blushed. Freddy wiped his glasses and waited; years of malice had enriched that sly congested expression.

"We both know a lady—" Piet began.

"We both know several ladies."

"A tall lady, with long blondish hair and a maiden name that's an animal."

"A lovely lady," Freddy said. "I hear she's wonderful in bed."

"I haven't heard that," Piet said. "However, she and I were talking—"

"Not in bed?"

"I think not. Over the phone, perhaps."

"I find phones, myself, so unsatisfying."

"Have you tried masturbation?"

"Piet my pet, I don't have much time. Spill it. I know what it is, but I want to hear you spill it."

"This lady has told me, or maybe she told somebody else who told me, that you know gentlemen who can perform operations of a nondental nature."

"I might. Or I might not."

"My guess is you might not." Piet made to shoulder past him to the closed door.

Freddy stayed him with a quiet touch, a calibrated technician's touch. "But if I might?"

"But do you? I must trust you. Answer yes or no."

"Try yes."

"Then, sweet Freddy, this lady needs your friendship."

"But old Piet, pious Piet, *friend* Piet, you speak of *her*. What about you and me? Don't *you* need my friendship too?"

"It's possible."

"Probable."

"OK. Probable."

Freddy grinned; one seldom saw Freddy's teeth. They were small and spaced and tartarish.

Piet said, "I hate this game, I'm going. You're bluffing, you bluffed her into getting me to betray us. You stink."

The bigger man stayed him again, holding his arm with injured warmth, as if their years of sarcasm and contempt had given him the rights affection claims. "I'm not bluffing. I can deliver. It's not easy, there's some risk to me, but it would be clean. The man's an idealist, a crackpot. He believes in it. In Boston. I know people who have used him. What month is she in?"

"Second. Just."

"Good."

"It really is possible?" The good news was narcotically spreading through Piet's veins; he felt womanish, submissive, grateful as a dog.

"I said *I* can deliver. Can *you* deliver?"

"You mean money? How much does he ask?"

"Three hundred. Four hundred. Depends."

"No problem."

"For the man, no. What about me?"

"You want money too?" Piet was happy to be again confirmed in his contempt for Freddy. "Help yourself. We'll raise it."

There was a fumbling at the door; Freddy called out, "*Uno momento*, Jeanette."

But it was Nancy's scared voice that answered: "When do we *go*, Daddy?"

Piet said, "One more minute, sweetie-pie. Go into the waiting room and look at a magazine. Dr. Thorne is giving me an X-ray."

Freddy smiled at this. "You've become a very inventive liar."

"It goes with the construction business. We were discussing money."

"No we weren't. Money isn't discussed between old friends like you and me. Surely, old friend, we've gone beyond money as a means of exchange."

"What else can I give you? Love? Tears? Eternal gratitude? How about a new skin-diving suit?"

"Boy, you do make jokes. You play with life and death, and keep making jokes. It must be why women love you. Piet, I'll give it to you cold turkey. There's an unbalanced matter between us: you've had Georgene—right?"

"If she says so. I forget how it was."

"And I, on the other hand, though I've always sincerely admired your bride, have never—"

"Never. She'd never consent. She hates you."

"She doesn't hate me. She's rather attracted to me."

"She thinks you're a jerk."

"Watch it, Handlebar. This is my show and I've had enough of your lip. I want one night. That's very modest. One night with Angela. Work it out, fella. Tell her what you have to. Tell her everything. Confession is good for the soul."

Piet said, "You're asking the impossible. And I'll tell you why you are: you have nothing to deliver. You are a slimy worthless creep."

With crooked forefingers Freddy made gay quick horns at his scalp. "You put 'em there, buddy. You're the expert. I'm just a gullible middle-class grubber who as far as we know hasn't made a career of screwing other men's wives." Freddy's hairless face became very ugly, the underside of some soft eyeless sea creature whose mouth doubles as an anus. "You dug this grave by yourself, Dutch boy."

Again Piet moved toward the door, and this time he was not prevented. He hauled it open, and hopped back, startled; Nancy, having disobeyed, was standing there listening. Her lips were pursed around the stem of a lollypop and her eyes, though she had no words, knew everything.

When over the phone Piet told Foxy of Freddy's proposition, she said, "How funny. I had assumed he and Angela did sleep together, or at least *had*."

"On what basis had you assumed this?"

"Oh, how they act together at parties. Very relaxed. Chummy."

"As far as I know, she's never been unfaithful."

"Are you bragging or complaining?"

"You're in a jolly mood. What do you suggest our next step should be?"

"Me. I don't have a next step. It's up to Angela, isn't it?"

"You're kidding. I can't put this to her."

"Why not?" Impatience surmounted fatigue in her voice. "It's not such an enormous deal. Who knows, she might enjoy getting away from you for a night."

He'll hurt her, Piet wanted to explain. Freddy Thorne will hurt Angela. He said, "But it means telling her all about us."

"I don't see why. If she loves you, she'll do it simply because you ask. If you do it right. She's your wife, let her earn it. The rest of us have been keeping you entertained, let her do something for the cause."

"You're tough, aren't you?"

"I'm getting there."

"Please, Fox. Don't make me ask her."

"I'm not *making* you do anything. How can I? It's between

you and her. If you're too chicken, or she's too holy, we'll have to work at Freddy some other way, or do without him. I could try throwing myself on the mercy of my Cambridge doctor. He's not a Catholic. I could say I was going to have a nervous breakdown. It might not be a lie."

"You honestly think it's possible for me to ask her? Would you do it, to save Ken?"

"I'd do it to save *me*. In fact, I already offered."

"You offered what? To sleep with Freddy?"

"Don't let your voice get shrill like that. It's unbecoming. Of course I did, more or less. I didn't pull up my skirt; but what else do I have for him? What else do men and women ever talk about? He turned me down. Rather sweetly, I thought. He said I reminded him too much of his mother, and he was afraid of her. But it may have given him the idea of having Angela. I think what he really wants is to get at *you*."

"Because of Georgene?"

"Because you've always scorned him."

"You don't think he just honestly wants *her*?"

"Please don't try to squeeze compliments for your wife out of me. We all know she's magnificent. I have no idea what Freddy honestly wants. All I know is what *I* honestly want. I want this damn thing to stop growing inside of me."

"Don't cry."

"Nature is *so* stupid. It has all my maternal glands working, do you know what that means, Piet? You know what the great thing about being pregnant I found out was? It's something I just couldn't have imagined. You're never alone. When you have a baby inside you you are not *alone*. It's a *person*."

He had already told her not to cry. "You really think . . . she might?"

"Oh for God's sake, she's human like everybody else, I don't know what the hell she'll do or won't do. You still seem to think there's a fate worse than death. She's your divine wife, settle it between yourselves. Just let me know how it comes out, so I can work on something else. I thought I'd done pretty well to get Freddy Thorne for us."

"You did. You're being very brave and resourceful."

"Thank you for the compliment."

Piet told her, "I'll try. You're right. I don't expect it to go. She may ask for a divorce instead, but if it does, Foxy, love—"

"Yes, love."

"If we do get out of this, it has to be the end of our—of us."

"Obviously," Foxy said, and hung up.

A morning later, Nancy described her first dream, the first remembered dream of her life. She and Judy Thorne were on a screened porch, catching ladybugs. Judy caught one with one spot on its back and showed it to Nancy. Nancy caught one with two spots and showed it to Judy. Then Judy caught one with three spots, and Nancy one with four. Because (the child explained) the dots showed how old the ladybugs were!

She had told this dream to her mother, who had her repeat it to her father at breakfast. Piet was moved, beholding his daughter launched into another dimension of life, like school. He was touched by her tiny stock of imagery—the screened porch (neither they nor the Thornes had one; who?), the ladybugs (with turtles the most toylike of creatures), the mysterious power of numbers, that generates space and time. Piet saw down a long amplifying corridor of her dreams, and wanted to hear her tell them, to grow older with her, to shelter her forever. For her sake he must sell Angela.

"Angel?"

"Mm?" They were in the dark, in bed, nearly asleep. They had not made love; Piet had no intention of making love to anyone ever again.

"Would you believe it," he asked, "if I told you I was in deep trouble?"

"Yes," she answered.

Surprised, he asked, "What sort of trouble?"

"You and Gallagher aren't getting along any more."

"True. But that's the least of it. I can work things out with Matt once I get myself straightened out."

"Do you want to talk about it? I'm sleepy but can wake myself up."

"I can't talk about it. Can you accept that?"

"Yes."

"Could you believe it if I told you you could help me greatly by doing a specific thing?"

"Like getting a divorce?"

"No, not that at all. Have you been thinking about that?"

"Off and on. Does that alarm you?"

"Quite. I love my house."

"But that's not the same as loving me."

"I love you too. Obviously." The word echoed dryly and he felt them drifting farther from the point, the question. Perhaps there was a way of making it also seem a drifting, a detail of fate. "No," he said, "the thing you could do for me would only take one night."

"Sleep with Freddy Thorne," she said.

"Why do you say that?"

"Isn't that right?"

In the softness of the dark Piet could find no breath to make an answer; he lay on the bed like a man lying on water, only his eyes and nostrils not immersed. Finally he repeated, "Why do you say that?"

"Because he's always told me he would get into bed with me some day. For years he's been wanting to get a hold over you. Now does he have it?"

Piet answered, "Yes."

"And is that what he wants?"

His silent nodding made the bed slightly shudder.

"Don't be shocked," Angela went on, in a voice soft as the dark, "he's been working on it for years, and would tell me, and I imagined I should laugh. What I always thought strange, was that he never just *asked* me, on his own merits, but assumed it had to be worked by bullying you. I don't love him, of course, but he can be appealing sometimes, and I've been unhappy enough with you so that it might have happened by itself, if he'd just been direct. Do you want to know something sad?"

He nodded again, but this time the trembling of the bed was a theatrical effect, deliberately managed.

She told him, "He's the only man in town who's ever been attracted to me. Eddie Constantine took me for that ride on his Vespa and never followed it up. I'm just not attractive to men. What's wrong with me?"

"Nothing."

"Well something must be. I'm not on anybody's wavelength. Not even the children's, now that Nancy's no longer a baby. I'm very alone, Piet. No. Don't touch me. It sometimes helps but it wouldn't now. I really don't seem to be quite *here*; that's why I meant it about psychiatry. I think I need a rather formal kind of help. I need to go to a school where the subject is myself."

He sensed a bargain forming in the shadows. The far lamps along Nun's Bay Road, the wavy-branched lilacs and vase-shaped elms, leafless, and the reflecting snow made patterns of light along the walls that would never occur in summer. He said, "Why not? If things straighten out."

Angela repeated, "If. One question. I'm incredibly curious, but I'll ask just one. Do you trust Freddy? To keep his end of this bargain."

"I don't know why, I do. He needs to impress me as a man of honor, maybe."

"He wants me only once?"

"That's what he said."

She laughed a syllable and turned her back on him. "I don't seem to arouse very strong passions in men." Her words were muffled but her accent sounded ironical.

He lifted himself on an elbow to hear her better. Was she crying? Would she die?

She answered his lurch, "I'd rather not do it here in town. There are too many cars and children to keep track of. Aren't the Thornes coming on the Washington's Birthday ski weekend?"

"Sure. They never miss anything."

"Well, the children will all be in the bunk rooms and we'll

probably be along the same hall. You've slept with Georgene?"

He hesitated, then saw that they had passed into another room of their life altogether, and admitted, "In the past."

"Well then. It's all very neat. No, Piet, don't touch me. I really must go to sleep."

The ski lodge still displayed on its bulletin board photographs of itself in summer, as if to say, *This is me, this soft brown lake, these leafy birches, not the deathlike mask of ice and snow in which you find me.* The defunct cuckoo clock still haunted the high corner misted with cobwebs, the television set crackled with ignored news, the elderly young proprietors came and went with ashtrays and ice trays, trailing an air of disapproval. The rates had been raised. The raisin sauce on the ham was less generous. A quartet of strangers played bridge, and the Tarbox couples played word games on the floor. Whiskey warmed their bodies with a triumphant languor—they were survivors, the fortunate, the employed, the healthy, the free. The slopes today had been brilliant, under the holiday sun that daily looped higher. The conditions had been icy at the top, powdery in the middle of the mountain and along the shaded trails, corny on the broad lower slopes, and slushy by the base lodge, where mud was beginning to wear through. The potent sun, the prickling scintillating showers of dry snow abruptly loosened from the pine branches overhanging the trails, the heavyish conditions, the massive moguls carved by two months of turning and edging all freighted the skiers' bodies with a luxurious lassitude. They began to retire earlier than they had last year, when Freddy Thorne regaled the Applesmiths with his fantasies. Now Jonathan little-Smith, nearly thirteen, was livelier than his parents, and made Frankie Appleby, two years younger and cranky from drowsiness, play one losing game of chess after another. The only way to get him to bed was for Harold and Marcia to go themselves, out to the gas-heated cottage where Julia and Henrietta already were sleeping. The Applebys promptly followed. This year both couples were in cottages—at opposite ends, Janet had insisted, of the row. Then the Guerins, though Freddy huggingly begged Roger to stay for another drink, and Bea cast wise swarming glances of farewell to Piet, went out into the night, barren of a moon, to their hissing cottage. This left the Gallaghers, Hanemas, and Thornes. The Whitmans did not ski. Eddie Constantine, promoted to ever greater responsibilities, was piloting a wonderful new jet, three-engined and hot, the Boeing 727, to San Juan. The Saltzes, who had announced this as the winter when they would take up skiing, were now authoritatively rumored to have accepted the Cleveland offer, to be leaving Tarbox; and instantly they had become pariahs. After some constrained banter Matt Gallagher primly coughed and announced that *he* was going to bed. The emphasis of "he" implied that Terry had been formally given freedom. She, who under circumstances confided only to Carol Constantine had stopped taking pottery lessons, promptly stood and said that so was *she*. When the Hanemas and Thornes were alone, disposed as couples face to face on the two sofas opposed across a maple coffee table stacked with back copies of *Ski* and *Vogue*, Freddy said to Piet, "You and Matt don't seem to have much to say to each other these days."

Piet told him, "He does his end, and I do mine."

Freddy smiled fishily. "Not much doing at your end these days, is there, Handball?"

"There will be soon. As soon as the frost breaks we'll be going back to Indian Hill. Six houses this summer is the plan." A year ago he would not have given Freddy the satisfaction of so full a response, almost an apology.

Angela sat up and parted an invisible drape with her hands. "Well. Is this the night?" Her face looked fevered from sun and windburn, and her eyes had been so steeped in unaccustomed exercise and the beauty of the day that the irises and pupils were indistinguishable. She had changed her ski costume for a looseknit mauve sweater and white pants flared at the ankles; she was barefoot. She had become Janet Appleby.

Georgene stood and said, "I'm not going to listen to this. I'm going to go to bed and lock the door and take a sleeping pill. You three do whatever you want. Don't involve *me*." She stood as if waiting to be argued with.

Freddy said, "But Georgie-pie, you started everything. This is just my tit for your tat. What's sauce for the goose, et cetera."

"You're contemptible. All of you." Her long chin flinty, she crossed through the light of several lamps to the stairs. The day's sun had already become on her face the start of a tan.

While she was still within earshot, Freddy said, "Oh hell. Let's call it off. I was just curious to see your reactions."

Angela said, "No, sir. There's some kind of a bargain and we're going to keep our side. We better go up now because all that fresh air is getting to me and I'll soon fall asleep."

Piet found he could not look at either of them: he felt their faces, blurs in his upper vision, as deformed, so deformed that if he dared to lift his eyes to them he might involuntarily whimper or laugh. He told his stockinged feet, "Let's give Georgene a minute to get into her room. Freddy, should you get your toothbrush or anything?"

Freddy asked, "She's on the pill, isn't she?"

"Of course. Welcome to paradise." Piet stayed sitting on the sofa as they went up. Angela kissed him good night on his cheek; his head refused to move. Her lips had felt weirdly distinct, the parted carved lips of a statue, but a statue warmed by fire. He dared look at her only as she disappeared up the stairs, gazing straight ahead, her gentle hair unbound from the scarlet ear-warmer she wore skiing. Freddy followed, his white hands held lamely at his chest, his mouth open as if to form a bubble.

The upstairs hall was hushed. A single light bulb burned. Georgene's door looked tight shut. The Gallaghers in the room adjacent could be heard murmuring. On silent bare feet Angela led Freddy into her room, and then without their touching excused herself to go back into the hall, to the lavatory. When Freddy in turn returned from the lavatory, she was in her nightie, simple cotton such as a child might wear, a green flower stitched at the neckline. The room's single window overlooked a shallow deck that in summer would be a sunporch; the banister supported baroque shapes of snow sculpted by the melting of the day and the night's refreezing. Within the room there was a double bed with a brass-pipe headboard, a porcelain washstand stained by the hot-water faucet's tears, a five-and-dime mirror, an old rocking chair painted Chinese red, a pine bureau painted bile green, a black bedside table nicked by alarm-clock legs and holding a paperbound copy of *Beyond the Pleasure Principle* and a gay small lamp whose shade was orange. When Angela, who had been brushing down her hair amid serene explosions of static, bent to turn out this lamp, the light pierced the simple cloth and displayed her silhouetted bulk, the pucker of her belly; her big breasts swayed in the poppy glow like sluggish fish in an aquarium of rosewater. The light snapped off and a ghost replaced her. Her voice from a frame of fluffed black hair asked Freddy, "Don't you want to take off your clothes?"

Snowlight from the window picked out along the rim of her hair those tendrils looped outwards by the vigor of the brushing. She had expanded expectantly. Freddy felt the near presence of her blood-filled body as an animal feels the nearness of water, of prey, or of a predator. He said, "Love to, but how would you feel about a drink first? You haven't anything in the suitcase, a little Jack Daniels, say?"

"We brought some bourbon but it's downstairs. Shall I go down and take it from Piet?"

"Jesus, no. Don't go near him."

"Do you really need a drink? I think you've had plenty."

The lining of his mouth felt scratchy, as if he had chewed and swallowed a number of square blocks. This ungainly squareness had descended, still abrasive, to his stomach. Her long-awaited nearness had crystallized his poisons. He said, "I see you're still reading Freud."

"I love this one. It's very severe and elegant. He says we, all animals, carry our deaths in us—that the organic wants to be returned to the inorganic state. It wants to rest."

"It's been years since I read it. I think I doubted it at the time." Paralyzed, he felt her unbuttoning his shirt. He was immobilized by the vision of a drink—amber, clouded with ice—and the belief that its smoky golden distillation would banish his inner kinks. He let her part the halves of his shirt and fumble at his fly until, irritated at her own inexpertness, she turned away. She went to the window, glanced out quickly, peeled off her nightgown, and jackknifed herself, breasts bobbling, into the tightly made bed. "Oh, it's icy," she cried, and pulled the covers over her face. "Hurry, Freddy": the call came muffled.

He imagined Piet downstairs with the whiskey bottle, in the long room golden from the fire, and undressed down to his underwear, and got into the bed.

"Hey," Angela said. "You're cheating."

"You scared me by saying the bed was so cold."

"Well. Let's warm it up." She touched him in front. "Oh. You're not excited."

"I'm in shock," Freddy told her, stalling, adjusting the covers. The tightly made sheets had virginally resisted his entry, and then tangled, exposing him behind.

"Piet never—" Angela stopped. Had she been going to say, "—is not excited"? She instead said, "I don't move you."

"You stun me. I've always loved you."

"You don't have to say that. I'm nothing special. Sometimes I look at myself in the mirror Piet gave Ruth and I see this knotty veiny fat peasant woman's body with tiny red feet and a dear little oval head that doesn't go with the rest. Piet calls me a dolphin." She remembered that he called her this in bed, when she turned her rump upon her husband and, holding him in herself, exposed her curved back to his smoothing rough hands.

"How are you and Piet getting along?"

She realized Freddy wanted to talk, and foresaw that talk would make her sleepy. She tickled the gap between his undershirt and pants elastic while answering, "Better, really. He's been bothered about something lately, but I think basically we're more *fun* for each other than we've been for years. I think it's taken me a year to forgive him for not letting me have the Robinson place. The Whitman place, I should say. Those people haven't made much of an impression on me." She lifted his shirt and snuggled against his bare chest.

"But—how do you reconcile this?" Freddy asked.

"With what?" His dumbstruck silence led her to laugh; fatty warm points, her breasts, shimmered against him, and the jiggled bed complained. "You and me in bed? He told me I should do it. The Hamiltons are always obedient wives. Anyway, I was curious what it would be like. And I must say, Freddy, you're being passive. Take off these insulting clothes."

She managed to lower his elastic waistband—unlike Piet's Paisley, he wore little-boy Jockey briefs. When he was naked, she explored with pinches his sides and the tops of his arms. "Freddy Thorne," she said, "you are pudgy." Her fingers went lower. "And still little," she accused. Delicate and tepid, his genitals lay in her hand like three eggs, boiled and peeled and cooled, she was carrying to the table. The sensation made Angela languorous. She hadn't dreamed men could be this calm with women. She could never have held Piet so long. Even asleep. Their sweetest phase. Not tucked safe inside like women. Committed to venture. More injurable.

Testingly Freddy placed his hand on her back, as if they were dancing. Her skin felt dark to him, oily and Negroid: flat wide muscles glidingly wedged into one another, massive buttocks like moons heaved from an ancient earth. Her body's bland power dismayed him. That Angela, the most aloof of women, whose shy sensitive listening had aroused in his talking tongue the eager art of a drill probing near pulp, should harbor in her clothes the same voracious spread of flesh as other women afflicted Freddy, touching his way across the smooth skin black as lava, with the nausea of disillusion. Her hand under his balls seemed about to claw. He begged, "Let's talk." He longed for her voice to descend from silence, to forgive him.

She asked, "Is there anything you'd like me to do? Anything special?"

"Just talk. Aren't you curious about what the bargain is?"

"No. It feels too scary to me, I don't want to hear it. I feel we've all gone too far to know everything. It's awful of me, but I've never wanted to know about Piet and his women. For me it's no more part of him than his going to the bathroom. You can't realize this, but he's terribly pleasant around the house."

"Tell me about it. I never can picture you and Piet fucking."

"How funny of you, Freddy. You've idealized me or mixed me up with somebody else. Piet and I don't"—she couldn't manage the word, out of consideration, it seemed, for *him*—"as often as he'd like, but of course we do. More and more, in fact."

"Have you ever slept with anyone except Piet?"

"Never. I thought maybe I should."

"Why?"

"So I'd be better at it."

"For *him*. Shit. Let's face it, Angela. You married a bastard. A bully boy. He's pimping for you. He's got you so intimidated you'll shack up with anybody he tells you to."

"You're not anybody, Freddy. I more or less trust you. You're like me. You want to teach."

"I used to. Then I learned the final thing to teach and I didn't want to learn any more."

"What final thing?"

"We die. We don't die for one second out there in the future, we die all the time, in every direction. Every meal we eat breaks down the enamel."

"Hey. You've gotten bigger."

"Death excites me. Death is being screwed by God. It'll be delicious."

"You don't believe in God."

"I believe in that one, Big Man Death. I smell Him between people's teeth every day."

He was hoping to keep her at a distance with such violence of vision but she nudged closer again, crowding him with formless warmth. Her toes engaged his toes; her chin dug into his chest, the hard bone to the right of the heart. "Piet's terrified of death," she said, snuggling.

Freddy told her, "It's become his style. He uses it now as self-justification. He's mad at the world for killing his parents."

"Men are so romantic," Angela said, after waiting for him to tell her more. "Piet spends all his energy defying death, and you spend all yours accepting it."

"That's the difference between us. Male versus female."

"You think of yourself as female?"

"Of course. Clearly I'm homosexual. But then, of the men in town, who isn't, except poor old Piet?"

"Freddy. You're just leading me on, to see what I'll say. Be sincere."

"I am sincere. Anybody with a little psychology can see I'm right. Think. Frank and Harold. They screw each other's wives because they're too snobbish to screw each other. Janet senses it; she's just their excuse. Take Guerin and Constantine. They're made for each other."

"Of course, Roger—"

"Eddie's worse. He's a suc*cess*ful sadist. Or Gallagher and Whitman. Spoiled priests. Saltz and Ong, maybe not, but one's moving and the other's dying. Anyway, they don't count, they're not Christian. Me, I'm worst of all, I want to be everybody's mother. I want to have breasts so everybody can have a suck. Why do you think I drink so much? To make milk."

Angela said, "You've really thought about this, haven't you?"

"No, I'm making it all up, to distract your attention from my limp prick; but it works, doesn't it? Piet stands alone. No wonder the women in town are tearing him to pieces."

"Is that why you've always hated him?"

"Hated him, hell. I love him. We both love him."

"Freddy, you are not a homosexual and I'm going to prove it." She pushed herself higher in bed, so her breasts swam into starlight and her pelvis was above his. She lifted a thigh so it rested on his hipbone. "Come on. Put it in me."

He had kept a half-measure of firmness, but the slick warmth of her vagina singed him like a finger too slowly passed through a candleflame.

Feeling him grow little again, she asked again, "What can I do?"

He suggested, "Blow me?"

"Do what? I don't know how."

Pitying her, seeing through this confession into a mansion of innocence that the Hanemas, twin closed portals, had concealed, Freddy said, "Skip it. Let's gossip. Tell me if you think Janet still goes to bed with Harold."

'She made a big deal of getting cottages at opposite ends of the row."

"Merely thirty or so yards, not very far even in bare feet, if your heart's in it. My thought about Janet is, being her father's daughter, she really believes in cures. She had the baby, then she took a lover, then she went into analysis; and still she wears that headachy expression."

"I want to go into analysis," Angela told him. Her voice was slow and her weight now rested all on the bed, depressing it in the middle so that Freddy had to resist rolling closer toward her. His voice stroking, his hand on her halo of hair, he talked to her about analysis, about himself, about Marcia and Frank, Irene and Eddie, about John Ong's cancer, about the fate of them all, suspended in this one of those dark ages that visits mankind between millennia, between the death and rebirth of gods, when there is nothing to steer by but sex and stoicism and the stars. Angela, reminded by his tone and rhythm of her parents and uncle talking, of the tireless Gibbs pedantry, the sterile mild preachiness descended from the pilgrims, in which she had been enwombed, and from which Piet had seemed to rescue her, dozed, reawoke, heard Freddy still discoursing, and fell irrevocably asleep. He, having held her at bay and deepened his shame and completed his vengeance, felt himself grow strong and adamant and masturbated toward her belly, taking care not to defile her. Then both, parallel, floated toward dawn, their faces slacker than children's.

Downstairs, Piet, having poured himself one more bourbon, had grown cold beside the dying fire, and bored, and outraged. He tried to use his parka as a blanket but it was too small. He tiptoed up the stairs, listened at his own door, and tapped at Georgene's. He tested the lock. It gave. Georgene, though at first overwhelmingly indignant about being discarded by her lover, betrayed by her husband, and treated like an insignificant counter in this game, accepted Piet into her bed, because there was really nowhere to sit, and it was cold. She vowed to him she would not make love. Piet agreed. But, as he lay meekly beside her, his proximity and the danger of insomnia conspired to render her resolve unreal. He offered to rub her back. She invited him into her body. As always, though many distorting months had intervened, they came together; her face snapped sideways as if slapped, a welling softness merged with his clangor, her thighs flared to take him more fully, and he knew that he had exaggerated his trouble, that fate could be appeased.

v. *It's Spring Again*

I N Boston Common there is a somber little pavilion surrounded by uneven brick paving and cement-and-slat benches for band concerts. Here Piet waited for Foxy to come down from a dentist's office in a mustard-colored six-story office building on Tremont Street. By this the middle of March few other idlers were present in the park. Some children in snowsuits were snuffing caps on the lip of the dry wading pool; a gray squirrel raced staccato across the dead grass, at intervals pausing as if to be photographed or to gauge the danger expressed by the muted gunshot sound of the caps. Piet's own scuffing footsteps sounded loud. There was a mist in which the neon signs along Tremont and Boylston distinctly burned. Sooty wet pigeons veered arrogantly close to the heads of hurrying passersthrough. Trees overhead, serene fountains of life labeled *Ulmis hollandicis*, dangled into the vaporous air drooping branchlets dotted with unbroken buds, having survived the blight to greet another year. The wheel turned. Time seemed to Piet as he waited a magnificent silence: the second hand of his watch circling the dial daintily, the minute hand advancing with imperceptible precision. He almost adored the heartlessness that stretched him here for hours, untouched by any news. RUBY GUILTY, TO DIE, said a discarded tabloid being mulched by footsteps into the mud and ice bordering the path. The palm of Piet's left hand tingled thunderously whenever he read the headline, or heard a child shout.

Freddy and Foxy had arranged the matter between them so efficiently Piet felt excluded. Neither wished to explain the arrangements to him. Foxy, pale on Charity Street, her nostrils pinched by wind, a tearing bag of groceries bulky in her arms, told him, "You don't have to do a thing. I'd rather you didn't ever know when it happens. Just tell me one thing now. Is it what you want? You want this child destroyed?"

"Yes." His simplicity shocked her; she turned paler still. He asked, "What are the alternatives?"

"You're right," she said coldly, "there are none," and turned away, the bag tearing a bit more in her arms.

She explained the plan to him later, reluctantly, over the phone. Ken had to go to Chicago three days for a biochemical symposium, in the middle of March, beginning on a Wednesday, the eighteenth. Wednesday was also Freddy's day off, so he could take her up to Boston to the idealist who for three hundred fifty dollars would perform the abortion. Freddy would stay with her and drive her back home to Tarbox. Alone in her home at the far end of the beach road, she would need only to feed herself and Tobias, who slept twelve hours a day. Georgene would come by in the mornings and evenings, and Foxy would be free to call her any time. If complications ensued, she could be admitted to the Tarbox hospital as a natural abortion, and Ken would be told the child had been his.

Piet objected to Georgene's knowing.

Foxy said, "She already knows there was some kind of hideous bargain. It's Freddy's decision, and he's entitled to it. If anything were to happen to me, you must realize, he'd be an accessory to murder."

"Nothing will happen to you."

"Let's assume not. Georgene can drop around in a way neither you or Freddy can. Marcia goes up and down that road all day. It is especially important that *you* stay away. Forget I exist." She

would not tell him the address of the abortionist until she had
talked to Freddy again. "Freddy's afraid you'll do something
dramatic and crazy."

"And are you?"

"No." Her tone was not kind.

Freddy called him that afternoon, gave him the address on
Tremont, absolutely forbade his coming in with them, and tried
to discourage his keeping watch from the Common. "What can
you do?" Freddy asked. He answered himself scornfully: "Pray.
If she's had it, son, she's had it." The ambiguity of "had it," the
suggestion of a finite treasurable "it" that Foxy could enclose and
possess, as one says "had him" of sleeping with a man, the faint
impression that Foxy was competing for a valuable prize, sent
ghosts tumbling and swirling through Piet, the ghosts of all those
creatures and celebrities who had already attained the prize. He
longed to call it off, to release Freddy from his bargain and let
Foxy swell, but that wouldn't do; he told himself it had gone
beyond him, that Freddy and Foxy would push it through re-
gardless: they had become gods moving in the supernature where
life is created and destroyed. He replaced the receiver physically
sick, his hand swollen like a drowned man's, the brittle Bakelite
more alive than he.

Yet last night, playing Concentration with his two daughters,
knowing he had set a death in motion, he cared enough to concentrate and win. Piling up cards under Nancy's eyes filling with
tears. She had thought the game hers. A little beginner's luck had
told her she owned a magic power of selecting pairs. Piet had
disillusioned her. A father's duty. But so jubilantly. Ruth had
watched his vigorous victory wonderingly.

A snuffly bum approached him, hand out, whiskers like quills.
Piet shied from being knifed. The other man confusedly flinched,
palm empty. Piet settled to listening; he was being asked for
something. Dime. Derelict wanted a dime. His voice retreated
behind the whiskers toward the mumbled roots of language. Piet
gave him a quarter. "Gahblessyafella." Angel in disguise. Never
turn away. Men coming to the door during the Depression. His
mother's pies. Bread upon the waters. Takes your coat, give him

your cloak. Asks a mile, go twain. Nobody believes. Philanthropy a hoax to avoid Communism. As a child he wondered who would eat wet bread. Tired old tales. Loaves and fishes, litter. Keep your Boston clean. He found himself hungry. A lightness in his limbs, strange sensation, how does it know food? Strange angels, desires. Come from beyond us, inhabit our machines. Piet refused his hunger. If he ran to the cafeteria burning at the corner, Foxy would die. He did without. His mother's beautiful phrase. *Well sen, do wissout.* Her floury arms upreaching to the pantry shelf. Glory. An engine of love ran through him, flattened his gut. Never again. *Moeder is dood.*

Cruel hours passed. The pavilion, the frost-buckled bricks, the squirrels posing for snapshots, the hurtling gangs of hoodlum pigeons, the downhanging twigs glazed with mist to the point of dripping became the one world Piet knew: all the others—the greenhouse, the army, the houses and parties of his friends in Tarbox—seemed phantom precedents, roads skimmed to get here. Hunger questioned his vaporous head, but he went without. Might miss Foxy's moment. The knife. Ask for a dime, give a quarter. Fifteen-cent profit. He was protecting his investment. His being expanded upward in the shape of a cone tapering toward prayer. Undo it. Rid me of her and her of it and us of Freddy. Give me back my quiet place. At an oblique angle she had intersected the plane of his life where daily routines accumulated like dust. Lamplight, breakfast. She had intruded a drastic dimension. He had been innocent amid trees. She had demanded that he know. Straight string of his life, knotted. The knot surely was sin. Piet prayed for it to be undone.

Overhead the elm branches were embedded in a sky of dirty wool: erosion deltas photographed high above the drained land: stained glass. Footsteps returning from lunch scuffed everywhere in the Common distinctly, as if under an enclosing dome. A small reddish bug crawled along an edge of brick. Happened before. When? His head tilted just so. Exactly. His mind sank scrabbling through the abyss of his past searching for when this noticing of an insect had happened before. He lifted his eyes and saw the Park Street church, stately. He looked around him at the grayly streaming passersthrough and all people seemed miraculous, that they could hold behind their glowing faces the knowledge that soon, under the whitewash-spattered sky, they would wither or be cut.

Church. Tolled. Three. He weakened, broke faith with himself, ran for coffee and one, no two, cinnamon doughnuts. When he emerged from the cafeteria the yellow sky between the buildings was full of Foxy. Coffee slopping through the paper cup and burning his fingers, he ran up Tremont, convinced of hopeless guilt. But Freddy's car, his yellow Mercury convertible, the canvas top mildewed from being buttoned up all winter, was still parked, half on the sidewalk, down a narrow alley off the street, near a metal door painted one with the mustard wall yet whose hinges, rubbed down to the bare steel, betrayed that it could be opened. So she was not gone. He went back across Tremont to the pavilion's vicinity and ate.

His feet grew numb. Boston danker than Tarbox: oily harbor lets in the cold sea kiss. More northern. To his dread for Foxy attached a worry that he would be missed at home. Gallagher, Angela, each would think the other had him. The sun slipped lower behind the dome of sky, to where the walls were thinner. Sunshine luminous as tallow tried to set up shadows, touched the tree plaques and dry fountains. In this light Piet saw the far door down the alley open and a dab that must be bald Freddy emerge. Dodging through thickening traffic, Piet's body seemed to float, footless, toward the relief of knowing, as when he would enter the Whitmans' house by the doorway crowded with lilacs and move through the hallway fragrant of freshly planed wood toward the immense sight of the marshes and Foxy's billowing embrace. Freddy Thorne looked up from unlocking his car door, squinting, displeased to see him. Neither man could think to speak. In the gaping steel doorway a Negress in a green nurse's uniform and silver-rim spectacles was standing supporting Foxy.

She was conscious but drugged; her pointed face, half-asleep, was blotched pink and white as if her cheeks had been struck, and struck again. Her eyes paused on Piet, then passed over him. Her hair flowed all on one side, like wheat being winnowed, and the collar of her Russian-general greatcoat, a coat he loved, was up, and buttoned tight beneath her chin like a brace.

Freddy moved rapidly to her side, said "Six steps," and, his mouth grimly lipless, one arm around her waist, the other beneath her elbow, eased her toward the open car door as if at any jarring she might break. The Negress in silence closed the metal door upon herself. She had not stepped into the alley. Piet's running had attracted the curiosity of some pedestrians, who watched from the sidewalk at the alley mouth yet did not step toward them. Freddy lowered Foxy into the passenger's seat, whispering, "Good girl." With the usual punky noise of car doors hers swung shut. She was behind glass. The set of her mouth, the tension above the near corner predicting laughter, appeared imperfectly transported from the past, a shade spoiled, giving her face the mysterious but final deadness of minutely imitated wax effigies. Then two fingertips came up from her lap and smoothed the spaces of skin below her eyes.

Piet vaulted around the front of the car. Freddy was already in the driver's seat; grunting, he rolled his window some inches down. "Well, if it isn't Piet Enema, the well-known purge."

Piet asked, "Is she—?"

"Okey-doak," Freddy said. "Smooth as silk. You're safe again, lover."

"What took so long?"

"She's been lying down, out, what did you think, she'd get up and dance? Get your fucking hand off the door handle."

Perhaps roused by Freddy's fury of tone, Foxy looked over. Her hand touched her lips. "Hi," she said. The voice was warmer, drowsier, than hers. "I know you," she added, attempting, Piet felt, irony and confession at once, the irony acknowledging that she knew very well this intruder whom she could not quite name. Freddy rolled up the window, punched down both door locks, started the motor, gave Piet a blind stare of triumph. Delicately, taking care not to shake his passenger, he eased the car down off the curb into the alley and into the trashy stream of homeward traffic. A condom and candy wrapper lay paired in the exposed gutter.

Not until days later, after Foxy had survived the forty-eight hours alone in the house with Toby and the test of Ken's return from Chicago, did Piet learn, not from Freddy but from her as told to her by Freddy, that at the moment of anesthesia she had panicked; she had tried to strike the Negress pressing the sweet, sweet mask to her face and through the first waves of ether had continued to cry that she should go home, that she was supposed to have this baby, that the child's father was coming to smash the door down with a hammer and would stop them.

After she confessed this to him over the phone on Monday, his silence stretched so long she laughed to break it. "Don't take it upon yourself that you didn't come break down the door. I didn't want you to. It was my subconscious speaking, and only after I had consciously got myself to the point of no return, and I could relax. What we did was right. We couldn't do anything else, could we?"

"I couldn't think of anything else."

"We were very lucky to have brought it off. We ought to thank our, what?—our lucky stars." She laughed again, a perfunctory rustle in the apparatus.

Piet asked her, "Are you depressed?"

"Yes. Of course. Not because I've committed any sin so much, since it was what you asked me to do, what had to be done for everybody's sake, really. But because now I'm faced with it again, *really* faced with it now."

"With what?"

"My life. Ken, this cold house. The loss of your love. Oh, and my milk's dried up, so I have that to feel sorry for myself about. Toby keeps throwing up his formula. And Cotton's gone."

"Cotton."

"My cat. Don't you remember him?"

"Of course. He always greeted me."

"He was here Wednesday morning catching field mice on the edge of the marsh and when I came back that night he was gone. I didn't even notice. Thursday I began to call, but I was too weak to go outdoors much."

Piet said, "He's out courting."

"*No,*" Foxy said, "he was fixed," and the receiver was rhythmically scraped by her sobs.

He asked her, "Why didn't you talk to me more, before we did it?"

"I was angry, which I suppose is the same as being frightened. And what did we have to say? We'd said it. You were too chicken to let me have it as if it were Ken's, and I've always known I could never get you away from Angela. No, don't argue."

He was obediently silent.

She said, "But what now, Piet? What shall we expect of each other?"

He answered, after thought, "Not much."

"It's easier for you," she said. "You'll always have somebody else to move on to. Don't deny it. Me, I seem stuck. You want to know something horrible?"

"If you'd like to tell it."

"I can't stand Ken now. I can hardly bear to look at his face, or answer when he talks. I think of it as *him* who made me kill my baby. It's *just* the kind of thing he'd do."

"Sweet, it wasn't him, it was *me*."

Foxy explained to him, what he had heard often before, how Ken, in denying her a child for seven years, had killed in her something only another man could revive. She ended by asking, "Piet, will you ever come talk to me? Just talk?"

"Do you think we should?"

"Should, shouldn't. Of course we shouldn't. But I'm down, lover, I'm just terribly, terribly down." She pronounced these words with a stagy lassitude learned from the movies. The script called for her to hang up, and she did. Losing another dime, he dialed her number from the booth, the booth in front of Poirier's Liquor Mart, where one of their friends might all too likely spot him, a droll corpse upright in a bright aluminum coffin. At Foxy's house, no one answered. Of course he must go to her. Death, once invited in, leaves his muddy bootprints everywhere.

Georgene, faithful to Freddy's orders, came calling on Foxy that Monday, around noon, and was shocked to see Piet's pick-up truck parked in the driveway. She felt a bargain had not been kept. Her understanding had been that the abortion would end Foxy's hold over Piet; she believed that once Foxy was eliminated her own usefulness to Piet would reassert itself. She prided herself, Georgene, on being useful, on keeping her bargains and carrying out the assignments given her, whether it was obtaining a guest speaker for the League of Women Voters, or holding her service in a tennis match, or staying married to Freddy Thorne. She had visited Foxy late Wednesday night, twice on Thursday, and once on Friday. She had carried tea and toast up to the convalescent, changed Toby's spicy orange diapers, and seen two baskets of clothes and sheets through the washer and dryer. On Friday she had spent over an hour vacuuming the downstairs and tidying toward Ken's return. Her feelings toward Foxy altered in these days of domestic conspiracy. Georgene, from her first glimpse, a year ago at the Applebys' party, of this prissy queenly newcomer, had disliked her; when Foxy stole Piet from her this dislike became hatred, with its implication of respect. But with the younger woman at her mercy Georgene allowed herself tenderness. She saw in Foxy a woman destined to dare and to suffer, a younger sister spared any compulsion to settle cheap, whose very mistakes were obscurely enviable. She was impressed with Foxy's dignity. Foxy did not deny that in this painful interregnum she needed help and company, nor did she attempt to twist Georgene's providing it into an occasion for protestation, or scorn, or confession, or self-contempt. Georgene knew from living with Freddy how surely self-contempt becomes contempt for others and was pleased to have her presence in Foxy's house accepted for what it was, an accident. Wednesday night, Foxy dismissed her with the grave tact of a child assuring a parent she is not afraid of the dark. She was weepy and half-drugged and clutched her living baby to her like a doll, yet from a deep reserve of manners thanked Georgene for coming, permitted her bloody bedsheets to be changed, accepted the injunction not to go up and down stairs, nodded gravely when told to call the Thornes' number at any hour, for any reason, even senseless fright. Thursday morning, Georgene found her downstairs, pale from lack of sleep; she had

been unable to breast-feed the baby and had had to come downstairs to heat up a bottle. Obedient, she had not attempted the
return trip upstairs, and with one blanket had made a bed for
them both on the sofa. Imagining those long moon-flooded hours,
the telephone offering a tempting release from solitude, Georgene
secretly admired the other's courage and pride. She helped her
upstairs and felt leaning upon her, naked under its robe and slip,
the taller, less supple, rather cool and dry and ungainly body her
lover had loved. Imagined love flowed from her. The current was
timidly returned. They were silent in unison. They moved together, in these few days, whose weather outside was a humid
raw foretaste of spring less comfortable than outright winter,
through room upon room of tactful silence. They did not speak
of Piet or of Freddy or of the circumstances that had brought
them together except as they were implied by Georgene's inquir-
ies into Foxy's physical condition. They discussed health and
housework and the weather outside and the needs of the infant.
Friday afternoon, the last day Georgene was needed, she brought
along little Judy, and in the festive atmosphere of recovery Foxy,
now fully clothed, served cookies and vermouth and persuaded
Georgene, after her exertions of cleaning, to smoke an unaccustomed cigarette. Awkwardly they lifted their glasses as if to toast
one another: two women who had tidied up after a mess.

Georgene had not been asked to return on Monday. But she
was curious to know how Foxy had weathered the weekend, had
put off Ken. She would ask if Foxy needed any shopping done.
Seeing Piet's truck in the driveway, she experienced a compounded jealousy, a multiple destruction within her: the first loss
was her tender comradeship with the other woman. Of Piet she
expected nothing except that he continue to exist and unwittingly
illumine her life. She had willed herself open to him and knew
that the chemistry of love was all within her, her doing. Even his
power to wound her with neglect was a power she had created
and granted; whatever he did he could not escape the province of
her freedom, her free decision to love. Whereas between her and
Foxy a polity existed: rules, a complex set of assumed concessions,
a generous bargain posited upon the presumption of defeat.

Georgene seldom visited the middle ground between female submission and sexless mastery, so her negotiated fondness for Foxy was rarer for her, more precious perhaps, than her love for Piet, which was predetermined and unchanging and somewhat stolid. Foxy's betrayal found her vulnerable. She was revealed to herself as not merely helpless but foolish. Helplessness has its sensual consolations; foolishness has none. She pushed through the door without knocking.

Piet and Foxy were sitting well apart, on opposite sides of the coffee table. Piet had not removed the zippered apricot suède windbreaker he wore to jobs, and the stub of a yellow pencil was tucked behind his ear. The morning marsh light struck white fire from the hem of Foxy's frilled nightie and froze into ice her pale hand holding a cigarette from which spiraled smoke sculptural as blue stone. Coffee equipment mixed arcs of china and metal and sun on the low teak table between them. Georgene felt she had entered upon a silence. Her indignation was balked by her failure to surprise them embracing. Nevertheless, Piet was embarrassed, and half rose.

"Don't get up," Georgene told him. "I don't mean to interrupt your cozy tryst."

"It wasn't," he told her.

"Just a meeting of souls. How beautiful." She turned to Foxy. "I came to offer to do your shopping and to see how you were doing. I see you're back to normal and won't be needing me any more. Good."

"Don't take that tone, Georgene. I was just telling Piet, how wonderful you were."

"*He* wasn't telling *you?* I'm hurt."

"Why are you angry? Don't you think Piet and I have a right to talk?"

Piet moved forward on his chair, grunting, "I'll go."

Foxy said, "You certainly will not. You just got here. Georgene, have some coffee. Let's stop playing charades."

Georgene refused to sit. "Please don't imagine," she said, "that I have personal feelings about this. It's none of my business what you two do, or rather it wouldn't be if my husband hadn't saved your necks at the risk of his own. But I *will* say, for your own good, unless you're planning to elope, it is very sloppy to have Piet's pick-up truck out where Marcia could drive by any minute."

"Marcia's at her psychiatrist in Brookline," Foxy said. "She's gone every day from ten to two, or longer, if she has lunch with Frank in town."

Piet said, wanting to have a conversation, a party, "Is Marcia going too? Angela's just started."

Georgene asked him, "How on earth can *you* afford it?"

"I can't," he said. "But Daddy Hamilton can. It's something the two of them cooked up."

"And what were you two cooking up, when I barged in?"

"Nothing," Piet told her. "In fact we were having some trouble finding things to say."

Foxy asked, "Why shouldn't I talk to the father of my child?"

Piet said, "It wasn't a child, it was a little fish, less than a fish. It was nothing, Fox."

"It was *something*, damn you. You weren't carrying it."

Georgene was jealous of their quarrel, their display of proud hearts. She and Freddy rarely quarreled. They went to sleep on one another, and kept going to parties together, and felt dreary all next day, like veteran invalids. Only Piet had brought her word of a world where vegetation was heraldic and every woman was some man's queen. That world was like, she thought, the marsh seen through the windows, where grasses prospered in salty mud that would kill her kind of useful plant. "I honestly think," she heard herself saying, "that one of you ought to move out of Tarbox."

They were amazed, amused. Foxy asked, "Whatever for?"

"For your own good. For everybody's good. You're poisoning the air."

"If any air's been poisoned," Piet told her, "it's your husband that's done it. He's the local gamesmaster."

"Freddy just wants to be human. He knows you all think he's ridiculous so he's adopted that as his act. Anyway, I didn't mean poison. Maybe the rest of us are poisoned and you two upset us with your innocence. Think of just yourselves. Piet, look at her.

Why do you want to keep tormenting her with your presence? Make her take her husband back to Cambridge. Quit Gallagher and go somewhere else, go back to Michigan. You'll destroy each other. I was with her at the end of last week. It's not a little thing you put her through."

Foxy cut in drily. "It was my decision. I'm grateful for your help, Georgene, but I would have gotten through alone. And we would have found a way without Freddy, though that *did* work out. As to Piet and me, we have no intention of sleeping together again. I think you're saying you still want him. Take him."

"That's *not* what I'm saying! Not at all!" There had been some selfless point, some public-spirited truth she had been trying to frame for these two, and they were too corrupt to listen.

Piet said, joking, "I feel I'm being auctioned off. Should we let Angela bid too?"

He was amused. They were both amused. Georgene had entertained them, made them vivid to themselves. Watching her tremblingly try to manage her coffee cup, a clumsy intruder, they were lordly, in perfect control. Having coaxed the abortion from their inferiors, they were quite safe, and would always exist for each other. Their faces were pleasant in sunlight, complacent in the same way, like animals that have eaten.

Georgene took a scalding sip of coffee and replaced the cup in its socket on the saucer and sat primly upright. "I don't know what I'm trying to say," she apologized. "I'm delighted, Foxy, to see you so happy. Frankly, I think you're a very gutsy girl."

"I'm *not* happy," Foxy said, protesting, sensing danger.

"Well, happier. I am too. I'm *so* glad spring is here, it's been a long winter up on my hill. The crocuses, Piet, are up beside the garage. When can we all start playing tennis?" She stood; there was no coat to slow her departure. On all but the coldest days of winter, Georgene wore no more than a skirt and sweater and a collegiate knit scarf. It was warming, on a January afternoon when the sun had slipped through a crack in the sky, to see her downtown dressed as if for a dazzling fall afternoon, leading snowsuited Judy over hummocks of ice, hurrying along full of resolution and inner fire.

. . .

Town meeting that spring smelled of whiskey. Piet noticed the odor as soon as he entered the new high-school auditorium, where orange plastic chairs designed to interlock covered the basketball floor solidly between the bleachers and the stage, beneath the high fluorescent emptiness hung with cables and gymnastic riggings. A few feet above the swamp of faces hovered a glimmering miasma of alcohol, of amber whiskey, of martinis hurriedly swallowed between train and dinner, with the babysitter imminent. Piet had never noticed the scent before and wondered if it were the warm night—a thawing fog had rolled in from the sea and suddenly dandelions dotted the football field—or if the town had changed. Each year there were more commuters, more young families with VW buses and Cézanne prints moving into developments miles distant from the heart of historical Tarbox. Each year, in town meeting, more self-assured young men rose to speak, and silent were the voices dominant when Piet and Angela moved to town—droning Yankee druggists, paranoid clammers, potbellied selectmen ponderously fending off antagonisms their fathers had incurred, a nearsighted hound-faced moderator who recognized only his friends and ruled all but deafening dissents into unanimity. At the first meeting Piet had attended, the town employees, a shirtsleeved bloc of ex-athletes who perched in the bleachers apart from their wives, had hooted down the elderly town attorney, Gertrude Tarbox's brother-in-law, until the old man's threadbare voice had torn and the microphone had amplified the whisper of a sob. Now the employees, jacketed, scattered, sat mute and sullen with their wives as year after year another raise was unprotestingly voted them. Now the town attorney was an urbane junior partner in a State Street firm who had taken the job as a hobby, and the moderator a rabbit-eared associate professor of sociology, a maestro of parliamentary procedure. Only an occasional issue evocative of the town's rural past—the purchase of an old barn abutting the public parking lot, or the plea of a farmer, a fabulous creature with frost-burned face and slow tumbling voice, that he be allowed to reap his winter rye before an S-curve in the Mather road was straightened—provoked debate. New schools and new highways, sewer bonds and zoning by-laws

all smoothly slid by, greased by federal grants. Each moderniza-
tion and restriction presented itself as part of the national necessity, the overarching honor of an imperial nation. The last oppo-
nents, the phlegmatic pennypinchers and choleric naysayers who
had absurdly blocked the building of this new school for a
decade, had died or ceased to attend, leaving the business of the
town to be carried forward in an edifice whose glass roof leaked
and whose adjustable partitions had ceased to adjust. There was
annual talk now of representative town meeting, and the quorum
had been halved. Among Piet's friends, Harold little-Smith was
on the Finance Committee, Frank Appleby was chairman of the
committee to negotiate with the Commonwealth for taxpayer-
subsidized commuter service, Irene Saltz was chairlady of the
Conservation Commission (and charmingly coupled her report
with her resignation, since she and her husband were with sincere
regret moving to Cleveland), and Matt Gallagher sat on the
Board of Zoning Appeals. Indeed, there was no reason why Matt,
if he believed the hint of the Polish priest, could not be elected
selectman; and Georgene Thorne had narrowly missed—by the
margin of a whiff of scandal—election to the school board.

Politics bored Piet. The Dutch in his home region had been
excluded from, and had disdained, local power. His family had
been Republican under the impression that it was the party of
anarchy; they had felt government to be an illusion the governed
should not encourage. The world of politics had no more substance for Piet than the film world, and the meeting of which he
was a member made him as uncomfortable as the talent auditions
at a country fair, where faces strained by stolen mannerisms lift in
hope toward wholly imagined stars. Piet went to town meetings
to see his friends, but tonight, though the Hanemas had arrived
early, it happened that no one sat with them. The Applesmiths
and Saltzes sat up front with the politically active. On the stage,
as observers, not yet citizens, sat the young Reinhardts, whom
Piet detested. The Guerins and Thornes had entered and found
seats by the far doors and Piet never managed to catch either
woman's eye. Bernadette Ong and Carol Constantine came late,
together, without husbands. Most strangely, the Whitmans did

388 : C O U P L E S

not attend at all, though they had now lived in Tarbox long enough to be voting citizens. At Piet's side Angela, who had to rush into Cambridge after nursery school every day and then fight the commuter traffic home, was exhausted, and kept nodding and twitching, yet as a loyal liberal insisted on staying to add her drowsy "Ayes" to the others. The train service proposal, at the annual estimated budget cost of twelve thousand dollars, on the argument that the type of people attracted to Tarbox by creditable commuter service would enrich the community inestimably, unanimously passed. The self-righteous efficiency of the meeting, hazed by booze, so irritated Piet, so threatened his instinct for freedom, that he several times left the unanimous crowd to get a drink of water at the bubbler in the hall, where he imagined that the town building inspector evaded his gaze and refused to return his hello. When the meeting, after eleven, was adjourned, he saw the other couples huddling by an exit, planning a drink at one of their homes. Harold's eager profile jabbered; Bea slowly, dreamily nodded. Angela mocked Piet's premonition of exclusion and said she wanted to go home and sleep. Before psychiatry, she would have equivocated. Piet could only yield. In the car he asked her, "Are you dead?"

"A little. All those right-of-ways and one-foot strips of land gave me a headache. Why can't they just do it in Town Hall and not torment us?"

"How did psychiatry go?"

"Not very excitingly. I felt tired and stupid and didn't know why I was there."

"Don't ask *me* why you're there."

"I wasn't."

"What do the two of you talk about?"

"Just *I'm* supposed to talk. He listens."

"And never says anything?"

"Ideally."

"Do you talk about me? How I made you sleep with Freddy Thorne?"

"We did at first. But now we're on my parents. Daddy mostly. Last Thursday it came out, just popped out of my mouth, that he always undressed in the closet. I hadn't thought about it for years. If I was in their bedroom about something, he'd come out of the closet with his pajamas on. The only way I could see him *really* was by spying on him in the bathroom."

"You spied. Angel."

"I know, it made me blush to remember it. But it made me *mad*, too. Whenever he'd be in there he'd turn on both faucets so we couldn't hear him do anything."

We: Louise, her seldom-seen sister, a smudged carbon copy, two years younger, lived in Vermont, husband teaching at a prep school. Louise married early, not the rare beauty Angela was, smudged mouth and unclear skin, probably better in bed, dirtier. He thought of Joop. His pale blond brother, flaxen hair, watery eyes, younger, purer, had carried on the greenhouse, should have married Angela, the two of them living together in receding light. Leaving him dirty Louise. Piet asked, "Did Louise ever see his penis? Did you and she ever talk about it?"

"Not really. We were terribly inhibited, I suppose, though Mother was always talking about how glorious Nature was, with that funny emphasis, and the house was full of art books. Michelangelo's, the ones on Adam, are terribly darling and limp, with long foreskins, so when I saw you, I thought—"

"What did you think?"

"I'll try to work it out with *him* what I thought."

The Nun's Bay Road was, since it had been widened, unlike the beach road, straight and rather bare, more like a Midwestern road, sparsely populated by a shuttered-up vegetable stand and, high on a knoll, a peeling gingerbread mansion with a single upstairs light burning, where a widower lived. Joop had had more Mama's eyes and mouth. Washed-out, unquestioning, shattered. He felt Angela beginning to doze and said, "I wonder if I ever saw my mother naked. Neither of them ever seemed to take a bath, at least while I was awake. I didn't think they knew a thing about sex and was shocked once when my mother in passing complained about the spots on my sheets. She wasn't really scolding, it was almost kidding. That must have been what shocked me."

"The one good thing Daddy did," Angela answered, "was to tell us to stand up straight when we began to get breasts. It made him furious to see us hunch over."

"You were ashamed of them?"

"Not ashamed so much, it just feels at first as if you can't *manage* them. They stick out and wobble."

Piet pictured Angela's breasts and told her, "I'm very hurt, that you talk about your father when I thought *I* was your problem. To be sure, he *is* the one paying for it."

"Why does that make you so angry? He has money and we don't."

The wheels of their car, her cream-colored Peugeot, crunched on gravel. They were home. Squares of windowlight transfixed shrubbery in misted crosshatch. The lawn felt muddy underfoot, a loose skin of thaw on winter's body. A maple sapling that had taken root near the porch, in the bulb bed, extended last summer's growth in glistening straight shoots red as thermometer mercury. Beside the black chimney the blurred moon looked warm. Gratefully Piet inhaled the moist night. His year of trouble felt vaporized, dismissed.

Their babysitter was Merissa Mills, the teen-age daughter of the ringleader of the old boatyard crowd, who years ago had divorced his wife and moved to Florida, where he managed a marina and had remarried. Merissa, as often with children of broken homes, was determinedly tranquil and polite and conventional. She said, "There was one call, from a Mr. Whitman. I wrote down the number." On a yellow pad of Gallagher & Hanema receipt forms her round bland hand had penciled Foxy's number.

Piet asked, "*Mr.* Whitman?"

Merissa, gathering her books, gazed at him without curiosity. Her life had witnessed a turmoil of guilt she was determined not to relive. "He said you should call him no matter how late you got back."

"He can't have meant *this* late," Angela told Piet. "You take Merissa home and I'll call Foxy in the morning."

"No!" In sudden focus Piet saw the two women before him as identical—both schooled prematurely in virtue, both secluded behind a willed composure. He knew they were screening him from something out there in the dark that was his, his fate, the fruit of his deeds. His tongue streaked tranced down the narrow path still open. "We may still need Merissa. Let me call Ken before we let her go."

Angela protested, "Merissa has school tomorrow and I'm exhausted." But her voice lacked fiber; he walked through it to the phone, his palms tingling. His movements, as he picked up the receiver and dialed, were as careful as those of a leper whose flesh falls off in silver shards.

Ken answered on the second ring. "Piet," he said. It was not said as a greeting; Ken was giving something a name.

"Ken."

"Foxy and I have had a long talk."

"What about?"

"The two of you."

"Oh?"

"Yes. Do you deny that you and she have been lovers since last summer?"

Ken's silence lengthened. An impatient doctor faced with a procrastinating hope. Piet saw that there was no glimmer, that the truth had escaped and was all about them, like oxygen, like darkness. As a dying man after months of ingenious forestallment turns with relief to the hope of an afterlife, Piet sighed, "No, I don't deny it."

"Good. That's a step forward."

Angela's face, forsaken, pressed wordless against the side of Piet's vision as he listened.

"She also told me that she became pregnant by you this winter and you arranged to have the pregnancy aborted while I was in Chicago."

"Did she though? While you were in the Windy City?" Piet felt before him an adamant flatness upon which his urge was to dance.

"Is that true or false?" Ken persisted.

Piet said, "Tell me the rules of this quiz. Can I win, or only lose?"

Ken paused. Angela's face, as something of what was happening

dawned on it, grew pale, and anxiously mouthed the silent syllable, *Who?*

Less disciplinary, a shade concessive, Ken said, "Piet, I think the
best thing would be for you and Angela to come over here
tonight."

"She's awfully tired."

"Could you put her on the phone, please?"

"No. We'll come over." Hanging up, he faced the rectangle
of slightly darker wallpaper where until recently a mirror had
hung. Angela had transferred it to Nancy's room because the
child expressed jealousy of her father's birthday gift of a mirror
to Ruth. He told Angela, "We must go," and asked Merissa, "Can
you stay?" Both acquiesced; he had gained, in those few seconds
over the phone, the forbidding dignity of those who have no
lower to go. His face was a mask while his blood underwent an
airy tumult, a boiling alternation of shame and fear momentarily
condensing into those small actions—a sticky latch lifted, a
pocket-slapping search for car keys, a smile of farewell at Merissa
and a promise not to be long—needed to get them out of the
house, into the mist, on their way.

By way of Blackberry Lane, a winding link road tenderly
corrupted from Nigger Lane, where a solitary escaped slave had
lived in the days of Daniel Webster, dying at last of loneliness and
pneumonia, the distance from the Hanema's house to the Whitmans was not great. Often in summer Piet after his afternoon's
work would drive his daughters to the beach for a swim and be
back by supper. So Piet and Angela had little time to talk; Angela
spoke quickly, lightly, skimming the spaces between what she had
overheard or guessed. "How long has it been going on?"

"Oh, since the summer. I think her hiring me for the job was a
way of seeing if it would happen."

"It occurred to me, but I thought you wouldn't use your work
like that, I thought it was beneath your ethics to. Deceive me, yes,
but your men, and Gallagher . . ."

"I did a respectable job for her. We didn't sleep together until toward the end. It was after the job was done, when I had no reason to have my truck parked there, that it began to seem not right."

"Oh, it did seem not right?"

"Sure. It became very heavy. Religious, somehow, and sad. She was so pregnant." It pleased Piet to be able to talk about it, as if under this other form he had been secretly loving Angela, and now could reveal to her the height and depth of his love.

She said, "Yes, that is the surprise. Her being pregnant. It must be very hard for Ken to accept."

Piet shrugged. "It was part of her. I didn't mind it if she didn't. Actually, it made it seem more innocent, as if that much of her was being faithful to Ken no matter what we did with the rest."

"How many times did you sleep with her in all?"

"Oh. Thirty. Forty."

"Forty!"

"You asked." She was crying. He told her, "Don't cry."

"I'm crying because you seemed happier lately and I thought it was *me* and it's been *her*."

"No, it hasn't been her." He felt under him a soft place, a hidden pit, the fact of Bea.

"No? When was the last time?"

The abortion. She mustn't know. But it was too big to hide, like a tree. In its shade the ground was suspiciously bare. He said, "Months ago. We agreed it would be the last time."

"But after the baby had been born?"

"Yes. Six or so weeks after. I was surprised she still wanted me."

"You're so modest." Her tone was empty of irony, dead. A mailbox knocked cockeyed, toppling backwards forever, wheeled through their headlights. Ghosts of mist thronged from the marshes where the road dipped. Angela asked, "Why did you stop?"

Having withheld truth elsewhere, Piet lavished frankness here. "It began to hurt more than it helped. I was becoming cruel to you, and I couldn't *see* the girls; they seemed to be growing up without me. Then, with her baby, it's being a boy, it seemed somehow clear that our time was past." He further explained: "A time to love, and a time to die."

Her crying had dried up but showed in her voice as a worn place, eroded. "You did love her?"

He tried to tread precisely here; their talk had moved from a thick deceptive forest to a desert where every step left a print. He told her, "I'm not sure I understand the term. I enjoyed being with her, yes."

"And you also enjoyed Georgene?"

"Yes. Less complexly. She was less demanding. Foxy was always trying to educate me."

"And any others?"

"No." The lie lasted as they dipped into the last hollow before the Whitman's little rise.

"And me? Have you ever enjoyed being with me?" The desert had changed; the even sand of her voice had become seared rock, once molten, sharp to the touch.

"Oh," Piet said, "Jesus, yes. Being with you is Heaven." He hurried on, having decided. "One thing you should know, since Ken knows it. At the end, after I figured our affair was over, Foxy got pregnant by me, don't ask me how, it was ridiculous, and we got Freddy Thorne to arrange our abortion for us. His price was that night with you. It sounds awful, but it was the only thing, it was great of you, and it absolutely ended Foxy and me. It's done. It's over. We're just here tonight so I can get reprimanded."

They were at the Whitmans'. With the motor extinguished, Angela's not answering alarmed him. Her voice when it came sounded miniature, dwindled, terminal. "You better take me home."

"Don't be silly," he said. "You *must* come in." He justified his imperious tone: "I don't have the guts to go in without you."

Ken answered their ring. He wore a foulard and smoking jacket: the host. He shook Piet's hand gravely, glancing at him from those shallow gray eyes as if taking a snapshot. He welcomed Angela with a solicitude bordering on flirtation. His man's voice and shoulders filled comfortably spaces where Foxy alone had seemed adrift and forlorn. He took their coats, Angela's blue second-best and Piet's little apricot jacket, and ushered the couple down the rag-rugged hall; Angela stared all about her, fascinated by how the house that should have been hers had been renovated. She murmured to Piet, "Did *you* choose the wallpaper?" Foxy was in the living room, feeding the baby in her lap. Unable to rise or speak in greeting, she grinned. Lit up by her smile, her teary face seemed to Piet a net full of gems; lamplight flowed down her loose hair to the faceless bundle in her lap. The array of bottles on the coffee table glittered. They had been drinking. In the society of Tarbox there was no invitation more flattering than to share, like this, another couple's intimacy, to partake in their humorous déshabille, their open quarrels and implicit griefs. It was hard for these couples this night to break from that informal spell and to confront each other as enemies. Angela took the old leather armchair, and Piet a rush-seat ladderback that Foxy's mother, appalled by how bleak their house seemed, had sent from Maryland. Ken remained standing and tried to run the meeting in an academic manner. Piet's itch was to clown, to seek the clown's traditional invisibility. Angela and Foxy, their crossed legs glossy, fed into the room that nurturing graciousness of female witnessing without which no act since Adam's naming of the beasts has been complete. Women are gentle fruitful presences whose interpolation among us diffuses guilt.

Ken asked them what they would like to drink. The smoking jacket a prop he must live up to. Outrage has no costume. Angela said, "Nothing."

Piet asked for something with gin in it. Since tonic season hadn't begun, perhaps some dry vermouth, about half and half, a European martini. Anything, just so it wasn't whiskey. He described the smell of whiskey at the town meeting, and was disappointed when no one laughed. Irked, he asked, "Ken, what's the first item on your agenda?"

Ken ignored him, asking Angela, "How much did you know of all this?"

"Ah," Piet said. "An oral exam."

Angela said, "I knew as much as you did. Nothing."

"You must have guessed something."

"I make a lot of guesses about Piet, but he's very slippery."

Piet said, "Agile, I would have said."

Ken did not take his eyes from Angela. "But you're in Tarbox all day; I'm away from seven to seven."

Angela shifted her weight forward, so the leather cushion sighed. "What are you suggesting, Ken? That I'm deficient as a wife?"

Foxy said, "One of the things that makes Angela a good wife to Piet, better than I could ever be, is that she lets herself be blind."

"Oh, I don't know about that," Angela said, preoccupied with, what her shifting in the chair had purposed, pouring herself some brandy. It was five-star Cognac but the only glass was a Flintstone jelly tumbler. Foxy's housekeeping had these lapses and loopholes. Admitted to her house late in the afternoon, Piet would see, through the blond rainbow of her embrace, breakfast dishes on the coffee table unwashed, and a book she had marked her place in with a dry bit of bacon. She claimed, when he pointed it out, that she had done it to amuse him; but he had also observed that her underwear was not always clean.

Unable to let Angela's mild demur pass unchallenged, she sat upright, jarring the sleeping bundle in her lap, and argued, "I mean it as a compliment. I think it's a beautiful trait. I could never be that way, the wise overlooking wife. I'm jealous by nature. It used to kill me, at parties, to see you come up with that possessive sweet smile and take Piet home to bed."

Piet winced. The trick was not to make it too real for Ken. Change the subject. A mild man innocently seeking information, he asked the other man, "How did you find out?"

"Somebody told him," Foxy interposed. "A woman. A jealous woman."

"Georgene," Piet said.

"Right," Foxy said.

Ken said, "No, it was Marcia little-Smith. She happened to ask me the other day downtown what work was still being done on the house, that Piet's truck was parked out front so often."

"Don't be ridiculous, that's what the two of them cooked up to say," Foxy told Piet, "Of course it was Georgene. I knew when she found us together last week she was going to do something vicious. She has no love in her life so she can't stand other people having any."

Piet disliked her slashing manner; he felt they owed the couple they had wronged a more chastened bearing. He accused her: "And then you told him everything."

The gems in her face burst their net. "Yes. Yes. Once I got started I couldn't stop. I'm sorry, for you, and then not. You've put me through hell, man."

Angela smiled toward Ken, over brandy. "They're fighting."

He answered, "That's their problem," and Piet, hearing the unyielding tone, realized that Ken did not view the problem, as he did, as one equally shared, a four-sided encroachment and withdrawal. Ken's effort, he saw, would be to absolve, to precipitate, himself.

Angela, frightened, with Piet, of the other couple's rising hardness, inquired softly, her oval head tilted not quite toward Foxy, "Georgene found you together a week ago? Piet told me it was all over."

Foxy said, "He lied to you, sweet."

"I did *not*." Piet's face baked. "I came down here because you were miserable. We didn't make love, we hardly made conversation. We agreed that the abortion ended what should have been ended long ago. Clearly."

"Was it so clear?" Eyes downcast. Velvety mouth prim. He remembered that certain subtle slidiness of her lips. Her demeanor mixed surrender and defiance. Piet felt her fair body, seized by his eyes, as a plea not to be made to relive the humiliation of Peter.

Ken turned again on Angela. "How much *do* you know? Do you know the night of the Kennedy party they were necking in the upstairs bathroom? Do you know he was having both Georgene and Foxy for a while and that he has another woman now?"

"Who?"

Angela's quick question took both Whitmans aback; they looked at each other for a signal. Piet saw no sign from Foxy. Ken pronounced to Angela's face, "Bea."

"Dear Bea," Angela said, two fingertips circularly lingering on the brass stud second from the top along the outer edge of the left leather arm. *Pain so aloofly suffered. The treachery of Lesbians. Dress in chitons and listen to poetry. Touch my arm. Hockey.*

Piet interposed, "This is gossip. What evidence do you two have?"

"Never mind, Piet," Angela said aside.

Ken resumed the instructor's role; lamplight showed temples of professorial gray as he leaned over Angela. "You know about the abortion?" His face held a congestion his neat mouth wanted to vent. A pudgy studious boy who had been mocked at recess. *Never tease, Piet, never tease.*

Piet asked Foxy, "Why doesn't he lay off my wife?"

Angela nodded yes and with a graceful wave added, to Ken, "It seems to me they did that as much for you as for themselves. A cynical woman would have had the child and raised it as yours."

"Only if I were totally blind. I know what a Whitman looks like."

"You can tell just by listening," Piet said. "They begin to lecture at birth."

Ken turned to him. "Among the actions I'm considering is bringing criminal charges against Thorne. You'd be an accessory."

"For God's sake, why?" Piet asked. "That was probably the most Christian thing Freddy Thorne ever did. He didn't have to do it, he did it out of pity. Out of love, even."

"Love of who?"

"His *friends*." And Piet pronouncing this felt his heart vibrate with the nervousness of love, as if he and Freddy, the partition between them destroyed, at last comprehended each other with the fullness long desired, as almost had happened one night in the Constantines' dank foyer. Hate and love both seek to know.

Ken said, and something strange, a nasty puffing, an adolescent sneer, was afflicting his upper lip, "He did it because he likes to

meddle. But that's neither here nor there. It's been done, and I
see no way back through it."

Angela understood him first. She asked, "No way?"

Ken consented to her implication. "I've had it. To be technical:
there are reactions that are reversible and those that aren't. This
feels irreversible to me. Simple infidelity could be gotten around,
even a prolonged affair, but with my *child* in her belly—"

"Oh, don't be so superstitious," Foxy interrupted.

"—and then this monstrous performance with Thorne . . ."

Angela asked him, "How can you judge? As Piet says, in
context, it was the most merciful thing."

Piet told him, "She wrote me long letters, all summer, saying
how much she loved you." But even as he pleaded he knew it was
no use, and took satisfaction in this knowledge, for he was loyal to the God Who mercifully excuses us from pleading, Who
nails His joists of judgment down firm, and roofs the universe
with order.

As Ken spoke, still standing above them like a tutor, his voice
took on an adolescent hesitancy. "Let me try again. It's clear I
don't count for much with any of you. But this has been quite a
night for me, and I want to have my say."

"Hear, hear," Piet said. He waited happily to be crushed, and
dismissed.

"In a sense," Ken went on, "I feel quite grateful and benevo-
lent, because as a scientist I supposedly seek the truth, and tonight I've gotten it, and I want to be worthy of it. I don't want
to shy from it."

Piet poured more gin for himself. Foxy blinked and jostled
the baby; Angela sipped brandy and remained on the edge of
the huge leather chair.

"In chemistry," Ken told them, "molecules have *bonds;* some
compounds have strong bonds, and some have weaker ones, and
though now with atomic valences we can explain why, originally
it was all pragmatic. Now listening to my wife tonight, not only
what she said, the astonishingly cold-blooded deceptions, but the
joyful fullness with which she spilled it all out, I had to conclude
we don't have much of a bond. We should, I think. We come

from the same kind of people, we're both intelligent, we can stick to a plan, she stuck with me through a lot of what she tells me now were pretty dreary years. She told me, Piet, she had forgotten what love was until you came along. Don't say anything. Maybe I'm incapable of love. I've always assumed I loved her, felt what you're supposed to feel. I wanted her to have my child, when we had room for it, I gave her this house—"

Foxy interrupted, "You gave yourself this house."

Piet said, "Foxy."

Ken's hands, long-fingered and younger than his body, had been groping into diagrams on a plane in front of him; now they dropped rebuked to his sides. He turned to Piet and said, "See. No bond. Apparently you and she have it. More power to you."

"*Less* power to them, I would think," Angela interposed.

Ken looked at her surprised. He had thought he had been clear. "I'm divorcing her."

"You're not."

"Is he?"

Angela had spoken to Ken, then Piet to Foxy. She nodded, gems returning to her pink face, burning, eclipsing the attempted gaze of recognition, the confession of hopelessness, toward Piet. He was reminded of Nancy in the instant of equilibrium as she coped with the certain knowledge that she was going to cry, before her face toppled, broke like a vase, exposing the ululant tongue arched in agony on the floor of her mouth.

"If you divorce her, I'll have to marry her." Piet felt the sentence had escaped from him rather than been uttered. Was it a threat, a complaint, a promise?

Drily Foxy said, "That's the most gracious proposal I've ever heard." But she had named it: a proposal.

"Oh, my God, my God," Angela cried. "I feel sick, sick."

"Stop saying things twice," Piet told her.

"He doesn't love her, he doesn't," Angela told Ken. "He's been trying to ditch her ever since summer."

Ken told Piet, "I don't know what you should do. I just know what *I* should do."

Piet pleaded, "You can't divorce her for something that's over.

Look at her. She's repentant. She's confessed. That's your child she's holding. Take her away, beat her, leave Tarbox, go back to Cambridge with her, anything. But no reasonable man—"

Ken said, "I am nothing if not reasonable. I have legal grounds six times over."

"Stop being a lawyer's son for a second. Try to be human. The law is dead."

"The point of it is," Ken said, sitting down at last, "she's not repentant."

"Of *course* she is," Piet said. "*Look* at her. Ask her."

Ken asked gently, as if waking her from sleep, "Fox, are you? Repentant?"

She studied him with bold brown eyes and said, "I'll wash your feet and drink the water every night."

Ken turned to Piet, his experiment successful. "See? She mocks me."

Foxy stood tall, placed the infant on her shoulder, and rapidly drummed its back. "I can't stand this," she announced, "being treated as a *thing*. Excuse me, Angela. I'm truly sorry for your grief, but these *men*. All this competitive self-pity." She paused by the doorway to retrieve a blanket from a chair, and in the motion of her stooping, in the silence of her leaving, Tobias burped.

At the little salutary hiccup, so portentously audible, Angela's shoulders jerked with laughter. She had hidden her face in her hands. Now she revealed it, as if, her own acolyte, she were reverently unfolding the side wings of a triptych. It was a face, Piet saw, lost to self-consciousness, an arrangement of apertures willing, like a sea anemone, to be fed by whatever washed over it. "I want to go home," she told Ken. "I'm tired, I want a bath. Is everything settled? You're going to divorce Foxy, and Piet's going to divorce me. Do you want to marry me, Ken?"

He responded with a gallantry that confirmed Piet in his suspicion, from infancy on, that the world was populated by people bigger and wiser, more graceful and less greedy, than he. Ken said, "You tempt me. I wish we had met years ago."

"Years ago," Angela said, "we would have been too busy being good children." She asked Piet, "How shall we do? Do you want to move out tonight?"

Piet told her, "Don't dramatize. Nothing is settled. I think we all need to get some daylight on this."

Ken asked, "Then you're already backing out on your offer?"

"What offer?"

Ken said, "Piet, there is something you should know about us, you and me, that for some reason, modern manners I suppose, I don't seem able to express, and that I don't think this discussion has made clear to you, from the way you're sitting there smiling. I hate your guts." It sounded false; he amended it, "I hate what you've done to me, what you've done to Foxy."

Piet thought Angela would defend him, at least vaguely protest; but her silence glided by.

Ken went on, "In less than a year you, you and this sick town, have torn apart everything my wife and I had put together in seven years. Behind all this playfulness you *like* to destroy. You love it. The Red-haired Avenger. You're enjoying this; you've *enjoyed* that girl's pain."

Bored with being chastised, Piet rebelled. He stood to tell Ken, "She's your wife, keep her in your bed. You had lost her before you began. A man with any self-respect wouldn't have married her on the rebound like you did. Don't blame me if flowers didn't grow in this" —at the mouth of the hall, following Angela out, he turned and with whirling arms indicated to Ken his house, the Cambridge furniture, the empty bassinet, mirroring windows, the sum of married years—"test tube." Pleased with his rebuttal, he waited to hear Angela agree but she had already slammed the screen door. Outside, in sudden moist air, he stepped sideways into the pruned lilacs and was stabbed beneath an eye, and wondered if he were drunk, and thus so elated.

The car hurtled through mist. Angela asked, "Was she that much better in bed than me?"

Piet answered, "She was different. She did some things you don't do, I think she values men higher than you do. She's more insecure, I'd say, than you, and probably somewhat masculine.

Physically, there's more of *you* everywhere; she's tight and her responsiveness isn't as fully developed. She's young, as you once said."

The completeness of his answer, as if nothing else had convinced her that he had truly known the other woman, outraged Angela; she shrieked, and kneeled on the rubber car floor, and flailed her arms and head in the knobbed and metal-edged space, and tried to smother her own cries in the dusty car upholstery. He braked the Peugeot to a stop and walked around its ticking hood to her side and opened her door. As he pulled her out she felt disjointed, floppy as a drunk or a puppet. "Inhale," he said. The beach road dipped here, low to the marsh, and the mist was thick, suffused with a salinity that smelled eternal. Angela recovered her composure, apologized, tore up some wands of spring grass and pressed them against her eyelids. A pair of headlights slowly trundled toward them in the fog and halted.

A car door opened. Harold little-Smith's penetratingly tipped voice called, "All right there?"

"We're fine, thanks. Just enjoying the sea breeze."

"Oh, Piet. It's you. Who's that with you?"

"Angela.'

"Hi," Angela called, to prove it.

Piet called to the others over the glistening car roof, "How was the party?"

Harold guiltily answered, "It wasn't a party, just a beer. *Un peu de bière.* Carol looked for you but you'd gone out the other exit."

"We couldn't have come, thanks anyway," Piet said, and asked, "Who's that with *you?*"

"Marcia. Of course."

"Why of course?"

Marcia's voice piped through the fog. "Cut it out, Piet. You're a dirty old man."

"You're a doll. Good night, all."

"Good night, Hanemas." The pair of red tail lights dwindled, dissolved. In the silence then was the sighing of the sea rising in the marsh channels, causing the salt grass to unbend and rustle and suck. Her shrieks had been animal, less than animal, the noise of

a deranged mechanism. Piet could hardly believe that the world
—the one-o'clock mist, the familiar geography of Tarbox—
could reconstitute itself after such a shattering. But Merissa, as
Angela thanked her and told a lie about their going out again
("Their baby was having colic and they panicked; it's their first,
you know."), noncommitally gathered together her books, having been reading in the light of television. As Piet drove her home
she exuded a perfume of tangerines and talked about the dreadful
earthquake in Anchorage. Returning, he found his downstairs
lights off and Angela upstairs in the bathtub. The veins in her
breasts turquoise, the ghost of a tan distinct on her shoulders and
thighs, she was lying all but immersed, idly soaping her pudenda.
She scrubbed circularly and then stroked the oozy hair into
random peaks and then shifted her body so that the water washed
over her and erased the soap. Her breasts slopped and slid with
the pearly-dirty water; her hair was pinned up in a psyche knot,
exposing tenderly the nape of her neck.

Piet said, "Pardon me, but I must sit down. My stomach is a ball
of acid."

"Help yourself. Don't mind me."

He opened himself to the toilet and a burning gush of relief
mixed with the fascinating sight of her toes—scalded, rosy, kittenish nubs. Foxy had long prehensile toes; he had seen her one
night at the Constantines' hold a pencil in her foot and write
Elizabeth on the wall. He asked Angela, "How do you feel?"

"Desperate. If you'll pass me the razor, I'll slash my wrists."

"Don't say things like that." A second diarrheic rush, making
him gasp, had postponed his answer an instant. Where could so
much poison have come from? Did gin kill enzymes?

"Why not?" Angela rolled a quarter-turn. The water sloshed
tidally. "That would save you all the nuisance of a divorce. I
don't think my father's going to let me be very generous."

"Do you think"—a third, reduced rush—"there's going to be
such a thing? I'm scared to death of that woman."

"I heard you propose to her."

"She made it seem that way. Frankly, I'd rather stay married to
you."

"Maybe I'd rather not stay married to you."

"But who do you have to go to?"

"Nobody. Myself. Somehow you haven't let me be myself. All these parties you've made me go to and give so you could seduce the wives of all those dreary men."

He loved hearing her talk with such casual even truth; he loved agreeing with her, being her student. "They *are* dreary. I've figured out there are two kinds of jerks in this town, upper-middle-class jerks and lower-middle-class jerks. The upper went to college. My problem is, I'm sort of in the middle."

She asked, "What did you think of Ken?"

"I hated him. A real computer. Put in some data and out comes the verdict."

"I don't know," Angela said, moving her legs gently apart and together and apart in the water. "I think he showed more courage than any of us have."

"Talking about divorce? But he has no intention of divorcing her. All he cares about is frightening her and me and you and protecting his schoolboy honor."

"She didn't seem frightened to me. It's just what she wants. Why else would she tell him so much, all night?"

Now a coldness cut into his voided bowels. He wiped himself and flushed; the odor in the little room, of rotten cinnamon, embarrassed him before his wife. She held a washcloth to her face and moaned through it, "Oh God, oh my God."

He asked her, "Sweet, why?"

"I'll be so alone," she said. "You were the only person who ever tried to batter their way in to me."

"Roll over and I'll scrub your back." Her buttocks were red islands goose-bumped from heat. A slim bit of water between. Her back an animal brown horizontally nicked by the bra strap and starred by three dim scars where moles had been removed. "It won't happen," he told her, smoothly soaping, "it won't happen."

"I shouldn't even let you stay the night."

"Nothing will happen," he told her, making circles around and around her constellation of scars.

"But maybe something should happen," she told him, her voice small in submission to his lulling laving. But when he quit, and she stood in the tub, Angela was colossal: buckets of water fell from the troughs among her breasts and limbs and collapsed back into the tub. Her blue eyes seemed wild, her bare arms flailed with an odd uncoördination. Tears glazed her cheeks while steam fled her skin in the coolness of their eggshell bedroom. "Something *should* happen, Piet. You've abused me horribly. I've asked for it, sure, but that's my weakness and I've been indulging it."

"You're beginning to talk like your own psychiatrist."

"He says I have no self-respect and it's true. And neither do you. We were with two people tonight who have some and they rolled right through us."

"It was his inning. I've had mine."

"Oh, I can't *stand* you when your face gets that stretched look. That's the thing you don't know. How your face looked tonight. When you said you'd have to marry her, there was this incredible, I was stunned, happiness, as if every question ever had been answered for you."

"That can't be true. I don't want to marry her. I'd rather marry Bea Guerin. I'd rather marry Bernadette Ong."

"You've slept with Bernadette."

"Never. But she's bumped me and her husband's dying." He laughed. "Stop it, angel. This is grotesque. I have no desire to marry Foxy, I love you. Compared to you, she's such a bitch."

Her neck had elongated; though exactly her height, he felt he was looking up at her—her thoughtful pout so tense her nostrils were flared, the breasts over which she had defensively flung an arm. "You like bitches," she said. Another thought struck her: "Everybody we know must think I'm an absolute fool."

He calculated he must do something acrobatic. Having removed all his clothes but his Paisley shorts, Piet threw himself on his knees and wrapped his arms around her thighs. The hearthbricks were cold, her body still steamy; she protestingly pushed down on his head, blocking an amorous rise. Her vulva a roseate brown. Parchment. Egypt. Lotus. "Don't make me leave you," he begged. "You're what guards my soul. I'll be damned eternally."

"It'll do you good," she said, still pushing down on his head.

"It'll do Foxy good too. You're right, Ken is not sexually appealing. I tried to get the hots for him tonight and there was nothing, not a spark."

"God, don't joke," he said. "Think of the girls."

"They'll be fine with me."

"They'll suffer."

"You used to say they should suffer. How else can they learn to be good? Stop nibbling me."

Embarrassed, he got to his feet. Standing two feet from her, he removed his undershorts. He was tumescent. "God," he said, "I'd love to clobber you."

She dropped her arm; her breasts swung free, livid and delicate as wounds. "Of course you would," she said, confirmed.

His fist jerked; she flinched and aloofly waited.

Through the April that followed this night, Piet had many conversations, as if the town, sensing he was doomed, were hurrying to have its last say in his ear. Freddy Thorne stopped him one rainy day on Divinity Street, as Piet with hammer and level was leaving the Tarbox Professional Apartments, once Gertrude Tarbox's shuttered hermitage. "Hey," Freddy said, "what have you done to me? I just got a paranoid letter from Ken Whitman about the, you know, the little pelvic orthodonture we performed. He said he had decided not to take legal action at the present time, but, cough, cough, reserved the intention to do so. The whole thing was psychopathically formal. He cited four laws I had broken chapter and verse, with the maximum penalties all neatly typed out. He's anal as hell. Wha' hoppen, Handlebar?"

Piet, who lived now day and night behind glassy walls of fear, clinging each evening to the silence of the telephone and to Angela's stony sufferance, while his children watched wide-eyed and whimpered in their sleep, was pleased to feel that at least he had been redeemed from Freddy Thorne's spell; the old loathing and fascination were gone. Freddy's atheism, his evangelical humanism, no longer threatened Piet; the dentist materialized in the drizzle as a plump fuzzy-minded man with a squint and an old woman's sly mouth. A backwards jacket peeked white under his raincoat. If any emotion, Piet felt fondness, the fondness a woman might feel toward her priest or gynecologist or lover—someone who has accepted her worst. Piet decided not to tell him that Georgene had betrayed them to Ken; he owed the Thornes that much. He said instead, "Foxy broke under the tension and blurted it all out to him the night of town meeting."

And he described briefly the subsequent confrontation of the two couples.

"The old mousetrap play," Freddy said. "She wants you bad, boy."

"Come on, she was hysterical. She couldn't stop crying."

Freddy's lips bit inward wisely. "When that golden-haired swinger has hysterics," he said, "it's because she's punched the release button herself. You've been had, friend. Good luck."

"How worried about Whitman are you?"

"Semi-semi. He's not going to press anything, with Little Miss Vulpes pulling the strings."

"Freddy," Piet said, "you live in a fantasy world of powerful women. I haven't heard from her since. In fact, I'm worried. Could you possibly send Georgene down to see how things are?"

"I think Georgene's errand days are over," Freddy said. "She really blew up after finding you and Foxtrot together; I had a vicious creature on my hands for a few days. The less you and she see each other, the better we'll all be. Keerect?"

"Is that why we're not being invited to parties any more?"

"What parties?"

Georgene phoned him Friday afternoon, while he was leafing through Sweet's Light Construction Catalogue File, looking for flanged sheathing. Two of the houses on Indian Hill had complained about leaks last winter, and Piet wanted to improve the new houses, whose foundations were already being bulldozed. Gallagher sat listening in his cubbyhole, but Piet let Georgene talk. Her clubwoman's quick enunciation, and the weather outside hinting of tennis and sunporches again, made him sentimental and regretful. He could see larches leaning, remembered the way the inside tendons of her thighs cupped and her pupils contracted as her eyelids widened and how afterwards she would tell him he gave her her shape. "Piet," she said, in syllables from which all

roughnesses of love and innuendo had been burred, leaving a
smooth brisk sister, "I drove down to the Whitmans today,
Freddy mentioned you were worried, and there's nobody there.
It doesn't look as if anybody has been there for a while. Four
newspapers are bunched up inside the storm door."

"Does Marcia know anything?"

"She says there hasn't been a car in the drive since Tuesday."

"Did you look inside a window?" The open oven. The gobbled
sleeping pills. The hallway where a lightbulb has died above a pair
of ankles.

"Everything looked neat, as if they had tidied up before going
away. I didn't see the bassinet."

"Have you talked to Carol or Terry? Somebody must have the
answer. People just don't vanish."

"Easy, dollink, don't panic, you're not God. You can't protect
the Whitmans from what they want to do to each other."

"Thanks. Thanks for the pep talk. And thanks a bushel for
telling Whitman in the first place."

"I told him almost nothing. I admit I did, more or less maliciously, ask him why your truck was parked down there, but then
he jumped all over me with questions, he was really hungry for it.
Clearly he had half guessed. I *am* sorry, though. But, Piet—are
you listening?—it made me mad the way I came in there that
Monday all anxious to be Sue Barton and somehow I was turned
into the cleaning lady who invites herself to tea."

He sighed. "OK, forget it. Truth will out, it may be best.
You're a good woman. A loyal wife and dutiful mother."

"Piet—I wasn't right for you, was I? I thought we were so
good, but we weren't?"

"You were a gorgeous piece of ass," he told her patiently. "You
were too good. You made it seem too easy and right for my
warped nature. Please forgive me," he added, "if I ever hurt you.
I never meant to."

It was Gallagher, of all people, who had the answer. Having
overheard this conversation, he called Piet into his inner office,
and there, as the late light died in measured segments, without
turning on a lamp, so his broad-jawed pentagonal face became a
murmuring blur, told Piet of a strange scene. Early Tuesday

morning, earlier than the milk, Ken Whitman had appeared at their house. He was soaked and rumpled and sandy; he had spent the night walking the beach in the mist and had taken a cramped nap in his MG. Silent, Piet guiltily remembered how Monday night he had slept warm beside Angela, as soundly as the just, amid irrelevant dreams about flying. Ken explained himself. He had come to the Gallaghers because Matt was the one man in Tarbox he could respect, the only one "uninvolved." Also Terry, he tried to say, could understand Foxy, perhaps. What did he mean? Were they alike? They were both "proud." Here Matt hesitated, caught in private considerations, or debating with himself how much Piet should be told. But having commenced, his Irish blood demanded the tale should continue fully. Piet pictured that early-morning kitchen, the postcard print of Dürer's praying hands framed above the stainless-steel sink, Terry's rough bright tablecloth and the bowls she had clumsily turned, three drowsy mouths sipping coffee, and heard himself being discussed, deplored, blamed. Ken asked them what he should do. Both of course told him to go back to Foxy; he loved her, they had a son now to think of, they were a handsome couple. Everybody, Terry said, lapses—or is tempted to. Piet suspected Matt had added the qualification in his own mind. But they found Ken adamant. Not vindictive. He spoke of the people concerned as of chemical elements, without passion. He had thought it through by the side of the ocean and could make no deduction but divorce. Terry began to cry. Ken ignored her. What he was curious to know from *them* was whether or not they thought Piet would divorce Angela to marry Foxy. If they thought yes, then the sooner the better. If they thought Piet would be "bastard enough"—Matt tactfully paused before releasing the expressions —to "let her stew," then maybe they at least should wait, merely separate. He was going to go back to Cambridge, she should stay in the house. Would they keep an eye on her? Of course they would. Terry then gave him a long lecture. She said that he and Foxy had been different from the rest of them because they had no children, and that because of this they were freer. That, despite what the Church said, she did not think a marriage sacred and irrevocable until the couple produced a third soul, a child. That until then marriage was of no different order than kissing your first boy; it was an experiment. But when a child was created, it ceased to be an experiment, it became a fact; like papal infallibility or the chromatic scale. You must have such facts to build a world on, even if they appeared arbitrary. Now Ken might still feel free, he seemed very slow to realize that he had a son—

Piet asked, "She told him that?"

"Yes. She's never liked Whitman much."

"How nice of Terry."

Terry had gone on, Ken might imagine he was free to make decisions, but Piet certainly wasn't. He loved his children, he needed Angela, and it would be very wrong of Ken to try to force him, out of some absurd sense of honor that hasn't applied to anybody for centuries, to give up everything and marry Foxy. Piet just wasn't free.

"And how did Ken take all this?"

"Not badly. He nodded and thanked us and left. Later in the morning Terry went over to see Foxy, since Ken has somehow chosen us, and she was packing. She was perfectly calm, not a hair out of place. She was going to take the baby and go to her mother in Washington, and I assume that's where she is."

"Thank God. I mean, what a relief she's all right. And that she's out of town."

"You honestly haven't heard from her?"

"Not a whisper."

"And you haven't tried to reach her?"

"Should I have? No matter what I said, that would only have meant to her that I was still in the game and confused things. What's your advice?"

Matt spoke carefully, picking his words in such a way that Piet saw he was no friend; one did not have to speak so carefully to friends. Matt had grown to dislike him, and why not?—he had grown to dislike Matt, since he had first seen him, in a pressed private's uniform, his black button eyes as shiny as his shoes: an eager beaver. "Terry and I of course have discussed this since, and there is one thing, Piet, we agree you should do. Call his bluff. Let them know, the Whitmans, either by phone to Ken or by letter to Foxy, you surely can find her mother's address, that you will *not* marry her in any case. I think if they know that, they'll get back together."

"But is that necessarily good? Them coming back together to make you and Terry and the Pope comfortable? Georgene just told me I shouldn't try to play God with the Whitmans."

The other man's skull, half-lit, lifted in the gloom, one tightly folded ear and the knot of muscle at the point of the jaw and the concavity of his temple all bluish-white, for beyond the office window the carbon-arc streetlight on Hope Street had come on. Piet knew what had happened and what would: Matt had mis-judged the coercive power of his moral superiority and would retreat, threatened by Piet's imperfect docility, into his own impregnable rightness. Matt slammed shut a steel desk drawer. "I don't like involving myself with your affairs. I've given my advice. Take it if you want this mess to have a decent outcome. I don't pretend to know what you're really after."

Piet tried to make peace; the man was his partner and had transmitted precious information. "Matt, frankly, I don't think I'm calling any of the shots any more. All I can do is let things happen, and pray."

"That's all you ever do." Matt spoke without hesitation, as a reflex; it was one of those glimpses, as bizarre as the sight in a three-way clothing-store mirror of your own profile, into how you appear to other people. *The Red-haired Avenger.*

At home Angela had received a phone call. She told him about it during their after-supper coffee while the girls were watching *Gunsmoke.* "I got a long-distance call today, from Washington," she said, beginning.

"Foxy?"

"Yes, how did you know?" She answered herself, "She's been calling you, though she told me she hadn't."

"She hasn't. Gallagher told me today where they both were. Ken apparently went over there Tuesday and told his sad story."

"I thought you knew that. Terry told me days ago."

"Why didn't you say so? I've been worried sick."

"We haven't been speaking." This was true.

"What did the lovely Elizabeth have to say for herself?"

Angela's cool face, slightly thinner these days, tensed, and he knew he had taken the wrong tone. She was becoming a disciplinarian. She said, "She was very self-possessed. She said that she was with her mother and had been thinking, and the more she thought"—Angela crossed her hands on the tabletop to control their trembling—"the more she felt that she and Ken should get a divorce now, while the child was still an infant. That she did not want to bring Toby up in the kind of suppressed unhappiness she had known as a child."

"Heaven help us," Piet said. Softly, amid motionless artifacts, he was sinking.

Angela lifted a finger from the oiled surface of the cherrywood dining table. "No. Wait. She said she called not to tell me that, but to tell me, and for *me* to tell *you*, that she absolutely didn't expect you to leave me. That she"—the finger returned, weakening the next word—"loves you, but the divorce is all between her and Ken and isn't because of you really and puts you under no obligation. She said that at least twice."

"And what did you say?"

"What could I? 'Yes, yes, no, thank you,' and hung up. I asked her if there was anything we could do about the house, lock it or check it now and then, and she said no need, Ken would be coming out weekends."

Piet put his palms on the tabletop to push himself up, sighing. "What a mercy," he said. "This has been a nightmare."

"Don't you feel guilty about their divorce?"

"A little. Not much. They were dead on each other and didn't know it. In a way I was a blessing for bringing it to a head."

"Don't wander off, Piet. I didn't have anything to say to Foxy but I do have something to say to you. Could we have some brandy?"

"Aren't you full? That was a lovely dinner, by the way. I don't know why I adore lima beans so. I love bland food."

"Let's have some brandy. Please, quick. *Gunsmoke* is nearly over. I wanted to wait until the children were in bed but I'm all keyed up and I can't. I must have brandy."

He brought it and even as he was pouring her glass she had begun. "I think Foxy's faced her situation and we should face ours. I think you should get out, Piet. Tonight. I don't want to live with you any more."

"Truly?"

"Truly."

"This does need brandy, then. Now tell me why. You know it's all over with Foxy."

"I'm not so sure, but that doesn't matter. I think you still love her, but even if you don't, they mentioned Bea, and if it's not Bea it's going to be somebody else; and I just don't think it's worth it."

"And the girls? It's not worth it for them either?"

"Stop hiding behind the girls. No, actually, I *don't* think it's worth it for them. They're sensitive, they know when we fight, or, even worse I suppose, don't fight. Poor Nancy is plainly disturbed, and I'm not so sure that Ruth, even though she inherited my placid face, is any better."

"I hear your psychiatrist talking."

"Not really. He doesn't approve or disapprove. I try to say what I think, which isn't easy for me, since my father always knew what I should think, and if it bounces back off this other man's silence—I hardly know what he looks like, I'm so scared to look at him—and if it still sounds true, I try to live with it."

"Goddammit, this is all because of that jackass Freddy Thorne."

"Let me finish. And what I think is true is, you do not love me, Piet Hanema. You do not. You do *not*."

"But I do. Obviously I do."

"Stop it, you *don't*. You didn't even get me the house I wanted. You fixed it up for her instead."

"I was paid to. I adore you."

"Yes, that says it. You adore me as a way of getting out of loving me. Oh, you like my bosom and bottom well enough, and you think it's neat the way I'm a professor's niece, and taught you which fork to use, and take you back after every little slumming expedition, and you enjoy making me feel frigid so you'll be free—"

"I adore you. I need you."

"Well then you need the wrong thing. I want out. I'm tired of being bullied."

The brandy hurt, as if his insides were tenderly budding. He asked, "Have I bullied you? I suppose in a way. But only lately. I wanted *in* to you, sweet, and you didn't give it to me."

"You didn't know how to ask."

"Maybe I know now."

"Too late. You know what I think? I think she's just your cup of tea."

"That's meaningless. That's superstition." But saying this was to ask himself what he contrariwise believed, and he believed that there was, behind the screen of couples and houses and days, a Calvinist God Who lifts us up and casts us down in utter freedom, without recourse to our prayers or consultation with our wills. Angela had become the messenger of this God. He fought against her as a raped woman might struggle, to intensify the deed. He said to her, "I'm your husband and always will be. I promise, my philandering is done, not that there was awfully much of it. You imagine there's been gossip, and you're acting out of wounded pride; pride, and the selfishness these fucking psychiatrists give everybody they handle. What does he care about the children, or about your loneliness once I'm gone? The more miserable you are, the deeper he'll get his clutches in. It's a racket, Angel, it's witchcraft, and a hundred years from now people will be amazed that we took it seriously. It'll be like leeches and bleeding."

She said, "Don't expose your ignorance to me any more. I'd like to remember you with some respect."

"I'm not leaving."

"Then I am. Tomorrow morning, Ruthie has dancing class and she was going to have lunch with Betsy Saltz. Nancy's blue dress should be washed and ironed for Martha Thorne's birthday party. Maybe you can get Georgene to come over and do it for you."

"Where could you go?"

"Oh, many places. I could go home and play chess with Daddy. I could go to New York and see the Matisse exhibit. I could fly to Aspen and ski and sleep with an instructor. There's a lot I can do,

Piet, once I get away from you." In her excitement she stood, her
ripe body swinging.

The upsurge of music in the dark living room indicated the end
of the program. Cactuses. Sunset. Right triumphant. He said, "If
you're serious, of course, I'm the one to go. But on an experimental basis. And if I'm asked politely."

Politeness was the final atmosphere. Together they settled the
girls in bed, and packed a suitcase for Piet, and shared a final
brandy in the kitchen. As he very slowly, so as not to wake the
sleeping girls, backed the pick-up truck down the crunching
driveway, Angela made a noise from the porch that he thought
was to call him back. He braked and she rushed to the side of his
cab with a little silver sloshing bottle, a pint of gin. "In case you
get insomnia," she explained, and put the bottle dewy in his palm,
and put a cool kiss on his cheek, with a faint silver edge that must
be her tears. He offered to open the door, but she held the handle
from the other side. "Darling Piet, be brave," she said, and raced,
with one step loud on the gravel, back into the house, and doused
the golden hallway light.

He spent the first weekend in the Gallagher & Hanema office,
sleeping under an old army blanket on the imitation-leather sofa,
lulling his terror with gin-and-water, the water drawn from the
dripping tap in their booth-sized lavatory. The drip, the tick of
his wristwatch left lying on the resounding wood desk, the sullen
plodding of his heart, the sash-rattling vibration of trucks changing gears as they passed at all hours through downtown Tarbox,
and a relentless immanence within the telephone all kept him
awake. Sunday he huddled in his underwear as the footsteps of
churchgoers shuffled on the sidewalk beside his ear. His skull
lined like a thermos bottle with the fragile glass of a hangover, he
felt himself sardonically eavesdropping from within his tomb.
The commonplace greetings he overheard boomed with a sinister
magnificence, intimate and proud as naked bodies. On Monday
morning, though Piet had tidied up, Gallagher was shocked to
find his office smelling of habitation. That week, as it became
clear that Angela was not going to call him back, he moved to the
third floor of the professional apartment building he himself had

refashioned from the mansion of the last Tarbox. The third floor had been left much as it was, part attic, part servants' quarters. The floorboards of his room, unsanded, bore leak stains shaped like wet leaves and patches of old linoleum and pale squares where linoleum had been; the oatmeal-colored walls, deformed by the slant of the mansard roof outside, were still hung with careful pastels of wildflowers Gertrude Tarbox had done, as a young single lady of "accomplishments," before the First World War. When it rained, one wall, where the paper had long since curled away, became wet, and in the mornings the heat was slow to come on, via a single radiator ornate as lace and thick as armor. To reach his room Piet had to pass through the plum-carpeted foyer, between the frosted-glass doors of the insurance agency and the chiropractor, up the wide stairs with an aluminum strip edging each tread, around past the doors of an oculist and a lawyer new in town, and then up the secret stair, entered by an unmarked door a slide bolt could lock, to his cave. A man who worked nights, with a stutter so terrible he could hardly manage "Good morning" when he and Piet met on the stairs, lived across the stair landing from Piet; besides these two rooms there was a large empty attic Gallagher still hoped to transform and rent as a ballroom to the dancing school that now rented the Episcopal parish hall, where Ruth took her Saturday morning lessons.

Though work on Indian Hill had begun again, with hopes for six twenty-thousand-dollar houses by Labor Day, Jazinski could manage most problems by himself now. "Everything's under control," Piet was repeatedly told, and more than once he called the lumberyard or the foundation contractors to find that Gallagher or Leon had already spoken with them. So Piet was often downtown with not much to do. On Good Friday, with the stock market closed, Harold little-Smith stopped him on Charity Street, in front of the barber shop.

"Piet, this is a terrible. *C'est terrible.* What did the Whitmans pull on you?"

"The Whitmans? Nothing much. It was Angela's idea I move out."

"*La belle ange?* I can't buy that. You've always been the

perfect couple. The Whitmans now, the first time I met them I could see they were in trouble. Stiff as boards, both of them. But it makes me and Marcia damn mad they've screwed you up too. Why can't *tout le monde* mind their own business?"

"Well, it's not as if I had been totally—"

"Oh, I know, I know, but that's never really the issue, is it? People use it when they need to, because of our moronic Puritan laws."

"Who used who, do you think, in my case?"

"Why, *clairement*, Foxy used you. How else could she get rid of that zombie? Don't be used, Piet. Go back to your kids and forget that bitch."

"Don't call her a bitch. You don't know the story at all."

"Listen, Piet, I wouldn't be telling you this just on my own account, out of my own reliably untrustworthy neo-fascist opinion. But Marcia and I stayed up till past three last night with the Applebys talking this over and we all agreed: we don't like seeing a couple we love hurt. If I weren't so hung, I'd probably put it more tactfully. *Pas d'offense*, of course."

"Janet agreed too, that Foxy was a bitch and I'd been had?"

"She was the devil's advocate for a while, but we wore her out. Anyway, it doesn't mean a fart in Paradise what we think. The thing is, what are you going to do? Come on, I'm your friend. *Ton frère.* What are you going to do?"

"I'm not doing anything. Angela hasn't called and doesn't seem to need me back."

"You're waiting for her to call? Don't wait, go to her. Women have to be taken, you know that. I thought you were a great lover."

"Who told you? Marcia?" Harold's twin-tipped nose lifted as he scented a remote possibility. Piet laughed, and went on, "Or maybe Janet? A splendid woman. Why I remember when she was a prostitute in St. Louis, the line went clear down the hall into the billiard room. Have you ever noticed, at the moment of truth, how her whole insides kind of *pull?* One time I remember—"

Harold cut in. "Well I'm glad to see your spirits haven't been crushed. Nothing sacred, eh Piet?"

"Nothing sacred. *Pas d'offense.*"

"Marcia and I wanted to have you over for a drink sometime, and be serious for a change. She's all in a flap about it. She went over to your house, and Angela was perfectly polite, not a hair out of place, but she wouldn't unbend."

"Is that what Marcia likes, to bend people?"

"Listen, I feel I've expressed myself badly. We care, is the point. Piet, we *care*."

"*Je comprends. Merci. Bonjour.*"

"OK, let's leave it at that," Harold said, miffed, sniffing. "I have to get a haircut." His hair looked perfectly well-trimmed to Piet.

The invitation to a drink at the little-Smith's never came. Few of the friends he and Angela had shared sought him out. The Saltzes, probably at Angela's urging, had him to dinner by himself, but their furniture was being readied for moving, and the evening depressed Piet. Now that they were leaving, the Saltzes could not stop talking about themselves as Jews, as if during their years in Tarbox they had suppressed their race, and now it could out. Irene's battle with the school authorities over Christmas pageantry was lengthily recounted, her eyebrows palpitating. The fact of local anti-Semitism, even in their tiny enlightened circle of couples, was urgently confided to Piet. The worst offenders were the Constantines. Carol had been raised, you know, in a *very* Presbyterian small-town atmosphere, and Eddie was, of course, an ignorant man. Night after night they had sat over there arguing the most absurd things, like the preponderance of Jewish Communists, and psychoanalysts, and violinists, as if it all were part of a single conspiracy. Terrible to admit, after a couple of drinks they would sit around trading Jewish jokes; and of course the Saltzes knew many more than Eddie and Carol, which was interpreted as their being ashamed of their race, which she, Irene, certainly, certainly was *not*. Piet tried to tell them how he felt, especially in the society of Tarbox, as a sort of Jew at heart; but Irene, as if he had furtively petitioned for membership in the chosen race, shushed him with a torrent of analysis as to why Frank Appleby, that arch-Wasp, always argued with her, yet couldn't resist arguing with her, and sought her out at parties. In fairness, there were two people among their "friends" with whom she had never felt a trace of condescension or fear; and one was

Angela. The other was Freddy Thorne. "That miserable bastard," Piet groaned, out of habit, to please; people expected him to hate Freddy. The Saltzes understood his exclamation as a sign that, as all the couples suspected, Freddy and Angela had for ages been lovers.

Piet left early; he missed the silence of his shabby room, the undemandingness of the four walls. Ben put his hand on his shoulder and smiled his slow archaic smile. "You're down now," he told Piet, "and it's a pity you're not a Jew, because the fact is, every Jew expects to be down sometime in his life, and he has a philosophy for it. God is testing him. *Nisayon Elohim.*"

"But I clearly brought this on myself," Piet said.

"Who's to say? If you believe in omnipotence, it doesn't matter. What does matter is to taste your own ashes. Chew 'em. Up or down doesn't matter; *ain ben David ba elle bador shekulo zakkai oh kulo chayyav.* The son of David will not come except to a generation that's wholly good or all bad."

Piet tried to tell them how much he had liked them, how Angela had once said, and he had agreed, that the Saltzes of all the couples they knew were the most free from, well, crap.

Ben kept grinning and persisted with his advice. "Let go, Piet. You'll be OK. It was a helluva lot of fun knowing you."

Irene darted forward and kissed him good-bye, a quick singeing kiss from lips dark red in her pale face, rekindling his desire for women.

Later in the week, after cruising past her house several times a day, he called Bea. He had seen her once downtown, and she had waved from across the street, and disappeared into the jeweler's shop, still decorated with a nodding rabbit, though Easter was over. Her voice on the phone sounded startled, guilty.

"Oh, Piet, how are you? When are you going back to Angela?"

"Am I going back? She seems more herself without me."

"Oh, but at night it must be terrible for her."

"And how is it for you at night?"

"Oh, the same. Nobody goes out to parties any more. All people talk about is their children."

"Would you—would you like to see me? Just for tea, some afternoon?"

"Oh, sweet, I think not. Honestly. I think you have enough women to worry about."

"I don't have any women."

"It's good for you, isn't it?"

"It's not as bad as I would have thought. But what about us? I was in love with you, you know, before the roof fell in."

"You were lovely, so alive. But I think you idealized me. I'm much too lazy in bed for you. Anyway, sweet, all of a sudden, its rather touching, Roger needs me."

"How do you mean?"

"You won't tell anybody? Everybody's sure you're keeping a nest of girls down there."

"Everybody's wrong. I only liked married women. They reminded me of my mother."

"Don't be uppity. I'm trying to tell you about Roger. He lost a lot of money, one of his awful fairy investment friends in Boston, and he really came crying to me, I loved it."

"So because he's bankrupt I can't go to bed with you."

"Not bankrupt, you *do* idealize everything. But scared, so scared—oh, I must tell somebody, I'm bursting with it!—he's agreed to adopt a child. We've already been to the agency once, and answered a lot of insulting questions about our private life. The odd thing is, white babies are scarce, they have so many more Negroes."

"This is what you've wanted? To adopt a child?"

"Oh, for years. Ever since I knew I couldn't. It wasn't Roger, you know, it was me that couldn't. People poked fun of Roger but it was *me*. Oh, Piet, forgive me, I'm burdening you with this."

"No, it's no burden." Floating, he remembered how she floated, above the sound of children snowballing, as evening fell early, through levels of lavender.

She was sobbing, barely audibly, her voice limp and moist, as her body had been. "It's so rotten, though, that you need me and I must say no when before it was I who needed you, and you came finally."

"Finally. Bea, it's great about the adoption, and Roger's going to the poorhouse."

A laugh skidded through her tears. "I just can't," she said, "when I've been given what I've prayed for. The funny thing is, you helped. Roger was very frightened by you and Angela breaking up. He's become very serious."

"He was always serious."

"Sweet Piet, tell me, I was never very real to you, was I? Isn't it all right, not to? I've been dreading your call so, I thought it would come sooner."

"It should have come sooner," he said, then hastened to add to reassure her with, "No, you were never very real," and added finally, "Kiss."

"Kiss," Bea faintly said. "Kiss kiss kiss kiss kiss."

Sunday, bringing his daughters back from a trip to the Science Museum in Boston, Piet was saddened by the empty basketball court. This was the time of year when the young married men of Tarbox used to scrimmage. Whitman was gone, Saltz had moved, Constantine was flying jets to Lima and Rio, Thorne and little-Smith had always considered the game plebeian. Weeds were threading through a crack in the asphalt and the hoop, netless and aslant, needed to be secured with longer screws. Angela greeted them outdoors; she had been picking up winter-fallen twigs from the lawn, and sprinkling grass seed in the bare spots. Seeing the direction of his eyes, she said, "You should take that hoop down. Or would you like to invite your gentlemen friends to come play? I could tolerate it."

"I have no gentlemen friends, it turns out. They were all your friends. Anyway, it would be artificial and not comfortable, don't you think?"

"I suppose."

"Mightn't Ruth ever want to use the hoop?"

"She's interested right now in being feminine. Maybe later, when they have teams at school; but in the meantime it looks hideous."

"You're too exquisite," he said.

"How was your expedition? Artificial and not comfortable?"

"No, it was fun. Nancy cried in the planetarium, when the machine made the stars whirl around, but for some reason she loved the Transparent Woman."

"It reminded her of me." Angela said.

Piet wondered if this bit of self-disclaiming wit was the prelude to readmitting him into their home. Sneakingly he hoped not. He felt the worst nights of solitude were behind him. In loneliness he was regaining something, an elemental sense of surprise at everything, that he had lost with childhood. Even his visits to Angela in their awkwardness had a freshness that was pleasant. She seemed, with her soft fumbling gestures and unaccountable intervals of distant repose, a timid solid creature formed from his loins and now learning to thrive alone. He asked her, "How have you been?"

"Busy enough. I've had to reacquaint myself with my parents. My mother says that for ten years I snubbed them. I hadn't thought so, but maybe she's right."

"And the girls? They miss me less?"

"A little less. It's worst when something breaks and I can't fix it. Ruth was very cross with me the other day and told me I was stupid to lose their Daddy for them by being so pushy in bed. I guess Jonathan or Frankie at school had told her I was bad in bed, and she thought it must mean I didn't give you enough room. Oh, we had a jolly discussion after that. Woman to woman."

"The poor saint. Two poor saints."

"You look better."

"I'm adjusting. Everybody lets me alone, which in a way is a mercy, since I don't have to play politics. The only people I talk to all day some days are Adams and Comeau; we're doing some cabinets for a new couple toward Lacetown."

"I thought you were on Indian Hill."

"Jazinski and Gallagher seem to be managing that. They're working straight from canned plans that don't fit the slope at all."

"Oh. They had me over, with some North Mather people I hated. Money sort of people. Horsey."

"Matt's on the move."

"Terry seemed very bored."

"She'll be bored from here on in. And you? Bored? Happy? Fighting off propositions from our gentlemen friends?"

"A few feelers." Angela admitted. "But nothing serious. It's a different kettle of fish, a separated woman. It's scarier for them."

"You do think of us as separated?"

Rather than answer him, she looked over his shoulder, toward the corner of woods where scilla was blooming and where he had buried Ruth's hamster and where the girls, in a burst of relief at being released from the confinement of their father's embarrassingly rattly and unwashed pick-up truck, had, still in their Sunday expedition clothes, sought their climbing tree, a low-branching apple stunted among maples. Angela's face was recalled to animation by remembered good news. "Oh Piet, I must tell you. The strangest nicest thing. I've begun to have dreams. Dreams I can remember. It hasn't happened to me for years."

"What kind of dreams?"

"Oh, nothing very exciting yet. I'm in an elevator, and press the button, and nothing happens. So I think, not at all worried, 'I must be on the right floor already.' Or, maybe it's part of the same dream, I'm in a department store, trying to buy Nancy a fur hood, so she can go skiing in it. I know exactly the size, and the kind of lining, and go from counter to counter, and they offer me mittens, earmuffs, galoshes, everything I don't want, but I remain very serene and polite, because I know they have them somewhere, because I bought one for Ruth there."

"What sweet dreams."

"Yes, they're very shy and ordinary. *He* doesn't agree, or disagree, but my idea is my subconscious tried to die, and now it's daring to come back and express things I want. Not for myself yet, but for others."

"He. You're having dreams for *him*. Like a child going wee-wee for her daddy."

She retreated, as he desired, into the enchanted stillness that, in this square yard, this tidy manless house, he liked to visit. "You're such a bully," she told him. "Such a jealous bully. You always dreamed so easily, lying beside you inhibited me, I'm sure."

"Couldn't we have shared them?"

"No, you do it alone. I'm discovering you do everything alone. You know when I used to feel most alone? When we were making love." The quality of the silence that followed demanded she soften this. She asked, "Have you heard from Foxy?"

"Nothing. Not even a postcard of the Washington Monument." His lawn, he saw, beside the well and barn, had been killed in patches where the ice had lingered. Hard winter. The polar cap growing again. The hairy mammoths will be back. "It's kind of a relief," he told Angela.

The girls returned from the woods, their spring coats smirched with bark. "Go now," Nancy said to Piet.

Ruth slapped at her sister. "Nancy! That is *not* very nice."

"I think she's trying to help," Angela explained. "She's telling Daddy it's all right to go now."

"Mommy," Nancy told her, her plump hand whirling with her dizzy upgazing, "the stars went round and round and round."

"And the *baby cried*," Ruth said.

Nancy studied, as if seeking her coördinates, and then sprang at her sister, pummeling Ruth's chest. "Liar! Liar!"

Ruth bit her lower lip and expertly knocked Nancy loose with a sideways swerve of her fist. "*Baby cried*," she repeated, "*Hurting Dad*dy's *fee*lings, making him *take* us out *ear*ly."

Nancy sobbed against her mother's legs. Her face where Piet would never be again. Convolute cranny, hair and air, ambrosial chalice where seed can cling. "I'm sure it was very exciting," Angela said. "And that's why everybody is tired and cranky. Let's go in and have supper." She looked up, her eyes strained by the effort of refusing to do what was easy and instinctive and ask Piet in too.

Bernadette Ong bumped into Piet on the street, by the door of the book store, which sold mostly magazines. He was entering to buy *Life* and she was leaving with a copy of *Scientific American*. Her body brushing his felt flat, hard, yet deprived of its force; she was sallow, and the Oriental fold of upper-lid skin had sagged so that no lashes showed. She and Piet stood beneath the book-store awning; the April day around them was a refraction of apical summer, the first hot day, beach weather at last, when the high-school students shove down the crusty stiff tops of their convertibles and roar to the dunes in caravans. Above downtown Tarbox the Greek temple on its hill of red rocks was limestone white and the gold rooster blazed in an oven of blueness. Bernadette had thrown off her coat. The fine chain of a crucifix glinted in the neck of a dirty silk blouse. Descending into death, she had grown dingy, like a miner.

He asked her, immediately, guiltily, how John was, and she said, "About as well as we can expect, I guess." From her tone, her expectations had sunk low. "They keep him under drugs and he doesn't talk much English. He used to ask me why nobody visited him but that's stopped now."

"I'm so sorry, I thought of visiting him, but I've had my own troubles. I suppose you've heard Angela and I are separated."

"No, I hadn't heard. That's *terrible*." She pronounced it "tarrible"; all vowels tended in her flat wide mouth toward "a." *Whan do I gat my duty dance?* "You're the last couple I would have thought. John, as you've probably guessed, was always half in love with Angela."

Piet had never guessed any such thing. Impulsively he offered, "Why don't I visit him now? I have the time, and aren't you on your way back to the hospital?"

The Tarbox Veterans' Memorial hospital was two miles from the center of town, on the inland side. Built of swarthy clinker bricks, with a rosy new maternity wing that did not quite harmonize, it sat on a knoll between disused railroad tracks and an outlay of greenhouses (Hendrick Vos & Sons—Flowers, Bulbs, and Shrubs). Behind the hospital was a fine formal garden where no one, neither patients nor nurses, ever walked. The French windows of John Ong's room opened to a view of trimmed privet and a pink crabapple and a green-rusted copper birdbath shaped like a scallop shell, empty of water. Wind loosened petals from the crabapple, and billowed the white drapes at the window, and made the coarse transparent sides of the oxygen tent beside the bed abruptly buckle and snap. John was emaciated and, but for the hectic flushed spots, no larger than half dollars, on each cheekbone, colorless. So thin, he looked taller than Piet had remembered him. He spoke with difficulty, as if from a diminished pocket of air high in his chest, near the base of his throat. Only unaltered was the quick smile with which he masked imperfect comprehension. "Harya Pee? Wam weller mame waller pray terrace, heh?" Bernadette plangently translated: "He says how are you Piet? He says warm weather makes him want to play tennis."

"Soon you'll be out there," Piet said, and tossed up and served an imaginary ball.

"Is emerybonny?"

"He asks how is everybody?"

"Fine. Not bad. It's been a long winter."

"Hanjerer? Kiddies? Feddy's powwow?"

"Angela wants to come see you," Piet said, too loud, calling as if to a receding car. "Freddy Thorne's powwow has been pretty quiet lately. No big parties. Our children are getting too big."

It was the wrong thing to say; there was nothing to say. As the visit grew stilted, John Ong's eyes dulled. His hands, insectlike, their bones on the outside, fiddled on the magazine Bernadette had brought him. Once, he coughed, on and on, an interminable uprooting of a growth with roots too deep. Piet turned his head away, and a robin had come to the lip of the dry birdbath. It became clear that John was drugged; his welcome had been a strenuous leap out of hazed tranquillity. For a moment intelligence would be present in his wasted face like an eager carnivorous power; then he would subside into an inner murmuring, and twice spoke in Korean. He looked toward Bernadette for translation but she shrugged and winked toward Piet. "I only know a few phrases. Sometimes he thinks I'm his sister." Piet rose to leave, but she sharply begged, "Don't go." So he sat fifteen more minutes while Bernadette kept clicking something in her lap and John, forgetting his guest, leafed backwards through *Scientific American*, impatiently skimming, seeking something not there. Rubber-heeled nurses paced the hall. Doctors could be heard loudly flirting. Portentous baskets and pots of flowers crowded the floor by the radiator, and Piet wondered from whom. McNamara. Rusk. The afternoon's first cloud darkened the crabapple, and as if held pinned by the touch of light a scatter of petals exploded toward the ground. The room began to lose warmth. When Piet stood the second time to break away, and took the other man's strengthless fingers into his, and said too loudly, too jokingly, "See you on the tennis court," the drug-dilated eyes,

eyes that had verified the chaos of particles on the floor of matter, lifted, and dragged Piet down into omniscience; he saw, plunging, how plausible it was to die, how death, far from invading earth like a meteor, occurs on the same plane as birth and marriage and the arrival of the daily mail.

Bernadette walked him down the waxed hall to the hospital entrance. Outdoors, a breeze dragged a piece of her hair across her eye and a sun-shaped spot on the greenhouses below them glared. Her cross glinted. He felt a sexual stir emanate from her flat-breasted body, her wide shoulders and hips; she had been too long torn from support. She moved inches closer, as if to ask a question, and the nail-bitten fingers rising to tuck back the iridescent black strand whose windblown touch had made her blink seemed to gesture in weak apology for her willingness to live. Her smile was a grimace. Piet told her, "There *are* miracles."

"He rejects them," she said, as simply as if his assertion, so surprising to himself, had merely confirmed for her the existence of the pills she administered daily. A rosary had been clicking.

The adventure of visiting the dying man served to show Piet how much time he had, how free he was to use it. He took long walks on the beach. In this prismatic April the great Bay was never twice the same. Some days, at high tide, under a white sun, muscular waves bluer than tungsten steel pounded the sand into spongy cliffs and hauled driftwood and wrack deep into the dunes where tide-change left skyey isolated pools. Low tide exposed smooth acres that mirrored the mauves and salmons and the momentary green of sunset. At times the sea was steeply purple, stained; at others, under a close warm rain sky, the no-color of dirty wash; choppy rows hurried in from the horizon to be delivered and disposed of in the lick and slide at the shore. Piet stooped to pick up angel wings, razor-clam shells, sand dollars with their infallibly etched star and the considerate airhole for an inhabiting creature Piet could not picture. Wood flecks smoothed like creek pebbles, iron spikes mummified in the orange froth of oxidation, powerfully sunk horsehoe prints, the four-tined traces of racing dog paws, the shallow impress of human couples that had vanished (the female foot bare, with toes and a tender isthmus linking heel and forepad; the male mechanically shod in the waffle intaglio of sneaker soles and apparently dragging a stick), the wandering mollusk trails dim as the contours of a photograph overdeveloped in the pan of the tide, the perfect circle a blade of beach grass complacently draws around itself—nothing was too ordinary for Piet to notice. The beach felt dreamlike, always renewed in its strangeness. One day, late in an overcast afternoon, with lateral flecks of silver high in the west above the nimbus scud, he emerged from his truck in the empty parking lot and heard a steady musical roaring. Yet approaching the sea he saw it calm as a lake, a sullen muddy green. The tide was very low, and walking on the unscarred ribs of its recent retreat Piet percieved—diagnosed, as if the sustained roaring were a symptom within him—that violent waves were breaking on the sand bar a half mile away and, though little of their motion survived, their blended sound traveled to him upon the tranced water as if upon the taut skin of a drum. This effect, contrived with energies that could power cities, was his alone to witness; the great syllable around him seemed his own note, sustained since his birth, elicited from him now, and given to the air. The air that day was warm, and smelled of ashes.

In his loneliness he detected companionship in the motion of waves, especially those distant waves lifting arms of spray along the bar, hailing him. The world was more Platonic than he had suspected. He found he missed friends less than friendship; what he felt, remembering Foxy, was a nostalgia for adultery itself— its adventure, the acrobatics its deceptions demand, the tension of its hidden strings, the new landscapes it makes us master.

Sometimes, returning to the parking lot by way of the dunes, he saw the Whitmans' house above its grassy slope, with its clay scars of excavation and its pale patches of reshingling. The house did not see him. Windows he had often gazed from, euphoric and apprehensive, glinted blank. Once, driving past it, the old Robinson house, he thought that it was fortunate he and Angela had not bought it, for it had proved to be an unlucky house; then realized that they had shared in its bad luck anyway. In his solitude he was growing absent-minded. He noticed a new woman downtown— that elastic proud gait announcing education, a spirit freed from the peasant shuffle, arms swinging, a sassy ass, trim ankles. Piet hurried along the other side of Charity Street to get a glimpse of her front and found, just before she turned into the savings bank, that the woman was Angela. She was wearing her hair down and a new blue cape that her parents had given her, as consolation.

How strange she had been to be jealous of his dreams, to accuse him of dreaming too easily! Perhaps because each night he dosed himself with much gin, his dreams now were rarely memorable —clouded repetitive images of confusion and ill-fittingness, of building something that would not stay joined or erect. He was a little boy, in fact his own father, walking beside his father, in fact his own gandfather, a faceless man he had never met, one of hundreds of joiners who had migrated from Holland to work in the Grand Rapids furniture factories. His thumbs were hugely callused; the boy felt frightened, holding on. Or he was attending John Ong's funeral, and suddenly the casket opened and John scuttled off, behind the altar, dusty as an insect, and cringing in shame. Such dreams Piet washed away along with the sour-hay taste in his mouth when, before dawn, he would awake, urinate, drink a glass of water, and vow to drink less gin tomorrow. Two dreams were more vivid. In one, he and a son, a child who was both Nancy and Ruth yet male, were walking in a snowstorm up from the baseball diamond near his first home. There was between the playground and his father's lower greenhouses a thin grove of trees, horsechestnut and cherry, where the children would gather and climb in the late afternoon and from which, one Halloween, a stoning raid was launched upon the greenhouses that ended with an accounting in police court and fistfights for Piet all November. In the dream it was winter. A bitter wind blew through the spaced trunks and the path beneath the snow was ice, so that Piet had to take the arm of his child and hold him from slipping. Piet himself walked in the deeper snow beside the tightrope of ice; for if both fell at once it would be death. They reached the alley, crossed it, and there, at the foot of their yard beside the dark greenhouses, Piet's grandmother was waiting for them, standing stooped and apprehensive in a cube of snowlessness. Invisible walls enclosed her. She wore only a cotton dress and her threadbare black sweater, unbuttoned. In the dream Piet wondered how long she had been waiting, and gave thanks to the

Lord that they were safe, and anticipated joining her in that strange transparent arbor where he clearly saw green grass, blade by blade. Awake, he wondered that he had dreamed of his grandmother at all, for she had died when he was nine, of pneumonia, and he had felt no sorrow. She had known little English and, a compulsive housecleaner, had sought to bar Piet and Joop not only from the front parlor but from all the downstairs rooms save the kitchen.

The second dream was static. He was standing beneath the stars trying to change their pattern by an effort of his will. Piet pressed himself upward as a clenched plea for the mingled constellations, the metallic mask of night, to alter position; they remained blazing and inflexible. He thought, *I might strain my heart,* and was awakened by a sharp pain in his chest.

Foxy was back in town. The rumor flew from Marcia little-Smith, who had seen her driving Ken's MG on the Nun's Bay Road, to Harold to Frank to Janet to Bea and Terry in the A & P and from there to Carol and the Thornes, to join with the tributary glimpse Freddy had had of her from his office window as she emerged that afternoon from Cogswell's Drug Store. The rumor branched out and began to meet itself in the phrase, "I know"; Terry, acting within, as she guessed at her duties, the office of confidante that Ken had thrust on the Gallaghers that dawn a month ago, phoned and gingerly told Angela, who took the news politely, as if it could hardly concern her. Perhaps it didn't. The Hanemas had become opaque to the other couples, had betrayed the conspiracy of mutual comprehension. Only Piet, as the delta of gossip interlaced, remained dry; no one told him. But there was no need. He already knew. On Tuesday, in care of Gallagher & Hanema, he had received this letter from Washington:

Dear Piet—

   I must come back to New England for a few days and will be in Tarbox April 24th, appropriating furniture. Would you like to meet and talk? Don't be nervous—I have no claims to press.

Love,

F.

After "press" the word "but" had been scratched out. They
met first by accident, in the town parking lot, an irregular asphalt
wilderness of pebbles and parked metal ringed by back entrances
to the stores on Charity Street—the A & P, Poirier's Liquor Mart,
Beth's Books and Cards, the Methodist Thrift Shop, even, via an
alleyway sparkling with broken glass, the Tarbox Professional
Apartments. He discovered himself unprepared for the sight of
her—from a distance, the candence of her, the dip of her tall
body bending to put a shopping bag into her lowslung black car,
the blond dab of her hair bundled, the sense of the tone of muscle
across her abdomen, the vertiginous certainty that it was indeed
among the world's billions none other than she. His side hurt; his
left palm tingled. He called; she held still in answer, and appeared,
closer approached, younger than he had remembered, smoother,
more finely made—the silken skin translucent to her blood, the
straight-boned nose faintly paler at the bridge, the brown irises
warmed by gold and set tilted in the dainty shelving of her lids,
quick lenses subtler than clouds, minutely shuttling as she spoke.
Her voice dimensional with familiar shadows, the unnumbered
curves of her parted, breathing, talking, thinking lips: she was
alive. Having lived with frozen fading bits of her, he was not
prepared for her to be so alive, so continuous and witty.

"Piet, you look touchingly awful."

"Unlike you."

"Why don't you comb your hair any more?"

"You even have a little tan."

"My stepfather has a swimming pool. It's summer there."

"It's been off and on here. The same old tease. I've been
walking on the beach a lot."

"Why aren't you living with Angela?"

"Who says I'm not?"

"She says. She told me over the phone. Before I wrote you I
called your house; I was going to say my farewells to you
both."

"She never told me you called."

"She probably didn't think it was very important."

"A mysterious woman, my wife."

"She said I was to come and get you."

He laughed. "If she said that, why did you ask why wasn't I living with her?"

"Why aren't you?"

"She doesn't want me to."

"That's only," Foxy said, "half a reason."

With this observation their talk changed key; they became easier, more trivial, as if a decision had been put behind them. Piet asked her, "Where are you taking the groceries?"

"They're for me. I'm living in the house this weekend. Ken's promised to stay in Cambridge."

"You and Ken aren't going to be reconciled?"

"He's happy. He says he works evenings now and thinks he's on to something significant. He's back on starfish."

"And you?"

She shrugged, a pale-haired schoolgirl looking for the answer broad enough to cover her ignorance. "I'm managing."

"Won't it depress you living there alone? Or do you have the kid?"

"I left Toby with Mother. They get along beautifully, they both think I'm untrustworthy, and adore cottage cheese."

He asked her simply, "What shall we do?" adding in explanation, "A pair of orphans."

He carried her bag of groceries up to his room, and they lived the weekend there. Saturday he helped her go through the empty house by the marsh, tagging the tables and chairs she wanted for herself. No one prevented them. The old town catered to their innocence. Foxy confessed to Piet that, foreseeing sleeping with him, she had brought her diaphragm and gone to Cogswell's Drug Store for a new tube of vaginal jelly. As he felt himself under the balm of love grow boyish and wanton, she aged; his first impression of her smoothness and translucence was replaced by the goosebumped roughness of her buttocks, the gray unpleasantness of her shaved armpits, the backs of her knees, the thickness of her waist since she had had the baby. Her flat feet gave her walking movements, on the bare floor of Piet's dirty oatmeal-walled room, a slouched awkwardness quite unlike the casually springy step with which Angela, her little toes not touching the floor, moved through the rectangular farmhouse with eggshell trim. Asleep, she snuffled, and restlessly crowded him toward the edge of the bed, and sometimes struggled against nightmares. The first morning she woke him with her hands on his penis, delicately tugging the foreskin, her face pinched and blanched by desire. She cried out that her being here with him was wrong, wrong, and fought his entrance of her; and then afterwards slyly asked if it had made it more exciting for him, her pretending to resist. She asked him abrupt questions, such as, Did he still consider himself a Christian? He said he didn't know, he doubted it. Foxy said of herself that she did, though a Christian living in a state of sin; and defiantly, rather arrogantly and—his impression was—prissily, tossed and stroked back her hair, tangled damp from the pillow. She complained that she was hungry. Did he intend just to keep her here screwing until she starved? Her stomach growled.

They ate in the Musquenomenee Luncheonette, sitting in a booth away from the window, through which they spied on Frank Appleby and little Frankie lugging bags of lime and peat moss from the hardware store into the Applebys' old maroon Mercury coupe. They saw but were not seen, as if safe behind a one-way mirror. They discussed Angela and Ken and the abortion, never pausing on one topic long enough to exhaust it, even to explore it; the state of their being together precluded discussion, as if, in the end, everything was either too momentous or too trivial. Piet felt, even when they lay motionless together, that they were skimming, hastening through space, lightly interlocked, yet not essentially mingled. He slept badly beside her. She had difficulty coming with him. Despairing of her own climax, she would give herself to him in slavish postures, as if witnessing in her mouth or between her breasts the tripped unclotting thump of his ejaculation made it her own. She still wore the rings of her marriage and engagement, and, gazing down to where her hand was guiding him into her silken face, her cheek concave as her jaws were forced apart, he noticed the icy octagon of her diamond and suffered the realization that if they married he would not be able to buy her a diamond so big.

She did not seem to be selling herself; rather, she was an easy and frank companion. After the uncomfortable episode of tagging the furniture (he was not tempted to touch her in this house they had often violated; her presence as she breezed from room to room felt ghostly, impervious; and already they had lost that prerogative of lovers which claims all places as theirs) she walked with him Saturday along the beach, along the public end, where they would not be likely to meet friends. She pointed to a spot where once she had written him a long letter that he had doubtless forgotten. He said he had not forgotten it, though in part he had. She suddenly told him that his callousness, his promiscuity, had this advantage for her; with him she could be as whorish as she wanted, that unlike most men he really didn't judge. Piet answered that it was his Calvinism. Only God judged. Anyway he found her totally beautiful. Totally: bumps, pimples, flat feet, snuffles, and all. She laughed to hear herself so described, and the quality of her laugh told him she was vain, that underneath all fending disclaimers she thought of herself as flawless. Piet believed her, believed the claim of her barking laugh, a shout snatched away by the salt wind beside the spring sea, her claim that she was in truth perfect, and he hungered to be again alone with her long body in the stealthy shabby shelter of his room.

Lazily she fellated him while he combed her lovely hair. Oh and lovely also her coral cunt, coral into burgundy, with its pansy-shaped M, or W, of fur: kissing her here, as she unfolded fom gateway into chamber, from chamber into universe, was a blind pleasure tasting of infinity until, he biting her, she clawed his back and came. Could break his neck. Forgotten him entirely. All raw self. Machine that makes salt at the bottom of the sea.

Mouths, it came to Piet, are noble. They move in the brain's court. We set our genitals mating down below like peasants, but when the mouth condescends, mind and body marry. To eat another is sacred. *I love thee, Elizabeth, thy petaled rankness, thy priceless casket of nothing lined with slippery buds.* Thus on the Sunday morning, beneath the hanging clangor of bells.

"Oh Piet," Foxy sighed to him, "I've never felt so taken. No one has ever known me like this."

Short of sleep, haggard from a month of fighting panic, he smiled and tried to rise to her praise with praise of her, and fell asleep instead, his broad face feverish, as if still clamped between her thighs.

Sunday afternoon was his time with the children; at Foxy's suggestion the four of them went bowling at the candlepin alleys in North Mather. Ruth and Nancy were wide-eyed at the intrusion of Mrs. Whitman, but Foxy was innocently intent on bowling a good score for herself, and in showing the girls how to grasp the unwieldy ball and keep it out of the gutters. When it went in, Ruth said, "*Merde.*"

Piet asked her, "Where did you learn that word?"

"Jonathan little-Smith says it, to keep from swearing."

"Do you like Jonathan?"

"He's a fink," Ruth said, as Angela had once said of Freddy Thorne, *He's a jerk.*

On the second string Piet bowled only 81 to Foxy's 93. She was competition. The outing ended in ice-cream sodas at a newly reopened roadside ice-cream stand whose proprietor had returned, with a fisherman's squint and a peeling forehead, from his annual five months in Florida. To Piet he said, putting his hand on Ruth's head, "This one is like you, but this little number"—his brown hand splayed on Nancy's blond head—"is your missus here all the way."

Foxy had planned to fly back to Washington late Sunday, but she stayed through the night. "Won't Ken guess where you've been sleeping?"

"Oh, let him. He doesn't give a damn. He has grounds enough already, and anyway the settlement's pretty much ironed out. Ken's not stingy with money, thank God. I've got to admit, he's the least neurotic man I ever met. He's decided this, and he's going to make it stick."

"You sound admiring."

"I always admired him. I just never wanted him."

"And me?"

"Obviously. I want you. Why do you think I came all this way?"

"To divide the furniture."

"Oh who cares about furniture? I don't even know where I'm going to be living."

"Well, I suppose I *am* up for grabs."

"I'm not so sure. Angela may just be giving you a holiday."

"I—"

"Don't try to say anything. If you're there, you're there; if not, not. I must make myself free first. I'll be away for a long time now, Piet. Six weeks, two months. Shall I never come back?"

"Where are you going?"

"I don't know yet. Ken's father thinks it should be a western state, but a friend of ours in Cambridge went to the Virgin Islands and that sounds like more fun than some desert ranch full of Connecticut menopause patients whose husband shacked up with the secretary."

"You're really going to go through with it?"

"Oh," she said, touching his cheek in the dark curiously, as if testing the contour of a child's face, or the glaze on a vase she had bought, "absolutely. I'm a ruined woman."

Later, in that timeless night distended by fatigue, demarcated only by a periodic rising of something within him yet not his, a surge from behind him that in blackness broke beneath him upon her strange forked whiteness, Foxy sighed, "It's good to have enough, isn't it? Really enough."

He said, "Sex is like money; only too much is enough."

"That sounds like Freddy Thorne."

"My mentor and savior."

She hushed his lips with fingers fragrant of low tide. "Oh don't. I can't stand other people, even their names. Let's pretend there's only us. Don't we make a world?"

"Sure. I'm a ticklish question, and you're the tickled answer."

"Oh sweet, I do ache."

"You think I don't? Oooaaoh."

"Piet."

"Oooaauhooaa."

"Stop it. That's a horrible noise."

"I can't help it, love. I'm in the pit. One more fuck, and I'm ready to die. Suck me up. Ououiiiyaa. Ayaa."

Each groan felt to be emptying his chest, creating an inner hollowness answering the hollowness beneath the stars.

She threatened him: "I'll leave you."

"You can't. Try it yourself. Groan. It feels great."

"No. You're disciplining me. You're under no obligation to marry me, I'm not so sure even I want to marry you."

"Oh, do. Do. Uuoooiiaaaugh. Oh, mercy. You are tops, Fox."

"Mmmmooh. You're right. It does relax."

He repeated, "Oh, mercy," and, as the wearying wonder of her naked sweated-up fucked-out body being beside his sank in, said with boneless conviction, "Ah, you're mine." She put her blurred cheek against his. The tip of her nose was cold. A sign of health. We are all exiles who need to bathe in the irrational.

Monday morning, sneaking downstairs, they met the other tenant of the third floor returning, a small bespectacled man in factory grays. Freezing on the narrow stair to let them pass, he said, "G-g-g-gu-ood mur-mur—"

Outdoors, in the parking lot, beside the glittering MG, Foxy giggled and said, "Your having a woman scared the poor man half to death." Piet told her No, the man always talked like that. The world, he went on, doesn't really care as much about lovers as we imagine. He saw her, said his farewell to her, through a headachy haze of ubiquitous, bounding sun; her pale brave face was lost, lightstruck. He saw dimly that her eyes above their blue hollows had been left soft by their nights, flowers bloomed from mud. Called upon by their circumstances to laugh joyfully, or to weep plainly, or to thank her regally for these three slavish days, or even to be amusingly stoical, he was nothing, not even polite. She gave him her hand to shake and he lifted it to his mouth and pressed his tongue into her palm, and wished her away. He leaned into the car window and blew on her ear and told her to sleep on the plane. Nothing had been concluded; nothing wanted to be said. When, after a puzzled flick of her hand and the sad word "Ciaou," learned from movies, her MG swerved out past the automatic car-wash and was gone, he felt no pang, and this gravel arena of rear entrances looked papery, like a stage set in daylight.

Loss became real and leaden only later, in the afternoon. Walking along Divinity Street with an empty skull and aching loin muscles, he met Eddie Constantine, back from the ends of the world. Eddie was rarely in town any more, and perhaps Carol had just filled him in on a month's worth of gossip, for he gleefully cried in greeting, "Hey, Piet! I hear you got caught with your hand in the honeypot!"

One Sunday in mid-May Piet took his daughters to the beach; the crowd there, tender speckled bodies not yet tan, had herdlike trapped itself between the hot dunes and the cold water, and formed, with its sunglasses and aluminum chairs, a living ribbon parallel to the surf's unsteady edge. Nancy splashed and crowed in the waves with the three Ong boys, who had come with a grim babysitter; Bernadette's final vigil had begun. Ruth lay beside Piet unhappily, not quite ready to bask and beautify herself like a teen-ager, yet too old for sandcastles. Her face had thinned; the smoky suggestion across her eyes was intensifying; she would be, unlike her mother, a clouded beauty, with something dark and regretted filtering her true goodness. Piet, abashed, in love with her, could think of no comfort to offer her but time, and closed his eyes upon the corona of curving hairs his lashes could draw from the sun. Distant music enlarged and loomed over him; he saw sandy ankles, a turquoise transistor, young thighs, a bikini bottom allowing a sense of globes. *How many miles must a man* . . . Folk. Rock is out. . . . *the answer, my friends* . . . Love and peace are in. As the music receded he closed his eyes and on the crimson inside of his lids pictured globes parting to admit him. He was thirsty. The wind was from the west, off the land, and tasted of the parched dunes.

Then the supernatural proclaimed itself. A sullen purpling had developed unnoticed in the north. A wall of cold air swept south across the beach; the wind change was so distinct and sudden a unanimous grunt, *Ooh*, rose from the crowd. Single raindrops heavy as hail began to fall, still in sunshine, spears of fire. Then the sun was swallowed. The herd gathered its bright colors and hedonistic machinery and sluggishly funneled toward the board-walk. Brutal thunderclaps, sequences culminating with a splinter-ing as of cosmic crates, spurred the retreat. The livid sky had already surrounded them; the green horizon of low hills behind which lay downtown Tarbox appeared paler than the dense atmosphere pressing upon it. A luminous crack leaped, many-pronged, into being in the north, over East Mather; calamitous crashing followed. There was a push on the boardwalk; a woman screamed, a child laughed. Towels were tugged tight across huddling shoulders. The temperature had dropped twenty degrees in five minutes. The beach behind Piet and his children was clean except for a few scoffers still lolling on their blankets. The plane of the sea ignited like the filament of a flash bulb.

A moment before Piet and his daughters reached the truck cab, the downpour struck, soaking them; rain slashed at the cab's windows and deafeningly drummed on the metal sides. WASH ME. The windshield had become a waterfall the wipers could not clear. Bits of color scurried through the glass, and shouts punctured the storm's exultant monotone. In their space of shelter his daughters' wet hair gave off an excited doggy smell. Nancy was delighted and terrified, Ruth stoical and amused. At the first slight relenting of the weather's fury, Piet put the truck in gear and made his way from the puddled parking lot, on roads hazardous with fallen boughs, via Blackberry Lane, flooded at one conduit, toward the crunching driveway of Angela's house. In the peril his dominating wish had been to deliver his daughters to their mother before he was overtaken: he must remove his body from proximity with theirs. He refused Angela's offer of tea and headed into the heart of Tarbox, unaware that the year's great event had begun to smolder.

The cloudburst settled to a steady rain. Houses, garages, elms and asphalt submitted to the same gray whispering. Thunder, repulsed, grumbled in retreat. Piet parked behind his building and there was a sudden hooting. The Tarbox fire alarm launched its laborious flatulent bellow. The coded signal was in low numbers; the fire was in the town center. Piet imagined he scented ginger. Quickly he ran upstairs, changed out of his bathing suit, and came down to the front entrance. On Divinity Street people were running. The ladder truck roared by with spinning scarlet light and firemen struggling into slickers, clinging as the truck rounded Cogswell's corner. The fire horn, apocalyptically close, repeated its call. The section of the town leeward from the hill was fogged with yellow smoke. Piet began running with the rest.

Up the hill the crowds and the smoke thickened. Already fire hoses, some slack and tangled, others plump and leaking in graceful upward jets, filled the streets around the green. The Congregational Church was burning. God's own lightning had struck it. The icy rain intensified, and the crowds of people, both old and young, from every quarter, watched in chilled silence.

Smoke, an acrid yellow, was pouring neatly, sheets of rapidly crimping wool, from under the cornice of the left pediment and from the lower edge of the cupola that lifted the gilded weathercock one hundred twenty-five feet into the air. Down among the Doric columns firemen were chasing away the men of the church who had rushed in and already rescued the communion service, the heavy walnut altar and pulpit, the brass cross, the portraits of old divines, stacks of old sermons that were blowing away, and, sodden and blackening in the unrelenting rain, a few pew cushions, new from the last renovation. As a onetime member of the church Piet would have gone forward to help them but the firemen and police had formed a barricade through which only the town dogs, yapping and socializing, could pass. His builder's eye calculated that the bolt had struck the pinnacle, been deflected from the slender lighting-rod cable into the steel rods reinforcing the cupola, and ignited the dry wood where the roofline joined the straight base of the tower. Here, in the hollownesses old builders created for insulation, between the walls, between the roof and the hung plaster ceiling of the sanctuary, in the unventilated spaces behind the dummy tympanum and frieze and architrave of the classic façade, amid the hodgepodge of dusty storage reachable by only a slat ladder behind the disused choir loft, the fire would thrive. Hoses turned upon the steaming exterior surfaces solved nothing. The only answer was immediate axwork, opening up the roof, chopping without pity through the old hand-carved triglyphs and metopes. But the columns themselves were forty feet from porch to capital, and no truck could be worked close enough over the rocks to touch its ladder to the roof, and the wind was blowing the poisonously thickening smoke straight out from the burning side into the throats of the rescuers.

A somewhat ironical cheer arose from the theater of townspeople. Buzz Kappiotis, his swollen silhouette unmistakable, had put on a smoke mask and, ax in hand, was climbing a ladder extended to its fullest to touch the great church's pluming rain gutter. Climbing slower and slower, his crouch manifesting his fear, he froze in a mass of smoke, disappeared, and reappeared inching down. A few teen-agers behind Piet booed, but the crowd, out of noncomprehension or shame, was silent. Another fireman, shiny as a coal in his slicker, climbed to the ladder's tip, swung his ax, produced a violet spurt of trapped gas, so his masked profile gleamed peacock blue, and was forced by the heat to descend.

Now flames, shy flickers of orange, materialized, licking their way up the cupola's base, along the inside edges of the louvered openings constructed to release the sound of the bell. The bell itself, ponderous sorrowing shape, a caped widow, was illumined by a glow from beneath. Jets of water arched high and fell short, crisscrossing. Spirals of whiter smoke curled up the painted cerulean dome of the cupola but did not obscure the weathercock turning in the touches of wind.

The fire signal sounded a third time, and engines from neighboring communities, from Lacetown and Mather, from as far away as Quincy and Plymouth, began to arrive, and the pressure generated by their pumps lifted water to the flickering pinnacle; but by now the tall clear windows along the sides had begun to glow, and the tar shingles of the roof gave off greasy whiffs. The fire had spread under the roof and through the double walls and, even as the alien firemen smashed a hundred diamond panes of glass, ballooned golden in the sanctuary itself. For an instant the Gothic-tipped hymnboards could be seen, still bearing this morning's numerals; the Doric fluting on the balcony rail was raked with amber light; the plush curtain that hid the choir's knees caught and exploded upwards in the empty presbytery like a phoenix. Gone was the pulpit wherein Pedrick had been bent double by his struggle with the Word. The booing teen-agers behind Piet had been replaced by a weeping woman. The crowd,

which had initially rushed defenseless and naked to the catastrophe, had sprouted umbrellas and armored itself in raincoats and
tarpaulins. There was a smell of circus. Children, outfitted in
yellow slickers and visored rainhats, clustered by their parents'
legs. Teen-age couples watched from cars cozy with radio music.
People crammed the memorial pavilion, clung to the baseball
screen. The gathered crowd now stretched far down each street
radiating from the green, Divinity and Prudence and Temperance, ashen faces filling even the neon-scrawled shopping section.
Rain made dusk premature. The spotlights of the fire trucks
searched out a crowd whose extent seemed limitless and whose
silence, as the conflagration possessed every section of the church,
deepened. Flames, doused in the charred belfry, had climbed
higher and now fluttered like pennants from the slim pinnacle
supporting the rooster. With yearning parabolas the hoses arched
higher. A section of roof collapsed in a whirlwind of sparks. The
extreme left column began to smoulder like a snuffed birthday
candle. Through the great crowd breathed disbelief that the rain
and the fire could persist together, that nature could so war with
herself: as if a conflict in God's heart had been bared for them to
witness. Piet wondered at the lightness in his own heart, gratitude
for having been shown something beyond him, beyond all blaming.

He picked up a soaked pamphlet, a sermon dated 1795. *It is the
indispensable duty of all the nations of the earth, to know that the
LORD he is God, and to offer unto him sincere and devout
thanksgiving and praise. But if there is any nation under heaven,
which hath more peculiar and forcible reasons than others, for
joining with one heart and voice in offering up to him these
grateful sacrifices, the United States of America are that nation.*

Familiar faces began to protrude from the citizenry. Piet spotted the Applebys and little-Smiths and Thornes standing in the
broad-leafed shelter of a catalpa tree near the library. The men
were laughing; Freddy had brought a beer. Angela was also in the
crowd. She had brought the girls, and when they spoke to him it
was Ruth, not Nancy, who was weepy, distressed that the man
Jesus would destroy His church, where she had always wiped her

feet, timid of the holy, and had dutifully, among children who were not her friends, sung His praise, to please her father. Piet pressed her wide face against his chest in apology; but his windbreaker was soaked and cold and Ruth flinched from the unpleasant contact. "This is too damn depressing for them," Angela said, "we're going back." When Nancy begged to stay, she said, "The fire's nearly out, the best part is over," and it was true; visible flames had been chased into the corners of the charred shell.

Nancy pointed upward and said, "The chicken!" The rooster, bright as if above not only the smoke but the rain, was poised motionless atop a narrow pyre. Flames in little gassy points had licked up the pinnacle to the ball of ironwork that supported the vane's pivot; it seemed it all must topple; then a single jet, luminous in the spotlights, hurled itself higher and the flames abruptly vanished. Though the impact made the spindly pinnacle waver, it held. The flashbulbs of accumulating cameras went off like secondary lightning. By their fitful illumination and the hysterical whirling of spotlights, Piet watched his wife walk away, turn once, white, to look back, and walk on, leading their virgin girls.

Pedrick, his wiry old hair disarrayed into a translucent crest, recognized Piet in the crowd, though it had been months since he had been in the congregation. His voice clawed. "You're a man of the world. How much in dollars and cents do you estimate it will take to replace this tragic structure?"

Piet said, "Oh, if the exterior shell can be salvaged, between two and three hundred thousand. From the ground up, maybe half a million. At least. Construction costs increase about eight per cent a year." These figures bent the gaunt clergyman like a weight on his back; Piet added in sympathy, "It *is* tragic. The carpentry in there can never be duplicated."

Pedrick straightened; his eye flashed. He reprimanded Piet: "Christianity isn't dollars and cents. This church isn't that old stump of a building. The church is people, my friend, people. *Hu*man *be*ings." And he waggled a horny finger, and Piet saw that Pedrick too knew of his ouster from his home, his need to be brought into line.

Piet told him in return, "But even if they do save the shell, the walls are going to be so weakened you'll have to tear it down anyway." And as if to bear him out, fresh flames erupted along the wall on the other side and leaped so high, as the hoses were shifted, that a maple sapling, having ventured too close to the church, itself caught fire, and dropping burning twigs on the shoulders of spectators.

The crowd churned to watch this final resurgence of the powers of destruction, and Piet was fetched up against Carol Constantine. She carried an umbrella and invited him under it with her, and two of her children, Laura and Patrice. Her show of sorrow touched him. "Oh Piet," she said, "it's too terrible, isn't it? I loved that church."

"I never saw you in it."

"Of course not, I'm a Presbyterian. But I'd look at it twenty times a day, whenever I was in our yard. I'd really be very religious, if Eddie weren't so anti-everything."

"Where is Eddie? On the road?"

"In the sky. He comes back and tells me how beautifully these Puerto Rican girls lay. It's a joy to see him leave. Why am I telling you all this?"

"Because you're sad to see the church burn."

The gutted walls stood saved. The pillars supported the pediment, and the roof beam held the cupola, but the place of worship was a rubble of timbers and collapsed plaster and charred pews, and the out-of-town firemen were coiling their hose, and Buzz Kappiotis was mentally framing his report, and the crowd gradually dispersing. Carol invited Piet in for a cup of tea. Tea became supper, spaghetti shared with her children. He changed from his wet clothes to a sweater and pants, too tight, of Eddie's. When the children were in bed it developed he would spend the night. He had never before slept with a woman so bony and supple. It was good, after his strenuous experience of Foxy, to have a woman who came quickly, with grateful cries and nimble accommodations, who put a pillow beneath her hips, who let her head hang over the side of the bed, hair trailing, throat arched, and who wrapped her legs around him as if his trunk were a stout trapeze by which she was swinging far out over the abyss of the world. The bedroom, like many rooms in Tarbox that night, smelled of wet char and acidulous smoke. Between swings she talked, told him of her life with Eddie, his perversity and her misery, of her hopes for God and immortality, of the good times she and Eddie had had long ago, before they moved to Tarbox. Piet asked her about their affair with the Saltzes and whether she missed them. Carol seemed to need reminding and finally said, "That was mostly talk by other people. Frankly, she was kind of fun, but he was a bore."

Larry & Linda's Guest House
Charlotte Amalie, St. Thomas, V.I.
May 15

Dearest Piet—

Just to write your name makes me feel soft and collapsing inside. What am I doing here, so far from my husband, or my lover, or my father? I have only Toby, and he, poor small soul, has been sunburned by his idiot mother who, accustomed to the day-by-day onset of the Tarbox summer, has baked both him and herself in the tropical sun, a little white spot directly overhead no bigger than a pea. He cried all night, whenever he tried to roll over. Also, this place, advertised as "an inn in the sleepy tradition of the islands of rum and sun" (I have their leaflet on the desk, the very same one given to me by a Washington travel agent), is in fact two doors up from a steel band nightclub and the slanty little street where blue sewer water runs is alive most of the night with the roar of mufflerless VW's and the catcalls of black adolescents. So I have fits all night and droop all day.

Just then a maid with slithery paper sandals and a downcast lilt I can hardly decipher as English came in. From the way she stared at Toby it might have been a full-grown naked man lying there. I don't suppose too many tourist types bring babies. Maybe they think babies come to us in laundry baskets, all powdered and blue-eyed and ready to give orders.

Peace again. The girl cuddled him at my urging and made the beds and pushed some dust here and there and left and he went back to sleep. Trouble is, his mother is sleepy too. Outside the street is incandescent but in here sun lies slatted like yellow crayon sticks on the gritty green floor—Piet, I think I'm going to love it here, once I stop hurting. On the ride from the airport in I wanted to share it with you—just the way they build their houses, corrugated iron and flattened olive oil cans and driftwood all held together by flowering bougainvillaea, and the softness of the air, stepping from the plane in San Juan, like a kiss after fucking—oh lover, forgive me, I am sleepy.

After her restorative nap, the fair-haired young soon-to-be divorcee swiftly arose, and dressed, taking care not to abrade her sunburned forearms and thighs and (especially touchy) abdomen, and changed her youngling's soiled unmentionables, and hurled herself into the blinding clatter of the tropical ville in a heroic (heroinic?) effort to find food. No counterpart of the Tarbox A & P or Lacetown IGA seems to exist—though I could buy bushels of duty-free Swiss watches and cameras. The restaurants not up on the hills attached to the forbidding swish hotels are either native hamburgeries with chili spilled all over the stools or else "gay" nightclubs that don't open until six. At this time of year most of the non-Negroes seem to be fairies. Their voices are unmistakable and everywhere. I finally found a Hayes-Bickford type of cafeteria, with outrageous island prices, up the street near the open market, which meets my apparently demanding (sweet, I'm such an old maid!) sanitary standards, and gives me milk for Toby's bottle in a reassuring waxpaper carton. Larry and Linda aren't much help. They are refugees from New York, would-be actors, and I have the suspicion she rescued him from being gay. He keeps giving me his profile while she must think her front view is the best, because she keeps coming at me head on, her big brown bubs as scary as approaching headlights on a slick night. I was shocked to learn she's five years younger than me and I could see her tongue make a little determined leap to put me on a first-name basis. They seem waifs, rather. They talk about New

*York all the time, how horrible it was etc., love-hate as Freddy
Thorne would say, and are in a constant flap about their sleepy
elusive unintelligible help. Though the evening meals Linda puts
on are quite nice and light and French. American plan—they give
you breakfast and supper, forage as best you can in between. $18
per diem.*

*But it's you, you I think about, and worry about, and wonder
about. How grand we were, me as a call girl and you as a gangster
in hiding. Did I depress you? You seemed so dazed the last
morning, and pleased I was going, I cried all the way into B.U.,
and let Ken take me to lunch at the faculty club and cried some
more, so the tables around us became quite solemn. I think he
thought I was crying for* him, *which in a way I was, and I could
see him fighting down a gentlemanly impulse to offer to call it all
off and take me back. He has become so distinguished and courtly
without me—his female students must adore him. He had bought
a new spring suit, sharkskin, and seemed alarmed that I noticed, as
if I were wooing him again or had caught him wooing someone
else, when all the time you were flowery between my legs and I
was neurotically anxious because we had left Toby in Ken's lab
with his technicians and I would go back up the elevator and find
him dissected. Horrible! Untrue!! Ken was very cute with the
baby, and weighed him in milligrams.*

---

*Days have passed. My letter to you seemed to be going all
wrong, chattery and too "fun" and breezy. Rereading I had to
laugh at what I did to poor Linda's lovely bosom—she and
Larry are really a perfectly sweet phony fragile couple, trying to be parental and sisterly and brotherly all at once to me,
rather careful and anxious with each other, almost studiously
sensual, and so lazy basically. I wonder if ours was the last
generation that will ever have "ambition." These two seem so sure
the world will never let them starve, and that life exists to be
"enjoyed"—barbarous idea. But it is refreshing, after our awful
Tarbox friends who talk only about themselves, to talk to people
who care about art and the theater (they invariably call it, with
innocent pomp, "the stage") and international affairs, if that's*

*what they are. I've forgotten what else "affair" means. They
think LBJ a boor but feel better under him than Kennedy because
K. was too much like the rest of us semi-educated lovables of the
post-Cold War and might have blown the whole game through
some mistaken sense of flair. Like Lincoln, he lived to become a
martyr, a memory. A martyr to what? To Marina Oswald's sexual rejection of her husband. Forgive me, I am using my letter
to you to argue with Larry in. But it made me sad, that he
thought that somebody like us (if K. was) wasn't fit to rule us,
which is to say, we aren't fit to rule ourselves, so bring on em-
perors, demigods, giant robots, what have you. Larry, inciden-
tally, has let me know, during a merengo at the Plangent Cat,
which is the place down the street, that his sexual ambivalence
(AC or DC, he calls it) is definitely on the mend, but I declined,
though he does dance wonderfully, to participate in the cure. He
took the refusal as if his heart hadn't been in it.*

*Which brings us to you. Who are you? Are you weak? This
theme, of your "weakness," cropped up often in the mouths of
our mutual friends, when we all lived together in a magic circle.
But I think they meant to say rather that your strengths weren't
sufficiently <u>used</u>. Your virtues are obsolete. I can imagine you as
somebody's squire, maybe poor prim fanatic Matt's, a splendid
redheaded squire, resourceful, loyal, living off the land, repairing
armor with old hairpins, kidding your way into castles and inns,
making impossible ideals work but needing their impossibility to
attach yourself to. Before I knew you long ago Bea Guerin
described you to me as an old-fashioned man. In a sense if I were
to go from Ken to you it would be a backwards step. Compared
to Ken you are primitive. The future belongs to him or to chaos.
But my life belongs to me now, and I must take a short view. I am
not, for all my vague intellectual poking (about as vague as
Freddy's, and he knew it), good for much—but I know I could
be your woman. As an ambition it is humble but explicit. Even if
we never meet again I am glad to have felt useful, and used.
Thank you.*

*The question is, should I (or the next woman, or the next)
subdue you to marriage? How much more generous it would be*

*to let you wander, and suffer—there are so few wanderers left.
We are almost all women now, homebodies and hoarders. You
married Angela because your instinct told you she would not
possess you. I would. To be mastered by your body I would tame
you with my mind. Yet the subconscious spark in me that loves
the race wants instead to give you freedom, freedom to rape and
flee and to waste yourself, now that the art of building. belongs
entirely to accountants. Ever since you began to bounce up to my
empty house in your dusty pick-up truck and after an hour rattle
hastily away, I have felt in you, have loved in you, a genius for
loneliness, for seeing yourself as something apart from the world.
When you desire to be the world's husband, what right do I have
to make you my own?*

*Toby is crying, and Linda is here. We are taking a picnic to
Magen's Bay.*

---

*Night. The steel band down the street makes me want to go
outdoors. What I wrote this afternoon please read understanding
that its confusions are gropings toward truth. I am unafraid to
seek the truth about us. With Ken I was always afraid. Of coming
to the final coldness we shared.*

*You would have loved it where we went. Coral sand is not like
silica sand; it is white and porous and <u>breathes</u>, and takes deep
sharp footprints. My feet look huge and sadly flat. The shells are
tiny and various, baby's fingernails for Carol. Remember that
night? I was so jealous of Angela. Magen's Bay has sea-grape
bushes for shade. I am getting a tan. Linda has talked me into a
bikini. We roof Toby's basket with mosquito netting and he is
turning caramel through it. I have learned to drive on the left-
hand side of the road and am mastering my routines. The lawyers
are dreadful. You would hate the process. Marriage is something
done in the light, at noon, the champagne going flat in the sun,
but divorce is done in the dark, where insects scuttle, in faraway
places, by lugubrious lawyers. But at the end of the main street
where it stops selling watches there is an old square Lutheran
church smelling of cedar, with plaques in Danish, where I went
Sunday. The congregation was plump colored ladies who sang*

even the hymns of rejoicing wailingly. The sermon, by a taut young white man, was very intellectual—over my head. I liked it. The Negroes are lovely, softer than the Washington ones I rather dreaded as a child, without that American hardness and shame. I even like the fairies—at least they have made a kind of settlement and aren't tormenting some captive woman. The boats in the harbor are fascinating. Linda has rummaged up a baby carriage and I push Toby a half-mile each way along the quay. My father would tell me about boats and I find I still know a ketch from a yawl. I marvel at the hand-carved tackle on the old fishing boats from the more primitive islands. Not a bit of metal, and they hold together. The clouds are quick, translucent, as if Nature hardly intends them. When it rains in sunlight, they say, the Devil is beating his wife.

Are you well? Are you there? If you have gone back to Angela, you may show this to her. Think of me fondly, without fear. Your fate need not be mine. I will write again, but not often. There are things to do even here. Linda has put me in charge of the morning help, for a reduction in fee, and has begun to confess to me her love life.　　　　　*I am your*

Foxy

P.S.: Larry says that man is the sexiest of the animals and the only one that foresees death. I should make a riddle of this.
P.P.S.: At the Plangent Cat down the street I have danced now with Negroes, greatly daring for a Southern girl—the last one who touched me was the nurse in the dentist's office. They are a very silky people, and very innocently assume I want to sleep with them. How sad to instinctively believe your body is worth something. After weeks of chastity I remember lovemaking as an exploration of a sadness so deep people must go in pairs, one cannot go alone.
P.P.P.S.: I seem unable to let this letter go. A bad sign?

John Ong died the same day that France proposed another conference to restore peace to Laos, and Communist China agreed to loan fifteen million dollars to Kenya. Piet was surprised by the length of the obituary in the Globe: born in P'yongyang, political refugee, asylum in 1951, co-discoverer in 1957, with a Finn, of an elementary particle whose life is measured in millionths of a second, list of faculty positions, scientific societies, survived by wife and three sons, Tarbox, Mass. Private services. No flowers. Their friend. Piet walked through the day lightened, excited by this erasure, by John's hidden greatness, imagining the humming of telephone wires among the couples he and John had once known. The same covey of long-haired boys gathered on Cogswell's corner after three, the same blue sky showed through the charred skeleton of the burnt church, topped by an untouched gold rooster.

That same week, on an errand of business, trying to locate Jazinski, who seemed now to hold all of Gallagher's plans and intentions in his head, Piet went to the boy's house, an expanded ranch on Elmcrest Drive, and saw Leon's new golf bag in the garage. Not only were the clubs gleaming new Hogans but the handle of each was socketed in one of those white plastic tubes that were the latest refinement in fussy equipment: pale cannons squarely aimed upward. The bag, black and many-pocketed, was tagged with the ticket of a new thirty-six-hole club, in South Mather, that Piet had never played on. Piet, who played with an originally odd-numbered set filled in with randomly purchased irons whose disparate weights and grips he had come to know like friends, recognized that he must yield to the force expressed by this aspiring bag, mounted on a cart the wheels of which were spoked like the wheels of a sports car. When Leon's pretty wife, her black hair bobbed and sprayed, answered the side door, he read his doom again in her snug cherry slacks, her free-hanging Op-pattern blouse, the bold and equalizing smile that greeted her husband's employer, qualified by something too steady in the eyes, by a curious repressing thoughtful gesture with the tip of her tongue, as if she had often heard Piet unfavorably discussed. Behind her (she did not invite him in; his reputation?) her kitchen, paneled with imitation walnut and hung with copper pâté molds, seemed the snug galley of a ship on its way to warmer waters.

And before May was out Gallagher called Piet in for a serious talk. Matt asked if Piet thought Leon was ready to supervise construction, and Piet answered that he was. Matt asked if Piet didn't feel that over the last year their ends—sales and building—had begun to pull in opposite directions, and Piet responded that he was proud of how promptly the first three houses on Indian Hill had sold. Matt admitted this, but confessed that instead of these half-ass semi-custom-type houses he wanted to go into larger tracts—there was one beyond Lacetown he was bidding for, low clear land swampy only in the spring—and try prefab units, which would be, frankly, a waste of Piet's talents. Personally, he thought Piet's real forte was restoration, and with Tarbox full of old wrecks he would like to see Piet go into business for himself, buying cheap, fixing up, and selling high. Piet thanked him for the idea but said he saw himself more as a squire than a knight. Matt laughed uneasily, hearing another voice or mind emerge from Piet's disturbingly vacant presence. By the time a partnership dissolves, it has dissolved. In consideration for his half of their tangible assets—including a few sticks of office furniture, an inventory of light equipment and carpentry tools and the pick-up truck, a sheaf of mortgages held on faith, and a firm name that sounded like a vaudeville team (here Matt laughed scornfully, as if they had always been a joke)—he offered Piet five thousand, which to be honest was goddam generous. Piet, rebellious as always when confronted with pat solutions, suggested twenty, and settled for seven. He had not imagined himself getting anything, having forfeited, he felt, by his weekend with Foxy, all his rights. To placate his guilt he satisfied himself that Gallagher, who knew the value of their parcels better than he, would have gone higher than seven. They shook on it. The points of Gallagher's jaw flinched. He said earnestly, sellingly, that he wanted Piet to understand that this had nothing to do with Piet's personal difficulties, that he and Terry still believed that he and Angela would be reconciled. Piet was touched by this deceitful assurance for, though Matt had come to relish hard dealing, his conception of himself did not permit him, usually, to lie.

Meanwhile, across the town, Bea Guerin delighted in her

454 : C O U P L E S

adopted baby, its violet toenails, its fearless froggy stare. It was a
colored child. "Roger and I have integrated Tarbox!" Bea ex-
claimed breathlessly over the phone to Carol. "You know we're
the last crusaders in the world, it's just that we couldn't bear to
wait!" Bernadette Ong awoke to widowhood as if the entire side
on which she had been sleeping were torn open, a mouth the
length of her, where her church's balm burned like salt; she had
respected John's desire to be buried without religion, and was
bathed in a recurrent guilt whose scalding was confused with the
plucking questioning hands of her children. "Daddy's gone away.
To a place we can't imagine. Yes, they'll speak his language there.
Yes, the Pope knows where it is. You'll see him at the end of your
lives. Yes, he'll know you, no matter how old you've grown." She
had been beside the bed when he died. One moment, there was
faint breathing; his mouth was human in shape. The next, it was a
black hole—black and deep. The vast difference haunted her,
gave the glitter of the mass a holocaustal brilliance. Marcia little-
Smith received a shock; having twice invited the Reinhardts to
dinner parties and been twice declined, she went to visit Deb
Reinhardt, a thin-lipped Vassar graduate with ironed hair, who
told her that she and Al, though they quite liked Harold and
Marcia in themselves, did not wish to get involved with their
friends, with that whole—and here her language slipped unforgivably—"crummy crowd." So the Reinhardts, and the young so-
ciologist who had been elected town moderator, and a charmingly yet unaffectedly bohemian children's book illustrator who
had moved from Bleecker Street, and the new Unitarian minister
in Tarbox, and their uniformly tranquil wives, formed a distinct
social set, that made its own clothes, and held play readings, and
kept sex in its place, and experimented with LSD, and espoused
liberal causes more militantly than even Irene Saltz. Indignantly
the Applesmiths christened them "the Shakers."

Georgene Thorne suffered a brief vision. Heartsick over Piet's
collapse, and her final loss of him, and her own rôle in bringing
it about, she had turned to her children, and as the weekend
weather softened took Whitney and Martha and Judy on long
undesired expeditions to museums in the city and wildlife sanc-

tuaries well inland and unfamiliar beaches far down the coast. At one beach she was walking in from the parking area with her children when the laughter of a couple knee-deep in the icy ocean struck her as half familiar. The man was old and bearded and goatish, with knotted yellow legs, skimpy European-style bathing trunks, and a barrel chest coated in gray fur; coarsely hooting, rapacious, he was splashing seawater at a shrieking tall slender woman with tossing dark hair, girlish in a black bikini, Terry Gallagher. The man must be her lute teacher's husband, the potter. Georgene steered her children down the beach past some eclipsing rocks and never breathed a word of this glimpse to anyone, not even to Freddy, not even to Janet Appleby, who, in the course of their confidential outpourings following the discovery of Janet's note to Freddy, had become her closest friend.

Janet too had her secrets. One Saturday afternoon late in May, driving home from the little-Smiths', she noticed Ken's MG parked in the Whitmans' driveway, and impulsively stopped. She walked around the nursery wing, where Foxy's roses were budding, and found Ken at the front of the house, burning brush. In the light off the flooding marsh his hair was white. At first she talked in pleasantries, but he sensed in her, because he had always liked her, a nervous stalled fullness unbalanced by the beauty of the day. She moved the conversation toward his state of mind, to the loneliness she presumed was his and, unstated beyond that, the shame; and then she offered, not in so many words but with sufficient clarity, to sleep with him, now, in the empty house. After consideration, and with equal tact and clarity, he declined. It was the best possible outcome. "I've been burned, you see; I can't be hurt," had been the basis of her offer; and his refusal was phrased to enhance rather than diminish her notion of her worth: "I think we both need time to generate more self-respect." There was an island of brambles, hawthorn and alder, in the marsh too small to support even a shack, and as they watched, a cloud of starlings migrating north passingly settled here; even before the last birds of the flock alighted, the leaders lifted and fled. So their encounter, amid the quickening and the grass-smoke and the insect-hum and the tidewater overflowing its rectilinear channels, was sufficient consummation, an exercise for each of freedom. The first breath of adultery is the freest; after it, constraints aping marriage develop. Janet and Ken were improved for having stood, above the glorious greening marsh, in this scale, fit to live in such an expanding light. Their faces seemed each to each great planetary surfaces of skin and tension, overflowing dazzlingly at the eyes and mouths. She lowered her gaze; wind unsmoothed his hair. Her offer had been instructive for him; his refusal for her. For years they treasured these minutes out of all proportion to their circumspection.

The couples, though they had quickly sealed themselves off from Piet's company, from contamination by his failure, were yet haunted and chastened, as if his fall had been sacrificial. Angela, unattached now, was a threat to each marriage, and, though the various wives continued for a time to call on her politely, to be rebuffed by her coolness and distance, and to return home justified in their antipathy, she was seldom invited to parties. Indeed, parties all but ceased. The children as they grew made increasingly complex and preoccupying demands. The Guerins and Thornes and Applebys and little-Smiths still assembled, but rather sedately; one night, when once Freddy would have organized a deliciously cutting psychological word game, to "humanize" them, they drew up two tables and began to play bridge; and this became their habit. The Gallaghers, without the link of the Hanemas, drifted off to consort with the realtors and money-men of the neighboring towns, and took up horse riding. The Saltzes sent cards to everyone at Christmas. The Jazinskis have moved to an old house near the green and become Unitarians. Doc Allen has learned, the newest thing, how to insert intrauterine loops. Reverend Pedrick, ecstatic, has been overwhelmed by contributions of money, from Catholics as well as Congregationalists, from Lacetown and Mather as well as Tarbox, toward the rebuilding of his church. The fire was well publicized. One national foundation, whose director happened to be reading the *Herald* over breakfast at the Ritz that Monday, has offered to match private contributions dollar for dollar, and reportedly federal funds are available for the restoration of landmarks if certain historical and aesthetic criteria can be met. But the rumor in town is that the new building will be not a restoration but a modern edifice, a parabolic poured-concrete tent-shape peaked like a breaking wave.

The old church proved not only badly gutted but structurally unsound: a miracle it had not collapsed of itself a decade ago. Before the bulldozers and backhoes could munch through the building, the rooster was rescued by a young man riding a steel ball hoisted to the tip of an enormous crane. The elementary-school children were dismissed early to see the sight. Up, up, the young rider went, until he glimmered in the sun like the golden bird, and Piet Hanema, who in his unemployment was watching, and who knew what mistakes crane operators could make, held his breath, afraid. Gently the ball was hoisted and nudged into place; with surprising ease the young man lifted the gilded silhouette from its pivoted socket and, holding it in his lap, was swiftly lowered to the earth, as cheers from the schoolchildren rose. The weathercock measured five feet from beak to tailfeathers; the copper penny of his eye was tiny. As the workman walked across the green to present it to Pedrick and the two deacons waiting with him, the clustering children made a parade, a dancing flickering field of color as they jostled and leaped to see better the eye their parents had told them existed. From Piet's distance their mingled cry seemed a jubilant jeering. The grass of the domed green was vernally lush. The three stiff delegates of the church accepted the old emblem and posed for photographs absurdly, cradling the piece of tin between them; the man on Pedrick's right had hairy ears, the one on his left was a jeweler. The swarming children encircled them and touched the dull metal. The sky above was empty but for two parallel jet trails.

Affected by this scene of joy, seeing that his life in a sense had ended, Piet turned and realized he was standing where he had first glimpsed Foxy getting into her car after church, the spot where later they had met in the shadow of her mother's arrival, her tall body full, she in her pale turban; and he was glad that he would marry her, and frightened that he would not.

Is it too severe? I'd take it off but it's pinned.

It's great. It brings out the pampered pink of your face.

God, you're hostile.

I may be hostile, but I adore you. Let's go to bed.

Wouldn't that be a relief? Do you know how many days it's been since we made love?

Many.

Now, though it has not been many years, the town scarcely remembers Piet, with his rattly pick-up truck full of odd lumber, with his red hair and corduroy hat and eye-catching apricot windbreaker, he who sat so often and contentedly in Cogswell's Drug Store nursing a cup of coffee, the stub of a pencil sticking down from under the sweatband of his hat, his windbreaker unzippered to reveal an expensive cashmere sweater ruined by wood dust and shavings, his quick eyes looking as if they had been rubbed too hard the night before, the skin beneath them pouched in a little tucked fold, as if his maker in the last instant had pinched the clay. Angela, who teaches at a girls' school in Braintree, is still seen around, talking with Freddy Thorne on the street corner, or walking on the beach with a well-tailored wise-smiling small man, her father. She flew to Juárez in July and was divorced in a day. Piet and Foxy were married in September. Her father, pulling strings all the way from San Diego, found a government job for his new son-in-law, as a construction inspector for federal jobs, mostly military barracks, in the Boston-Worcester area. Piet likes the official order and the regular hours. The Hanemas live in Lexington, where, gradually, among people like themselves, they have been accepted, as another couple.

A Note about the Author

JOHN UPDIKE was born in 1932, in Shilling-ton, Pennsylvania; he attended Harvard College and the Ruskin School of Drawing and Fine Art, in Oxford, England. From 1955 to 1957 he was a staff member of The New Yorker, *to which he has contributed stories, essays, and poems. His previous novels are* The Poorhouse Fair *(1959),* Rabbit, Run *(1960),* The Centaur *(1963), and* Of the Farm *(1965). He lives with his wife and four children in Massachusetts.*

A Note on the Type

The text of this book was set on the Linotype in Janson, a recutting made direct from type cast from matrices long thought to have been made by the Dutchman Anton Janson, who was a practicing type founder in Leipzig during the years 1668–87. However, it has been conclusively demonstrated that these types are actually the work of Nicholas Kis (1650–1702), a Hungarian, who most probably learned his trade from the master Dutch type founder Kirk Voskens. The type is an excellent example of the influential and sturdy Dutch types that prevailed in England up to the time William Caslon developed his own incomparable designs from these Dutch faces.